The Wolf Inside

Book One of the Wild Hunt

Tyler W. D. Stewart

Supposed Crimes LLC • Matthews, North Carolina

All Rights Reserved
Copyright © 2016 Tyler W. D. Stewart

Published in the United States.

First Edition

ISBN: 978-1-938108-89-1

www.supposedcrimes.com

This book is typeset in Goudy Old Style, licensed by
Ascender Corporation.

Dedicated to the memory of *Mary Stewart*.

May we all overcome adversity.

PART I.
MOUNTAINS (LATE SUMMER)

One
Survive

Iridescent light beamed through wavering branches and flickering leaves as the sun's glow cascaded down the wooded mountainside. Birds chirped and sang throughout the green treetops, greeting the morning warmth spreading through the lingering chill. Thick droplets of rain fallen the previous night slickened the meadow's path, and the soft soil sunk under each careful step.

Snap.

It flicked its ears, craning its neck toward the trees. Nervous eyes scanned the thicket, wary of darkness the sun's glow couldn't abate.

She remained still, engulfed by shadows misting the edge of the forest. Her lungs burned but refused air; the deer lowered its gaze, keeping its ears fixated on her direction. Noise would reveal her presence, reassuring its urge to flee. She silently cursed the brittle branch that had crunched noisily beneath her boot, then shifted weight to her left leg. The deer, its fear temporarily slaked, resumed grazing in the long, browning grass. She crouched low and carefully eased closer.

She slid the bow off her shoulder and breathed deeply to relax. The handle was still slick and polished, meticulously kept clean from dirt and grime even as the years wore on. Though the red paint faded, as did the elasticity in its old limbs, it had once been a treasure from her family's past before the world fell apart. Now it was their means of survival, merely a faint echo of what used to be.

The arrow slipped over her shoulder as she pulled it from her quiver. She moved slowly, drawing the bowstring without groaning complaints of the flexing wooden ends. She peered down the makeshift sights, squinting one eye as the arrow shaft trembled between her pinched fingers. *Compensate for the breeze...* She shivered as a gentle breath caressed her perspiring skin.

She nudged the bow to the right and released the arrow.

It lunged from the bowstring and sailed, but wobbled and slapped into the dirt near the deer's hooves. Her fingers enclosed around the shaft to another arrow when the startled deer jumped. She pulled the bowstring as far back as she could, and again it snapped another arrow loose. It missed the fleeing deer as well, striking the ground where it stood only moments before. Another arrow docked and aimed, but she cried out in frustration when the deer disappeared into the morning fog.

"You're too impatient."

She sighed, unable to face her father. His gruff voice dripped disappointment, and her belly swelled with it. She felt sick, and not just from missing the shot. Hunger pangs plagued her gut and stiffened her muscles.

"Next time, steady your bow."

She turned with her throat tightening and eyes shut to wall away spilling tears. "I can't do it."

"I taught you how to fire a rifle," he barked. Even accustomed to his gritty tone, his harsh words still made her flinch. "I'll teach you how to use this as well."

The bow was suddenly dead weight in her sweaty palm. "Why can't I just use the rifle?"

It was a useless question, one she knew better than to mutter redundantly. When she looked up at him, he had the same hardened look on his face he always wore when he'd rebuke her. His eyes were brown, murky like puddled mud under thick rainfall. He arched his brow, his mouth curving into a deep frown. His long, dark hair and beard were peppered grey, his skin tanned from the sun's onslaught. His clothes were stained with dirt, sweat, and dried blood. They hung from his gaunt frame like stripped rags, the colors long faded and worn.

"You know why," he finally replied in a harsh whisper. "There's barely a few dozen bullets between the weapons we have. We conserve ammo."

"I don't think I can do it," she repeated. She concealed herself behind a sturdy wall of stubbornness. *That, at least, I learned from you.*

He reached for the bow in her hand. "You'll learn." He turned and tossed it over his shoulder, his boots slopping through the muddy trail back up the mountainside. She stood there, basking under the sun's warm embrace yet feeling cold as winter's touch.

"Come on!" he called out. "We can check the snares for some dinner."

They trudged through the wet grass and mud, through the shade with the occasional twinkle of sunlight bursting through the forest canopy. She could hear the river rushing in the distance, a constant roar resonating along the mountainside, drowning their words and stifling them silent. Her father kept a quickened pace, but she heard the wheeze in his throat and labored gasps while he struggled for air. It worried her.

He'd never been one to show pain. He would grimace through it and bear the weight of the world before he succumbed to its gnawing hurt. He leaned to the right when he walked, and she knew the injury in his knee flared up once more. Medication used to dull the pain, but they'd quickly exhausted the supply. It had been nearly a decade since they'd taken residence in the mountains. That sparked another potential wildfire through her heart.

"Maybe we should find a town," she finally said, appeasing her welling curiosity. "You know, for a supply run."

"What?"

"We can't stay here forever." *So much for subtlety.* She bit her lip.

He grunted back at her. "It's worked so far."

"I understand you're scared..."

"No," he said quickly, "I understand you've forgotten exactly what's out there."

"We haven't seen one in years," she countered.

"Those aren't the only monsters I'm worried about."

Her questions would not be smothered. "What if the world is becoming normal again?"

He didn't need to answer. *The world had long gone to hell before everything fell to shit,* he'd say to her over the firelight, finding small comfort in the fleeting warmth. *It was over before it began.*

She followed her father into a small clearing. The river bowed around the shoreline; trees and brush concealed the rushing water except for one small opening her father had carved out with a machete weeks before.

"Check the first two," he ordered curtly, pointing away from the river. "I'll see if there's any fish."

She knew better than to prod his soured mood. He was like an agitated bear shaken from its slumber during winter months. Mud splashed up his jeans as he stomped away from her, his mutterings like threatening growls.

I'll do better next time, she promised, her heart longing to heal his shattered soul.

She neared the snares they'd set the night before. The top of one sapling curved downward, the line and hook still set along the base. Twigs and pine needles camouflaged the shoestring noose, also undisturbed. The other sapling stood straight just a few feet away. Dangling from the noose, a small, brown rabbit battered helplessly against the sapling trunk, the shoestring tight around its leg. Blood soaked the fur where it had rubbed raw into its skin. Her mouth watered at the thought of roasting meat sizzling just above the tongues of flame, but a lump formed in her throat as the rabbit squealed in her grasp. She whispered her apologies before twisting its neck.

She called to her father with a wide grin, triumphantly parading the limp rabbit in her hands. He was too busy crouched near the shoreline, grumbling and splashing his face with river water.

"Goddamnit," he said, groaning as he stood. When she queried the problem, he grunted and replied, "Wolves." He pointed to the sapling. It stood straight on the bank of the river, the line ripped and dangling above rushing water. "Took the fish and ruined the snares."

"How do you know it was wolves?" She asked. "Bears frequent this river as well."

He gestured to the shoreline. Fresh paw prints stamped the mud in both directions, from the snare then back into the woods. Too small and narrow for a bear. "They're hunting closer and closer to where we are."

"We've got rabbit," she offered quietly.

It wasn't enough for him. It never was. "Only good for the damn night."

"And fish would have lasted us until morning," she tried reasoning. "I'll get the deer tomorrow."

"If we can even track it again." His accusing words stung. Oblivious, he continued, "I should be tracking these damn wolves."

"We could always hike further into the mountains, an overnight hunt," she said. "Or maybe follow the river and see if there's a better fishing spot."

He wrinkled his brow. "I know what you're trying to do."

"Because we're running out of options."

"We're doing just fine."

"We're not doing fine." *Why can't you see that?* Her mind screamed. Her mouth wouldn't form the words.

"We are!" He roared back. He gritted his teeth and bunched his shoulders. "I will not put us at risk like that again! We barely survived!"

"You can't protect me forever."

He snarled, "Don't you think I know that?" Before she stormed off through the woods, he said, "I'm not going to be around much longer."

She blinked back her tears. "Don't talk like that."

He pulled her close, and she fell into his embrace. His clothes were musty, and she could smell the sweat clinging to his body from the day's walk, but she never felt safer. She refused to think he could ever leave her side.

"I can't lose you like I lost your mother and brother," he choked, his voice shaking. "I can't lose you."

"You won't," she promised. "Now let's set these snares again." She coaxed his tears away with a mischievous smile. "I could eat this whole rabbit myself."

He nodded. "Right. These two are ruined."

"We've got copper wire back at the cabin."

He spat by his feet. "No, we need that for the fence. My boot strings will have to do for now."

"A supply run wouldn't be that bad," she pointed out playfully. His mouth nearly twitched into a grin.

"We'll switch the location of our snares tomorrow," he said. "No point in feeding the wolves as well. That problem needs to be dealt with soon."

"They're just like us, dad," she said over her shoulder. "Trying to survive."

The fire crackled and spat; sparks twinkled through the air like fleeing fireflies and singed the roasting meat. Embers sizzled as juices dripped into the fire's pit. Her stomach growled like a cornered animal. The crisping rabbit's succulent smell twisted her gut. She stared at its charring tips and drooled. She sat with her elbows on her lap, resting her head lazily in her palms.

It had been nearly a week since they'd had meat. Her father had planted plenty over the summer; he'd tamed the wild raspberries and even transplanted asparagus. He'd also gathered various plants he knew to be safe. Some he knew the names to, others they compensated for by creating their own names, a game they'd played for as long as she recalled. He knew to pick her favorite, goldenrod, a tall flower with a long green stalk and curving leaves, while the yellow tops bloomed like scattered sunshine. It smelled wonderful and tasted even better. Savoring its sweet fragrance lured her deep inside memories still warm with her mother's presence.

"Celeste," her father whispered, pulling her back from the depths of her mind. "Is something wrong?"

She blinked. In her mindless gaze, her eyes had dried from the fire's heat. She was enthralled by the flame's voracious hunger as her stomach echoed her own. "Nothing," she offered with a raspy voice. "Just thinking about mother."

She could see his eyes shimmer from across the fire when she looked up at him. Just the mention of her mother had tears threatening to spill and his voice wavering as he replied, "I think about her all the time."

"I know, dad." She took a drink to ease her parched throat. They'd boiled river water over the fire, but it still retained its murky color. It almost tasted like mud and coated the inside of her throat with a slimy residue, but it helped ease the thirst. *Somewhat.*

"And your brother."

She offered him the bottle of water, but he shook his head and turned the roasting rabbit over the flame. "Dad, do you think mom would have wanted to stay up here all these years?"

"Yes," he finally said, "and no." At her puzzled glance, he smiled and wrinkled his face. "It was her idea to go deep into the mountains, but she was never one to remain in one place very long. She would have wanted to leave eventually. Celeste, you were young, but I'm surprised even you don't remember how bad it was."

She did remember. Fragments, pieces... but she remembered. Screams haunted her dreams until they burned into hellish nightmares; tearful sobs and gunshots echoed as her dad held her close and ran, his frantic cries for her mother to hurry. Her tearful cry of love for them both as death dragged her away...

"We barely made it out alive."

She knew that as well, but the loneliness began devouring her heart. It was a burning, bitter feeling, a cold chill through her spine. Alone.

"The disease is still rampant," her father continued, his eyes a menacing dark. "Or have you forgotten that as well?"

She hadn't.

It had been a few years ago during a brutal mountainous winter. They had just settled into their cabin, their aging cow safe within a makeshift bunker surrounded by a shabby, wooden fence she'd helped her father build during autumn. She'd been sitting near the fireplace, prodding the glowing embers with a stick when her father barged through the door, the wintry wind howling at his backside until he kicked the door shut again. He had an armful of sticks and logs, frozen solid from the icy storm. He'd tapped the snow from his boots and dropped the bundle by the fireplace.

"Cold, huh?"

She nodded.

"You hungry?"

"Not particularly."

A grunt. "Did you finish your reading?"

"Yes."

Another grunt in return. He brushed the snow from his brown beard. "I'm thirsty, myself. Snow's too damn cold for my tongue."

He was gulping down the bottle of water when they both heard the agitated cow cry out through the wailing wind. She jumped to her feet, but he held out a hand, stopping her.

They listened.

Again, they heard the cow. Her father didn't waste another moment. He tugged his handgun free from the holster, a grey revolver with a long barrel, and told his daughter to stay. She feigned obedience and waited until he'd eased the door closed behind him to grab her rifle. He'd recently shown her how to shoot, so she loaded it with shaky hands then stepped out into the blustery night.

The frosty wind whipped at her face, and she pulled her torn coat close while peering through the darkness. She made out the fence posts near her and the copper wire that ran between them. Trees groaned and even the cabin creaked from the wind's ill-tempered assault. Her fingers became numb from damp gloves, but she trudged through the snow and followed her father's path. Beyond, two shadows blotted the side of the cow's shelter.

"... Bullshit, I don't believe him."

"Gotta be others around here, too."

Her heart nearly burst free from her chest. She finally breathed with relief when she heard her father's rough voice. "It's only me here."

"Well, this crapshack is ours now," the first man declared with a squeaky voice. The second mumbled his agreements then coughed hoarsely.

"Feeling sick?" Despite sounding friendly, she knew her father wore a grim expression on his face.

"Damn right he's feeling sick," the first man stated. "It's freezin' out here."

Her father chuckled. Shivering and teeth chattering, he replied, "Seems more like the disease than a mere winter cold."

"Shut the hell up," the second man wheezed. "What would you know?"

"Absolutely nothing," the first man replied. The gun cocked in his hands.

She muttered her thanks that the wind howled loudly enough to conceal her terrified yelp. She lifted her rifle.

"Any last words, asshole?"

"Whether or not I kill you here," he promised, hissing through clenched teeth as the man coughed again. "You're dead anyway."

"See you in hell," the first man declared smugly, a moment before a bullet blew the side of his face into bloody chunks of flesh. His body slumped beside her father, the gaping hole in his head oozing blood into frozen white. The second man turned and fired his gun blindly into the snowy night. She ducked as they whistled past, then aimed her rifle again.

But it was too late. Her father's blade slid effortlessly from the sheath on his waist then into the man's abdomen. He pulled the knife free only to plunge it through his gut with another thrust. Then another. And another. A scream rivaled the tempestuous wind as her father forced the bloodied blade through the wound with a final thrust. The man squeezed the trigger, firing a useless round into the snow. He fell to his knees when her father stuck the blade into his neck, and the man went down with a gurgled grunt.

Her father collapsed in the snowbank, panting and wiping the blood from his knife. She walked up cautiously, rifle in hand, and gazed over two motionless bodies. Dark, almost black liquid pooled under the second man's body.

"He was infected," her father pointed out breathlessly, sheathing his knife. "The disease was going to kill him. Maybe turn him. Stay away from him, and me for that matter."

She stared into the bloody snow until he ordered, "Get a fire started. We're going to burn them."

She looked up at him, and he nodded sharply to give his thanks. But as her eyes fell to the first man, now without a face, her belly turned and twisted.

She'd spent the rest of that evening vomiting.

Her throat tightened, the once sweet roasting rabbit now smelling like putrid, dirty flesh as it burned to ash.

"I remember, dad," she said. He handed her the smoking rabbit meat. She choked down a mouthful. "So what if there's nothing left? What if the world is already gone?"

"We survive."

Two
Nightmares

Despite the lambent embers and the occasional flare of flame as her father stoked the fire, the night chilled her bones. During the afternoon on a clear day, the mountains fell victim to torrid summer heat, sweltering conditions which browned grass and killed most trees not hardy enough to withstand the sun's brutality. It became a desert with patches of green occasionally cropping up amidst a sea of dead.

This year hadn't been particularly awful. The rain fell constantly, and the river flowed strong as winter receded. At night though, the cold seemed to emanate from shadows lingering long after the sun fell into slumber. She shivered, dozing to her father mumbling curses in a wearied tone.

A hallway, long and narrow, with one dim light flickering like a struggling flame as darkness loomed beyond. Her lips parted, but her screams were muffled.

Smoke. She choked on it. Where was it coming from? She turned, but her knees buckled.

Blood. It slimed her leg. She smelled it. Tasted it.

Arms wrapped around her waist before she collapsed to the dirty tile floor. Whisked away, her fingertips skimmed across pooling blood. She panicked, until she nestled into familiar warmth, and the fragrance of summer's blooming beauty flooded her nose.

Mother.

"I've got you, baby," she whispered. Her mother's calm voice soothed fears, and coaxed the pain in her side to a dull throb. "Stay with me, baby."

"Dad…"

"He's getting your brother, and we're getting out of here." Mother's unsteady tone and hammering heart worried her. "It's going to be okay."

"No," came a strange voice, echoing down the corridor. Her mother stopped and slowly turned, panting and cursing in between. "It won't be."

Her mother screamed, "Just let us go, you prick!"

Celeste whimpered like a wayward stray then buried her face into mother's sweater.

"I can't do that."

A familiar click echoed through his droll words. Shivering, she peeked over the rumpled fabric. A whimsical smile befell his face when his gaze settled into hers. Eyes like shards of ice pierced through her. It was him; the man who'd ripped her from mother's clutches, and made sure she'd heard her brother's screams through the paper-thin walls of their confinement.

The Blonde Man!

"You've done too much damage."

"Let her go," her mother sobbed. Like the gentle pitter-patter of rain she used to feel strolling to school with her parents on a cloudy day, teardrops fell and soaked her hair. "Please, let her go."

"You both have to come with me now. I'm sorry." But he wasn't. His eyes gleamed presentiment, a promise blood would soon spill.

A ghostly growl rose through the darkness. "Put the gun down."

The man never lowered his weapon, but turned his head to shout gleefully, "I'll shoot both of them if you don't put your goddamn hands where I can see them!"

"I'm not going to tell you again, asshole," the familiar voice hissed. He stepped through the black veil looking young but worn, with short brown hair kinked around his forehead. Patches of stubble shaded his face. Blood painted his clothes an ominous red, and the thick-bladed machete in his hand still dripped the same crimson liquid. The putrid, puddled mess *squished* noisily under his boots as he stepped forward.

The man chuckled. "You're pushing it! I'll kill them both!"

"Either way, you die," father replied grimly.

The Blonde Man whipped his arm to her father. The gun bellowed. Blood splattered the side of the wall. The bullet lodged into her father's shoulder, but he kept pace and severed The Blonde Man's arm with one fierce swing. A bloodcurdling scream tore through the ringing in her ears. Then the next blow silenced him. The blade sawed through the man's jaw and *crunched* into his skull, then he fell to the floor a bloody mess. Her father left the machete embedded in the man's head as a river of red covered the floor in slick death.

His boots slid through the bloody muck. Embraced by her parents, she knew she was finally safe again.

"Where is he?" Her mother whispered, fear shaking each word as it tumbled from her tongue. "Is he alright?"

Her father didn't answer. He stepped away from them, holding her close while her mother tore from her clutches. It was like cold wind between them, a wall of ice numbing her heart as her mother cried out and ran past the bloody scene.

She turned her head to gain a better view, her sight partially obscured. A small figure slumped against the wall. Skin hung in flaps from his forehead over his eyes. Blood dripped like a leaky faucet, a haunting echo down the lonely corridor.

Brother?

But behind them, the corpse stirred. Blood bubbled and skin split as a shadow ripped through dead flesh and roared for their blood.

The Blonde Man wasn't finished with them yet.

Incandescent light blinded her as she opened her eyes to the sun glaring through the window. Perspiration soaked her musty pillow and clothes, the blankets like fire as they bunched around her, suffocating her. She choked under the heat, and kicked the woollen traps off, her mind still raw from a nightmare's relentless grip.

Was it a nightmare? Something nipped at her thoughts. An uneasy feeling rose from the pit of her gut. *Mom. Brother.*

As she stretched, hammer strikes echoed from outside. Crows cawed in the treetops, taunting and calling to each other.

A murder of crows, she mused silently, her mouth arching in a sloppy grin. She recalled when her father had explained that.

"How ominous," she'd said, staring up into the trees as black birds blended with the scattered shadows.

"My mother," he had told her, "your grandmother, believed souls of the ones you love will always find a way to watch over you."

"So they come back as crows?" *How silly,* she recalled thinking at the time.

"She believed so, yes," he said with a sigh. "It used to drive me crazy, her beliefs. Now I like to think she was right. That she's somewhere up there watching over us."

She found herself oddly clinging to that hope as well. "I miss everyone."

"I do too, Celeste."

The sight of her mother, covered in blood and with her brother's limp body in her clutches rattled her free of warm memories. Regret panged like a blunt blade to her chest, twisting through her heart cruelly. She inhaled sharply. Dust caked her tongue, and she coughed, then spat into the ashy fireplace. Her saliva sizzled on dulling embers.

Why can't I remember more?

The sun's brilliance felt like a comforting embrace as she stepped outside. She eased the old cabin door closed, shielding her eyes and glimpsing her father by the cow's shelter. Since they'd first settled, the shelter had transformed from poles and a makeshift roof into an enclosed barn. She'd lost count of the seasons he'd spent crafting it, all the while teaching her how to survive.

"Dad?" She called out.

He greeted her as she approached. Her fingers trailed along the copper wire that made up the fencing between posts. The old cow grazed within the enclosure, barely glancing at her. Instead, the old girl flicked her tail and munched yellow grass. She didn't need much to keep her in. She was happy to stay as long as there was plenty to eat.

"Looked like you needed the rest," he commented, pulling the dirty glove off his hand. The sun bore down relentlessly, coating his forehead in sweat.

She bit her tongue and quelled her curiosity for the moment. "What are you doing?"

He grunted, then scratched at his greying beard. It was unruly, as was his tangled hair, reaching down to his shoulders. "Fixing the fence." He gestured to the wooden pole. It leaned and shifted out of the dirt, useless. "Old girl decided to wander this morning."

"Must be hungry," she said, welling with guilt. Her belly was still full.

He nodded. "I'll get her some grass after I'm done." He strained to keep his voice sturdy. She knew the sun's heat wearied him. "She needs water, too. Rain barrel is getting low. The others are already drained."

"I can help you with that," she promised. It was a chore, but the river wasn't far from where they lived. "I'll gather some grass as well." Her father became increasingly paranoid about letting the old girl graze without a fence. *Wolves*, he'd mutter, *will take the only reliable thing we have left.*

"I think you better leave that to me," he grumbled, already turning his cold gaze back to the fence.

"I'm going," she replied adamantly. When he glared at her over his shoulder, she did her best to match his fiery stare.

"Take your rifle." He turned without another word. It was his way of consent.

Yes!

She collected her rifle, checked twice to see if it was loaded, then decided against changing her clothes.

When we fill the barrels, she thought, *I can wash the day's grime off in the river.*

She grabbed the twisted metal wire they used for bundling grass together and coiled it around her wrist. Her hand brushed against the hunting knife sheathed at her waist. She breathed, comfortable, and set out the door once again.

She veered left, away from the fenced-in cow and her father meticulously hammering a post back into the ground. Old Sally groaned, clearly displeased with her dwindling grass nubs and the newly patched fence.

Pine trees and a mixture of other spruces and birch towered over her, casting a shadowed ocean which stretched through the woods. Others barely reached over her head, their trunks covered in needled twigs or bright green, glimmering leaves. Pinecones and browned needles crunched under her boots.

The rifle strap dug into her shoulder, and the edge chafed against her neck as the gun swayed at her side. It felt familiar though, a reassurance of safety while she trudged deeper through the dense trees. The river thrashed against the bank when she neared the top of the grassy knoll. Further down, near the brush dotting the shoreline, tall stalks of grass poked through the damp soil, glistening with the river's spray. She seized a handful, pulled her knife free, and ran the edge of the blade along the bottom stalks. She cut them from their roots and tossed them by her feet, then repeated.

By the time she finished, her hair flattened against her forehead from perspiration. Dirt caked her face where she'd wiped sweat away with her filthy sleeves. She scrunched her nose after smelling her shirt.

Ugh. I definitely need a wash.

She wrapped the steel wire around the bundle of grass several times, then twisted both ends together. It was more than she planned on carrying, but she'd cleared another path to the river. A place away from the wolves.

She expelled an exaggerated sigh and leaned back against the bundled stalks, enjoying the crisp chill the shade provided. Songs from various birds perched in branches above were drowned by the river's ravenous roar.

Her eyes shot open, and her fingers slipped around her rifle.

I must have dozed off!

No longer under the cooling shade, the sun had cooked the left side of her face. She barely noticed as her eyes flitted around her surroundings. She eased the rifle back to her lap.

She heard it again, the distinct *crunch* of discarded pine needles and prickled cones. The rifle's barrel swayed back and forth, but there was nothing. No one in sight, no animal lurking in the receding shadows... no monsters from her nightmares.

She finally drew a breath in, her own heartbeat matching the river's ferocity. She set her weapon down. *How long have I been here?*

The bundle of tall grass she'd gathered suddenly seemed a pittance. The old girl would be grateful but would devour it in minutes. *There's grass aplenty behind the cabin,* she thought sourly. *Stubs, but better than nothing. Maybe I can get dad to let her graze if I keep watch with the rifle.*

Not like I could hit the broad side of a barn, as he would say.

However unlikely it was, she shrugged and hauled the bundle up the rugged hillside.

A twinge of unease followed her, like a malevolent stare from the shadow's depths. The bundle chafed her hip as she walked, and she stumbled after every awkward glance she threw over her shoulder. Chills tickled the back of her neck, the gun strap on her shoulder now only a small comfort.

Descending the other side, her calves cramped. She listened to the river's rumble became a dull groan in the distance. Her forearm rested lazily on her rifle. She scanned the wooded area twice, but still the foreboding persisted.

Her gaze fell to the ground. She observed her own boot prints through the brittle needles and dirt but nothing else. No paw prints or animal droppings. Just barren forest floor. Even the flowers refused to bloom. After a few more moments of unsettled rest, she heaved the bundle from the ground and continued to the cabin.

The tall, brown trees surrounding their home that once seemed so beautiful now felt like bars to a prison she couldn't escape from. It suffocated her. Part of her reasoned that beyond their haven, the world was still aflame. But curiosity would not be slaked by bitter memories and dire warnings. She longed to leave, then shivered at the thought. She couldn't be alone, yet her father couldn't bear to be far from their cabin.

A supply run, she thought. *I can convince him slowly that we can't live here forever.*

Her blood ran cold.

A throaty growl seized her spine like the chilling grip of mountain wind. She cocked her head, already loosening her hold on the twisted wire. She was quick, but the ravaged being behind her might be quicker.

It was mangy, gaunt... cadaverous. It crouched, its ears flat against its skull. Rows of yellow teeth lined the inside of its scarred snout. Lolling its tongue, frothy saliva dripped by its paws. Its fur was jet black, its eyes a menacing yellow, brighter than the stains on its jagged teeth. It eased its skeletal frame closer, panting, then sniffed the air between them. Another growl, this time from beyond the beast. She caught the glare of more yellow eyes skulking in the shadows.

Wolves.

The bundle dropped from her grasp. The metal twine untwisted and spilled the grassy contents over dead leaves and broken branches. She lifted her rifle with a sudden yell, but the wolves remain undeterred. Hunger fueled their limbs. Their snarling snouts drooled from the smell of her flesh. She aimed her rifle, yelling once more.

Then, the first wolf leapt.

She stumbled, tripping and falling, but kept her rifle steady and squeezed the trigger. Her shoulder jolted from the kickback as the gun slammed against bone, and her head *smacked* off the piney forest floor.

The shot rang through the forest, echoing in the distance, making birds flee from the rippling treetops. She panicked, losing sight of the wolves. A shriek pushed past her pursed lips. Her hands found the rifle, her finger over the trigger.

Except they were gone.

The weapon bobbed in her hands, but not a trace of the wolves remained. Just her unsteady nerves and shallow breaths.

"Celeste!" Her father's voice boomed and carried through the woods like the cry of a violent storm.

He came barging through the thicket, his silver revolver brandished in one hand while he reached for her with the other. Wherever his eyes fell, the revolver glared as well.

"I'm okay, dad," she lied between breaths. "A bear startled me, that's all."

"Are you sure it's gone? It might have cubs."

"No," she said quickly. "It wasn't a mama."

She still heard the wolf's growl as she stared blindly into the shadows. As much as it had frightened her, a small sliver of sympathy glimmered in her heart. She knew the pangs of hunger, the desperation it seeped into one's blood as the body weakened and mind fogged beyond comprehendible thought.

We were once those wolves.

"Are you sure you're okay?" He helped her up, but she nodded. Sweat glistened his brow, with droplets forming on the edges of his beard. "How many times have I told you not to wander long in these hills?"

"Dad, I said I'm alright!" she barked back, pulling away from his embrace. "I'm not a child, I know how to handle myself! I don't need you to hold my hand all the damn time!"

Her face burned red when she recalled her fleeting bravery against the charging wolf. Her furrowed brow eased into repentance, and worry curved her mouth into a frown.

He looked away from her. "Dad..." She began, but her words trailed into bitter silence, her venomous tone already succeeding in casting him aside.

"I'll see to moving the snares," he replied as she leaned down to twist the wire around the bundle of stalks. Before she could protest, he said, "We'll get water before dawn breaks."

He set off without another word or backward glance, then disappeared into the brush.

She refused to spill any tears.

Dusk settled as sunlight trickled away. The land was awash in an ember glow from the sun's last defiant shine when her father finally returned home. He smiled widely through his grey speckled beard as he strolled up the path. He held up an arm victoriously, greeting her warmly with two large rabbits. They dangled limply, clutched by their ears in his bloody fist.

By the time she'd cleared the fire pit from the previous night's ashes and charred bits, her father had the rabbits skinned and skewered. He chuckled lightly as her stubborn flame snuffed itself out before it could spread across the tinder.

She scowled back at him. "This would be a lot easier if you let me use the matches."

He shook his head, still grinning. "Those are for emergencies only. You know that. Now come on, hurry up. Rabbits are going to rot."

"I'm not taking that long," she said dully, countering his sarcastic tone. "Were those rabbits on our old snares?"

She chipped the edge of a steel knife against the jagged side of a rock in her hand. A flash, but no spark. She tried again, this time generating enough to smoke the edges of her gathered tinder.

"There was nothing at our old site," he replied, peering over her shoulder. "I moved them upstream. I was lucky to stumble across these guys. There were more of them, at least a dozen. Could only catch two. Hopefully the snares will trap a couple more."

Another trail of sparks followed her blade's strike. "We still need supplies," she hinted casually. Smoke rose from the burning grass. "Yes!" She exclaimed. Her father handed her logs as the flame devoured her tinder and reached for the moss clinging around broken branches strewn over the pit. She smiled, the chill of nightfall finally vanquished.

My fire.

"It's about time you learned to do that without the luxury of matches, or hell forbid, a *lighter*." He grinned, propping the skewered pink flesh over the fire.

She scrunched her face into a sneer. "Mother taught me."

He laughed in return, though his eyes held a frosted despair. "She always liked doing things the easy way."

Her gaze was spellbound, lost in the memory, seduced by fire's light as it danced and melted with shadows around them.

"There," her mother had declared, pulling away from the billowing black smoke. "Simple as that."

"Be careful how often you use that," her father had chided her, whispering harshly as he eyed the surrounding darkness. The road beneath her had been frigid. She remembered its cold embrace as she huddled close to her mother.

"Oh hush," mother replied. "Is he talking yet?"

"Not a word since." Haunting silence, broken only when the fire spat sparks into the night air. "Fever," he managed to choke out without a sob.

"He'll be okay," Her mother breathed, then shuddered.

"Mom?"

Her mother looked down, walnut hued hair falling over her face. "Yes?"

"I'm hungry."

"Daddy's going to get something for us all." She looked back to her husband. "How is your shoulder?"

"Hurts like a son of a bitch."

"I can't believe you took that big of a risk."

He scoffed, "He wasn't going to kill you. He wanted you and the kids alive."

"Jesus Christ," she whispered. "What they were doing to those people... They were going to do that to us. To our children. That place was supposed to be different... What's happened to this world?"

"It went to hell."

"Then where's heaven?"

"There's only more nightmares."

She shook her head. "Real frickin' heartwarming."

Heavy footsteps faded into the night as he stomped away. Her mother couldn't stop shaking.

"Mom? The fire's going out."

She wiped her eyes. Blood still stained her face, layered over dirt and grime from weeks on the road. Yet when her mother would smile, her heart filled with more warmth than flames provided.

"Thanks, baby." She reached into her jacket pocket. "Do you want to learn how to light a fire? That way you'll never be cold."

When she nodded, mother dropped the object in her hands. She gazed at it curiously. It was purple, and nearly the size of her hand. It had a steel tip, with a red button on one side. *Lighter!*

She'd often seen her mother smoking, sometimes white, tube shaped cigarettes and bigger ones the color of dried mud. It all smelled foul and obnoxious, and clung to the curtains. She would hide behind them so only her feet were sticking out of the bottom and giggle quietly to herself that she obtained the ideal hiding place. Then, she'd gag from the stale stench of smoke on the fabric.

"Let me show you how to use it properly, Celeste," her mother said gently.

"Celeste?"

"Mom?" She looked up at her father. "Oh, sorry dad."

He averted his gaze from hers, scratching at the wild tangles in his beard. "Rabbit's done," he said in a low voice.

"Your beard," she said, taking the smoking meat. This time the smell didn't revolt her. "Mom used to cut it."

He scratched at it again, then he chewed a mouthful of rabbit. "Yeah," he answered after he swallowed. He took another bite. "She used to cut my hair, too."

"You need a cut," she mused. He grunted his acknowledgment. "I could cut it for you, dad."

He eyed her over his meat. "I don't think I'd trust those clumsy hands near my throat."

"Don't be mean." She playfully stuck out her tongue. "You look like a wild beast." *Or a starving wolf.* She grinned, speaking through partially chewed meat, "I'm giving you one after dinner."

After they'd picked the bones clean of all the moist meat and lobbed jabs at one another over their ragged looks, her father bunched grassy tinder around a reddened coal, completely smothering the fire.

The cabin had fallen to the cold clutches of night, so he rekindled the fire as she readied a chair and bucket of water.

"That's for drinking," he remarked, a dirty finger pointing to the bucket.

"You should have been back on time," she chided while she ushered him to take a seat. "We'll get more in the morning, remember?"

"I still can't believe you finished mending the fence on your own." It had taken her most of the day to accomplish. Her father had been so preoccupied with snares, he'd left her to wander back to the cabin alone. Racked with guilt, she finished his chores then tackled her own. She'd hoped it would make him would smile.

"Must be getting older," she replied drolly. She eyed him seriously and wiped the blade clean. "I'm not helpless, dad."

"I know, Celeste," he said. "I just miss you being my little girl, that's all." He reached into the bucket and scrubbed his beard and hair. Grimy water dripped to the floor like mud as it splashed off his face.

"Sit back," she told him.

After she chuckled for a moment, he finally asked, "What is it?" She shook her head. "Your beard. It's greyer than I thought. It was just filthy."

He tugged at it and blushed. "It's been a long week. Just thank the stars you didn't get my wild hair. You have your mother's. Tinged red. Like autumn."

"Stop talking," she said, steadying her voice. "I don't want to slice you open."

She remembered watching her mother with a pair of silver scissors in her hand, weaving the twin blades in and out of her father's curly hair with a smile. She would chide him gently, reminding him that care kept it from being wild, then laugh to herself as he mumbled his indifferent replies. She seemed so content with her father... like the world had never ended. Celeste wanted to feel that, to know some part of her hadn't been butchered by their newfound reality.

Hell on earth. A world of nightmares.

She was careful with the blade's edge, cutting entangled strands of hair knotted and matted to his scalp from years of neglect. It didn't take long; grey still scattered among the brown, but no longer did it reach down to his shoulders like a wild mane. Unruly curls still gnarled together while other patches were short, protruding from his scalp.

Scars.

She discovered many. Fleshy pink lines which curved neatly like a blade's tip or ended with jagged notches. She traced her thumb along one resembling a crescent moon, the flesh still missing from beneath the sealed wound.

"Are you finished?"

Startled, she fumbled the blade as she snatched her other hand from his shortened hair. "No," she said. "Your beard is next."

She realized there were more scars across his face and neck the closer she cut to his skin. She took extra care around his throat, careful not to expose anymore scars. She wasn't certain what kind of memories they could drag to the surface of his mind, and he was fragile enough without the bitter past biting his heart. By the time she'd reduced his beard to unruly stubbles, his head lolled to the side with his cheek against his shoulder. She set the knife down on the table near her, smiled, and wondered if this was the tranquility her mother felt all those years ago.

Something caught her eye, just above the collar of his plaid shirt. Curving above the edges of the dirty red fabric was another scar, a small, discolored blemish nestled below his collarbone. Her fingers pushed his shirt down a bit more to reveal the bullet wound she recalled from her nightmare.

"What are you doing?"

She pulled back. "You were shot."

He tugged his collar over the scar. "You still don't remember?"

Looking aside, she conceded, "Bits and pieces. Brother... What happened?"

He ignored her for several moments, and instead shook his shirt free from clumps of curled hair. He scratched at his shortened beard. She stared after him with fiery eyes, and inwardly cursed the fractured memories.

Blood and smoke. It burned her nostrils and back of her throat, her hands slicked with crimson...

"Dad!"

"Another night," he responded tersely, his back turned while he prodded the fire. It roared as he overturned a charred log and fed another to the eager flames.

Tears. She couldn't stop them. "I can't remember the day they left anymore," she choked out between sobs. "Just the feeling that I'll never see them again."

"I remember." Solemn. Cold. He was angry, but she didn't care.

"All I remember," she cried, "is the blood... the fire... you could have saved them."

"I did what I could!" Wood splintered from the old chair crushed under his boot. He stomped the floor again. She cringed as he bellowed.

He snarled back at her, "I tried my best."

"But they're gone," she whispered bitterly, misty eyes glaring up at him. "They're dead."

It was a dagger through his heart, plunged deep enough to maim his soul. "They're dead," he whispered in agreement. His eyes darkened. "They're dead."

She couldn't disperse the hate from her thoughts. It infected every word she muttered like a disease.

"Sit down, Celeste," he finally said. "Let me remind you of our nightmare."

Three
Scarlet Rivers

The fetor of death pervaded the dank dungeon. It was dark. Faint light ebbed from a sole lantern high against the stone wall. The floor was smeared with macabre décor; blood trailed hauntingly from the prison bars to the putrid piles of torn flesh, discolored organs, and broken, jagged bones. Flies clung to the rot in the stale air and favored the decomposing mess. Others buzzed around the far corner of the jail cell where fear had loosened the bowels of prisoners awaiting the final strike of death's scythe.

Blood bubbled by his mouth when he sighed, his face flat against the stone floor. The wound on the back of his head was still a hellish fountain of gushing red. Pain dishevelled his thoughts until all he could do was close his eyes against the dull ache in his body. He was tired.

When his eyes opened next, the silence had been overshadowed by frantic, shallow breaths.

"Hello?" He tried choking out through a broken voice.

"Y-you're alive?" A small voice ventured from the dark corner of the cell. Tiny, fragile, and sounding too young to be in hell with him.

"Yes," he managed to mutter. "What's your name?"

She began to answer, but only produced a small whimper. Like a frightened cub or a toddler on the verge of tears. Pain pumped from her heart just as sure as blood while she finally muttered, "I don't want to die. I want my mommy."

"It's okay," he promised. With a grunt, he pushed himself up from the frigid grip of the stone floor. He leaned against the bars, still weak without support. The light was too dim to see much, but he peered through the shadows at the girl huddled in the corner.

Her legs were slick with waste, her clothes tattered and bloody, barely hanging to her bony frame. Her bleached hair matted with dirt and her skin colored with grime, but her bright eyes glimmered as the candle's glow reached her. Sadness welled in her widened eyes as she tried crawling even further from him, as if the bowel-spattered wall wasn't there to stop her. She held one tiny, shaky fist to her mouth as she burst into tears. She wouldn't stop calling for her mommy.

"What happened to your mommy?"

"T-they took them. My daddy," she blurted through the tears. "He was really hurt."

"We'll find them," he told her. "I promise we will."

"I'll take you to them right now," came a chilling voice. "If you want to see them, that is."

The Blonde Man edged into the firelight, one hand propped against the holstered pistol on his waist while the other held a burning cigarette to his lips. The cherry brightened like a blossoming rose as he drew in and savoured a long drag. He exhaled the bitter smoke as he neared, clouding the inside of the cell with its rancidity. "They're waiting for you outside."

A whimper escaped her trembling lips, his calm demeanor and tone enticing a deeper fear from her heart than the blood and torn body parts. His lies enclosed around her like a coffin. He smiled at her.

"You don't want to keep them waiting," The Blonde Man coaxed, gently tapping his boots against the floor. More stale smoke billowed into the cell.

"Don't you dare touch her," he threatened his captor with a growl, seething anger through the bars. "I swear, I'll kill you."

The Blonde Man smiled, the grin of a predator spotting prey. Sweat gleamed from his grimy forehead as he licked his lips. "You should be worrying about your own family."

He crashed against metal, his arms lunging between the bars to wrench his hands around his captor's throat. The Blonde Man stepped back, seized the outstretched limbs, and heaved.

His scream muffled the *crunch* of his nose as his face smashed against the metal bars. The Blonde Man spat his cigarette stub to the floor and yanked the pistol from the holster on his hip.

"You think you have a say in what happens to you or your family? You came here! You were welcomed with open arms, friend! What do you do?"

He struggled against his captor's grip, but again his face *smacked* against the bars. Blood dripped from his nose and puddled on the cement floor.

"You try and kill us! We clothed you, fed you... HELPED YOU!"

Smoke and a rotting odor more pungent than decomposing bodies stung his nostrils. He glared at his captor, his shoulder wedged painfully between the bars.

Bits of saliva sprayed rained from thunderous words. "WE SAVED YOUR BLOODY LIVES!"

Cold metal nudged his chin. Another smile found its way across the Blonde Man's face. "Now they're going to pay for your mistake. Yes, that's right. We caught them trying to escape."

"No!" His face flushed red from rage, and then with blood. The Blonde Man's gun bounced off his skull repeatedly, a sickening *thud* resounding off the barren walls with each hit. The little girl sobbed after each meaty blow.

"You piece of shit." The Blonde Man spat in his face before letting him slump against the prison bars. Blood streamed, his world a disorderly circus of nausea and hurt. The voices above him seemed like whispers from miles away, conversing quickly as they stepped around his limp body. Footsteps all around him. The girl... she was screaming.

"Now, I'd like you to pay attention to this part, friend." Someone knelt beside him, using the cold barrel of a gun to lift his head from the bloodied floor. "This is the glory that will befall humanity." The prison doors slammed.

No.

He pushed himself off the floor. Blood still soaked his hair and rushed down his neck in reddened streams. More people shuffled through the room. Two were clothed as military, a mix of shaded red and black, with machine guns strapped to their waists. The girl struggled in their grip. One clamped his hand over her mouth, smothering her scream to the dull hum of a desperate tune. A third man in a surprisingly clean white overcoat pushed a gurney under her. He appeared young and grew increasingly nervous as the others strapped the girl down. He looked awry, as if stricken ill by her sorrowful pleas. She sobbed and called out for her mother.

"You son of a bitch," he muttered, cursing as more blood streamed from his nose.

"Now this is where it gets interesting." The Blonde Man paced in front of the prison bars, grinning back with rotting teeth. "When the revolution first began..."

"It's a goddamn disease."

"It is not!" Furor poured from his outburst. "Naïve. We heal slowly, we age... Compared to other species, we're weak and harmless. Truly, our only remarkable feat is the brain. Our intelligence serves us more than any other animal." He tapped his skull. "But even then we are limited."

"What the hell are you saying?"

The Blonde Man laughed. The nervous man in the white overcoat pulled a syringe from its wrapping. "It took me a long time to procure this specimen. You should be thanking whatever deity you worship. You're able to witness a new dawn." The needle jabbed her arm, drawing blood.

"You speak of this epidemic as a good thing!" He wiped the blood from his mouth. "As though you've somehow changed as well." He watched the girl's blood squirt into a vial. The liquid shifted blue.

"Ahh, but I have." The blonde man turned to the others. "Is she prepped?"

The nervous man nodded. "Yes. She tested positive."

"Good," The Blonde Ban replied, visibly relieved. He turned to the prison bars. "You've seen what roams the night now, haven't you? The monsters conjured from the wickedest nightmares of the devil himself. Beings neither dead nor alive, trapped in bloodthirsty limbo. Where you see fear, some see power." His captor nodded to the nervous man beside him, an eager smile creeping up his face. "Do it."

He screamed and bashed his fists against the bars, threatening and spitting at them all. But the screech of a buzz saw ripping into the girl's skull overwhelmed his cries and The Blonde Man's rapacious chuckle. The bastard didn't even flinch as her blood spattered his face with a coat of red slime.

"You know," the blonde man continued as the saw whirled to a stop.

"I'm not a callous man. You think of this as a horror, a monstrous act that should be remedied. You don't see the potential for this change. You don't see that I'm saving this girl's life, giving her the strength she will need to survive in this savage new world. You don't understand." His eyes darkened. "But we're going to fix that."

"She's ready." One of the men pulled the skin on the girl's head back, revealing white skull with fleshy, pink mass underneath.

Her brain.

The nervous man fumbled with another needle, casting a quick glance back at the blonde man. He then jabbed the tip into the girl's brain.

"Bypasses the immune response," The Blonde Man said, almost snickering. "Immediate change. Fascinating, isn't it? You're witnessing evolution. This decimated our population but changed few; that is evolution, my friend. Only the strong continue."

"You monster," he hissed through the bars. "You're a coward!"

"Hush, friend. Your family will get their turn. Whether they test positive or not, I have..." He licked his lips. "*Plans.*"

"Leave them alone!"

"IT'S TOO LATE!" Silence engulfed the room until footsteps echoed from beyond the doorway. Another man appeared, clad in the same military garb as the others. Perspiration soaked his young face, and he fought to regain his breath.

"Sir," he said, "we have a problem."

"Then deal with it," The Blonde Man replied venomously. "I'm busy."

"Sir," he repeated. He quickly looked aside as a fierce glare burned into him. "T-the woman killed Jenson, sir. She also grabbed the girl."

A glimmer of hope. It was enough.

"She's going to escape," he sneered at his captor through bloodied bars. "But first I'm going to kill you all."

The Blonde Man smiled and pulled his thick-bladed machete free from his belt. "Here," he said. He handed it to one of the men restraining the girl. "If the prisoner gives you any trouble, take his head off. Though I prefer him alive."

"Sir, they're getting away."

Amidst the rotting mess of the prison cell, he smiled at the soldiers and promised, "They're getting out. And I'm going to keep my word. You're all dead."

He was ignored.

"You," The Blonde Man ordered with a finger pointed at the cohort in white. "Make sure the girl transforms. You two," he said to the others, then jerked his thumb over to the prisoner. "Break his arms and legs. I'm sick of hearing anything but pain from him."

His captor turned to the door and pulled the bloodied pistol from its holster. "And *you...*" The man standing in the doorway – a *boy*, really – began fleeing as a flash erupted from the barrel, his mouth hanging open in a final gasp or frantic plea before the bullet pierced his skull. The back of his head burst. Red and pink splotched the wall, and he crumpled to the cement. "Don't interrupt me again." He sloshed through the boy's blood as he left.

The prison bars swung open.

He cowered as both men approached. He pleaded, sobbed, and begged for their mercy. They only laughed and reached for him with eager fists.

He sprang from the cold prison floor and swung wildly. His knuckles slapped off one man's chin, and he fell back with a grunt. The other charged and wrapped his calloused hands around his neck. It felt like his head would burst as the guard squeezed his throat shut. His lungs begged for air, a fiery yearning that would not cease under the man's crushing grip. He was thrust against the wall. His vision darkened.

"Ya little shit, don't give a damn what orders are. I'm going to squeeze the life outta ya," his attacker hissed in a thick accent. Then he shrieked.

Both thumbs plunged into the guard's eyeballs, plucking each from its socket. Blood squirted and streaked up his forearms. The attacker fell to the floor, writhing in pain and blindly reaching for his weapons.

The yelling ceased when his boot stomped down and crushed the guard's skull. The other man, still dazed and picking himself off the cement floor, never saw the blade coming. It lodged into his head, splitting his skull open like an axe striking firewood.

Barely pausing to catch his breath, he grabbed their weapons, a small machine gun and a blade, then embraced a bitter, deathly taste as he waded through the ocean of red.

The nervous man in white stood behind the gurney. "Don't hurt me, please."

He didn't answer. Trembling hands displayed his anger, and the bloody girl mutating before them weighed heavily on his heart. Her skin darkened and peeled from the bone. Blood streaked from her eyes. She was changing.

His lips curled into a snarl. *I'll show them monsters.*

"Please," the nervous man begged. "I'm not like them."

"Can you stop it?" His words were like a blade to the man's throat, the question already sealing his fate. The nervous man shook his head slowly.

He walked up to the gurney with tears in his eyes he'd promised to never spill again. Not in this world. Not since he'd nearly lost everything... Yet, they fell. Death. So much of it.

The world is hell, he thought, *flooding with rivers of blood.*

He turned his back on them both.

"I'm not like them!" The man shouted as he pushed past the gurney. He didn't answer, forcing the man to yell again, "Please! They said they would kill me if I didn't help! I'm one of the good guys!"

He stopped at the doorway. "There are none left."

He raised the gun and fired a single shot. The man shrieked, staggering. He clutched at the bloody hole in his thigh, pleading with tearful sobs. His words fell upon deaf ears. The door was shut and latched, leaving the man trapped in a room of death.

He wasn't alone.

The nervous man screamed as horror took shape. He pleaded and battered helplessly against the locked door until he gurgled on his own blood. Until his sputters of garbled words ceased, and his last breath inaudible as the flesh ripped from his broken bones.

The corridors were dim, a huddle of shadows and emptied rooms that seemingly led nowhere. Rot was heavy in the air, and his tongue swam in its stagnant taste. Disgusted, he grimaced and slowed his pace at the sound of faint voices. He chanced a quick peek around the corner.

Two men. Each with long white overcoats like the nervous man back in the room of death. *No others,* he thought, gazing beyond the approaching cohorts. *For now.* He stepped around the corner.

They stopped abruptly. Gaze falling to his gun, one of the men turned to escape. He quickly fell to the floor, remaining still after bullets chewed into the wall beside him.

Shaking, the man turned and muttered, "I'm sorry, I'm sorry."

"Shut up," he said tersely, holding both weapons steady. "Where is the boy?"

"What?" Asked the man on the right. He pushed up his square framed glasses, his shaking hands betraying his calm demeanor. "You'll have to be more specific."

Bullets sprang from the barrel, a short burst that sank into the man's chest and pushed him back against the wall. He grunted and looked down in disbelief. His heart pumped the last of his life out of the wounds. He collapsed, dead.

"Where is the boy?" Still smoking, he held the weapon at the second man.

"Don't! I'll tell you," he pleaded. "Down the hall, on the right. There's a room. You need clearance. Here." He fumbled with the strap around his neck and handed him a small identification card. It was white, with the man's name and picture. Jon Wern, Head of Genetic Research.

He looked back at Jon, but the man had his face cradled in his hands, sobbing like the little girl in the room of death... "Please," he continued, "I don't want to die." He choked out another sob, but more merciless bullets silenced his pitiful pleas. Crimson spilled from the holes on the back of his white overcoat, and he slumped forward, still sobbing.

The corridor seemed endless, and blood was thick in the air. He finally came to a white door. Through the stained glass, he glimpsed gurneys strewn throughout the room. Shadows occupied them, their faces unrecognizable in the darkness. He swiped the key card, and the door slid open.

He nearly keeled over.

They were all young children, bound to makeshift beds with chains and leather straps. Some had dark skin, blending with the shadows enveloping them. Others' scalps were peeled back, red staining the dullish white bone. Some had portions of their skulls removed, exposing their fleshy brains amidst pooling black blood.

"No..."

There were rows of them. Dozens of children. Kids.

What the hell? This is madness. We came all this way... lost so many friends, good people... family. For this?

"Jacob..."

His boy lay motionless on the gurney in a far corner, dark blood staining his pale face. "I'm going to get you out of here, okay, buddy? Just stay with me." He pulled the straps loose and carefully eased the boy into his arms. "I'm here for you, little man."

Tears blurred his vision but he stood, blade in hand, as monsters stirred to life around him.

"Is she asleep?"

"Yes," she replied softly. "She fell asleep after helping me with the fire."

He nodded. "We leave at first light. I want to put as much distance between us and this... place."

"You made sure to kill them all?"

The fire spat angrily. He looked away from her inquisitive glance, his hands still warm from blood. "Yes."

"Good," she breathed. "Those bastards deserved it. I'm glad I got to watch that facility burn to ashes."

"I know."

She noticed the open backpack by his feet. "You went through them again?"

"Yeah," he answered solemnly. It detailed the infection, the various types and mutations of the strain, even the experiments being developed – yet nothing to remedy his son's condition. The creatures themselves emitted the virus, and those infected passed it on as well. It mutated so often that it was theorized a vaccine could never be developed accurately.

"Have you checked on Jacob?"

It was her turn to look aside. "He's getting worse."

"We'll find help," he began, but she shook her head.

"He's not going to make it."

"Don't speak like that!"

"I'm not going to make it either."

"What?"

She withheld a sob, but tears fell and glimmered hauntingly in the firelight. "I'm sick." She rolled up her ragged sleeve, showing him the putrid wound. Dark, bloody ooze seeped from the blackened flesh. "That bastard got me."

"No," he whispered. "No, no."

"I'm sorry..."

"Why didn't you say anything?"

"I didn't want you to worry..."

He shouted back, "Well, I'm worrying now!"

"I want you to take Celeste and find somewhere to keep her safe," she said as he turned away from her. "Please."

He fumbled through his pack, procuring a bundled folder from its depths. "Maybe we can find something... something to reverse it. We have their notes!"

She placed her arms around his waist, and hugged him from behind. He was shaking under her embrace, choking on the words his tongue could not utter. "I'm glad you stopped them, but baby... We read those files through and through. There's no mention of a cure. Only..."

"... How fast the disease spreads," he finished tearfully. "That asshole..."

"Baby..."

"I couldn't protect you," he choked out. "I couldn't..."

"Stop," she said sternly. "I love you, and I know you're hurting. But you have to stop."

But his tears wouldn't. "I love you."

"Take Celeste, and go to the mountains like we planned."

"I'm not leaving you and Jacob behind," he replied. "Besides, we don't even know if it's even still safe up north."

"It has to be," she asserted. "Have faith in what your brother said."

"I lost that a long time ago."

She smiled at his bitter words. "I know, baby. I know. But try."

"I can't leave you..."

She pulled him closer. "You watched what happened to that blonde bastard after you killed him... He changed. He became a monster. And not like the others. He was... *different.*"

"He was a living weapon."

"I'm not going to turn into *that,*" she declared with a fiery tone. "I'm not going to let our son..."

They spent the next hour holding each other, their gentle bickering a calm familiarity in a world consumed by darkened flames. She kissed him gently, knowing it would be the last. She savoured it, the lulling bliss of his lips against hers. The bitter taste of dirt and blood, the fears weighing heavy on her broken heart... it all washed away once she fell in his embrace.

Celeste slept soundly by the dying fire as he packed what he was able to carry comfortably. He clutched the old map in his hand, his brother's scrawl nearly faded from the surface.

You'll know where to find us. Frontlines. We could use you, brother. To reclaim our world. Come back to the safe zone when you can.
Jordan.

It had been nearly a year since his brother gave him the map. After discovering the brutality, he'd decided a military operation was no place to try and rebuild his family's lives, but his brother had insisted they stay. In the end, he left in the dead of night. His brother must have known. Miles from the safe zone, he opened his pack only to find the map neatly tucked inside, his brother's handwriting etched along the front.

Part of him had longed to return, but even he knew a year could change a lot. The camp might not be there anymore. Or it could be destroyed. Jordan could be dead.

Maybe if I'd stayed, none of this would have happened. The refugee camp they'd stumbled across on their journey north turned into a slaughter farm. Still, there were other safe zones, all marked on the map. He scowled at the crinkled paper another moment, then shoved it back into his bag.

"Good-bye, Celeste," his wife whispered softly, fingers entwined in their daughter's hair. "I love you so much." She pulled the greying wool blanket over her small body as the fire dwindled to an ember's glow.

"How much time does he have left?"

He shook his head as he stood. "I don't know. The girl transformed almost immediately... He's changing at a slower pace." Bitter, cold and final words. His son was nearly gone.

"Mine is spreading quickly."

"How am I supposed to just leave the both of you here?" He couldn't do it. He knew his heart wouldn't let him.

She smiled back at him. Still beautiful, despite the grime and blood. Still his, at least for now. He couldn't leave that.

"I can't do this without you." She kissed him one last time. "I love you."

"I love you too..."

"Do you remember where we spent our first summer together? The river we used to drive to in the mountains?"

He nodded. "Yeah, I do. When we first met."

She smiled and whispered, "Where we first kissed."

"We always talked about going back there someday..."

"I wish we did," she said. "It was my favorite place in the world."

He cradled both of them in his arms, squeezing tight as if he could stop their lives from slipping away. They wept as their son's chest fell one last time, and he was finally still.

He whispered in her ear, reminding her of the love swelling in his heart for her, the memories he could never forget. Moments later, her eyes fluttered. A pained moan escaped her lips. She shuddered and sucked in a small breath of air as the blade slid between her ribs.

Soon, they were both gone. Scarlet flowed rivers between them, and he wept over their lifeless bodies until dawn broke through the malefic night. He wept even as his daughter watched, her own tears streaming down her blanched face. She found herself without a world.

And he found himself without his heart.

Four
Wolf

Night. With it came the baleful chill and restless shadows which haunted the edges of firelight. Crickets chirped monotonously along with the crackling fire, a desolate melody, a symphony of loneliness. It was a plague of despair. A nauseous madness twisting the inside of her gut. Words were smothered by welling tears, her tongue knotted.

"I'm sorry, Celeste."

She shook her head, unwilling to face the pain in his eyes.

"There was a lot I promised to protect you from..."

"It's okay," she croaked out at last. "It's strange. I can't recall anything. Only the day they were gone."

"I couldn't hide that from you, but I didn't want the burden of their deaths to fall on your shoulders as well."

"It wasn't your fault," she started, but he nearly shouted back, "It was!"

She flinched. "What those people did... They were the real monsters, dad."

"If I hadn't killed them... I could have escaped with your mother..."

"No," she interjected. "We could have all died."

"You cried for days after we had... the burial." He fed another log to the ravenous fire. It roared its gratitude as he continued, "You wouldn't abandon their graves. I had almost given up on convincing you to leave. Thought of building a shelter right there."

"I don't remember any of that," she admitted. The chill ate at the back of her neck while the fire's warmth coaxed her closer. "I mean, I remember their graves but not much else."

"Everyone handles grief differently," he told her. "After about a week though, you woke up different. Content. Like you said, barely remembering anything. After that, we left."

"And eventually came here," she finished.

He nodded and replied softly, "Yes. Though that path wasn't easily traversed either."

Her tone grew stern, "This is what the world is, dad."

"I know that," he replied curtly. "Perhaps better than most."

"Then we can't hide forever."

"We can try."

Sparks *popped* and drifted along with the night's chilling breeze like fiery snow.

She scoffed, "Is that it, dad? You're giving up?"

"I'm keeping you alive!"

"You're giving up," she accused, her words dripping venom. "Mom would *hate* you for it."

The blood drained from his face, his skin ashen as he stared at her from across the room, a ghost surrounded by shadows. He got up abruptly, his shaking hands clenched tightly into fists. She refused to meet his sullen gaze. He left without another word.

But she wanted to call after him, mend his tattered heart. But her own wallowed in toxicity. Her austere life grated her fleeting spirit. Her father's despair plunged her through trepidation and somber dreams born from the shadows of their past, demons he couldn't shake off. It was killing him inside, and that infection spilled into her own soul.

She cried until the fire withered to embers glowing beneath charred remains. Her thoughts were like algid wind through her mind, her heart falling victim to the same desolation as her father.

This is all there is?

Memories gushed from her mind like feelings from a broken heart. *I want no part of it.* The serenity she once found in the mountains, the happiness it exuded for years now slipped through her fingers.

I'm sorry, mother. We can't stay here, he's killing us.

Surely, she would perish from a lonely heart sooner than succumb to the world's hellish flames. She barely felt alive.

Her tears ceased as the last ember crumbled to ash, but still she remained shrouded in the shadows she had once been frightened of. Now it was like darkness permeated through every thought and feeling her fractured mind mustered, the malignant night and her soul becoming entwined with pell-mell hatred. She wallowed in fading, discrete dreams.

She shivered from the chill when her father finally returned from outside. She couldn't see his face, and only imagined the dismal look he wore as he rekindled the fire. She wasn't ready to face him. She shut her eyes against the luminosity of rising flames.

"Celeste."

She refused to yield to his sincerity. His words should be bitter, cruelly rolling off his tongue, harming her heart the way she'd always harmed his. Yet, she found respite in his tone, and felt the unconditional love push past the frosted edges of her heart. His forgiveness warmed her like a fire's gentle touch.

"Dad..."

"Here." She looked up. Cold enveloped her as her father stood between her and the fire. His face was lost to the depths of ebbing darkness, but she muttered her apologies with teary eyes all the same.

"What is it?" She asked.

He dropped a bag into her lap, and she stared at it for a moment. Light from the fire revealed a carefully wrapped plastic bag as he stepped aside. She gave him a curious glance before he told her to open it. So she did. She tore the old, sticky tape sealing the bag shut and pulled out a large bottle. The glass was stained dark with a peeling white label. The words were faded beyond legibility, the paper brittle and crumbling under her touch. The liquid inside the bottle sloshed as she turned the smooth glass in her hands. The back had another label with small words printed on the side.

Blackberry, raspberry... Wine? How long had it been hidden in the barn or buried beside the cabin? Years? Since we'd first settled and called the mountains our new home?

"Your mother's favorite," he mused, rousing her from a daze. "Cheap stuff, but does the trick. Tastes foul."

She shot him a puzzled look. "Then why would she drink it?"

"To ease her troubles," he answered with a smile. He scratched his stubbly beard.

"I don't see how that would help," she replied tartly. She looked down at the dark bottle. *Her favorite...*

"I taught you a lot," he said, reaching for the bottle with a sigh. "How to read, write, hunt, fight... kill. Survive." He ripped the plastic from the bottle's neck. "But I've never taught you how to drink."

She watched him untwist the lid and scrunch his face from the mephitic contents of the bottle. He smiled, shrugged, and gulped down a mouthful. He cringed and shook his head, nearly choking on its repulsive taste.

"Smooth," he lied, a devilish grin peeking through his short, ruffled beard. She snatched it from his grasp and eyed the liquid swirling inside. It had a pungent odor. Bitter berries that she'd expected to be sweet. She took a drink, choked, and spat most of it out.

"This is awful," she sputtered. She wiped the dripping wine from her chin and spat again. Her tongue felt slimy with its soured taste. "I don't like it."

"Acquired taste. Take another."

She did. And it was just as awful as the first.

"You'll get used to it," he said with a small shrug.

She handed the bottle back to him.

"Your mother," he said gently, "was an avid drinker." He took another sip, the bottle glinting from the fire's eerie glow. "Before you came along, most nights she would have one of these." He laughed. It was different than his usual dreary chuckle. It boomed happiness. "Not to say she had a problem. She was always amazing. Worked hard. But she liked to partake in the devil's nectar." He passed the bottle to her again. "She stopped once she had you."

"Why?" Another bitter mouthful, though a trace of sweet lingered on her tongue. She took another drink, suddenly parched.

"Slow down, Celeste," her father chided.

He took the bottle from her. "Mostly, because you were a handful," he said with a wink. "You had my withdrawn, calm appearance... but you were a crafty little devil. Just like your mother. Two years in a row you managed to find your Christmas presents early. Opened every single one." He took another swig. "Actually, you opened *all* of them, ours included!" Another hearty laugh to rival the crackling fire, an infectious bellow she soon mimicked.

"I did not!"

"No word of a lie!" He chuckled. "I thought your mother was going to kill you."

She giggled, and her father smiled back at her. "I can't believe it!" Either she'd tilted, or the world had. She caught herself from falling off the side of her chair, and could only laugh. Everything spun, her belly burned, and she was filthy. Yet, she'd never felt so content. "So, what did she do?"

He passed the bottle off to her again. She took it and gingerly sipped the diminishing wine.

He answered, "She wanted to be mad. She was certainly furious with me. But once she'd seen how happy you were... I mean, it was Christmas."

"I miss the holidays," she recalled fondly. "Chocolate, toys... Santa!" She tossed her head back and laughed deeply like her father, nearly falling off the chair a second time.

"We still have holidays!"

Even the bleak darkness looming over them couldn't dampen her spirits or wane her rosy mood. "Last winter you gave me my own knife."

"I sharpened it," he replied stolidly. He gestured for the bottle.

With a sly grin, she took another drink. "You dulled it in the first place."

He plucked the wine bottle from her greedy grasp.

"Just like your mother," he playfully accused. "You drink too fast and can't appreciate luxury."

"I liked it," she admitted sheepishly. "But it was still *my* old knife."

"I've given you plenty of other gifts."

She rolled her eyes. "You gave me a cow."

He gasped dramatically, "But you love Sally!"

"We were supposed to eat her, remember?" She reached for the wine, but he held it out of her reach and took another drink.

"The old girl grew on me," he said with a shrug. She finally snatched the bottle from him. "Besides," he told her. "I like having fresh milk. I just wish I had some cereal to enjoy with it."

Wine splashed down her pants as she tried to clasp her hands together. "Ha!" She exclaimed. "That's what I was trying to remember! Cereal. Sugary cereal."

"You and your brother ate that crap every morning." He sighed. "Your mother always spoiled you both with food."

She tried taking another drink, spilling most of it on her chin. Her father chuckled and took the wine from her.

"I wish I had some cereal, dad." She hiccupped and managed not to sway over the edge of her seat. "Just once more."

He sighed wearily. The warmth from alcohol's dizzying shine faded as penitence crept through each coherent thought once again. "I've kept you here for too long," he muttered, his eyes swimming in sorrow. "You're not letting this go, are you?"

He took one last drink of the wine then grimaced from its bitter bite. He gave his daughter the final sip. She took the bottle and looked back at him with one eye shut. She felt weird. Almost sick.

"One last drink, Celeste. This one's for your mother and brother. Wherever they are, they've found peace. Hopefully, we may as well." He nodded his head to her, and she drained the last of the bottle.

Tears spilled, but she hid her face from her father. The bottle felt oddly cold in her hands. Empty like her heart. *Mother.*

"I promised myself I would never lose you like I lost them," he said, rubbing his eyes. "But maybe I've been the one killing you slowly... inside."

"Dad..."

"The world isn't going to rebuild itself, Celeste. It's dark out there. A nightmarish wasteland with shadows deeper than a moonless night."

"You don' know that," she countered, her tongue stumbling and slurring her speech. "It coulda' got better." She hiccupped.

"It hasn't." He pulled something from his coat pocket. Yellowed paper, frayed at the edges, with words connected in swirls and lines she couldn't read in the dimming glow of the fire. "When the disease first became public, the governments assured us it would be contained. It wasn't. It spread through our airports, touching down on every country and in every city. It mutated and became airborne, and it hit us hard. Governments created quarantine zones, working on finding a cure and isolating those who were spreading or at risk for the disease. We were all forced into them. Some people disliked the military's rule over them, and rebel camps began to fight back. That's when the military responded with lethal force."

"They killed them?"

"They killed a lot of them. Innocent people, too."

She frowned. "They just wanted their freedom."

"I know," he replied with a single nod. "But they had no clue just how deadly that disease was becoming. Quarantines were breached. Most rebels gathered their sickly loved ones and left. News hadn't spread as fast as the disease. No one knew of the mutations it could lead to. God knows how many of those torture facilities cropped up..."

"The experiments." Her stomach turned.

"Yes," he said. "The disease killed most people, but a select few were mutated into something far more sinister than military."

"I remember." Dark creatures melting into shadows and stalking from its depths. Hellish monsters taming her fiercest nightmares.

"Quarantine zones fell once the infected began to mutate. The military split into various forms of governments. Each waged war against each other for diminishing supplies. They didn't even bother saving anyone after that. It was a lot of death, Celeste. Bombs dropped on major cities with vain hopes of eradicating the infected before more mutations occurred. The country became a barren wasteland. Most military branches still had quarantine zones... though they became death sentences. No one ever left alive. Whatever hadn't fallen to the military's grasp, the creatures claimed as their own. Cities, towns, highways... Forests, beaches, deserts, and anywhere on this forsaken earth you can think of... It wasn't safe from them."

"We haven't seen one since I was a kid."

He scoffed, "For good reason. There's barely enough food to sustain us. Even the wolves are starving. There's nothing for them deep in these mountains. Soon, there'll be nothing left in this ashy world."

"It hasn't fully burned yet."

"It will." He sighed again, shadows shrouding them both before her father fed another log to the starving fire. "The world hasn't changed, and I know it. Humanity won't change. You have your mother's optimism... her hope. She had faith everything could return to normal one day. I tried to build us normalcy, but it appears I've only succeeded in pushing you away."

His determination cut off her response. "No. I know how you've been feeling lately. If you still want to go out there, after everything I've told you and warned you against... I'm not going to stop you."

"What?"

He hardened his gaze. "I'll be going with you, of course. And it wouldn't be for a few weeks. We could find somewhere else to hold up for the winter." He smiled. Uncertainty dwelled within his eyes, but his sincerity swelled her heart. "Maybe find some cereal."

She blinked her tears away as he handed her the folded yellow paper. She took it, careful not to rip its edges even more as she opened it. She steadied her blurry eyes and leaned closer to the fire. Lines crossed and stretched across the entire page, some grey and black, others red and blue curving around blotches of darker blue and black circles with names scrawled beside them. Pale patches and green swirls. One area closest to the mountains had been encircled with a red marker, the words *safe zone* above in the same bright ink. *A map?* There were others as well, some crossed out with an X and others with a question mark.

"This is where we are," he explained. His finger traced along the edges. "Somewhere past here." There were no red or black lines leading up to the edges, no towns or cities dotting the vast expanse nearby. Only a faint trace of blue trailing back to the clusters of lines and names. *The river.* "It's quite a long hike back to the highways, at least a few weeks of steady walking. We'll take our time and hunt along the way."

"You mean it?" She barely breathed the words.

"Yes," he responded warmly. "After winter, we can make our way to the safe zone. See if it's still standing after all these years."

"Safe zone?" She stared at it curiously. It seemed like such a short leap from the mountains, barely a hand's length away on the map. "What's there?"

"My brother," he said, his tone as dark as nightfall. "Your uncle." He added grimly, "Maybe."

Uncle? "Why haven't you told me about him before?" She held a hand against her grumbling stomach. Her head lolled to one side as she swayed awkwardly in her seat.

"Because he fought for the military." Her father shook his head. "They were trying to find a cure, I think. But afterwards, they just started killing the infected. No chances. I disagreed with their actions, so we parted ways."

"I don't think I'd like to meet him, then," she declared. "Everyone deserves a chance to live."

"Their actions are despicable to some, but to others they're heroes. They were trying to rebuild. He swore they would reclaim this land from raiders, rogue military, and those creatures. He promised to fix the world." His grim chuckle sounded more like a grumbling bear. "Always had grandiose dreams."

"Do you think he's still fighting?"

"Possibly." He yawned. "We'll find out when the time is right."

"I don't feel good," she blurted.

"And here I thought you'd be happier," he said sarcastically, then laughed. She tried to stand but found the ground spun uncontrollably beneath her. "I told you I'd teach you how to drink. Unfortunately, this is a repercussion of it. Good news is you'll probably never want to do this again."

She opened her mouth, intending a witty response to remind him that she was her mother's daughter. *I can drink as much wine as my mother. In fact, I may have more once we find a town with decent supplies.*

All her thoughts were smothered by a wave of nausea, and she retched instead.

That was the last thing she recalled before everything went black.

Then, she woke in a panic.

Her heart palpitated as she shot upright. Perspiration soaked her face and tangled her hair, the cold, musty cabin chilling her damp clothes. She stumbled out of her blankets, and the floor still tilted under her feet. The contents of her belly churned, and she nearly vomited again. Her foul breath resembled the bitter wine which left nothing but a sharp throb in the back of her head.

"Dad?" She called out, uncertain what woke her. Then she heard it.

"Dad!"

She fumbled through the darkness until her hands reached the rifle propped by the door. The cold metal stung her palms. She called out to her father once more. Light flashed through the window, and she nearly dropped the weapon as the sound of thunder *boomed* outside.

No. It wasn't thunder.

Gunshots!

She pushed past the disorientation clouding her thoughts. The door swung open, and she leapt out into the numbing cold.

"Dad!"

Sally, the old cow, bellowed in agitation. Snarls and growls emanated from the darkness, as well as her father's grunts and yells.

Another flash from his gun.

Blotches of black blurred around him in the brief moment of light. Wolves snapped their jaws at Sally's bloody side, and around her father's legs. Then, darkness wrapped its deathly arms around them all again.

"Daddy!" She'd already cleared the fence.

Sharp rocks and twigs jabbed her bare feet as she ran. Her frantic cries rivaled a mighty wolf's howl. Another gunshot echoed, another muzzle flash blinded her as she raised her rifle. She pulled the trigger.

The first bullet hit a patch of blurred black, and the wolf yelped in pain. It stumbled to the ground, lifeless. Her father yelled and fired again. Bright crimson sprayed along the stubby grass as another beast fell. It tried standing, then whimpered and wheezed out its last breath. The third shot hit another beast, but it merely snarled at her in return. Blood trickled down its fur. The fourth shot slapped into the earth by its paws. The beast blurred out of sight. She heard them howling and snarling through the darkness in their retreat.

"Dad!"

He was on the ground amidst the lifeless wolves. The moon beamed through a parting curtain of dark clouds like an eerie lantern casting spectral light over the scene. Blood spurted from the gaping wound in his throat and gathered in a puddle of sickly red around him. Each breath labored as his lungs filled with its spillage. It rushed past her fingers with each erratic beat of his weakening heart. She couldn't stop it.

"Don't die, daddy! Please, stay with me. Stay with me," she pleaded tearfully. "You can't die, daddy!" She pushed harder on his wound. *More pressure!* She leaned over him, but blood still leaked past her hands. "You can't die! I love you, dad! You can't leave me alone, I need you!"

He looked up at her, his brown eyes gleaming under the moonlight. Red stained his lips and trailed down his cheeks. He smiled at her.

"I'm sorry, daddy," she sobbed. "We can stay here, I promise. I don't want to go anywhere, not without you. Dad!"

The blood rushing through her fingers lessened, and her eyes found his. Time shattered, and she became lost in memories flooding her mind like blood through the dirt around her knees. His smile broadened as he stared lovingly at her, and he whispered her mother's name through the bubbling fluid in his throat. His heart pumped out the last of his life, a final spill of crimson flowed through her hands.

"Dad?"

She called for him until her throat burned, until her screams grew hoarse between sobs. His blood remained warm, her hands still clasped around his neck trying to close the jagged wound as if she could somehow reverse the damage. Ghostly brown eyes stared up to her, his faint smile an echo of the love taken from her.

She kneeled beside her father as the wolves howled their appetence for blood from the shadows. Their avidity for meat kept them close.

"Go away!" She shrieked wildly. "Get the hell out of here!" They growled in unison, refusing to abandon their kill. "Leave us alone!"

She reached for her rifle and fired the final shot blindly into the night. The muzzle flash revealed the cadaverous wolves cloaked in shadowy fur, their yellow, hungered eyes glaring back. She heard their growls fade as they slipped back into the forest, unwilling to risk another clash. Her hands dripped with death, smearing the old rifle with thick globs of her father's blood. The weapon slipped from her grasp. She fell over his body and wept.

With sunrise came purpose.

Before dawn, she'd spent the hours awash in blood, her own sick, and a noxious feeling of utter loneliness. Her heart drowned in disbelief. The frightened child in her, the part of her who remained a small girl seeking safety in her father's arms, wished vainly he'd wake from the perennial slumber his wounds inflicted. The other side of her, the cold settling in her soul, knew he was simply gone.

His body stiffened as she clutched his coat and held herself close. He'd left her, just like her mother and brother. Finally alone, she found the world seemed impossibly large, too abhorrent to endure.

She hadn't noticed the horrors of the previous night until lurid sunlight flourished across a bleak sky. Away from her father's cold form, away from the wolves soaking in their own filth... far from the wounded cow, and the sickly scent of blood, there were flowers.

By the cow's shelter, a large wooden enclosure, stood a row of green stalks slowly reaching for the brightening sky and its warming touch. Rows of aureate petals blossomed and dangled from the stalk's leafy grasp like bursting sunlight.

Goldenrod.

Her father must have planted them in spring. She'd never be able to thank him, or tell him how much their beauty resonated through her soul. She never even noticed.

But the tears wouldn't fall anymore.

Her gelid heart pumped icy remnants of hatred through her veins.

Her mind embroiled with malice. Enmity struck until every thought was as bitter as bile burning the back of her throat. Her stiff fingers released his coat, and she parted from his final embrace. Soon, she held his machete and silver revolver in her hands. She stood over his bloody corpse, her gaze never leaving those flowers.

After a long while, she set off into the woods. She followed the tracks and spilled sanguine fluid from the wounded wolf. It led her on a winding trail through thickets of trees and verdure, through fallen pine needles, and sharp cones that dug into her bloody feet with each swift step. The chill clung to the shadows as she moved through them. She was a ghost moving silently between the trees.

She came through the brush into a clear opening. Brown, parched grass prickled her feet when she stepped onto the field. Her chest burned, and sweat matted her hair. About to catch her breath, she heard a solitary yelp in the distance, followed by a distressed growl.

They were close.

Adrenaline accelerated her fragile heart. She spurred through brittle grass like death itself nipped at her heels. Her blade gleamed between the red blotches along its edges. The hammer of her revolver *cocked.*

Darkness swallowed a portion of the hillside, partially concealing the opening to a paltry cave. Her steeled eyes met a minacious yellow glare from the pit of the shadowy curtain, and then another. It was a clamor of hungered beasts, a frenzy of snarls and barks. They blurred from the shadows with frothing jaws and lolling tongues. The blood soaked to her clothes and skin coaxed them across the field. She kept her pace as the first wolf surged for her.

They were no longer the hunters of these woods, the killers of the forest; they were to be prey to her predatory will, to be the meat between her teeth. She was the wolf, and they were food. Their spilled blood would be the vengeance that quelled her ravenous gut.

She howled like the beast she'd reverted to, a crazed animal tainted with fury, cornered and trapped. She raised her father's revolver. Her cries were silenced by a thunderous clap.

Blood fanned across dead grass as a bullet sank into the wolf's skull. Its limp body slumped then rolled through the dirt by her feet. She kept charging. The other wolves burst from the shadows.

Another bullet grazed the shoulder of the next wolf, and then her gun *clicked,* empty.

Rotting, carnivorous teeth ripped her sweater as the animal's jaws closed around her arm. Blood drenched her face. Her blade carved into its neck and wedged in its spinal column. The wolf collapsed as the third one attacked.

She screamed rabidly, first in an angered daze when the wolf knocked her to the ground, and then in pain as a cloud of red misted from her right shoulder. She struggled against its hold, but the wolf pinned her to the dirt. Flesh tore from her shoulder. Warmth spread down her breast and side, saturating her grimy coat and pants. Fiery pain followed, and she belted out another agonized scream.

The wolf lunged again.

She couldn't pull the machete free from its bony imprisonment. Saliva and her own blood rained down as the wolf's jagged teeth reached for her neck. She braced, striking the wolf with the empty revolver. The beast yelped, clubbed again. The third hit dazed the gaunt beast long enough for her to crack its skull with another hefty blow. She didn't stop until her arm became too weak to pummel its dead flesh any longer.

As she emerged triumphant, she thought her anger would ease and her heart would no longer beat a funereal tune. Instead, she suffocated in despondency and the remnants of the reaper's visit. The blood around her was like deathly brush strokes to a satanic painting. It soaked into the soil. Crimson dripped from the gun's silver nozzle as she clutched it in one small, trembling hand.

Death.

It was all around her. In her heart, in her mind. Its rancidity stained each thought, burned her nostrils, and left its foul filth clinging to her tongue until she lost the remaining contents of her belly in a dark stream of vomit.

She wanted to leave, but succumbed to her mournful wails and writhed in the blood she'd spilled. She called out for her father, hoping he could somehow hear her tearful pleas, her bellows of anger, and her vain hopes that he'd save her breaking heart.

She was lost.

She heard it long before she cared to open her stinging eyes. It was a whimper, followed by a small, frightful bark. Despite her head feeling full of cement, she sat upright and peered through the sun's blinding glare.

It was small, with mangy, black fur and a skeletal frame. It poked its dark nose into the air and sniffed curiously, distraught from the blood but eager to explore. It eased itself from the shadowed den, panting from the heat and revealing a small set of white teeth. It was still a pup, naïve and clouded in uncertainty as it barked and growled, trying vainly to stir its lifeless parents.

Her tears flowed like blood from a wound that could never heal.

PART II.
TOWN (LATE AUTUMN)

FIVE

INTO A DYING FIRE

IT TOOK her awhile to regain her composure.

Hours passed in a sickened swirl of disbelief that left her eyes bleary from constant tears. Sally had survived the attack, now warily grazing beside the cabin. Celeste left her there after salving her wounds with the leftover honey her father had collected and stored, an act which seemed to please the old girl enough to part with some of her milk.

She avoided her father. Fortitude wavered whenever his presence trickled into her thoughts. She couldn't bear to see him yet.

So she locked herself in their cabin and cleaned the death off of her. First, she stripped her bloodied clothes and tossed them near the fireplace. She would burn those later. Tears blurred her sight as she rummaged through his crumpled clothing. She chose an old sweater, dark blue and stained, with a hood dangling by a few stitches. But it still smelled like him, so she wore it. His jeans were too big, so she opted for his sweatpants instead, then collapsed on his bedding.

A growl roused her from a daze.

The wolfpup poked its nose up the edge of her father's bed. It cocked its head to the side, its ears perked and tongue hanging. It yelped at her.

Almost forgot about you. She retrieved the bucket of milk from the table, and the pup lapped it up eagerly.

She winced. Her wounded shoulder burned and rubbed against the woolly sweater. She peeled her clothing off again, using the last of their water to rinse her dirty wound. She applied the honey salve to it sparingly then dressed it with strips of fabric she tore from a cleaner shirt.

She burned her bloody clothes. The putrid smoke billowed into the room, and she choked on its thick rancor. But she adamantly remained to watch it wither into blackened ash. The pup beside her whined along with the crackling fire and buried its nose in its paws.

The first night alone nearly drove her to madness. Her heart tried *thumping* its escape through her ribcage, each beat a heavy pang of regret.

Sleep never came.

She spent the night clutching the soft fur of the pup, who howled along with her bellowed sorrow. A chorus of desolation.

The following morning, guilt settled like an insatiable hunger in the pit of her stomach. Shivering from the damp morning mist that fogged through her open window, she pulled herself free from her father's bedding and rubbed her blurred eyes. They burned raw in her skull, puffed from hours of crying and staring at the dark ceiling. Screaming until her voice went hoarse. She groaned as she swung her legs over the bedside and sloshed her foot through something warm.

She propped her head in her hand and looked at the puddle. The wolfpup whined quietly and stared back with round eyes, bright and vibrant gold.

She smiled. "You need to learn the rules if we're going to live together."

By the time she calmed her erratic heart, the sun had risen over the treetops and plunged part of the property in shade. It was warm when she stepped outside, but she couldn't stop trembling. Her blood ran cold.

She clutched his dark, red blanket close and circled the enclosure. Her father's body remained lifeless amidst the drying blood, now stained along the grass and soil. She cringed, eyes watering.

His wound was horrific, worse than she'd thought the previous night. His beard no longer peppered grey, instead speckled with crusted blood and dirt. Her legs threatened to buckle. She approached slowly, covering him with the blanket. Guilt fueled more tears. Insects had already started consuming him, and the decay from the sun's heat sickened her heart.

I should never have left him so long, undignified and alone.

The pup sat near the fence, wary of the dead wolves she refused to acknowledge.

It took her longer than she thought her stomach could last, but she dragged him closer to the cabin. Bemused by the apparent game, the wolfpup nipped at her hands and feet. She was exhausted. Worse, dusk reached across the sky and settled her surroundings in shadows. Night approached quickly.

I won't be sleeping tonight either.

She stayed close to her father's body, feeding tinder to the fire. She stared into its dim glow, lost in grief but too ravaged by fatigue to muster another tear or infuriated scream.

Over the fire, asparagus roasted. It was the last of what her father had planted, and she knew he'd been saving it for himself. She never liked it. It tasted foul and smelled worse. Yet she found herself nibbling on its charred ends, each soured bite filling her with an unbearable memory.

The wolfpup growled at her feet, hungry and unimpressed with his green dinner. She finally gave in, and fed the pup the last of the dried rabbit meat. She even gave him a few soft bones to chew on afterward. The pup's excited yelps and slobbered thanks had been the only moment capable of coaxing a smile from her sullen face.

As dawn broke through the gathered clouds and dreary night sky, she allowed the fire to die. She found herself in her father's garden, toiling away at his menial tasks he'd perform every morning. The cold lingered after sunrise, and she knew the comforting embrace of summer would soon yield to frigid snowfall and glacial winds. *I want to be far from here by then.*

Most of the berry bushes were picked clean. The vegetables long gone, eaten in place of meat when their snares were empty. She thought of checking them, but feared being far from her father. She couldn't, not yet.

She frowned and peered up into the treetops. Crows cawed and glared back with dark, beady eyes.

Damn it. Enjoying your free meal, arseholes?

She cursed. The pup yelped back, rolling lazily in the dirt by the cabin. "Oh hush," she grumbled.

Finally, she resolved to dig her father's grave. It was a decision weighing heavily against her heart. It was finality.

She walked, her mood somber and grim. The wolfpup's whimpers echoed her loneliness. She rounded the cabin, wiping the sweat from her forehead. Behind the dwelling, nestled right into the wood frame, was a shed nearly half the width of their home. It was small, but deep enough to step inside and close the door comfortably. He'd built it only a year ago to house tools, excess junk, and firewood.

She heaved the door open and brushed the cobwebs from the ceiling. Her father always left spiders alone, but she disliked their sticky traps entangled in her hair.

Gross!

She let the sunlight peer through the opening, and her heart burst. There were rows of shelves covered in cloth on each wall. On the floor, tucked into each corner, were almost a dozen jars, each packed full.

She reached down and plucked a heavy jar from the dusty floor. Crammed inside were thin strips of dark meat. The sweet, smoky scent drifted through the lid.

Jerky?

She grabbed another jar. Blackberries. Dried, wrinkled, and clumped together. Each jar had meat or various berries, and under the cloth there were more drying.

But how?

She ran her hands along the wall and finally found a latch above one of the shelves. She unlocked it and pulled the panel open. Sunlight flooded the shelf and lit the room up enough for her to see the other latches. The meat and berries still under the cloth had already lost moisture.

She marveled at her father's work, then shook her head and smiled at his stubborn stance.

He had food all along.

The old man taught her to hunt, and without procuring food, there had been consequences. The snares must have been motivation for her to succeed.

For so long, I cursed him for treating me like a child when all he was trying to do was help me survive.

So lost in her own angst, she'd never even noticed the food he'd worked hard to grow and kill, nor what he'd stored for them both. Suddenly ashamed to satisfy her grumbling stomach, she went back to her father.

The smell was horrendous, and guilt ate at her heart from her lack of decency. She'd been so consumed by grief... She hated herself for it.

But something nagged at the back of her mind, an incessant, jabbing thought.

She pulled part of the blanket from his body and reached into his pockets. Rummaging, she finally pulled it out of his coat. It was the yellowed and brittle map, now stained with his blood. She opened it, tracing her finger along the river leading out from their supposed position. She stopped at the words *Safe Zone*. There were many roads and rivers, lakes and cities and all sorts of unseen horrors in between.

Something else caught her eye.

You'll know where to find us. Frontlines. We could use you, brother. To reclaim our world. Come back to the safe zone when you can.

Jordan.

She spent the night gathering everything she wanted from the cabin, and packed it into her father's bag. She took her winter clothing, various tools for cooking, and provisions for water. She grabbed her father's favorite book, a withered old science fiction novel with a faded cover and yellowed pages. She even grabbed one she hated, a torn book with ripped pages called *Dictionary*. It had no story, no adventure... just words and more words to define those words. She abhorred it, recalling the days her father forced her to read, recite, and then explain what she'd learned. She stuffed it in her pack anyway. His machete found a place at her side along with the knife he'd given her repeatedly for their makeshift holidays.

She also cleaned her father's silver revolver, but left a trace amount of his blood on the handle. She tucked it away with her small supply of ammo.

She cleaned the rifle and adjusted the straps so it tied to the top of her bag. It left her shoulders free to carry her bow and quiver, though she only had a few arrows worthy of taking. The others were brittle and breaking, so she tossed them into the fireplace.

She found a second, smaller bag with bright colors tucked away under her father's bed. It had obviously belonged to her mother. Inside, there were letters, each addressed to her father and written in her mother's hand.

I can remember her writing, she thought with growing rancor. *But not the moment she vanished from my life.*

She tossed them on her father's bed before loading the dried meat and berries. She emptied most into fabric and containers she found that wouldn't shatter as she traveled. She fed the pup a gracious portion and filled her own belly as well.

Night reclaimed the land.

Her father had been moved into his own bed, her mother's letters clutched in his stiff fingers. Around the floor, she spread dried grass and brittle tinder, then surrounded his bed with remaining firewood. She stood with him, but couldn't find the strength to say anything. So she cried.

She sat on the steps of the cabin away from the glare of the fire pit. She found no comfort in its warmth. The wolfpup edged closer to her, still licking his lips with a pink tongue, grateful for the meat. She placed one hand on his head, and he nudged her gently. When he looked up at her with big, round eyes, she couldn't help but smile back. It was a radiant shine, a bright, golden gaze like the luminance of the sun. His eyes warmed her.

"You need a name," she said lightly, her voice cracking. She coughed, and said, "Would you like that?"

The pup flicked his ears at her words. She chuckled.

"Aurous," she declared, scratching the wolfpup's neck. "I think it suits you."

She thought the tears would finally stop, but as the fire caught along the tinder in the cabin, eventually consuming the entire structure, she cried out until her throat tore and her eyes stung. Until her heart burned along with her old life, charred and ashy like the cabin.

She sat in front of roaring flames, screaming hoarsely and braving its ferocity. Aurous howled beside her, stricken by her grief.

Weeks passed.

The memories bubbled to the surface of her thoughts, but pain no longer gripped and twisted her heart. It wasn't gone, but it dulled. She'd sat there until the cabin and her father had burned to ashes. She'd made sure of it. Sally had already wandered off, and the old girl only had a few more seasons left, if she even survived the winter. She'd contemplated taking the extra meat, but shuddered at the thought of killing the old cow. It had been hard enough to say goodbye.

Aurous grew. Instead of ragged fur and bony ribs, he was sleek with lean muscle. He excelled on a steady diet of meat, and even enjoyed the occasional berry if the night's hunting yielded nothing. Aurous had proven more resourceful, managing to plunge his snout in the rushing river to catch fish, and was more than happy to share. Though, he growled a dire warning that the guts were solely his.

Of course, she'd say, and slop entrails slop by his paws. She was more than happy to accommodate.

Her failure at hunting began to discourage her. Frequently, she'd been within range of a doe, but either fumbled with her bow long enough to rouse its suspicion, or Aurous would burst into a puppy frenzy and chase the deer deep into the brush. He'd return, panting and clearly impressed with himself, while she grumbled and tore a strip of jerky in half for them both.

She followed the rapid waters her father had marked on the map. It was a sinuous river with no trails or paths nearby she could safely traverse on. She spent the days trudging through untamed woods and hacking down thickets in her way. It was tiring, and everything she'd packed added to her exhaustion as the hours wore on.

Dusk and dawn she spent hunting, hoping to appease her belly's complaints. Squirrels, fish, and rabbit... but no large game. Nothing with richened flavor and enough fat to stop her own from deteriorating. Her body was lean like the wolf, though that did little to help build muscle.

Nightfall she spent huddled close to Aurous with her back against a fire, warding off the chill that bit her exposed skin and bound her heart in frigidity.

Life became arduous.

She figured it had been more than a month since she'd left home. The sun was setting as she gazed longingly up at the darkening sky. Stars blinked through the misty clouds while the crescent moon hung overhead with a lazy glare. The mountains were a jagged silhouette against the fiery sky. She heard the hum of the river off beyond the thicket. Trees became scarce, giving way to browning bush and tall, dead grass. Behind her, the makeshift path sloped into a steep climb and curved into the thick verdure.

Something foul burned her nostrils.

Aurous stood not far from her with his leg held high. A stream of yellow flowed and puddled by the patch of dead grass. He lolled his tongue at her proudly.

"Must you do that so close to where we sleep?"

Her nightly routine had turned second nature; she easily kindled a flame from bunched sticks and a small spark. She resolved to save the rest of her flint-rock, and instead bundled a burning coal to safely carry in the morning. Clean her weapons. Sharpen her blades. Push-ups until her arms burned.

Tonight, she settled for dried berries instead of hunting. Aurous growled but bitterly accepted. She gave him a handful more just to cheer him up.

The pup fell asleep by her feet rather quickly. She wriggled her blistered toes against the heat and then pulled them back into the cold. Her legs ached fiercely, but the fair weather dwindled with each passing day, and resting would only set her back.

"I want to visit a lake," she blurted out with a yawn. Stretching roused Aurous, and he opened one eye lazily to gaze up at her. "I'd like to find one before it gets too cold."

She trembled slightly every time her fingers brushed against her father's stained blood splattered across the aging map. She tugged it free from her coat and carefully unfolded it.

It was blank in the upper right corner. Except for a winding, blue line that led from the edge of the page down to the cross of roads and highways. The serpentine river branched off in several places, curving down. If she kept traveling along the same river, she would eventually reach what was called Highway 97, and from there it stretched down through various towns and crossed out settlements until it stopped at the Safe Zone. If she found where the river separated, it would lead her along the edge of the forest to a town that hadn't been crossed off with red marker. From there, it was a long but fairly straightforward journey to the marked safe zone.

If it's still there.

As she studied the map, she found various other settlements and cities marked *safe zone* were all impossibly far. At least during the winter months.

But this was the zone my father wanted to stop at first.

There was a lake she could visit along the way. The path would also give her ample time to hunt and gather in preparation for winter. She hoped dimly it wouldn't be as arctic as the mountains.

Sleep proved futile. Soon crickets ceased humming as birds chirped and sang to one another in the treetops. She yawned and tried not to stir Aurous from his slumber. The gun slipped out from under the bundle of clothes used as a makeshift pillow. Her fingers were stiff and sore from gripping the blood speckled handle throughout the night. Fog settled ominously around them. She shivered beneath her dampened blankets and shifted closer to the wolf.

But the wolf suddenly sprang to his feet and growled.

She was free of her blankets as he took off into the mist. Anxious, she forced both boots on her blistered feet then followed him through misted uncertainty.

"Aurous!" She whispered harshly, her eye glaring down the barrel. She held her arms straight, bracing for the gun's kickback. "Where are you?"

She heard another growl before he burst into view. He was crouched low, his ears perked up, slobber dripping from his snout. He gnawed on a white, glistening bone with strands of thick, red meat still clinging to it. She stared at him for a moment, bewildered, until her heart sank into her troubled gut.

No!

She ran back through the fog. Aurous sensed her panic and followed, though had difficulty balancing with the large bone in his jaws. She ignored the pain in her feet and legs, uncaring if each stomp through the dirt revealed her location.

By the time she reached her campsite, her brewing anger came to a boiling point, and spilled over into frantic cries and frustrated tears.

Everything had been taken.

All she had left was a smoldering fire.

Rocks and twigs jutted into her knees as she collapsed in anguish. Her food, weapons, clothing, and personal belongings had vanished. White smoke fueled the fog's density around her until embers dimmed to ash.

Aurous growled behind her, but cowered and crouched while she screamed with vehemence. The wolfpup whined at her sudden outburst, but she didn't care. For too long this storm gathered in her heart, brewed in part by turbulent thoughts and stubborn memories that wouldn't wither and perish.

She was sick of crying. Her father had left nothing to contingency, yet she'd grown careless too often since his absence. She'd failed at hunting, knowing if she could never master the bow's elegance she'd be forced to use the rifle. Limited ammo meant only a few hunts, and then her two steps forward would seem like three steps back. Even her snares turned up empty, neither tied nor bound with the same delicacy her father attained, but crude and bulky. After her berries vanished without her traps being disturbed, she suspected the animals were just plucking the bait and leaving. She could only imagine the snickering squirrel or rabbit that stumbled across a free lunch to enjoy. If it hadn't been for her father's food supply, she would have starved.

No, she thought, *not entirely true.* She had enough sense to know which wild berries were safe to eat. It wasn't much, but it would help. Aurous also proved to be a keen fisher and a loyal friend. *Without him...*

She bit her lip. "I'm sorry," she whispered, her voice trembling. "I'm sorry."

Aurous only growled in return.

Her chest twisted in knots as she turned to the wolfpup, but he had no eye for her tears. Instead, he nudged his nose into the dirt. She peered curiously over his shoulder until she distinguished the pattern of a shoeprint in the tussled up dirt. Shoeprints that led away from her campsite.

"Aurous, you're a genius!" She exclaimed with an enthusiastic scratch behind his ears. "And I love you," she added gently. He replied by nipping at her hand.

She followed as he dashed along the shoeprint trail, her revolver close to her side.

The wolf ran ahead. She moved carefully, gun in hand. He would parade into the fog, turn his head back to make sure she was still within view, and then proceeded to dash further along the makeshift trail. Caution flooded her mind, but her quickened heart fueled her focused ferocity. She needed to reclaim her belongings.

She quickly lost sight of the wolf, but another large shadow blemished the white curtain ahead. As quietly as she could, she cocked the hammer back on her revolver and approached the shadow.

Another distinctive *click* resounded throughout the foggy surrounding. Her speeding heart jumped up into her throat, and her blood chilled and drained from her face. Her arms trembled, unable to cope with the weight of her weapon.

"Drop the gun," a stern voice ordered. It was a woman, with a broken tone that cracked at the utterance of every word. "Drop it or so help me

God, I'll paint the ground with your brains."

She complied and eased the hammer back into place, letting her father's revolver slip from her fingers. It hit the ground with a weighty *thud* as cold metal jabbed the back of her head.

"Easy, girl. We don't want trouble."

"Then why did you take my stuff?" Celeste asked bitterly, silently cursing her foolishness.

"We just need your supplies," came the gruff reply. "Ellie, take this girl's weapon away."

"Yes, mama." A tiny girl, no taller than Celeste's hips, stepped out from the fog ahead of her. Dirty hair that had once been bright blonde jutted from her head like straw. Her skin was tanned from grime and dirt, not the sun. Her little pink dress hung in tatters around her shoulders. She clutched a brown, stuffed bear in her arms as she approached and wrapped her hands around the hefty weapon.

Celeste stared at the little girl named Ellie, her blood still frosty sludge pumping through her veins. She had her weapon cocked and her mind riddled with anger. One slip, one twitch... She could have killed that little girl.

"Now, you get far away from here," the woman began, but Aurous snarled and lunged for her.

His teeth ripped through the skin on the woman's arm, and Celeste heard the weapon drop to the ground. The woman shrieked, but Celeste had her knife free from its sheath.

"Aurous!" She yelled, kicking the rifle away from the woman's desperate grasp. "Enough!"

She had to tug at his fur, but eventually the frenzied pup abandoned his bloody grip on her arm. He snarled even as Celeste froze at the sight of the little girl aiming her own revolver back at her.

The gun's barrel wavered, and Celeste knew the girl would only be able to fire one shot before the kickback overwhelmed her tiny grasp. With luck, the bullet would miss her completely. She stood there, knife in hand and ready to pounce. *What would father do?*

Survive.

Revolted, she hesitated.

"Ellie, put down the weapon," the woman said gently, panting and clutching her bleeding arm. Crimson soaked her fingers and dripped into her lap. "No use getting us all killed."

Celeste hardened her heart as the child lowered the gun and eventually dropped it to the ground. She eased away from Celeste and clutched her teddy bear close.

Gun in hand, Celeste asked the woman for her belongings.

"In the house," she replied grimly. Celeste apologized for Aurous, but the woman waved her words away. She smeared blood across her wrinkled forehead trying to wipe away sweat.

At gunpoint, the woman retrieved Celeste's bags. She'd already gathered her rifle and after a quick browse through her pack, she found nothing missing.

"It's all there," the woman declared proudly. "I wouldn't lie." She glanced over her shoulder.

Someone coughed inside. Lightly at first, then they launched into a fit of gurgled sputters.

"Is someone hurt?" Celeste queried.

She lowered her revolver and reached into one of her bags. She pulled a small pile of folded cloth and handed the bunched material to Ellie.

The little girl stood puzzled at first, but moved toward the offering despite her mother's sharp refusal. Celeste opened the cloth, revealing strips of dried meat and berries clumped beneath.

The girl smiled at the sight of food and eagerly grabbed the cloth.

"Why are you doing this?" The woman asked. She ran her long fingers through her short, uneven brown hair. She shifted nervously, wary of the stranger's sudden kindness. "After we tried taking it all?"

Celeste shrugged. "You were just trying to survive."

The woman still would not yield to her sincerity. "Thanks," she replied coldly. "But once my husband gets over his sickness, we can get out of this forsaken place."

"Sickness?"

"Yeah," she said, a frown wrinkling her old face even more. "Caught a cold and wouldn't stay off his damn feet. Wouldn't listen until he was sick with fever."

Celeste glanced through the doorway. Past the fiery glow and the stale smell of perspiration, a balding man lay sprawled across the floor with blankets bunched around him. His skin looked charred, blackening like he sat in the pit of a fire becoming ash. Head glistening with sweat, he turned and glared back at her through the doorway. His eyes were flushed white, and blood dripped down the corner of his mouth.

No...

"I think you guys should leave here."

"What?" The woman asked, taken aback by her harsh tone. "What are you saying?"

"The disease," she whispered. She covered her mouth and nose with her dirtied shirt. "I know what it looks like. And that's it."

"You insolent brat!" The woman suddenly shrieked. "How dare you! Where are you parents, you sniveling child? Who taught you how to speak to your elders?"

Confused, Celeste said, "But you could catch the disease as well. If he turns, then you could die."

"From a cold? I admire your imagination, child," the woman sneered. Her fingers twisted the gold chain on her neck. A small t-shaped ornament hung from it. "I think you should go." She grabbed her daughter's hand and led her through the doorway.

The child's green eyes stared longingly at Celeste as the door closed. She couldn't help but think it was a silent plea.

So she left. The fog receded to a transparent cloud as she sat at the river's edge, her mind wandering far from her mundane tasks. Aurous tried his luck with the few small fish swimming along the shore while she filtered river water into canisters to boil.

Those sorrowful green eyes wouldn't fade from her thoughts. *Was that woman crazy, or am I?*

As night fell, she lit a small fire large enough to boil water. She was wary of revealing her campsite now, certain a presence lurked behind every shadow. She kept her weapons close, but it offered little comfort.

What if the thief happened to be another child? Would she pull the trigger carelessly? Those grim questions nagged at her restless mind as she shut away the world and feigned rest.

By morning, she sought to resolve the trepidation in her heart. She walked back through her previous campsite after she'd packed her belongings and cleaned her weapons. There was little fog, and the dark wood of the house blotted against the green trees and grass surrounding it in the distance. She approached cautiously, trying to hush Aurous as he growled.

She called out to the woman and her daughter so they wouldn't think her a trespasser. Then, she held up the water canisters and apologized loudly for her callous remarks.

No response.

Something clearly distressed Aurous. He growled lightly, and she inched closer to the dark house.

The door was ajar, only slightly, but even she began to smell the sickening scent of blood. She stopped at the doorway with her revolver drawn. Aurous crouched low by her boots, his ears flat against his skull and saliva bubbling around his sharp teeth. His bright, golden eyes glared into the darkness of the house. She cocked the hammer back on her revolver. Her finger trembled on the trigger guard as she pushed the door open with the barrel.

Blood slickened the wood beneath her boots. Thick globs streamed down the walls to create rivers and oceans of dark red. Wooden splinters scattered everywhere, along with larger broken fragments of furniture. Torn strips of blanket soaked in blood, while the food she'd given them still sat upon the counter, untouched.

There were no bodies... only fleshy chunks of crimson around a little pink dress and the grimy clothes the woman had worn. The brown teddy bear sat propped against the wall, saturated in death.

She closed the door and retched. Partially chewed berries and meat from her hastily eaten breakfast splattered the side of the house and her boots. She tried catching her breath, but her heart wouldn't stop hammering and battering her chest.

I could have helped them.

She clutched her rifle close and left as quickly as she could.

The unease ate at her mind for days. Even convincing herself there was little she could have done, the ache in her belly wouldn't cease. She packed and followed the river for an entire day and night before she stopped, too exhausted to continue. Then she slept, plagued by nightmares. Her clothing and blankets were soaked in sweat, and Aurous growled with worry by her side.

She walked mindlessly and gave up on hunting, then glimpsed a squirrel burying nuts by an old tree. The trunk warped, and now the top of the tree hunched over the river like an old, decrepit man, its leafy limbs skimming across the rushing water.

Aurous was behind her with his nose in the bushes, so he hadn't noticed the small animal or he would have surely given chase already. She eased her bags to the ground and reached for her bow, only to realize the arrowhead was larger than the creature. She cursed quietly, then spotted a small stone. Rough, with jagged edges and about the size of her palm, the stone was light enough to throw easily but heavy enough to hurt.

Her rifle slipped from her shoulder and crashed into the gravel, startling the squirrel. It dashed away from the tree. Aurous gave chase.

She took a chance and lobbed the stone as the squirrel shot up a nearby tree.

Thud!

The rock struck the poor animal off balance. Dazed, it slipped from the rugged tree bark. It panicked as reality settled into its frantic brain, but Aurous snatched the little creature before it smacked against the ground. Blood trickled from his frothy lips as he dropped the half-dead squirrel by her feet.

"Thanks," she said sincerely. "But next time try not to slobber on it."

Stomach satisfied, she set off the next morning with a smile on her face. The lake was now a short distance from her campsite.

More beautiful than she imagined, the water twinkled through the trees under the sun's blazing glare. It smelled foul, like the remnants of a gutted fish only Aurous and her father seemed to enjoy. The air was thick with it, and mosquitos thrived in swarms that nipped at her exposed skin. Aurous whined, biting his skin through his sleek, black fur.

The water was calm and graciously warm as she strolled along the shore. *Little Green Lake.* The name echoed through her mind. It was a tiny blip of blue on her father's map, but still important enough to garner a name.

And rightfully so, she thought, mesmerised.

The river flowed directly into the lake on one side. She noticed where it branched off into another rushing stream not far down the shoreline. The lake itself was shrouded in elegance. Its serene waters glimmered green under the sunshine. For a moment, she closed her eyes against bitter memories.

Sorrowful green eyes haunted her thoughts.

After an hour or so of washing her clothes, herself, and Aurous, she finally set off once more. Darkness loomed, so setting up camp in a suitable place became her priority. Aurous glared at her through the sopping fur over his eyes. She laughed. He didn't enjoy the water as much.

She was about to make camp as sunlight faded and plunged them back under night's haunting eye. The trees gave way to long green grass reaching up past her waist. Aurous yelped and growled at her, dashing and playing through the grass unseen. She'd reached the edge of the forest.

Her boots no longer slipped through soil, but *stomped* down on rubble. There was a road beneath her, cracked and crumbled as vegetation protruded from beneath. Beyond, under the fiery glow of a setting sun, she identified structures along the side of the overgrown road not far from where she stood. Even further, just beyond the slope of a mountain, she saw treetops, houses, and clear roads.

She tugged at the map inside her coat and unfolded it. Through the dim light, she read *Little Green Lake* and the snaking river she'd followed. *Antler Creek. What a strange name for a town.*

"Let's find a place to settle in for the night," she told Aurous.

She pulled her coat close as the wind howled its chilling wrath. The wolfpup growled in response, but strained his ears toward the forest. Amber eyes glanced through the darkness, then he followed her down through the overgrown verdure.

If the world had burned, she now found herself near its charred remains. She walked into a dying fire.

Six

Harbinger

Night descended quickly.

Shadows thrived as daylight waned into a fiery, dulcet glow. Pullulating darkness smothered everything in a haunting blanket of black. The moon peeked over the mountain, gazing over the forested top with dim, pale light like a ghostly lantern in the distance.

She dashed into the shadows despite her body's protests. Her bones ached, and her muscles frayed. Her feet were swollen, each step like a set of sharpened nails into her heels. Her shoulders chafed raw from the bow and heavy bags. Her chest pained, failing to grasp enough air with each ragged breath. Still, she didn't want to stop.

She kept her revolver cocked, past mistakes still freshly imprinted on her mind. Since, she remained wary, especially without the cover of trees. Or without daylight.

Aurous grumbled beside her but kept the same pace. He was weary as well, and favored his right foreleg. Sympathy pooled in her heart until she slowed her run into a cautious amble. But it wasn't until they reached the first building that she finally mollified her demands of them both and stopped completely.

She quietly eased her bags to the ground. She tried concealing her loud, labored gasps for air but couldn't. Her throat was raw and dry, yet she remained adamant on saving the last of her boiled water. At least until she found another source of hydration.

I could always double back to the river in the morning, she considered.

She holstered her revolver and plucked an arrow from her crumpled quiver. Aurous whined quietly, but she hushed him and ordered sharply, "Stay!"

He growled but sat, all too happy to pant and rest instead.

She ghosted along the side of the building. Near the edge, she crouched low into the long blades of grass and peeked around the corner. Overgrown shrubbery and weeds concealed the building's entrance. It looked undisturbed. She advanced slowly and docked the arrow on her bow.

She squinted through the darkness, observing only faint traces of scattered buildings ahead. No firelight shone from its corners, no windows with a dim glow... There were no smells of burning logs or roasting food, no sounds of nervous chatter around the warmth of a fire. Nothing. Just the dull hum of crickets in her ears.

She waited until her legs numbed and her eyelids sagged shut. Startling herself, she pulled free of her daze and stretched.

Doesn't seem to be any danger. For now.

Sleep would elude her, but she would be out of the wind. Its chill seemed to seep through to her soul. She shivered as she whipped the bow back over her shoulder.

Aurous had fallen asleep over her bags. She roused him gently and then carefully edged along the wall of the building. Again, she waited and peered around the corner, hesitant, fearing the fatigue brewing inside her. A whimper from Aurous convinced her to disregard the uneasy feeling in her gut. Though she kept her hand firmly around her holstered revolver.

The doorway had been completely covered with dense weeds and tangled brush, so she crept to the window frame next to it. Her eyes wouldn't focus on much through the darkness, just a splintered floor with jagged pieces of broken glass scattered throughout. She heard nothing emanating from within, and neither did she smell anything overly repugnant. Just stale air and a lingering sour scent tickled her nostrils.

She gently tossed her bags through, then heaved Aurous up as well. "Man, oh man," she whispered with a grunt. "You're getting too heavy."

Climbing up the sodden pane after him, she fell through its rot, glass, and splintered wood.

Damn it! She groaned and cursed her luck.

She gave Aurous a dour look, but he ignored her plight and wandered off with his nose against ground. Garbage, grime, and dirt littered the floor alongside jagged fragments of glass and saturated wood. Behind her stood rows of stands with emptied shelves. Some still intact, others destroyed and torn apart. Peering further into the dark room, she discerned nothing else of interest. Just a barricaded back door and another small, disheveled room.

She found Aurous claiming a corner of the building away from the frosty gale. She dropped her bags and sighed, already tiring of the dreary enclosure. Fire was not a luxury she could afford at the moment. She remained apprehensive about the entire area, especially with her sight obstructed. Tall grass, weeds, shrubs, dying trees, as well as unforgiving darkness shrouded her vicinity. All she could do was wait.

Their bellies growled in unison.

With a heavy heart, she rationed the last small jar tucked away at the bottom of her bag. It had strips of what smelled like venison. It tasted salty. Enough so that she felt inclined to share the last of her water, too.

Tomorrow. I can find more tomorrow, she assured herself, barely able to muster the thought. The last thing she recalled was fumbling for her revolver as she began to doze.

Sunlight scintillating off the shattered glass blinded her as she woke. Aurous slept soundly beneath her. Her head sank as he exhaled deeply, then rose when his lungs inhaled their fill.

She yawned and stretched, knowing too well the growing wolfpup would startle himself awake. He lightly nipped at her arm before sulking and resting his head back on his paws. Not even the euphonious chattering of morning birds or the sun beckoning her with its warmth could entice her from the comfort of Aurous' fur. His presence helped diminish the void in her heart and the shadows stirring in her mind. She smiled and slept a moment longer, until her swelling bladder nagged for relief.

Outside, it resembled a field. Long and narrow. The road she'd felt beneath her boots reached toward the few buildings not far down from where she'd slept, and then snaked around the mountainside. The cracking concrete was partially hidden beneath a wavering sea of green. Again, she spotted clear roads and houses beyond the rigid mountainside. Unease gnawed on her thoughts.

But her mind reeled as she turned to walk back to Aurous. A path had been carved through the grass just in front of the building – beyond where she'd ventured to leap through the rotting window. She stared at it and then back into the building. She had made *certain...*

Or was I that tired?

The wind unsettled the path in front of her. A closer inspection revealed no imprint or impression left in the hardened dirt. Her belly groaned its anticipation of food – *Maybe a deer,* a part of her hoped eagerly – but she kept her mind sharp. One hand fell to her revolver as she crept along the side of the building.

White paint peeled from the stained wood. Faded, illegible words were plastered all over. The only ones she could read clearly were *convenience, snacks* and *cigarettes.* They were in bright, bold letters and written under an unrecognizable drawing. Most of which had chipped from the brittle billboard.

Cigarettes.

As often as she recalled a sweet, flowered fragrance when dredging through memories of her mother, the bitter and stale stench that hung in the air after a late night or an argument with her father quickly followed. Though her heart longed for love, she blinked past tears and continued moving.

A few deteriorated structures stood amid the deadened grass. Mountains jutted out beyond the field of brown. They were everywhere, looming giants reaching toward a serene sky. She never realized how beautiful they were from afar.

The path through the tall verdure brought her past the flimsy wooden structures, guiding her to the other mountains. She strained her ears, but heard nothing through the tempered wind. Whatever animal it had been, it already wandered far from her vicinity. Far from her temporary shelter and away from their bellies. She couldn't help but grumble and sulk on her way back inside the building.

With daylight flooding the interior, she noticed just how dirty it was. Disuse allowed dust to settle along every surface. Grime stained everything, and dirt caked the once smooth and white floor. The shelves held nothing of interest. Empty wrappers of food long consumed. The counter near the back held a jar full of rusted nails behind a thick curtain of cobwebs. The building had been picked clean many years ago.

It must have remained abandoned ever since.

The room located near the back end of the building was more than disorganized. Twisted and broken metal shelves were stacked and jammed into the room. Various clutter, garbage, and other rusted junk piled and scattered on the floor. Cobwebs latched to her hair as she poked her head through the doorway. Still, nothing of use. She mumbled a few curses, then noticed something beneath the litter on the floor. She brushed the last of the cobwebs from her face and leaned into the grime.

Something was embedded in the tile. It resembled a handle, though it had rusted over and seemed unwilling to move. She pulled her knife free from the sheath on her belt and wedged the blade's point under the metal ring. A quick thrust, and the latch snapped free of its rusted hold.

Unfortunately, so did the tip of her knife. The point chipped into a jagged edge. She knew it would eventually happen, especially after years of sharpening then dulling with work.

Dad gave it to me so many years ago.

Winter. It suddenly dawned on her the chilly season quickly approached, and she would be alone for the first time in her life.

She sheathed her old knife and wiped away her tears.

Not completely alone. Her thoughts drifted to Aurous.

Whatever the handle opened, she couldn't budge it beneath all the clutter. She pulled at the gnarled metal, but it might as well have been a mountain.

Sunlight shone through the crumbled ceiling. It seemed no one deemed it of enough importance to clear the room of debris.

Or had little time for such an arduous task. Her mind circled back to her previous uneasy thoughts. *Why do the roads appear cleared closer to town, yet so wild here?*

After a few minutes, she heaved some of the twisted metal bars away from the apparent handle. She cleared the garbage and debris from the floor, then found hinges near the back when she squeezed under the broken shelving.

A door!

She opened it for a moment before the weight of the stacked rubble overpowered her weak muscles. Grunting, she fell back as it crashed down and slammed the floor-door shut.

Her backside ached as she stood, but she tried again, her curiosity piqued.

After a few dozen attempts, she wedged a thick piece of wood under the hatch. Peering through the opening, she saw nothing, but choked on the fetid air rising from it. It was nothing like the death she'd smelled before. But she cringed all the same, slightly repulsed.

Aurous slept by her bags. The pup breathed deeply, wearied from their journey through the mountains. It didn't help that they'd struggled for food, relying on the stash her father had left and stored for them. Now, they were dangerously low and without a means to procure more. They would have to hunt before sunset today. But first she wanted to know what was below.

She stepped as quietly as she could around Aurous while she searched the building for something she could use to pry the hatch open more. Her search availed little other than a second chunk of chopped wood.

Someone must have tried lighting a fire here at some point. She wondered if neglecting to build one the previous night had been good choice.

The piece of wood was larger than the one propping the hatch open. She jammed it under the opening with a few stomps of her ragged boot and covered her lower face with her sweater. Sunlight pouring in through the caved in ceiling couldn't reach the murky depths below her. She sighed and went back to her bags.

She crumpled and bunched loose papers and pieces of garbage then lit a small fire with the help of her flint-rock. She tore a few strips from her old, tattered clothing at the bottom of her pack and wrapped them tightly around a small, wooden stick. She lit the fabric evenly and then smothered her small fire with her boots.

She had limited time, so she moved quickly. There was a ladder on the side of the hatch the darkness had concealed. She double checked the wood that wedged the hatch open and then eased herself through.

The last thing I want was to be trapped under rubble.

She nearly squealed but suppressed her momentary fear. More cobwebs and dust clung to her loose hair as she climbed down the narrow ladder. Soon, her boot stomped against the concrete and echoed loudly. She turned and screamed.

Bony teeth flashed a deathly grin as the fire's ruby glow banished shadows to the edges of its flickering light. Empty sockets inside dull, white bone stared back as she fumbled the torch and nearly extinguished the flame.

She looked down at the skeleton by her boots. No flesh, no organs, or hair – just bones, clothes, and a rusted gun clutched inside a skeletal grip remained. She held the torch closer and glimpsed the small hole in the side of the skeleton's skull. Beside it, broken glass glowed like embers from the firelight and burned over a withered picture of purple wildflowers.

She stepped over the dusty bones and reached the shelves along the far end of the wall. Rows of cans stacked neatly, their labels covered with more dust. Below, clear bags had been torn through. Bugs squirmed through the few grains of white rice remaining, and mouse droppings surrounded the bags.

So much for that... She grabbed one of the cans, smearing the grime from the label. *Carrots? Peas?* Her stomach rumbled like the beginnings of a storm. She grabbed another can. *Corn! Chestnuts!*

There were dozens of cans, all unopened and seemingly fine. She stuffed her sweater pockets with a few and eased her way back toward the ladder. The fabric to her torch burned away, the edge of the stick now dull, glowing embers as she climbed back up to daylight.

Aurous finally awoke. He lounged outside, reveling in the warmth. Her nose alerted her to a fresh pile of wolf droppings that her boot nearly stomped through. She scrunched her face and called to the thinning pup, who wouldn't take his bright, honeyed eyes off the forest across the road. He sat with his head hunched low to his bony shoulders, ears flat against his skull. She followed his gaze, finding only a small hill shadowed by the rustic leaves of the woodlands.

"Aurous?" She shifted her gaze back to the parted grass behind her. *What the hell is going on?* "C'mon boy, I've got some food," she coaxed to no avail.

Again, she stared into the woods, and saw nothing but rustling leaves and trees. The wooded depths shadowed whatever agitated Aurous.

Still disheartened about her chipped blade, she grabbed her father's old machete and wiped the edge clean. She jabbed the blade into the top of the can and twisted the handle. The can's lid ripped into sharp corners and edges, and water splashed up her sleeve. Aurous finally left his ardent watch once the scent of old peas and carrots filled his nose. She found two old sheets of metal under the debris near the hatch, with jagged edges she'd dulled down by sliding across a patch of concrete outside. She slopped the entire contents of the can onto one sheet, which Aurous gratefully gobbled down.

The second can, chestnuts, had a small pull tab on top.

I've never eaten chestnuts before.

She found them delicious. She plucked them from the watery can one after another, stuffing them into her mouth until her cheeks swelled like a chipmunk. She chewed and swallowed more than her stomach needed. Aurous lapped up the last of his mushy peas, then eagerly watched her dwindling can of chestnuts. Rolling her eyes, she capitulated. He devoured the remaining chestnuts gleefully.

"There's plenty more," she told him with a smile he merely ignored. "So eat as much as you want."

He did. She went through all three cans. First, more peas and carrots. Then, they ate corn. They even drank the murky water left in the cans.

Satiated, with their bellies now groaning from overindulgence rather than hunger, they lounged until the warming rays of light itched her skin and chapped her lips. Suddenly parched, she opened her eyes to a fiery setting sun. Crimson reached across a darkening sky like streaks of blood, blanketing the land in a lambent, hellfire glow. They had tucked themselves near the back of the building, out of view but still close enough to hear movement throughout the grass. The wind had died to a mere whisper, the day's warmth now embracing them gently. She stood and nudged the lanky wolf-pup with her boot. Aurous yawned, then grudgingly followed her back inside the building.

After using the last of her old and torn spare clothes for a makeshift torch, she climbed back down the hatch to gather more cans of food. Once again, she stepped over the creepy skeleton slumped across the floor.

Something caught her eye. *What's this?*

Poking out of the red fabric draped around the skeletal frame was a crumpled piece of paper. It was old, like her map, and tore as she tried to unravel it. She succeeded after a few minutes of frustration in the dimming light of the torch, but couldn't read it quickly enough as the embers dulled. She climbed back up the ladder with an armful of cans, and brittle paper clutched under her chin.

Aurous slobbered on her face as she squeezed through the opened hatch. She wiped the globs of slime with her sleeve then rushed to the window. With the last of the day's light, she read what was written on the piece of tattered paper.

IF YOU SHOW THESE SYMPTOMS:
Nausea
Bloody mucus
Fever
Uncontrollable coughing, sore and swelling throat and/or congesting lungs
Bruising skin, especially around the mouth and eyes (rare)
CONTACT YOUR LOCAL HEALTH ADMINISTRATOR!
There has been a recent uprising in Influenza (Respiratory Infection and Collapse), and health officials are warning of its dangers. All traveling abroad are urged to get screened immediately.
Help keep your community safe!
Wash your hands!

The rest was illegible, lost to the friable edges. *Must have been before it started changing most people.* She still had trouble recalling those years.

Maybe it's not such a bad thing.

Turning the fragile paper, she discovered words etched to the back.

I'm sorry.
I wanted to save everyone, but I couldn't.
God is now punishing me for my sins.
I could have saved them, but I didn't.
Now I'm trapped.
Please, forgive me.

It was hastily written cursive, scrawled quickly with a drying pen. Whoever the skeleton once was, they had apparently committed terrible sins. She deduced he had selfishly hid in the bunker, trapping others outside with whatever dangers he perceived. Or still did.

She shivered.

Before nightfall brought more shadows to entrap them in darkness, they had another feast of old canned vegetables. They huddled inside the corner of the building away from the chilly wind blowing down the mountainside. There, she spoke emotively to Aurous about the memories she still recalled, the cordial thoughts of her bright-eyed little brother, how her mother would share her treasure cove of hidden candies. Or how her father used to chide her for eating too many sweets when she complained of a tummy ache. Regardless of how it stirred her cold heart, she spoke of the old sentiments casually, like a story her parents used to lull her to sleep with. Loneliness festered and marred her mind as she dozed off beside a snoring wolfpup.

She slept with a heavy heart.

It was the fear that woke her, the nightmares taking shape in the darkest crevices of her mind. Her eyes snapped opened, her mouth parting in a shrill scream. The clamor outside of the building chilled her blood.

Infected! She reached for the revolver, yelling frantically for Aurous to wake.

Only he wasn't there.

"Aurous!" She screamed, her voice lost to the ragged shriek outside of the window.

They're here!

It was like a malignant river burst through a brittle dam that was the window, and darkness surged inside like a steady stream of infected blood from a wound. Bony teeth snapped at the air, their screams fueled by bloodlust.

"Daddy!" She cried out, drowning beneath thrashing shadows.

No!

It took her a moment to realize she was truly awake. The sun glared through the window, blinding her.

It was just a nightmare, she reminded herself. But she couldn't stop trembling.

As morning waned, a thick curtain of fog impeded light and thwarted oncoming warmth. It crept through the open doorway and window, shrouding them in a murky cloud. Aurous stirred as she rose and kicked away the old cans of food they'd devoured the night before. He yawned and watched curiously with his bright eyes. She rearranged her bags and strapped the rifle to the larger one. She grabbed both and went back to the secured hatch in the back room.

She struggled to open the hatch again, and her wrists were sore from bracing against the weight of ceiling rubble as she wedged a piece of wood under the cover. She tossed her near empty bag down first. It *slapped* against the stone floor and resounded off the bare walls. She eased the bigger bag with her rifle down, then descended the rickety ladder. The old wood wiggled free from the nails in the wall and creaked loudly with each step.

Careful...

It was nearly pitch black. The hatch only opened a little, and fog obscured even more light. She had her flint-rocks and last torch already gathered at the top of her bag, and she fumbled for them blindly. Aurous growled by the opening. The dim light above blinked as he paced anxiously.

She finally lit the pile of paper and caught flames along the fabric surrounding the torch. Light flooded the bunker once more.

She took the rest of the vegetables. Part of the can near the back had ballooned out and nearly burst under her touch. It was pineapple slices, and she couldn't recall ever tasting them before. *From the state of the can, I won't anytime soon.* She left it and gathered the others.

Tucked away in the corner, just a few feet from the skeleton, sat a desk. Binders and yellowing papers were strewn across the top, none of which held anything interesting enough to grasp her attention for long. The drawers were full of the same, except the last one on the bottom. It was sealed shut, but the lock was weak enough for her to pry off with her machete blade. Her boots slid across the concrete and disturbed the skeletal remains as the lock suddenly broke.

The torch nearly burned itself out, her fingers now singed from falling embers.

The drawer held more binders. A quick glance through them, and she found each to be full of the same dizzying numbers and words she had no care for. Below the binder, however, she found something useful.

Flashlight!

She grabbed the black cylinder and unscrewed one end. A bulb fell out after she removed the glass piece, but landed safely on the pile of discolored binders in the opened drawer. There were no batteries, but the metal hadn't rusted. She smiled and quickly rummaged through the remainder of the drawer.

Using the last of the ember's attenuate glow, she managed to secure two packs of batteries wedged at the bottom of the drawer. One was already open with batteries too small to fit the flashlight, the other still tightly bound in packaging. She pocketed the first ones anyway, then ripped open the other pack. She found no flaws or leakage, and again made certain the flashlight hadn't rusted inside. Her father's caution echoed through each action. She smiled faintly.

A beam of light brightened the cellar's cement wall as she *clicked* the button. Overwhelmed by a wave of giddiness, laughter erupted from her, reminiscent of her father's heartiest chuckle.

Luck seems to finally favor me!

She left her bags in the cellar. She took only her revolver, bow, flashlight, knife, and machete. She contemplated carrying the rifle, too, but wanted to move swift and silent. A rifle only impeded her stealth. She tied her growing hair back and braced against the wind's chilling lashes.

Day trickled into dusk as she scurried through the tall grass. She strayed from the road so the soft soil and clumps of grass muffled her footsteps. Aurous sensed her determination and paced, his ears craned toward the darkened buildings.

She intended to scout and perceive any possible danger. Uncertainty dwelled in her thoughts, urging her to find another road bypassing the town. She had enough food that hunting wouldn't be an issue, though she knew not to solely rely on it for long. *I can double back to the river before first light tomorrow and find an alternate route. Something about that town ahead seems peculiar.*

Clear roads and maintained plant life... Yet, for two days now I've seen nobody.

Lungs aching, she stopped. She spied a few structures through the concealment of trees and brush. They were piles of rubble, slowly blanketed by green and brown grass. The far side of a building across the street had been partially torn down. The side of the wall lay in jagged pieces of rubble on the ground, while the crumbling roof folded over the gaping hole. She noticed the weakened floor sag from rot, soggy from rain and harsher elements. Stained steps led to a battered door. She couldn't even deduce its original color. Grime coated the building like it had her clothes and hands. She moved on.

Until something splashed up her boot. A chill seized her bones as Aurous growled deeply, his white teeth flashing brightly under the glaring moon. She looked down and ran her fingers alongside her tattered boot. Liquid.

Mud? But a darker thought followed. *It hasn't rained that much recently.* She held her fingertips to her eyes.

Blood. And hers ran cold.

Panic was her next thought.

Her quickened heart jumped up into her throat. Aurous wouldn't tear his gaze from the buildings ahead. Fingers twined with his fur, she hauled him through dying light.

Her eyes found the old, rusted sign. *Antler Creek, two kilometres.* To her right, just more flatland and trees, then a barricade of mountains. Her left, just a hillside, then mountains.

Damn it.

She gasped, certain her father whispered, "Go *around, love.*" And her heart echoed the same.

Her mind broached that more supplies meant less hunting, and less hunger pangs for her and Aurous. She shook her head. *No,* she thought rationally. *Daddy would never approve of such a reckless choice.*

Besides, how else would I learn how to properly hunt? Aurous seemed to be the only capable hunter out of them both.

Dad, I miss you.

She remained lost in contemplation until Aurous tore free from her grip. She stumbled and fell into the bloodied dirt. The snarling wolf ran, disappearing into the velvet black. She followed him deeper into night's obscurity after a harrowing moment of fear.

Eventually, the last buildings came into view. Still, no light of any kind radiated from the town in the distance, and again, she found herself with a limited ghostly glow from the moon and twinkling stars. The wind howled furiously. Its gelid grip reached through her coat, embracing her flesh with numbing cold. She followed the wolfpup's growls.

Her revolver sat heavily in her hand as she slowed her pace and peered through the dark opening. She heard Aurous inside, growling lightly from somewhere deep inside the building. She held her breath and stepped through the doorway.

Lightlessness blinded her. She whispered to Aurous several times before he answered with a throaty whine. She pulled the flashlight from her coat pocket and turned it on.

Then nearly screamed.

Blood pooled by her boots. Ribbons of pink flesh protruded from the sea of red. There were clumps of pulverised meat and torn organs. A body, or what was left of it, leaned against the wall by the window, its head slumped over the massive split in its chest. Blood still trickled slowly from the grisly wound. It was fresh.

Her stomach turned.

She found Aurous by the window. He stared through the opening with hollowed eyes. He no longer growled, but his lips curled into a snarl that could rival her father's. His black fur had been splashed with crimson. Bloodied paw prints trailed from the hellish ocean to the window. She lit up the window frame with her flashlight. Deep, jagged marks had torn through the blood-stained wood. With shivering hands, she turned to see the same deep claw-like marks in the floor near the blood.

What the hell...?

She left as quickly as she could.

Aurous followed, his bravery strangled by fearful worry. She ignored the aches in her legs, the burning of her lungs, and ran as fast as her tiring muscles allowed.

Her mind screamed to go back to the forest, through the cover of trees to circumvent the town and its hidden horrors. For a fleeting moment, her heart panged for home.

They blended with shadows. Aurous slowed as she whispered cautiously, and they both crept to the grassy doorway. She had her revolver ready. Aurous kept his nose to the ground as he followed her through the parted grass. She was blinded momentarily when she turned the flashlight on. Rows of rusting shelves still lined the inside of the building. The back room hatch was still concealed by the ceiling rubble. They stood alone in an empty building.

Or so she thought.

Aurous snarled and lunged at a black shadow behind them. Someone screamed. She reeled, but nearly lost her footing. Light flashed across someone struggling with her wolf. He had a large, ragged sweater with one sleeve now drenched in blood. Aurous clenched his teeth into the flesh on the stranger's arm. The unknown man screeched in pain then swiftly brought his boot up to bash the wolf's throat. A high-pitched yelp escaped Aurous. He released his hold and fell back.

She cocked the hammer on her revolver. The stranger charged.

She fired once, but the bullet lodged into the ceiling as she stumbled back. She dropped the flashlight, squeezing the trigger again. The man already gripped her arm and pulled the revolver from her hand as his own calloused fingers wrapped around her throat. She battered helplessly against his grip. He stared through the darkness into her eyes, then loosened hold.

His face looked filthy. Dirt clumped into his beard and long, unkempt hair. His eyes were wide and bloodshot, his breath like carrion as he breathed in her face.

"You're not..." He began.

The next instant she was covered in blood. The stranger crumpled, and she fell to the ground with him. She wiped the sticky, moist warmth from her face and fumbled for the fallen revolver.

A blade had wedged into his throat, soaking in red. With a sickening *crunch* and more spatters of blood, another stranger pulled the blade from the dead man's neck. He had his foot on her revolver, the weapon still a few feet from her grasp. She heard Aurous growling from somewhere in the darkness around them.

He looked down at her with cavernous eyes, his blade still dripping with deathly red. Scars gleamed through the dark, patchy stubble etched on his face. A long, black coat reached down to his knees, partially concealing the various weapons strapped to his belt.

"Well, well," he said. "Why don't ya come back to my campsite, girl?" His lips twitched into a sardonic grin. Bloody fingers groped the air for her hand. Sweat dripped from his aquiline nose. "Away from the monsters that roam the night."

"Ya not hungry?"

He slopped a chunk of meat over a rock and it *sizzled* loudly next to the fire. Juices seeped from inside the tender morsel and bubbled from the heat. The fire was furious. It roared inside its stony confinement as the logs below *crackled* and spat sparks into the night. Teeming shadows danced with lapping flames like nightmares hovering at the edges of their minds, a cold, polluting darkness that nipped at her frostbitten thoughts.

Narrow eyes greeted his hardened face from across the fire.

"I had to kill 'em," he continued explaining. Bloody fingers sank into the smoking meat as he flipped it and splattered more dark juice over the rocks and fire. "He would've killed ya." He tucked his receding chin to his chest and expelled a dramatic sigh, but kept his hawkish gaze level with hers.

"He had stopped," she countered fiercely, then looked aside from his rigid frown.

Aurous sat not far behind her; she glimpsed him over her shoulder. Tawny eyes gleamed against the firelight. He stood just out of warmth's reach, evanescing into the shadows surrounding them. She looked back at the man prodding the charring meat as he chortled and responded.

"Ya got no idea, girlie."

Emulating him, she grinned and cocked her head before saying, "Oh yeah? Then enlighten me."

That garnered her another chuckle. "No need to get snarky, girl," he replied, lightening his tone. "Do ya know what that means?"

She sneered and asked, "Do *you* know what *condescending* means?"

"Aren't ya clever," he remarked, then nodded his head to the roasting meat. "Ya want some?"

"I have my own food," she replied.

She had reluctantly gone back for her supplies, though she'd told the stranger to wait outside the building while she snuck back down into the bunker. She still didn't trust him. Aurous seemed wary of him as well, and flinched at any sudden movement he made. The wolf's gaze never strayed far from the strange man. He hadn't even touched his vegetables.

Maybe he wants meat.

She bit her lip, then asked suddenly, "Why do you talk like that?"

"Like what?"

She pursed her lips, uncertain if he continued to goad her. "Like you always have a mouthful of food."

Another smile.

Her stomach suddenly growled as the rich meat smoked and flooded her nose with its savory scent.

Maybe I want some too.

"I'm from the east, girlie," he said. His wide smile revealed scummy teeth jutting from stained gums. "Far east. Ya never been?" She shook her head. "Oi, but ya hafta. Beauty." He chuckled again as he noticed the sizzling meat entranced her more than his reminiscence.

"Ya want some?" He asked again. She refused, but he said, "Look, give me some of them greens, I'll give ya some meat." He shrugged. "Then ya won't feel like yer pretty lil' self owes me somethin'."

Seems fair.

She glanced back to Aurous as if seeking his approval. He stood still, as though encased in stone, barely sparing a breath as he glared mercilessly. She looked back at the man and nodded once. Very subtly.

He pulled his cleaver free and swiftly chopped the charred meat. It split in half, and more juices rained down into the greedy fire. He chopped at the steak again and held up a trim of fat. He lobbed it over her head at Aurous. The wolf snatched the stringy pink ribbons out of the air, baring his teeth menacingly as he chewed meat that was too hot for his tender tongue. His eyes still wouldn't wander far.

"Yer dog don't seem too friendly," he pointed out, handing her a thick slab of smoking meat. She cupped the steaming pile of mouth-watering grub and dropped it into an open can of corn. She tossed the man a second can she'd fished out from her bag.

"He doesn't like strangers," she said. *I don't either.*

"Caden," he muttered, then pressed a finger to the side of his nose. He blew a chunk of snot into the dirt by his feet. "That's the name my ma gave me."

"Celeste," she said in return through a mouthful of meat.

It was rough, stringy, and hard to chew. *Like gnawing on a leather boot.* But it tasted wonderful. Though what it was, she couldn't tell. "That's the name my father gave me."

I think. Another question burned, another answer lost. Bitter, she chewed another mouthful. *Of all the times I wished to be gone from that wretched cabin.* She smiled, almost amused by her constant angst. *Or maybe I'm going crazy...*

"Cheeky lil' brat, aren't ya?"

She barely heard his remark. His raspy voice became a distant echo down a long and empty tunnel. Warmth from the fire's incessant touch burned her eyes as each thought tumbled down into the fervid blaze. The food in her mouth felt like heavy ash along her tongue. She looked up to her father's rebuking eyes over the bright fire.

Except they weren't his. Caden stared at her, the corner of his mouth twitching in amusement. "Ya sure take compliments well," he said between mouthfuls of canned corn.

"What?" She asked stupidly. Her mind leapt from the embers and slammed back into her skull.

Dad...

"I said, that's a beautiful name."

She felt her face flush red, so she averted her eyes and fished her fingers through the can full of food. Her heart quickened, and her tongue tied itself into a knot as mumbled her thanks.

What the hell is wrong with me?

"What's a lil' girlie like yerself doin' out here anyway?"

"Looking for my father," she lied.

"Separated, were ya?"

She whispered grimly, "Something like that."

"Ahh," was all he offered in return. After he'd finished his corn, he belched and tossed the can into the dying fire, then grabbed another handful of tinder for the pit. When she pointed out that firewood burns longer, he eyed her carefully and said it wouldn't be wise to venture further than camp tonight.

"Why?" She asked. She tilted the can and emptied the remnants into her mouth.

"Stalker territory."

"What?"

"Stalkers," he repeated. "What, ya don't know about the bloody monsters?"

"Hunters?"

He laughed. "That's what ya call 'em?"

"Me and my dad," she said. "He called them Hunters, because that's what they're designed to do." She almost heard his voice whisper those words into her ear.

"Why can't we leave," she would ask as a young girl, her mother's old clothes much too big for her tiny frame. "Because," her father grumbled angrily. "We don't want to be attacked by Hunters, remember?" She bit her tongue and looked down into the dirt. Her father was an irascible man, yet it did little to stop questions from brewing in her mind and spilling past her lips. The alluring thought of a normal world... She'd just wanted her family back together again.

She still did.

"Aye," he agreed with a sigh. "We called 'em Stalkers. Because they hid in the damn shadows and followed ya 'til ya dropped yer guard." He stomped his foot down in the dirt and startled her. Aurous growled from the darkness. "Then they would strike. Take ya down in a mess of blood an' guts."

"Thrilling," she replied, the crackling fire smothering her droll tone.

"This is *their* territory, girlie," he replied. "Which is why I was surprised to find ya out here on yer own."

Her thoughts flashed back to the grisly scene she'd stumbled upon in the mountains, and then to the one from earlier in the evening.

That could have been me. Her dinner nearly found its way back up from her belly. *Disemboweled.*

Dead.

"I didn't know," she said, her voice trailing off into a delicate whisper.

"Which is why ya should turn back and go home."

She shook her head. "I can't. My... father is out there."

"He worth dyin' for, girlie?" He asked. "Would he want ya to die for him?"

No.

"Maybe," she said, but her heart refused to fuel the lie. She glared at him accusingly. "What are *you* doing in Hunter territory?"

He replied caustically, "I told ya... Ya got no idea."

"And I told you to enlighten me."

"I'm looking for the bastards who killed my family."

Her heart sank like a stone into her belly. "I'm sorry..."

"Nah," he said. "Ya didn't know."

There they sat, drowning in a deluge of silence. The fire *hissed* as she prodded the charred branches inside the pit.

"Was that man responsible?" She finally dared to ask. She met his hollowed stare, and he nodded sharply.

"That he was."

"Then he deserved to die."

He managed to smile. Her heart fluttered, and she couldn't help but smile back.

"That he did."

She looked away again, her face red. Aurous continued to growl lightly.

"Them bastards raided our camp," he explained. He spun the handle of his cleaver on the palm of his bloodied hand. "Killed almost everyone. My family... everyone else's families... it was a massacre. Goddamn raiders." He spat into the fire. "We hunted 'em down, few of us who made it out alive. Killed a few of 'em. They came through here, and the others with me... they were too afraid to be near Stalkers."

"The town doesn't look deserted."

"That's where the damn raiders have set up camp."

"How do you know this?" Suspicion reigned in her sympathy.

"Our camp used to trade with this town, before the Stalkers picked em clean. Somethin' happened in the city... The military stopped patrolling this area. The town was slaughtered a few weeks ago." He sighed again, his mouth curving up into a smile as if recalling a bright, sunny day.

Odd.

"I tracked the raiders all the way back here, then stumbled across ya. They probably don't know it's now Stalker land, just like ya had no clue."

"You don't seem afraid of monsters."

"Nothin' they can do to me those bastards haven't done to my heart already."

The wounds in her own heart still bled pain. She knew too well the burning lust for revenge, the insatiable thirst for blood.

The demons that pilfer your soul. "I hope you find peace."

"Why don't ya help me out?"

"Help you kill?" Uncertainty muffled her words.

He shrugged. "Why not?"

"I-I can't," she replied quickly. "I have to get to the city..."

"Ya help me out, I'll return the favor."

She cocked her head to the side. "How so?"

"I'll get ya safely around Stalker land."

"I can find my own way."

"Honestly, it's a miracle ya survived so long on yer own."

"I said I'm fine."

"Alright." He leaned back from the light, the night shrouding his face. "Don't say I didn't warn ya, girlie."

He cupped the back of his head in his hands and eased down to the dirt. She sat there, staring at the diminishing fire desperately trying to burn through ashy remains.

Could I? She'd certainly killed before. Lost within raging waters of despair and anguish, she'd slaughtered those responsible for that pain, that river of blood spilling from her fractured heart.

"There are things out there far worse than monsters, Celeste," she almost heard her father whisper. *"Remember that."* It was the gentle nudge of wisdom bestowed from a man she longed to see again. *What would you do, dad?* She struggled to tame her thoughts. *You've killed out of necessity... and sometimes because ignoring such evil would only darken one's soul.*

I remember.

"Alright," she finally conceded, wiping the sweat from her brow. The fire dulled to embers inside the pit, allowing darkness to blanket them in a deathly chill. "I'll help you."

"I knew ya would."

As Aurous growled behind her, she said, "Don't forget to help me afterwards, or else my dog might begin to dislike you."

He gave her a low, rustic chuckle in response, then dozed off. She sat near the edge of the fire pit, unable to sleep or loosen her grip on the revolver.

By morning, she'd grown weary of the chill numbing her toes through her boots. Her clothes were damp from the drizzle that persisted throughout the night. Fog ghosted along the edges of their campsite, curtaining their surroundings in a thick cloud of grey.

As Caden packed away what little belongings he had, she trudged off through the trees and into the dense smog to relieve herself. Aurous insisted on following her, acting as her guard. She kneeled behind a tree. *Good boy.* But she still found comfort when her fingers brushed alongside the handle of her revolver.

Caden led her through the haze and out of the thicket. They hadn't ventured far from the buildings she'd ran from, terrified and certain death was at her heels. She saw the *City Center* sign and the front of the building she knew concealed the bearded man's corpse. His blood had soaked into the floor, to add to the layers of rot and filth accumulated from years of disuse. It was there his life had been snatched away in one quick, bloody moment, and it was there he would begin to rot.

Don't think about it.

It would still be over an hour until they reached town, and she was already tiring. Her bags felt like swinging boulders as she walked, each step chafing her hips and thighs. Sensing her mounting frustration, he offered to carry one of her bags, but she crassly refused.

Trepidation roiled her mind, perturbing every thought as she followed the man into town. Walking a few paces behind, she winced at the blood splattered up his long coat. It stained the dull colored fabric, but blotches of faded red sullied his collar the most. The odor of spoiled meat clung to him. Its sultry smell flooded her nostrils.

Off to the side of the highway, Caden led her to a bridge with black wooden steps held together by flimsy, rusted bolts. Dense, green shrubbery twined around the bridge. Long stalks leaned over the embankment and covered the shore with a grassy jungle. When she'd asked why they were straying from the road, he'd scoffed and replied they weren't welcomed guests in a raider camp.

Doesn't have to be a sarcastic jerk about it. She helped him clear a small path through the lush greenery. *This is crazy.* She glanced back at Aurous, staring into his bright, amber eyes. *What am I doing?* Her legs twitched, and her eyes darted down the highway. *I could run. Go back to the mountains... Get away from everything.*

Run!

Except she didn't. She followed the stranger named Caden across the bridge.

Sunlight burst through parted clouds as they reached another emptied road. A few old cars barricaded one driveway, none with wheels. The insides were gutted like the corpse she'd found in the outskirts of town, now just rusted, broken frames blockading the house. The house itself looked to be in the same condition as the building she'd spent a few nights in; the windows were smashed, and the yellow painted panes dulled by grime. She could see through the various openings the state of rot the interior had succumbed to. Yet, the next house was immaculate. The paint still chipped away from years of wear, but the windows and doorways were closed to ward off the harsher elements. The yard also appeared well-maintained; a neglected garden withered near a small wooden porch protruding from the front of the house. *Someone lived here recently. Raiders, or the townsfolk before?* Even the lawn was recently trimmed. The grass was resplendent from light drizzle, like a sea of emeralds under the sun's brilliance.

"Keep yer weapon handy," Caden warned with a small whisper over his shoulder. She peeled her gaze from the lustrous shine of dewy grass, then pulled the weighty revolver from its holster. Aurous nudged her leg gently as he walked, keeping closer than ever while she trailed behind Caden. He stopped not far from the bridge and a few run-down houses, then nodded at the structure across the road.

"Check that one," he ordered gruffly, barely sparing her a second glance. "Leave yer bags at the door before you go in."

"And what happens if I find someone?"

He replied drolly, "Kill 'em, obviously."

Arsehole. "What if they're not raiders?"

"Then I suppose ya can ask 'em politely," he replied with a sly grin as he walked away from her. "But if ya get a bullet for an answer, probably a raider."

Because it's that easy, right?

Each step across the bare pavement *clapped* through the street like thunder. A quick look down each direction, and she found it as empty as it appeared the first time she'd glimpsed it from a distance.

What am I doing? She bit her lip anxiously as she neared the front entrance. Already, the putrid smell of rotting wood assaulted her nose. Even breathing through her mouth left a foul taste. *There could be raiders behind these walls, ready to fill me with bullets.*

Aurous poked his nose through the doorway and eased himself through, disregarding caution. She dropped her bags and followed the wolf in.

Or a goddamn Hunter.

His paws sank into the soggy floor. He held his snout high and sniffed the stale air. This house had obviously been abandoned long ago, and left that way even after the town's resettlement. The stench of neglect hung heavy in each room. If the house once held any belongings, they had already been taken. She found nothing but twisted bedframes, splintered furniture, and rotting wood.

She nudged the broken door at the end of the hall. It opened, revealing an empty room, same as the others. Except beside the door, there were pieces of an old dresser still intact that resembled the one her father fixed for use at their cabin.

She traced her fingers along the dark, cragged wood. Drawers had been ripped off or left jutting from the frame. Each emptied and smashed, except for one still partially closed at the bottom. When it opened, she found a slip underneath a net of cobwebs. It was small, about the size of her palm, and stiffer than paper. One word was inked on the back, nearly obscured by crinkled scars from numerous folds. It simply read *always*. The other side had nearly faded, but enough remained for her to see them. Two people smiled back at her, a girl with long, auburn hair and a man with a smooth face and bright eyes. They had their arms around each other, their fingers intertwined in her lap.

Her father's deep chuckle echoed through her thoughts, followed by the gentle hum of her mother's soothing whispers. They stared at her, lovingly, from the faded photograph.

Was this how happy you two were before?

She set the forgotten memory back down in the dusty drawer.

Another foul scent spread through the odorous mold of the house. Her boots nearly slid across the splintery debris with each descending step, and she scrunched her nose in disgust when she reached the bottom stair. She almost stomped through a large pile of wolf droppings near the door. She shook her head and muttered, "What is it with you and your need to do that *inside?*"

He lolled his tongue in reply.

The sun layered the dark pavement in sweltering heat with the absence of any cool breeze. She wiped her brow and squinted against the light, then tossed her bags back over her shoulder.

Where is he? There were only three houses until the road curved to the left and beyond the trees. *What if something happened?*

After a few vexing moments, she tucked her bags into the dense shrubbery outside of the next house across the road. She set her bow atop her bag and favored the bloodstained rifle instead. The old weapon dangled loosely from her shoulder as she stood, then bumped against her lower back with each stride. She kept one hand on her holstered revolver. The door slowly eased open.

Aurous sensed it before she did. A sharp growl erupted from his throat when he poked his head through the doorway. His frantic yelps were smothered by the deep growls of a larger creature. Her hands fell to the rifle at her side, but the wolf collided with her, and they both tumbled down the steps. The strap slipped from her shoulder as she hit the ground, and the rifle skidded from her clutches. Aurous scrambled to free himself of their entanglement, his paws digging into her ribs.

Something warmed the side of her face.

Blood.

Large claws raked across the wolf's chest. Crimson blemished his sleek fur and rained down in thick droplets. The wolf snarled, then lunged. Teeth sawed through flesh. The creature hissed wildly, claws outstretched. It bared its bloodied fangs as Aurous limped away from its scathing reach.

Red saliva dribbled from its sharp fangs. It was covered in tanned fur, except for a bright, white underbelly. It was lean, but not frail. She watched muscles bunch around its shoulders while it hunched forward and hissed again.

A mountain lion!

The wolf snarled. Blood spilled to the pavement, but Aurous remained between her and the mountain lion. He tried to attack.

The cougar was quicker. It pounced, a blur of tanned fur, fangs, and salient claws. She yanked the revolver from her belt, but the two beasts had their teeth and claws deep within flesh. She couldn't pull the trigger without the risk of hitting Aurous.

Damn it!

Aurous collapsed with a final weakened growl, bracing for the cat's final swipe.

Then, she fired.

The single shot nearly deafened her in one ear. A trickle of blood leaked through the lion's tanned fur, just above its hind leg. Her ears rung. She barely heard the cougar's screech when it turned its fangs on her.

Aurous snagged part of its throat with his teeth and jerked the cat downward. They both *smacked* against the pavement and slid into her before she could squeeze the trigger again. Air was driven from her lungs violently. Black blotted her vision as her head rocked off the ground.

Her fingers slipped around the hilt of her chipped knife, and she plunged it deep within the first patch of tawny fur she could distinguish. Blood sprayed up her forearm as the cougar screamed and pushed away from the wolf's jaws. Her knife slid free of its fleshy hold. It slipped from her fingers as she flung her arms around her wolf. She clutched at his bloodstained fur, halting his attack.

Then she heard the *click* of her rifle.

"No!" She screamed as Caden peered down the sights of her fallen weapon. She watched his finger twitch against the trigger, his eyes darting from her to the crouched cougar.

"Please, don't," she pleaded.

Only when he witnessed what she had did he finally lower the rifle. By the door sat two mewing kits, both slightly smaller than Aurous, with light fur and tanned spots. The mother cougar hissed again, but retreated cautiously as Celeste pulled her wolf away from the house.

Caden helped her to her feet. She swayed, but kept her grip on the wolf's bloodied fur. She motioned to the shrubbery not far from the spilled blood, and Caden retrieved both her bags as she gathered her bloody weapon. They quickly left the cougar's domain.

"Yer bloody insane," Caden grumbled, tossing the bags by her feet. "Which one, did ya say?"

"The smaller one," she replied coldly. "Where were you?"

He only grunted his response.

She furrowed her brow and parted the wolf's fur. *Damn it.* Blood seeped into her hands. *It's deep but still not as bad as I'd thought.* His flesh had been torn through, but nothing else appeared severely damaged. It would be a slow, painful heal... but it *would* heal.

All I can do is clean and dress it well.

"The small one," she ordered as he rummaged through her belongings. He finally procured the small jar of honey salve she'd been savoring.

So much for rationing it.

"Water, too."

The bottle held her last bit of clean water. She poured it over the serrated wound. Then, she scooped a glob of honey salve with her fingers and gently pushed it between the separated flesh. She steeled her heart as the wolf whimpered meekly under her touch. The blood slowed to a drip as the salve clumped inside the wound. She parted with a portion of her shirt and ripped strips from the bottom for a makeshift bandage.

"Insane," Caden whispered again, shaking his head in apparent disbelief. He scratched at his dark stubble. "Find somethin'?" He asked, referring to the emptied house she'd searched.

"Years of rot, grime, and abandonment," she said, each word laced with sarcasm. "Well worth the effort."

"I told ya to search one house." He spat by his feet and gave her a dark glare. "One I knew *had* to be empty."

"And how would you *know* this?" She stood to face him, but her chin barely reached his chest. She watched his ropy muscles flex as her hand fell to her gun side. "You told me the raiders have made camp in town. Where are the watchers? The scouts? If there had truly been a massacre here, then where are the bodies? Why would raiders stay in what they would most certainly now know to be Hunter territory?"

"Ya seem to be full of questions, girlie."

"Enough!"

He stared at her with hollowed eyes, then chuckled gently. Then he tossed her rifle down on her bags. "Ya got a lot of guts."

"I want to know what's going on."

"I told ya," he said. "I'm after the raiders."

Something doesn't feel right. The same unease that rooted in her thoughts before crossing the bridge into town now blossomed into fear. "There's no way a group of raiders would be running from one man."

She paused until his glare drifted to her hips, then she placed her hand atop the holstered revolver.

He glowered at her. He relaxed his shoulders, dropping his hands to his own belt. "Be careful, princess." Darkness soiled his eyes, his lips curling into a smile at her shallow, frantic breaths. "Yer actin' a bit insane again."

"You're not answering my questions!"

He scoffed and spat close to her boots. A quiet, throaty chuckle chilled her through the heated tension between them. "I told ya the damn truth."

It was a threatening growl from an injured Aurous that convinced her to go for her gun. Her hand slipped around the familiar handle, and she yanked the silver weapon from her belt. Caden flicked his dark coat and revealed the row of knives on the right of his tattered belt, then pulled his stained cleaver from its leather binding. The hammer on her revolver *clicked* back as she thrust it up into his neck. She felt the point of his own weapon nudge against her abdomen.

"Not a game ya want to play, girl," he snarled dangerously. She shivered as he spoke and warmed her ear with his stale breath. "Ya seem to be tad indecisive. Can ya make up yer mind and pull the trigger before I carve out yer neck? I think ya might lose this one."

"I'm going," she declared fiercely over Aurous' growls. "I'll find the city on my own."

Short, dark curls bounced as he shook his head. "Ya won't make it."

"I'll find a way."

He pulled his weapon away from her, and she lowered her own. She took one step back, reached for her bags, and then raised her revolver again. Caden refused to even flinch.

"Don't follow me," she ordered.

I have to get the hell out of here. But she couldn't pull the trigger. *What if I'm wrong?*

"Town could be full 'o raiders," he cooed, lazily scratching at the growing stubble around his neck.

"I'm willing to take that chance."

Aurous limped alongside. She kept her gun steady and eased away. After a few moments, he followed her. His boots lightly tapped against the pavement, but it echoed hauntingly around her.

He knows I'm not going to shoot. Caden had finally procured his own pistol, but made no move to fire it. *Why can't I just injure him?*

Because, whispered a familiar voice in her mind. *You're better than that.*

"Ya need me," he called out. "Just let me help ya out of the town!"

"I just want to go."

The wolf whined. Blood soaked through the grimy bandage on his side.

He needs rest.

Her bravery wavered. The muscles in her shoulder burned. Both bags offset her balance and caused her to stumble, but she turned and fled into the unknown. Various houses, run-down shacks, and makeshift fences; buildings congested the landscape and blurred past her.

Town.

Where do I go? She wondered, panic coursing through her thoughts. *He's still following me,* she realized with a nervous glance over her shoulder. He no longer called out to her, but each stride of his long legs seemed fueled with predacious purpose. His pallid face held a deeply set frown, and dark eyes seemed to prey upon her mending heart. Aurous attempted a growl as he limped by her side, but barely mustered a meek whimper.

The first house she passed was bright red and elongated. *Must have been recently painted.* She extended her arm behind her, the heavy revolver shaking in her hand.

Maybe he was telling the truth.

The next few houses were also well maintained, considering the conditions of the previous buildings she'd stumbled across. One even had *real* windows, and dappled brick along the bottom wall with fading green paneling across the top. But in her awe, she almost missed it; the glint under the sunlight, the sharp glare in her eyes as she turned her head and marveled at each house.

Oh crap!

"That's as far as you go, miss!"

She halted, but Aurous fell into a frenzy and snarled wildly. The gun dropped to her waist. She peered up through the fiery stare of the sun, glimpsing the barrel of a rifle similar to hers aimed down from a rooftop to her left. To her right, she heard footsteps. A man quickly approached, another long rifle pointed at her. He was heavily garbed, in thick layers of dark material she couldn't recognize.

"Drop the weapon!" He barked. "Drop it now!"

One on the roof. She slackened her grip on the revolver. Her heart threatened to burst free from her chest. *One in front.* As she shifted her weight and glanced to her left, she counted another figure standing at the door of a different house. There was nothing she could do. She gave a final glance down the road behind her, but Caden had vanished.

He was right. Raiders.

"What the hell are you doing here, little one?" the man approaching her asked. He nudged his rifle downward and opened his mouth to say something else when she didn't dare reply.

A stream of blood spurted from the man's neck. The first bullet ripped through the side of his throat. Confusion contorted his face. His hand slipped from his weapon then slowly reached up to his neck, vainly trying to clasp his wound shut. As he turned, two more shots echoed throughout the street, and his face exploded in a mist of red. He collapsed, bloody and dead.

Caden stood near the house to her right, his pistol now aiming past her, the barrel still smoking.

"Run!" he yelled, maddened. Then she was thrown into a storm of bullets.

EIGHT
DEATH BECOMES THEM

IT WAS a cannonade; an outburst of continuous thunder, a downpour
of lead. Bullets peppered the concrete and ricocheted past. Screams and
distant shouts were lost in the clamor.

Both bags slipped from her shoulder as she pushed against the wolf
with waning strength. She stumbled, and her boots slipped through the
spate of murky red under the faceless man's corpse. More bullets drilled
through dead flesh. She scrambled desperately for Caden.

His words were incomprehensible under the discharge of his pistol.
She felt his fingers entwine with her coat when she fell by his feet. Despite his forceful grip and fervent yell with each pull of the trigger, she
felt safe.

For now.

He hauled her through the doorway, and emptied the pistol into the
man atop the balcony of the dappled brick house.

"Yer not one for discretion, are ya?"

He thrust his shoulder against the door, slamming it shut. He ducked.
Three more shots pierced through the old wood.

Her heart sped erratically, and her mind refused to focus, but that
wasn't what worried her. As she pressed against her breast, warmth
trickled through her fingers. *Blood.* Caden peeked through the window
next to her, and dug through his pocket for another clip.

"Shit," he muttered. "At least four more comin' up the road." He jerked his thumb to the stairs. "Time to go, princess."

She didn't move. When he knelt down beside her, Aurous growled but mustered little more than that. Caden clawed at her coat the moment he noticed her bloody hand.

"Aye," he finally said, almost laughing. "There's an exit wound. Yer lucky. Now, time to get outta here."

She shook her head, unable to quell her rising dread. "We're hopelessly outnumbered."

"That we are," he agreed grimly. "Ya know how to shoot, girlie?" She nodded, her rifle still hanging at her side. "Good. I knew ya could. I'm going to draw their fire." He pointed down the hallway. "Ya go out back and flank the bastards."

"I don't have much ammo, Caden," she protested, her voice shaking. *How am I going to get out of this?*

"Make every shot count," he whispered harshly.

He stared at her for a moment longer with dark, ardent eyes, then pushed her back when gunfire erupted once more. More bullets bit through the wooden framing of the house.

"Go, Celeste!" He crouched near the shattered window, one hand bracing against the kickback of his pistol, while the other clutched Aurous close. The wolf watched her go with dimmed eyes and offered her a worried, throaty whine.

She fled through the narrow hallway, past the blur of faces inside dusty picture frames and pale peeling wallpaper, then into the kitchen. Her boots slapped against the grime of an unwashed floor. She barely glanced at the dirty dishes piled up along the counter. What finally stopped her determined pace was the table just beyond the back door.

Five chairs were still tucked neatly under the table edge, the dark cloth spread neatly across the surface. Plates had been set in front of each chair. Flies buzzed around rotting food in the center of the table, gorging on remnants of carrots, meat, beans, and other mush she couldn't recognize.

I shouldn't have doubted him.

Tall trees with light, craggy bark and branches thick with pine needles and cones blocked out sunlight in the backyard. Brisk shadows welcomed her reticent approach through the doorway. A rusted chain link fence enclosed the yard, partially bowed along one end. The aging metal *creaked* eerily from the errant breeze, muffling each step through dead, brittle grass.

Click. Her thumb nudged the hammer back on her revolver. Panic froze her blood. Distant gunshots echoed along with the wind's haunting harmony. Then she heard it.

Footsteps.

She swung her head as the barrel of a dark, sleek rifle poked over the bowed fence. She raised her revolver and braced against the forcible kick. Her eardrums nearly burst from the volley.

She threw herself back through the doorway, the ground near her feet spewing clumps of grassy dirt. Bullets drilled into the ground and paneling. Her shoulder bashed against the floor, but pain flared when her knee caught along the doorframe.

Click-click-click. The shooter had a jammed weapon.

Another echo of what used to warm her heart. *How I wished for those days to end.* She'd stand on the edge of the forest, her heart yearning for freedom, her thoughts beckoned by the fleeting wonder of a fallen world. *How I wanted to run away.* When the sweetened aroma of wildflowers drifted through the wind, she would remember the bright smile her mother gave her. Then reality would set in. "Celeste," her father called, his voice raw and ragged. Memories that seized her heart with a chilling grip still haunted him every night. His tortured screams never ceased. "It's time to continue." She would sigh, knowing her daily chores could not be avoided long. He would hand her a weapon, expecting her to clean and maintenance it regularly. Sometimes more than once if his mood was dour that day. All that seared into her being, becoming a mundane task she nonetheless partook in each night before closing her eyes and feigning rest.

Her weapons were always reliable.

Two gunshots smothered what little remained of her hearing. The first bullet ripped into the dirt by the rusting fence, but the other sank deep into the raider's abdomen. He grunted loudly and flinched. She pulled the trigger a third time.

Click.

Eyes wide, he turned to flee while she fumbled for her rifle.

Damn it!

Air couldn't satisfied her ragged lungs. She hopped over the bowed fence, giving chase to the raider. The bolt *snapped* back, and she knew there were mere seconds before he ducked into the next house. She had one shot. She aimed down the long barrel, neglected the flip-sight, and then pulled the trigger.

The rifle discharged with a mighty *roar*. The bullet missed the raider, but splintered the crest of the door frame.

Stumbling, she struggled to regain her balance. She pulled back on the bolt again and stepped over the empty casing, but winced as her shoulder jolted with pain. No others followed the raider into the yard. The distant gunfire had ceased.

Did Caden kill them all?

She slowed near the darkened house. Soiled sheets obscured the sunlight, creating a shadowy veil across the doorway.

It took a fearful moment for her eyes to adjust in the dimly lit room. She bobbed the rifle to each dark doorway beyond the small area, but discerned nothing. The pungent stench of rotted food pervaded the air. Like the previous house, it seemed the former residents had uprooted fairly quickly.

The raider probably circled around from the front. She stepped carefully, muffling noise. *Maybe Caden already killed him.* She couldn't supress the next grisly thought. *Or maybe they've already killed Caden.*

Back facing the doorway, her rifle was ripped from her hands. A yell rumbled in her throat, but blood spewed from her lips instead of words. Vision flashed white as bony knuckles rapped against the side of her head. She lunged blindly and snarled like her wolf. In one fluid motion, she pulled her knife free and stuck it into the raider's gut. Blood flecked across her face as the blade plunged deep through hefty flesh. She heard him gurgle then swear loudly, before a second blow battered against her face. Another yell was quickly cut short when cold, slick fingers tightened around her throat.

Her mouth gaped as she desperately fought for air. Thrust against the wall, her head jarred against the hard surface. Dirty fingernails clawed bloody rivulets into her attacker's forearms, but still his grip would not slacken. Like a ghost, his pale face melted through the shadows. A furrowed brow crested rapacious eyes, and bloody lips parted in a murderous smile that no longer concealed his few rotted teeth. With each wheezing breath, warm blood speckled her face. It bubbled in the back of his throat and pooled under his tongue, until he muttered another string of curses. Crimson spittle cascaded down his chin and spilled on her clothes as he leaned over her, his hands crushing her windpipe closed.

Dad! Help me... But the words didn't budge, the screams didn't echo throughout. Nobody would hear her plea.

Widened with surprise, the raider's eyes bulged from his skull. Filthy fingers groped the side of his face and pressed against his cold, pale skin. She felt the raider's grip loosen around her throat. His bloody lips parted in a final, fearful utterance of mercy.

Snap! His neck twisted abruptly with a quick, violent jerk. His body convulsed and slouched against the wall next to her. His head lolled past his shoulder, staring back at her with hollowed eyes.

His ghostly grip still burned her neck. Her lungs struggled for air. Caden left her sprawled across the dirty floor, but Aurous pushed against her shoulder with his snout, his worry manifesting as cautious whimpers through her ringing ears.

"Get up," Caden ordered harshly. "There's more comin'."

"I-I can't," she rasped, her eyes bleary with tears. "I'm almost out..."

Her stomach turned, and she nearly retched as the scent of blood filled her nose.

Caden grunted his reply, hunched his shoulders, and holstered his weapon. Shivering, she slowly stood and reached for her rifle.

The handle of her knife poked through the tattered remains of the raider's coat. She reached for it, watching blood ooze from the cavernous gash. Death smeared the blade red. Aurous growled, and a moment later she heard it too; more raiders in the distance, gathering and beginning to beset the house. But it was Caden's snarl that chilled her to the bone. She gasped at his rough grip around her collar.

"Listen," he hissed, his dark eyes glaring into hers. She shivered again, but said nothing. "Ya got one chance gettin' outta here alive, got it?" At her nod, he averted his gaze and stared past her. "Help me with that."

She followed him through the darkened room. Beyond, there was a table Caden cleared. She helped drag it across the sullied floor. They pushed the table flat against the opening, and he wedged several other pieces of broken furniture against it. It wasn't completely solid, but it would hold momentarily.

Not that it's going to help in the long run... She kept that grim thought to herself.

"How many rounds ya got in that rifle?" Caden asked, ghosting to the front of the house.

She followed him, her hand rubbing the raw skin around her throat. Aurous limped beside her. She scratched his ears and replied, "I only fired one shot."

"Good," he replied. "Ya go up top, take out as many as ya can from above."

"I still don't have much."

"Ammo?"

She bit her lip, ignoring the grime that fouled her tongue, then nudged her head at the window. Caden eased around the scummy curtain. He cursed silently.

"Ya left yer damn ammo in the bag. Any idea on how ya can get that shit back? Of course not," he muttered, each word a venomous barb piercing her heart. Not bothering to mask the anger in his voice, he barked, "Gimme the bloody rifle."

When she opened her mouth in protest, he yanked the bloodstained weapon from her flimsy grasp. "I'll go up top."

As he turned, he swiftly slammed his boot into the small desk near the stairs. It toppled over, a splintery mess. A sole picture frame landed with a *thud*, stopping after a short skid at her feet. An older woman smiled from behind the glass, her dress vibrant with purple floral patterns.

She fought welling tears and grabbed the polished black pistol he dangled in front of her. He dug through his pocket and produced a solitary clip. "This is all ya got, princess. Don't miss." He pointed to the overturned desk now blockading the hallway. "Use that for cover if they get in."

He reached for Aurous, but the wolf snapped at his fingers. With her urging, the wolf reluctantly left her side, though not without his bright, amber eyes staring back with worry.

I'll be okay. She feigned a smile at the rangy wolf.

Caden eased up the stairs after him, concealed in a cloak of shadows. Each step along the corroded wood cut through the haunting silence with a sharp *creak.*

"Kill anyone who comes near."

"Right," she mumbled, her heart throbbing madly. Her upturned belly made her queasy.

She stared at the curtain wavering from the wind, and tried to focus her capricious thoughts. The handle of Caden's gun was still warm to her touch. She carefully peeked past the makeshift curtain.

Across the road, two more raiders huddled behind a gutted vehicle, their long barreled weapons resting on the gnarled metal frame. One stood near the doorway to the house behind the others. She counted two others in the windows on the top floor, their guns glinting under the fading sunlight. She strained her eyes to the far left and caught sight of her bags.

Only both shooters in front are within range. She closed the curtain and leaned against the wall. The gun nearly fell from her trembling hands. *Can't get to my bags unless Caden takes out the bastards in the windows.*

"You really need to do this?" Someone shouted through the wind's furious howl. "You're only prolonging the inevitable!"

Each deep breath did little to calm her accelerating heart. Panic disheveled her thoughts.

C'mon, get it together. Dad would understand.

"You're a goddamn coward! A goddamn murderer!"

Caden fired the first shot. Like a detonating bomb, the rifle discharged with a deafening blast. The bullet *clanged* against the twisted car frame. Gunfire erupted throughout the empty street once more. She fired her own gun out the window through squinted eyes; wood splintered around the window frame and the stained curtain tattered as bullets ripped into the house. Through the clamor, a shrill voice shrieked for them to hold their fire. She ducked as the final bullets bit into the wall above, and then all was silent. Except for the incessant ringing in her ears.

"Enough!" Even from afar, the booming command carried throughout the house. The voice was raucous, raspy... and a woman's. "Girl! I know you're in there! Why are you doing this?"

Through the inundating silence, she heard the woman click her tongue in apparent impatience. "What has that man offered you in return for your aid?"

"Safe passage along the highway." Celeste's voice cracked as she spoke each word slowly. *No point in lying.* "That's it."

"Well, you could always help us instead of dying needlessly," the woman remarked wryly. "We *will* kill that man."

A pugnacious reply followed, "Don't listen to that bitch!"

Celeste heard the woman bidding her companion to hold his fire. The man beside her, kneeling behind the rusted car, left his weapon fixated on her window.

"Look," the woman went on. "I'm what some would call a sheriff. I make sure this place runs smoothly."

"This place looks like it's been to hell and back," Celeste called out, unable to still her shaking hands.

"That's because it isn't safe here anymore."

"Then why are you here?"

Another click of her tongue. "Girl, I'm offering you a chance to live. I'll grant you passage to the city, but I warn you, the roads are treacherous without the army patrols."

"I'll get ya across, girlie!" Caden yelled with a strained voice. *Aurous.* He growled through the wooden floorboards. "Military be damned! Don't worry yerself with these bastards!"

"We don't need no murderer's brat!"

"Kill them both!"

"Goddamn killers!"

Through the tumult, the woman's deep voice bellowed, "That's enough!" Silence followed her echoing command. "What will it be, girl? You don't need to pay for this man's crimes."

Crimes? She thought of the trail of dead he'd left since she'd met him, his coat and blades saturated with blood. Like a decomposing corpse, the rancidity of rotting meat lingered in the air around him. Yet he had saved her life more than once.

I nearly had us both killed.

"This is ridiculous, Kayla," the man behind the rusted car hissed, his harsh whispers barely audible through the blustery wind. "We can kill them both now!"

The woman named Kayla remained silent for another moment, then, "Okay, storm the building."

"Wait!"

Thunder rumbled through the tempestuous clouds gathering in the distance, echoing Celeste's frantic cry.

We survive, right, dad? She exhaled a shaky breath. *No matter what. Survive.*

"I'm coming out," she finally declared. *It's my only chance.*

Blood from her shoulder still seeped through her coat. She wiped sweat from her brow, but only smeared more of her red across her forehead. Shifting her belt, she stepped through the doorway.

"Don't ya do it, bitch!" She heard Caden's ragged voice resound through the house. His sharp tone chilled her heart. "I'll kill ya!"

"Take aim at that window, and put a bullet in his forehead if he tries to shoot her," Kayla ordered, loudly enough so her heartless command would reach Caden's ears. The man began to protest until she held up her hand, then reached for her own weapon. "Alright, girl. Come out, and I promise, no harm will befall you."

The cold wind nipped at her exposed skin. The light drizzle from the oncoming storm turned to squally rain, soaking her coat and matting her hair. The woman stood still as Celeste approached slowly, the sleek, black pistol hanging at her side.

"Holster the weapon."

It slipped into the large holster now on the front of her thigh. The woman nodded to the man on her right, and once his large rifle fixated on Caden's position in the upper window, the woman stepped out from behind the rusted car.

Gelid rain pelted them like sleet. Strands of dark, carmine hair dangled in front of Celeste's eyes, flickering slightly with each rapid breath she exhaled. The woman smiled, her bright blue eyes piercing through the rainy veil. She had sun-bleached blonde hair, tightly-bound and tied in the back. Her clothes were clean, not soiled or tattered like the others. She had a long, brown coat almost the same length as Caden's. Two pistols were holstered on each hip, the handles bobbing and swaying as she walked. She held a large rifle like the man behind the car, but she kept the barrel lowered to the ground. Brown freckles checkered her elegant, white skin. Her mouth twisted in a wry smile, curving up past her long, sharp nose.

"Don't do it!" Caden continued to scream fiercely, almost desperately, his words smothered by inclement wind. "They'll kill ya!"

"I'm Kayla," the woman said. Even through the heavy rainfall, her voice echoed. She stood straight, almost a foot taller than Celeste. She looked down and then back toward the house Caden concealed himself within. "And you seem to have found yourself some trouble."

"Seems that way," Celeste croaked in response, trying to steady her voice. *C'mon, get it together.* "I'm just looking for family in the city."

"Right," Kayla said. "Safe passage."

"You promised."

"I did." The woman eyed her carefully. "But first, we deal with that man."

"He saved my life," Celeste began, until Kayla's chilling glare cut her short.

"He's taken many others." The large weapon shifted in her hands. "Saving your life does not exonerate him for murdering others."

"I have another friend in there." Her numbed fingers trembled. *Aurous.*

"The deal was safe passage for *you* only." Words that chilled her more than a brewing storm. Kayla tossed a quick glance to the man behind her and said, "Get ready to shoot the prick and anyone else in that building." She turned back to Celeste with a sneer. "Little girl. Come with me."

Celeste smiled back at her. *I will not become prey again.* "You may be right. He killed those men." She stepped forward, her hand falling behind her back. *I was taught to survive by any means.* Her icy fingers wrapped around the hilt of her hidden knife. "But I am *not* a little girl."

Her knife lunged and sank into Kayla's neck with a meaty *thump.* A runnel of blood burst past the hilt, and her thin raspberry lips parted in a breathless gasp.

The man behind Kayla screamed before an eruption of rapid gunfire overwhelmed his angered bellows. Bullets ripped up the concrete by her feet, so Celeste pushed herself against Kayla, but the woman braced and lifted her own weapon. Bullets *zinged* past her ears and plunged into Kayla's flesh. The woman grunted and gurgled on more blood as it pooled in her throat. Her eyes fluttered, and she slouched, legs buckling.

They both slammed against the concrete. She struggled under Kayla's limp body, reaching for her holstered weapon as the man opened fire again. Through the clamor of gunfire, she heard the *blast* of her rifle, and red spattered the approaching man's chest. He fell with a grunt and rolled across the road as lifeless as the woman named Kayla.

"I got yer back, girlie!" She heard Caden yell. "Now get the hell outta there!"

She groaned, pushing herself up. Discordant screams, gusty winds, and merciless gunfire; her heart sped along with the chaos. Kayla's blood soaked into her clothes. More bullets trailed the concrete as she ran for her bags.

They were only a few feet away. Bullet holes punctured the outer lining, her clothes and various belongings now drenched from the rain. She secured her bow to the sodden bags and pulled the straps up to her shoulder. Peering through the rain, she witnessed scintillating light of gunfire erupting in the distance.

Zing!

Another bullet veered into the pavement beside her.

Zing!

A patch of concrete cracked by her feet. Still, she ran. Each *thud* of her boots against the road mimicked her quickened heart. Through the misty rain, more gunfire flashed like lightning and *boomed* like rumbling thunder. Caden's strident laughter followed every loud *clap* of her rifle.

"C'mon, girlie!" He yelled, another cackle haunting the streets. "The bastards are runnin' away!"

She threw herself in the doorway as the last shot echoed. She rolled into the wall, the contents of her bag tumbling through the ripped seams.

Damn it!

A wet nose nudged her face while she desperately caught her breath. The grimy, stale air stung her throbbing lungs. She buried herself in her wolf's shadowy fur, trying not to retch from the malodorous scent of blood and death. Heavy boot steps covered her small sobs.

Too much death. Kayla's blood dripped from her fingers.

"That was damn brilliant," Caden said, a devilish grin plastered on his face. A blatant fool. She glowered as he approached, her blood-stained rifle in his hands. "I knew ya wouldn't leave yer mutt."

"I don't know what you did," she whispered. Aurous growled in unison. "But I know this isn't for revenge." His eyes darkened, and he tucked his narrow chin to his chest. Before he could respond, she hissed, "I'll help you, then you show me the safest route to the city. We can part ways after that."

"Pout all ya want, Celeste," he replied drolly, her rifle shifting in his grasp. He sneered, "I know ya loved every damn minute. Can't wash that blood from yer hands now, princess."

A raspy chuckled hummed dully through heavy rain battering against the roof. Shivering, she stood and grimaced, more blood warming her shoulder. She stared into his eyes. Her mouth curved into a sharp frown, which he returned with a callous smile.

For a moment, she thought he was right. "Time to finish the hunt."

Nine
Stalker

DARKNESS REACHED across a storming sky. Inky shadows consumed the surroundings, blotting out buildings and mountains. Impetuous winds howled through the barren streets like fearful screams, drowning out the drum of pummeling sleet.

His boots slapped against the slick pavement as he ran, quick, ragged breaths fogging the air behind him. Her head bobbed along with every step, her arms tightly wrapped around his neck with her chin tucked into her sweater. He swore between desperate gulps of frigid air, his voice trembling as the cold encompassed them both.

She could hear them coming.

Voices bellowed through the roaring wind. She braced as their pursuers burst through darkness curtaining the road behind them. Light flashed and thunder erupted; bullets whistled past. Her father screamed and tightened his grip around her small body.

The sky blurred into the ground as they tumbled through the dirt. While his grip around her never slackened, confusion clouded her mind after countless blows against the dirt during their roll. Driven from her lungs forcefully, air wouldn't return with her panicked gasps. Her father groaned and coughed, a gentle mist warming her face. More warmth flooded against her chest. Blood. She wanted to scream, but couldn't. Her father tried to stand, only to groan again and sputter a curse before a final, thunderous gunshot shattered the ensuing silence.

Another dreaded memory blurred into reality. The darkening streets were slick with frozen rain and haunted by wailing winds. Her lungs pained with labored breaths.

Thud. Thud. Thud. Thud.

Like the steady beat of a war drum pounding within her ears, the thump of her quickened heart echoed her stomping boots. She moved swiftly, as much as her tired muscles would manage. With her bags discarded and only her most precious items safely within the pockets of her coat, she was more agile and moved nimbly through the streets.

Loose bullets jingled in her pockets. Her sweater bulged by her belly from the tattered book her father once forced her to read. Other items, such as the few dirty rings once belonging to her mother and gloves her father had worn every winter were also stuffed into her pants. Strapped to her belt, both her rusting, chipped knife and bloodstained machete dangled and swayed against her hip. Two pistols, both taken from Kayla's corpse, were tucked away near her backside. The flashlight was wedged beside the empty holster on her left. Her revolver remained drawn, still clutched between numbed fingers. Her faded red bow hung down her back over the quiver, the string strapped across her chest.

Caden matched her pace, slowing his long strides to stay beside her. Her rifle dangled from his shoulder while the dead man's weapon remained by his hip. His maniacal grin flashed bloodstained teeth.

He's enjoying himself.

They ran past the dappled brick house and gnarled vehicles, through the sopping grass, then up the crumbling stone walkway that shifted beneath each step. The remaining raiders retreated through the farthest house from the street. Far from their dead littered along the pavement.

"They ain't gonna be here," Caden remarked with a gruff whisper. "Bastards probably know we ain't playin' anymore."

"They're going further into town," she breathed, trying to steady her heart. "They could hide anywhere."

He shook his head. Droplets of rain and perspiration fell by his boots and splattered along the front of her coat. "Nah. They'll be haulin' ass outta here." He jerked his thumb over his shoulder, then smiled viciously. "Ya killed their leader."

Thankful for the rain masking the scent of spilled blood, she merely nodded her head and ignored the groaning protest of her stomach. *Too much death.*

"So, what now?"

He raised an eyebrow and asked playfully, "Eager to finish what ya started, princess?"

"What *you* started," she countered, still sickened.

His smile faded quickly, his rigid brow now furrowed as he growled back, "Ya would have been slaughtered without me." He leaned closer. Each breath he exhaled filled her nose with the stench of rotted meat. "Ya best remember that."

The rancidity stung her bleary eyes. "Feel like sharing your plan?"

He chuckled, running his dirty fingers through his sleek, wet hair. "Aye." He pushed the bullet riddled door open with his boot. "We go through the house. Follow their trail."

She frowned and stared into the dark doorway. "Why go through the house if we know they're not there?"

"One of them bastards has a scope."

"What?"

"A goddamn sniper." He patted her rifle. His fingers drummed against the faded bloodstain on the handle. "Almost took my head. Scared 'em off with this beauty."

"Extra cover," she said, "and a trail to follow."

"Now yer catching up."

She narrowed her eyes, glaring into the velvet shadows. "Lead the way."

Though they treaded lightly, the old, wooden floor still *creaked* and *groaned* with each carefully placed step. With one finger placed over his bloody, puckered lips, he nudged his head to the first room on their left. She nodded back, raising her revolver and gently easing the hammer back. *Click.* She felt Aurous brush up against her leg. He kept by her side as she moved away from Caden and into the blinding night.

The clamorous wind battered against the house, tearing the makeshift curtains and hastily nailed boards away from the windows. She braced against the bitter cold and clenched her teeth to stifle the chatter. Besides a few blankets disheveled from the bed and a pile of musty clothing in the far corner, the room was empty.

"Nothing here," Caden called to her. His rough voice echoed along with the rumbling of the storm.

After telling him the room was clear, she found him at the foot of a spiraling staircase, the marble winding up into the ceiling. Rubble and debris had fallen through the sodden roof, burying most of the staircase

"Nothing here, either," he muttered, then turned and walked to the back doorway.

She followed him with her fingers snagged in the wolf's black fur. Aurous lolled his tongue when her eyes drifted to his, provoking a smile and a warmth inside her heart the glacial storm and chilling death had yet to pierce. His eyes blossomed a bright gold, and his tail wagged gently while she combed her fingers through his matted fur.

"Stay close," she whispered softly.

I need you.

The frigid wind sent shivers slinking down her spine. Pain flared in her shoulder and knee when she stood and extended her arm toward the door.

Caden had been peering past the soggy curtain obscuring the far window. He barely gave a glance when her fingers curled around the doorknob, but turned and yelled for her to stop a moment later. Wood splintered from the door frame as a gunshot tore through the falling sleet. More exploded around the door as another bullet burst through and lodged into the wall behind them.

She crashed into the floor, her shoulder wound opening with a flood of warm blood. Caden had thrown himself into her, tumbling over her with his pistol discharging blindly through the wooden door. Caden's yells were muffled. He yanked her to her feet by the collar of her sweater. Blood had soaked through to her coat once more.

"Ya goddamn fool!" He cursed her after the gunfire ceased. "Take that bloody thing off!"

"Don't!" She slapped his hand away defiantly, her lips curling in a threatening snarl. Aurous mimicked her growl as she whispered gruffly as though he were her father, "I can take care of myself."

"Clearly," he replied, rolling his dark eyes.

Her face reddened, but she eventually took off her coat. After emptying the pockets and stuffing her sweater full, he shook his head but grinned, scratching at his stubble. "Ya got guts, girlie. I'll give ya that much."

She only glared in response.

He laughed and asked, "Ya ready to finally have some fun?"

The rain hadn't stopped, it merely froze. Thick clumps of ice pelted them. The cold wind bit at her skin, whipping hair wildly around her face. The chilling air frosted her lungs. Gloved fingers still clutched the revolver tight, while her other hand grazed Aurous' slick fur. Like a thick veil of fog, the sleety rain misted her surroundings with a deep white.

"There!" Caden whispered harshly, thrusting his finger to the faint flashes of light in the hazy cloud. "Get 'em, princess!"

The revolver bucked. Her muscles strained against its kick, but she braced and pulled the trigger. Again, a dull light flickered through the foggy sleet as another bullet *whizzed* past and sank into the dirt beside her.

Their pace never wavered. Houses beyond the tall, wooden fence shadowed the pearly mist like spilled ink staining a white sheet of paper. They both ducked, shoulders hunched, before colliding with the solid wood. She slid through the dirt first. The left side of her body *smacked* against the fence. Caden hit simultaneously. She peered through the cracks, but her lips barely parted with a swift yell as another light flashed through the sleet.

Caden threw his head back. A bullet chewed through the drab wooden fence. Mud blotched his coat as he rolled, more bullets rupturing the makeshift cover. Celeste scrambled, her back pushing against a frenzied wolf. Aurous howled along with the gunfire, resisting her retreat. Through the chaos and uproar, she heard the cacophonous laughter erupting from Caden as he stood and aimed the dead man's rifle.

He pulled the trigger.

It was like hell brewed its own dark, twisted storm. Bullets spat through the fiery blaze at the end of the barrel. The peal of discharging gunfire ripped through her eardrums, the force of each shot thundering against her chest. She stared at Caden with tumid eyes until she saw her father. His sharp frown beset by a blood-spattered beard, his cold, dark eyes under a creased brow... It was how she used to see him as a child, as a young girl who couldn't understand what horrors hid in a world she longed to know. He was her barrier, her shield against a darkness no light penetrated. Now he could no longer protect her.

But she wouldn't succumb to fear.

She was thrust back in reality. Her heartbeat pulsed in her ears, muffling the storm of gunfire and howling winds. The revolver steadied as the trembling in her hands ceased.

Survive.

She kept her head low and pushed past Caden, who ducked down to change the clip from his smoking rifle.

He practically screamed over the ringing in his ears. "You hear that bitch *roar?*"

She had no words for the maniac, only a quick glance into his icy, blue eyes that flushed her pallid face red once more. He laughed and lifted the rifle as she turned away from him. Her boots plopped through the mud, filling with thick, murky water and soaking the bottom of her pants. Her coat and sweater managed to keep her only partially dry. So far, her knees weren't drenched.

Yet, she thought sarcastically.

The yard stretched further into misty sleet, but the fence ended abruptly. Remnants of another lay scattered in the mud by her boots. To her right, there was another run-down house with boarded windows. Past the fence was still an aphotic haze.

Slop.

Someone was coming.

Before she pulled the trigger, a shadow blurred through the sleety veil.

Thump!

The dark wooden fence fractured alongside the top as a flurry of lead burst through the craggy edge. Shattered fragments rained down as she ducked and then slipped, her hands and revolver sinking into sludge.

Thump!

The figure unloaded his shotgun again. Lead sprayed the muddy ground beside her.

Click.

Her muddied revolver, raised, poised, and eager for flesh, wouldn't fire.

The raider pierced through the hazy curtain. His eyes were shadowed, his dark, tanned skin blending with his black clothes. Before the empty shell casing hit the ground after pumping the forend, another blast ripped through the stormy night.

There was only so much she could do. She rolled, or tried, through the muddy ground, but felt the sting in the side of her left leg, followed by a trickle of warmth down into her sock. She grunted, and reached for her belt while the raider pumped the forend again. Death's hollow eye stared back at her through the end of the shotgun's barrel.

Leaping over her, Aurous snarled and weaved through the muck for the raider. The man's heart must have pumped uncertainty. He hesitated, then lowered his shotgun to the charging wolf. Her own heart nearly succumbed to the same hesitation.

Aurous!

She tugged the dead woman's pistol from her belt and fired.

Blood sprayed into the sleety wind, and the raider dropped his weapon, grasping at his arm. The shotgun dangled at his side. Her panic stopped the wolf from lunging, but the raider cursed and vanished behind the broken fence.

"Thanks, boy," she whispered, her voice low and ragged. She couldn't catch her breath, and her hands trembled again.

It's almost over. She held on to Aurous, refusing to spill more tears. *Soon, we'll be safe.*

Then she was running. Again.

Through the rumblings of an irate sky, panicked screams and fervent cries harmonized with the deafening barrage of bullets. *Sniper.* She dashed through another muddied yard, keeping low and leaning against makeshift cover. Bullets seemed to trail her movements.

The bastard must have a clear view, she thought bitterly. *High point. Enough to slightly see through this freezing rain.*

"So, what are you going to do?"

She nearly screamed. Her father whispered in her ear, but when she turned, nobody stood behind her. There was nothing but footprints through the mud, a twisted wooden fence that had fallen long ago, and bullet holes in the ground now filling with mud water.

"Think, love," his disembodied voice commanded. "You could keep going, risk another ambush as soon as you pass the far side of this house."

"Or I could stay in the sniper's path." She shook her head. *Why am I talking to myself?* "Not a lot of great options."

She heard him chuckle. An echo of a memory that warmed her chilly heart. "There's always a smarter solution, Celeste."

It dawned on her. "The house."

Up the steps with ruptured, rotting wood and dark stains smeared along the panels was where her solution hid. As she neared the door with thick boards nailed across it, the stains became legible.

INFECTED. STAY OUT.

"This doesn't seem smart..."

But no reply followed. He was no longer with her, had never truly been there. She was still alone.

No, she thought ardently. *I'm not alone.* She smiled at Aurous, who whined with worry but stared with bright, wondering eyes.

"Hush. Since when have I ever been smart, anyhow?" She ripped the jagged boards down from the door and stepped into the house marked with death.

It stunk. Badly.

The first few corpses were disemboweled and slumped against the far wall, maggots and buzzing flies swarming the putrefying flesh. Their innards hung in bloody, discolored strands from their torn torsos. The moist, feculent air fouled the taste on her tongue. Every reluctant breath made her gag. Even though her clothes were still damp from the stormy weather, she bunched the front of her sweater in her palm and masked the bottom half of her face. She nearly retched into her cold, musty clothes.

Disgusting.

Clumps of meat squished and oozed under her boots as she stepped through the dark pool of crimson. The next room held a different corpse. The dead woman still had her flesh intact, slumped against the wall in a similar fashion of the first few bodies. Her face contorted in a grim smile, her gaze fixated on the pictures that lined the cabinet shelf across the room. Her throat had been gouged. Someone had thrust a knife into her neck, and carved instead of slit. Like sculpting the cur-vaceous smile of a Jack-o'-lantern. A chunk of flesh was missing. Blood peppered the white wall behind her, and stained the front of her yellow blouse. She held a knife in her curled, rigid fingers, the blade also smeared with dark ooze.

She killed herself... Horribly.

The pictures inside the cabinet were covered with dusty cobwebs. With all the insects feasting on the decaying ruins of a family, the spiders had found their haven.

Bright smiles greeted her through the grimy, faded photographs. Propped in a stained vase, long orchids hung over the brim. Brittle, plum-colored petals crumbled into dust between her fingers.

Why did I never have any pictures of my parents?

Aurous finally nudged her hand with his cold nose, and she wiped her tears.

Blood, guts and decay; a fetor she'd almost grown accustomed to. Until now. A wave of nausea churned her belly, and the little content it held came up in violent, watery spurts. Choking, she covered her face but retched more. Aurous panted, his wide, amber eyes brimming unease. Maggots squirmed under her boot. There were more bodies with bones jaggedly protruding through sundered flesh, the skin on their faces like dangling, bloody ribbons.

ABANDONED BY GOD

Above the wall in grubby, brown smears, the words were barely legible through pressing shadows. Loose bowels. The stench hung with the heavy odor of blood and guts. Below the message scrawled in human waste there was a final body. This corpse had not been cruelly desecrated like the others. Instead, its flesh appeared charred and blackened from the tongue of an angry flame. Misshapen points pierced through its split fingertips, its jaw crooked with carious fangs and bloodied eyes. The side of its skull bulged out like the bone ballooned beneath putrid, black flesh. Puncture wounds covered its body; it was riddled with lead.

Oh no... Her stomach twisted again.

Infected.

Her father's words echoed strongly throughout her mind, his low, growling voice repeating what she already knew from years of his incessant drills. *The most common spread is by blood, as well as other bodily fluids. As the host became more ravaged by the assaulting virus, they would most often fall victim to bouts of violent coughs — which expelled bloody mucus from the lungs. Those unlucky enough to mutate instead of withering in pain before dying continued carrying the virus. Different strains, various infection rates... All deadly.*

She'd covered her face knowing the house to be infected as she entered, but had carelessly sloshed through tainted blood. The open wound on her shoulder throbbed, as well as the small punctures on her left leg.

I've got to be more careful. She peered down, worried, but no blood except her own stained her pants. *They were beginning to change.* She glanced back to the woman in the other room, still haunted by her ghostly, chilling smile. *I can still catch it from infected blood.* She shuddered from a chill festering in her heart. *I knew it would be diseased, but I never thought it would have progressed this far.*

Voices.

Dim light cut through the darkness from cracks in the boarded up windows. There was no front door, just a long hallway leading down to various rooms. *Must be on the side.* Again, she heard muffled tones through the walls. Aurous growled, but she leaned down, soothing his fur to silence him. Careful to avoid the sludgy, dark blood saturated into the carpet by the black corpse, she eased toward the large boarded window.

"... I don't see either of them, Jerry," one of them whispered, his voice low and rough. "Could've gone around us."

"Nah," the man named Jerry replied, not bothering to conceal his lightly toned voice. "Bitch doesn't look like much of a fight, and Eli still has one of them pinned down with the scope. The others will have plenty of time to escape this madness."

The first man snorted loudly then hushed his voice. He replied nervously, "You see that bitch, Jer? One hit and Kayla was down. And that woman helped us through a lot of shit. Scary shit. I've seen her take down droves of infected."

"Yet she was taken down by a runt. The bitch got lucky, Bill." He laughed. "Couldn't even kill you with a full clip."

"Messed my arm up," Bill grunted. "Hurts to hold this damn shotty."

"Well, stay ready. They could pop around these corners at any time."

Bill whispered bitterly, "We best shut the hell up then."

Ambush. Clever bastards.

She'd almost walked into a trap. *Thanks, dad.* Another growl filled the eerily silent room. Her lips parted in a snarl that quickly curved into a sharp, bloodthirsty smile.

The wolf in her attacked first.

Gripping the small, black pistol she'd looted from Kayla's corpse, she stepped back and squeezed the trigger. Her aim wavered; the kickback jolted her shoulder, and each bullet veered further from her intended target. After a series of bewildered cries, lead viciously greeted her in return.

They all fired blindly.

The side of the house nearly burst apart from the cannonade. Splinters and dusty debris clouded the room as bullets ripped through both ends of the wall. She leaned close to the floor, careful not to drench her hands on the soggy carpet, and pulled the trigger until the clip emptied. A pained scream followed the *clap* of her last bullet leaping from the barrel and drilling through the punctured wall.

"Shit, Jer!" There was a loud grunt and a gurgling wheeze. "I'm hit pretty bad!"

"C'mon, Bill!"

Pale light poured through the holes, illuminating the black blood stained along the wall and floorboards. Shaken by the clamorous commotion, Aurous lay by her feet, covered in settling dust. Her arm ached and so did her hips. Crimson snaked down the back of her hands like bloody rills, dripping down her fingers and the black gun in her grasp. She rolled up her sleeves, but found only a few small wounds on her forearm and left shoulder. *Grazed.* Her hip had been slightly singed as well.

It could have been a lot worse. She grinned stupidly, lost with euphoric adrenaline.

"I know you're scared, boy," she said through chattering teeth. Her body trembled like the nervous wolf beside her. She took one last steadying breath. "But we have to finish this."

Her bloody fingers coiled around a familiar handle. The machete cleaved a path through the splintered boards, and once more she found herself in the heart of a storm.

The raiders retreated through the fog ahead of her. Gunshots echoed beyond the slaughterhouse against her back.

Caden... She shook her head. *Focus.*

The frame was slick from rain, and the string *creaked* when she eased it back. Her shoulder burned, like hot embers pressing against her muscles. She grimaced, but held the bow steady with the string pinched between her fingers, her gaze transfixed on the blurry shadows in the distance. The bowstring released with a *twang* and the arrow snapped forward, leaping up into the air before carving a downward path and striking the ground near the dark blots in the distance. She cursed, plucking another arrow from of her leathery quiver.

Steady.

"How many times do I have to remind you?" Her father gibed from nowhere, though his tone conveyed no malice. "How long until you get it?"

"Steady breathing," she whispered, her eyes now squinting to focus on the shadowy blurs. "Compensate for the wind. And only take the shot..." The barbed missile lobbed through the gelid rain, swiftly sailing toward her mark. "... When you're ready." Like the talons of a hawk ripping into the flesh of its unknowing prey, the arrow dropped and pierced through the blurred shadow.

Yes!

Elated, she had trouble suppressing a broadening smile. *About time I hit something!*

Aurous' troubled whine dampened her celebration. When she looked to the wolf, he thrust his nose into the air. Then the concrete by her boots ruptured. Thunder echoed through the neighborhood, though she knew too well it wasn't a bellow from the storm above. The sniper had his sights fixated on her through the sleet, and a sickened feeling settled in her belly before two muffled gunshots clapped through the storm's patter.

Caden!

The smile returned, and she slipped the bow over her shoulder. After nudging Aurous playfully, the two wolves hastened down the frozen road to claim their fallen prey.

Slick ice coated the concrete. She slipped occasionally, her boots gliding across the frosty road while Aurous scampered to catch up. He continued to limp from his injury.

The blots in the distant haze stopped, and she knew one had taken a direct hit.

It's over.

She ran past charred houses, some gutted from fire and others burned to nothing but dark ash. *This whole block was practically destroyed... and what wasn't became condemned.*

The shadows were moving again. The outline of a tall building loomed like a giant mountain in the hazy horizon. The shadows vanished.

Damn.

A sign near the stone walkway read *Evergreen Apartments* in faded letters. Blood left a haunting trail along the muddied stone, and she followed its winding lead to the front of the building. Grinning wolfishly, she pulled the second black pistol from her belt and eased the door open.

Stepping into the solid darkness, her muscles tensed. Her finger hovered over the trigger, stiff from the cold piercing her damp gloves. Her heart slowed its heavy beat, her lungs refusing air. She'd been expecting something – anything but a deluge of shadows and the minacious clutches of its silence. She was treading lightly when Aurous sauntered past her with his snout to the floor, his short, rapid pants echoing loudly down the long corridor. The slim wolf growled lightly. Curious, she reached for her flashlight.

Light beamed through the darkness. On the floor, by her boots and even further along the tile by Aurous, were thick droplets of blood. It was hard to see, the floor itself was covered in muck and grime, but splatter marks gleamed under the light. Aurous also followed the makeshift trail with his nose, looking back with fiery eyes to make sure she stayed close.

Many of the doors were boarded up like the previous home she'd gone through, with the same warnings scrawled above. *Infected.*

"Hush," she whispered, silencing the wolf's uneasy growl. With her pistol poised, she flicked the flashlight down the muddy corridor. Nothing. Aurous craned his neck and snarled as she heard the chilling echo of a forend shift.

THUMP!

The shotgun blast ripped into the wall beside her. Debris showered her, and the attacker pumped the forend again. Undeterred, the wolf snarled madly and lunged.

"No!" She shrieked. The pistol trembled in her hands. The wolf's jaws closed around the man's throat, and they both fell back against the floor as the shotgun discharged down the corridor again. Sparks flared, and lead sprayed along the walls.

"Aurous!"

She left the flashlight on the floor behind her, the corridor ahead now swallowed by her shadow. The wolf's jagged teeth had torn into the man's neck, and blood rushed through gorged flesh. Aurous was ready to attack again, but the man raised his shotgun with shaky hands, his sputters and grunts lost under the drumming of her erratic heart. She heard the forend of the shotgun shift, the barrel aimed at her wolf.

Blood. Her body seemed to be losing a lot of it. It flowed from her torn shoulder and down her chest. It pooled in her gloves and boots. Every healing wound on her body ripped open again as she slammed into

Aurous. The wolf yelped. They collided, launching through the nearest door. The wood groaned before bursting in a cloud of splinters. The blast savagely tore through the corridor, shredding the walls and ceiling.

Her lungs burned. The dusty debris clogged her throat when she inhaled sharply. The wolf tried to stand, but she scrambled through the shattered remnants of the wooden door and pushed against the shaken animal again.

THUMP!

Glass shattered and sprayed behind her. Debris scattered along the floor. Pain came from everywhere, every muscle and fiber of her bruised being. She was rattled. She couldn't hear past the high-pitched squeal resounding through her ears. She waited, fighting for air that still wouldn't soothe her aching lungs, certain death loomed, ready to pierce through her soul with its scythe.

Bloody mucus dribbled down her chin as she coughed, pushing herself up from the rubble. Pieces of fractured wood dug into her hip like a serrated blade. Eyes bleary and stinging, she looked up.

Nobody stood in the doorway.

Brightness beamed across the wall from her fallen flashlight in the corridor. Black coursed down the faded paint like oozing shadows.

What the hell? The whimpering wolf shook the dust from his fur while she stood and wiped her brow. Sweat, blood, and grime.

I'm a goddamn mess.

She gave Aurous a lackluster grin, her gun already raised.

But we could be dead.

She approached the corridor cautiously. Rigid muscles, strained eyes, and bloody wounds – she was on the verge of collapse. *Where did that bastard go?* But there was nobody in the corridor either. Nothing but black slime crawling down the wall.

Blood. Fear swelled inside her mind, bulging through every thought. *Black blood.* Light flickered through the corridor as she snatched the fallen flashlight. Aiming it at Aurous, her heart chilled. The same black blood stained his teeth and muddied his pink gums.

That man was infected!

Even with a rupturing heart, tears couldn't spill through her stinging eyes. *You never told me if animals could be affected,* she thought, clenching her teeth. A rancorous fire raged through her mind. *I never thought to ask...*

Now I'll never get to.

The pain had dulled in recent days, but now it flared like a fresh wound, seeping bloody loneliness and despair. *First my mother and my brother.* Her throat tightened. *My father.*

"I can't lose you too," she whispered, her hands buried in the wolf's black, bristly fur.

Shadowed palm prints were stamped and smeared along the wall down the corridor. She followed the blood, her looted pistol resting on the flashlight. Her extended arms quivered, the weight of her weapon too much for her aching muscles.

The hallway ended at a door with a handle coated in thick, black blood. Already slightly open, she *clicked* her flashlight off and pushed against the door with her foot. It groaned as it slowly swung open. Aurous growled, and she heard it a moment later. Short, shallow breaths. Rapid.

Someone coughed and choked, gurgling on blood in their throat before spewing it on the floor with a sickening *splat.*

"That's... far enough," the man managed to gasp. He sat, slumped in the corner, holding a small, dull grey pistol. It looked no bigger than his palm, but he grasped and leveled it with her head despite a shaking hand. The barrel of her own weapon had its sights on him as well.

"This... was supposed to be for... me," he continued muttering through pooling blood, gesturing to his poised weapon. "After I... killed you."

"Change of plans," she replied coldly.

"I... knew I was sick." He coughed. "Turn it... on." After a moment, she complied and switched on her flashlight.

His skin darkened like a deep bruise. Shadows streamed from his eyes like muddy tears. Flesh was beginning to peel from his fingers like melting wax running down the side of a lit candle. She could see the glistening bone poking through rancid meat. In his leg, part of her arrow still jutted out through his bloody jeans.

He smiled at her disgusted look, his twisted teeth black from the blood in his mouth. "That bad... huh?"

When she didn't answer, he continued, "I wanted... to stay behind. I was... dying anyway. After killing you... I would have killed... myself."

"Then why didn't you kill me?"

Blood seeped through his clenched teeth as he hissed, "I want you...

to suffer!"

He raised his other arm. His dark, rippled skin had been slashed along his wrist. Frayed flesh clung by bloody strings as his hand dangled. He grinned madly, his lips black and peeling from his face. Sharpened teeth sawed through the messy clumps of tattered flesh.

Dad had always warned me about this!

She remembered his late night lectures, the stories she thought were only meant to frighten her, to make her wary of a world she longed to dwell within. Fear roared through her, as it had all those years ago.

I need you... Mother, father... brother!

"Remember what I taught you, Celeste," she heard him whisper. His dark, fiery eyes stared back at her from the shadowed edge of the flashlight's beam. Brown, unruly hair dangled down his neck, and he smiled through a blood-splattered beard. "Within a healthy host, the virus replicates and spreads at a slower rate. Metamorphosis occurs. But when the host is dying before that can happen – well, the virus doesn't want to die either. So it begins its assault early, corrupting DNA and altering the host quickly. Those... things will never fully transform, but that doesn't mean they're to be taken lightly. They're maddened, vicious, and able to spread their infection. Tread carefully, love."

Her bereavement seemed endless, but his ghostly words warmed through the ice forming around her mind. He was gone after she blinked, her tears fresh and soothing to her sore eyes.

I will, dad.

A terrible screech brought her back to the horrors of reality.

Like he was thrown into the pit of a fire, black skin melted from his face. Bones crunched, and his chest burst; black sprayed against the wall beside her, misting the room and coating it in sludge. She covered her face and fell back.

She raised her weapon and leaned over Aurous. The wolf howled wildly and trembled beneath her. The man named Bill dropped his small, silvery gun. He convulsed, but snapped his teeth like a frenzied, hungered beast.

The head! Dad said, always shoot the head before it's too late!

She squeezed the trigger. More black blood rained against the floor. The creature's head slammed back against the wall, but a vengeful wail still rang through the *blast* of her gun.

Now emptied, she tossed the looted pistol aside and dragged the wolf back through the door. Aurous snarled, eager to rake his teeth through the strange being.

It stood, awash in blood and filth. Torn flesh fell to the floor along with its tattered clothes. Its black skin glistened under the bright flashlight, and serrated bones protruded from its hands like claws. Gnarled teeth and deep, bloodied eyes glared back ravenously.

Then it lunged at them.

TEN

FANGS

THEY TUMBLED back through the entryway. Her damp, gloved fingers slipped from the handle as the door slammed shut behind her. She turned, fleeing, panic surging like a voracious fire through her veins. Then her legs tangled with the wolf.

Smack!

Pain pervaded her mind, muddling her thoughts. Blood soaked her gloves when she rubbed the back of her head. She groaned, almost certain the blow had shattered her skull. Her sight flickered faintly as the flashlight rolled along the floor.

A forceful crash rattled walls and echoed down the dark corridor, the commotion matched only by the terrible screech piercing through the rickety door.

Not exactly using my head, she thought, dizzied. *I have to get out of here!*

The wolf's anger refused to simmer. Aurous snarled and howled while the creature battered its black, bloodied body against the door.

"Aurous," she mumbled, heaving from the nauseating throb in the back of her head. The door and walls tremored from the creature's force. "We have to go!" Tugging at the wolf's fur, she found unsteady footing and pulled him away.

Behind them, the wood ballooned then shattered into a storm of splintery shards. The ravaged being screeched and clawed across the rubble, mincing the walls with sharp, bony barbs.

Damn!

She fought against the rabid wolf's strength. He snapped his frothy jaws, twisting his body to loosen her grip.

The creature was gaining on them. Quickly.

Jagged fangs snapped at the wolf's fur. Her revolver cleared the holster, but Aurous tore himself from her grip. Thrown into the wall, she stumbled, then stuck her revolver into the swirling shadows behind her.

Her wolf lunged and rived black flesh from the creature's torso. The strange being's lopsided jaws nipped at empty air while it fell forward. Aurous twisted his neck for another attack, but a swift swipe of the creature's bony claws lacerated his shoulder. The next blow bashed the wolf against the torn wall.

Two rounds burst from her revolver, and black blood slimed the floor. The creature wavered, but its misstep didn't slow its pace. Instead, bony spines raked through the floor like the vinyl tile were loose dirt. She pulled the trigger a third time, and the creature screeched madly through the fiery blast of her gun. The bullet lodged deep into the ceiling after ricocheting off monster's skeletal head. Teeth threatened to snare her flesh, but the wolf collided with them both.

Caught between two beasts and forcibly pulled toward the floor, she thrust the revolver against pulpy, black flesh, and pumped another round into its malformed abdomen. Claws scythed through her coat.

The wolf's teeth sawed through part of the creature's neck. Pinned, the creature wailed and struggled like a rabbit in a snare, but the wolf's claws sank into its deformed face. As with a mutt unearthing a bone in the yard, Aurous dug through its clumpy flesh. Both red eyes were shredded into bloody strings. It howled and raged, sputtering through the leathery flesh ripping around its face.

By the time she scrambled to her feet, pale bone glistened beneath streams of sludgy black. Her fingers twined with the wolf's matted fur, her revolver poised – but the creature struck first. It batted them away like insects, mere annoyances.

She hit the wall, the air forced from her lungs, and she suddenly felt every wound on her body. Pain flared throughout with every deep pump of her speeding heart. Nothing else mattered. It seared her mind and seized her muscles. She wanted to scream, to cry out against the agony brewing inside. *Oh, death, please come swiftly.*

Warmth embraced her heart. Thoughts were of her mother's welcoming arms, the gentle smile spreading across her face, and soft lips pressing against her cheek. Her father's disappointment shadowed the joy. A giggle from her brother echoing distantly... *All I have to do is step over the edge.*

Dad, I'm sorry. You can't save me this time.

But he never had to.

It was Aurous who brought her back from the brink of despair. Ripping and wringing her coat sleeve, he yanked her down the dark corridor. Still disoriented, her thoughts were clouded and unfocused, her belly turned with sickness, and her legs barely withstood her weight as she stumbled over the splintered remnants of the door. She felt worse than she had after slaking her curiosity with wine during the summer.

At least that had numbed some of the ache.

Horror pursued through the dark. Piles of noisome flesh splattered under her boots as she ran, the creature's gurgling wail haunting the corridor behind them. Fresh air flowing through the rancid cloud of death guided them through the darkness.

She stopped only for a moment to avoid tumbling through the infected slush. The creature barreled after her, colliding with the blood smeared wall. Bony claws ripped through the dusty air, but she was already gone.

Light streaming through the cracks of the boarded door ahead of them was a blinding but welcoming sight through the dense, smothering black. The wolf dug his paws into the panels while her shoulder slammed against it. Ignoring the pain, she thrust herself against the boarded door again, but again it refused to budge.

"I'm sorry, boy," she whispered softly. *I'm not going to risk your life any longer.*

She pushed against the wolf, hurling his frail body into the wall. With a whine, he slumped over, and her blood soaked fingers curled around the handle of her machete. She raised the revolver, pulling the trigger. Another bullet thundered through the corridor and plunged into the charging creature's rotting chest. It kept charging, and she greeted its bony barbs with her machete blade.

Glass and splintered wood showered her with jagged debris. Her head rocking against the metal frame jarred and disheveled every panicked thought. The machete was torn from her grip. She fell with the bursting glass, the blackened monster overtop of her. The next moment, there was nothing but pain.

Stone steps broke her fall. The monster collided with her, crushing the air from her lungs. As they tumbled, her face *smacked* against the ground before they rolled through the muddied grass. Blood leaked past her lips. She pushed herself up, revolver raised. The monster clawed through the dirt after her, but the barrel met its voracious stare. She grimaced and pulled the trigger, hoping it would finally be over.

Click.

Empty.

No!

The cylinder spun open, but her legs buckled under the creature's force. It rammed her chest with its bony shoulder, and once more she crashed against the muddy ground. Again, death bared its bloodied fangs, eager to drag her to its fiery Hell.

Except it didn't move. It stood over her, its twisted fists raised and ready to pulverise her into bloody sludge. Its partially severed neck wrenched to the side, its emptied sockets glaring into the haunting brume.

Dumbstruck, she scarcely believed it. Plunging her hand deep into her coat pocket, her numb fingers fumbled for survival. The creature hissed, its bloody saliva slopping down its bony chin. The cylinder spun and snapped into place. The hammer *clicked* back.

"You suffered worse, *asshole*," she whispered through clenched teeth. When the creature once known as Bill turned its ravaged head to her, she thrust the barrel of her gun into its mouth. Gnarled teeth closed around the dull, silver revolver as she pulled the trigger.

The blast tore through its head. Its malformed skull fractured and split. Brain, bits of flesh, and black, tainted blood coated the ground and the remains of the apartment doors. The twisted creature went limp, then fell back into its own sundered filth, dead.

But she wasn't safe yet.

Despite the torturous strain her body endured, she stood with her revolver raised. It was empty, she knew, but she also knew something had been watching them. Bleary eyes scanned the haze, her gun wavering with each glance. Nothing. She finally collapsed into the mud.

Tears fell, carving clear pink trails through the grime on her face. Her aching body didn't matter anymore. *Survive.* But she still shut her eyes, ashamed to feel so weak. *I'm not like you, dad...*

I'm not strong.

When her eyes snapped back open, the beginning of nightfall shrouded the fog blanketing the town. Stormy clouds continued to blot out the evening sky, but the rain finally ceased. She tried moving, a weary groan escaping her bloody lips. Her muscles felt shredded, and her bones ached like they'd been bludgeoned to pieces under bruising flesh. All of it was forgotten when something stirred by her side.

Hastily scrambling to her feet, she lost her balance and fell back into the cold mud. She kept her frigid fingers around the revolver, her frantic heart *thumping* against her tender ribs.

It was only her wolf, with muddy, blood-soaked fur, trembling near the creature's corpse. *Aurous.* He was alive, though terribly wounded.

He cringed when she yelped suddenly, and watched apprehensively while she tore her filthy clothes off.

She was covered in wounds. Red blood dried and crusted to her bare, pale skin. She inspected every bloody abrasion, laceration, and any other jagged opening in her flesh. Then, she took her clothes and turned them inside-out, checking the material closely. Black stained the exterior of her coat, and nearly seeped through her sweater. But the infected blood had no contact with any of her wounds. To be safe, she splashed her face and rinsed her hair with murky mud water, then grudgingly washed her wounds with it too. *I'm all out of salve.* Sorrow found a way to shadow the constant throb throughout her frail body.

Dad...

She shivered from the wintry breeze, then crossed her arms over her bare chest. Her eyes searched the surrounding fog. *Now what?* When she glanced back to the wolf, old fears gnawed at her heart. *What about him?*

Aurous showed no signs of malady. Granted, he was as bloody and bruised as she was. He'd been panting and lapping up the muddy water by his paws, so the black staining his teeth and gums had faded. He looked exhausted, and cold. So was she.

Her clothes were saturated with deathly black. *What am I going to do?* She almost heard her father again, his whispers echoing her thoughts. *Fire. Burn it all.*

She couldn't. Not that she'd become particularly modest, but her skin flushed red from the wind's frosty bite. With chattering teeth, she carefully reached through her coat. The book had been bound in a silky, black material. It was still supple and dry, warm to her frigid hands. She unraveled it carefully, running her numb, swollen fingers along the silk. *Mother...*

Though memories of her mother warmed a heart beset by cold, the bitter rancidity of loss quickly clouded her thoughts afterward. Where her father had been a source of safety, a shelter from the perceived hell encompassing their world, her mother had been the reason for their strength, the smiles they gave each other every day, and the warmth blossoming between them. When she'd died, along with her brother, her father had changed. She knew he loved her, but he'd been cold and resentful, unwilling to accept her death. Unable to stop the pain of loving her mother.

Her mother's belongings had been hidden inside their cabin, locked away from Celeste's eyes until she'd been certain of her father's absence one evening. She scrounged through his things and found it, the small box he kept under the floorboards by his bed. Wonderment pooled in her bright, brown eyes as she sifted through it all.

Jewelry. Peculiar rings, some plain and ordinary or with brightly colored gems, a few odd ones were shaped like bowties, ice-cream cones, and kittens. There were necklaces, some gold and others twined with brittle string and beads. She found letters addressed to her father, and she recognized her mother's writing. She smiled with brewing curiosity, but quickly decided they were his to treasure alone. What truly caught her eye had been the elegant, silky black material folded at the bottom of the box. It appeared to be hand-woven, with dark and dulling beige thread adroitly stitched throughout in alluring patterns. Points jutted from a spherical sun. Beside it, a fading crescent moon. Other small, grey stars dotted the dark scarf.

A few nights later, after summoning enough courage, she broached him about her mother's things. Instead of reacting with anger like she'd expected, he explained it all to her. Why he'd kept it hidden. He wanted his daughter to have them all so she would remember the beautiful wildflower her mother had been. The sun, the moon and stars... The scarf had been for her. One last gift for her daughter.

Celestial.

Which is why tears fell when she ripped it into pieces.

After rinsing herself with dirty slush again, she proceeded to bind each wound tightly, unwilling to risk infection.

If I don't already have it, the bitter thought weighed heavily on her mind. *Aurous...*

After tending her wounds, she saw to his. Timid under her touch, guilt panged through her worry. He flinched as she ran her fingers through his coarse fur. "I'm sorry," she whispered softly. She carefully peeled away the makeshift bandage she'd wrapped around the jagged tear in his flesh and was elated to find it wasn't festering. The honey salve worked. *Thanks again, dad.* Her heart sank as she finished securing the last of the torn fabric around the wolf's front leg.

The scarf was gone.

Sickness wormed into her gut, but she resolved that tears would change nothing. *Survive first,* her thoughts echoed the gruff words her father had seared deep within her mind.

Mother would understand.

Smiling, she almost thought she whiffed the sweet fragrance of flowers.

She emptied her ragged coat, and stuffed her mother's rings in her socks. They'd probably pinch her feet when she slipped her boots back on, but she didn't want to risk losing them. The damp map had been tucked tightly into her jeans, along with her book. She wanted to keep the gloves, but knew better. They had been soaked and stained with black blood, and even if the virus no longer thrived in the saturated fabric, she did not wish to remember these moments. She tossed them in the discarded pile of crumpled clothing.

She secured her bandages once again, then slowly slid back into her jeans. They were drenched and cold, like a sheet of ice gliding up her pale thighs. She shivered and grudgingly grabbed her sweater, knowing it would yield little warmth. When she was fully dressed again, it seemed colder than letting the crisp wind embrace her bare flesh.

Three bullets. She unclenched her fist and dropped the gold-tinted projectiles into her revolver. *I only have three more shots, and Caden still has my rifle... If he's still alive.* She strained to hear anything other than the ghostly howl of the wind.

Nothing.

Suddenly, being so close to the open road seemed foolish. She grabbed her bow and quiver, then nudged her drowsy wolf. It was time to go.

She carefully roamed through the receding fog and ventured further into town. Houses eventually gave way to taller buildings and emptied parking lots. Some had boarded up windows, curtains drawn across each frosting window. She passed what resembled a gas station, but the pumps were run-down and the building itself collapsed inward. Still, she faintly recalled the lingering sour smell of diesel when her father would pick her up in his truck. It had been so big, he had to lift her into the seat. She smiled, then continued treading through the rising shadows.

It wasn't long before she came across deep impressions in the mud. *Footprints.* She leaned down, pushing against the wolf's curious nose. *Fresh too.* She grinned, setting her hand on her holstered revolver. *If not, the storm would have obscured them.* Another lesson her father had drilled into her mind.

More tears would have to wait.

They both hurried through the darkening alleys. Pursuing the snaking, muddied trail, the makeshift path led away from the hauntingly barren streets and condemned buildings.

Dissipating, murky clouds rumbled gently, scattering across a dimming skyline. The tumultuous wind eased into a chilling breeze. The dying breath of a tempest. Purpose fueled her aching muscles. She no longer loathed the hunt, instead driven by the promise of blood. *Prey,* whispered the wolf in her heart.

They ran through the blinding gloom. She kept pace with the wolf, stopping momentarily to find the trail again. Soon, the footprints overlapped. Same prints. It seemed like whoever it was went in circles.

Trying to find the sniper.

Caden. She couldn't dwell on it. Not now. *It might be him.*

She saw him the same moment he turned his gaze toward her. She'd stopped, her mouth slightly agape with surprise, and he cocked his head before his eyes widened.

Gunfire erupted from the weapon at his side as she yanked her revolver from the holster. She ducked and pulled the trigger, firing one shot in return. Bullets ripped into the muddy concrete. She stumbled. The revolver bucked twice, jarring her wounded shoulder.

Click. Click.

"Aw, shit!" He cursed loudly.

The man pulled a small, rusting blade from his boot, then stopped his approach. Grinning, she pulled the trigger.

Her weapon was empty.

"Bitch!"

Slopping through the mud, he slashed his rusted blade wildly with a wavering balance. Its serrated edge carved through the air and lunged for her neck like it hungered for her flesh. He missed, but she didn't. Taking advantage of the blade's lengthy reach, she swung her machete. The blade bit through his tightly coiled fingers, severing the digits and knife from his hand. Red spurted from the stumps. He screamed and bellowed another curse. She brought her machete down again.

His knuckles struck her jaw. She slipped into the mud, disoriented and grimacing from the warm blood flecking her face. He stood over her, clutching his bloody hand. He beamed victoriously.

Aurous snarled, bewitched by the spilling blood. Panicking, the man's boots sank through the marshy ground as he reeled and stumbled into an unsteady, frantic run.

The wolf gave chase.

The man went down in a blur of claws, fangs, and blood. He thrashed wildly, pummeling his fist into the wolf. Like billowing smoke, steam puffed from the warm blood spilling around him.

"Aurous!"

The wolf halted his onslaught. His snout, stained bright red, still dripped with death. The man cowered beneath Aurous. She approached slowly, and he flinched at each gentle *tap* of her boots against the muddy pavement.

"How dare you," he muttered, nursing his bleeding stumps. "You come into my town and slaughter my people! You and that mutt are going to die tonight! You hear me?"

"He's a wolf," she corrected with a soft whisper. She stopped at the edge of his pooling blood, letting it stream around her boots. "And so am I." His widening eyes followed the machete's swift movement, and his body convulsed in apparent fear. "Let me show you my fangs!"

The blade ripped through the flesh on his arm with the first strike, grinding down to the bone. The second nearly cleaved through his neck. He trembled as the last of his vital fluid tickled down the blade's edge. He was finally dead.

But someone else had their eyes on her.

It was nothing but a shadow in the distance, a blip between two buildings which quickly vanished into gathering darkness. Flattening herself against the wall, she peered through the gloomy night. Discerning no further movement, she lowered her head and cautiously approached.

Beside her, the rising moon glared off the chain link fence with barbed wire spiraling across the top. Her nostrils burned. *Smoke.* To her left, a fire had gutted everything under the building's brick overlay. *This place went to hell.* She reached the end of the alleyway.

Muddy footprints led to the door of a small, rickety brown house. Years of grime or faded paint, she couldn't tell. *Another ambush?* There were no other prints aside from the few leading into the dwelling. *Two sets, at least.* Her knuckles whitened from gripping the machete. *No ammo, bow is practically useless in close combat.* She sighed wearily. *I'm at a clear disadvantage... But I should be close to the highway by now. I don't want any surprises once I'm there.*

"Sorry, boy," she said, scratching the wolf behind his ears. "I'm not putting you in danger again. You're sitting this one out." *He looks like he's going to collapse from exhaustion.*

Worry shadowed his radiant eyes. He whined over the creak of the opening door. "It's almost over." She stepped inside, becoming shrouded in shadows, then closed the door behind her.

Faint moonlight slithered through torn, makeshift curtains. Exposed to the ferocity of the elements, dark blemishes had formed down the walls and floor under the windows. The wood sank under her weight. Mud had splattered along the floor, curving around a corner and ending at a far doorway. She nudged the door, easing it open. Voices emanated from the darkness below. Whispers. It wasn't the boastful banter she'd heard from the previous raiders. It seemed more like fearful mutters.

Other than the dull glow of the curtained window, the room drowned in a sea of black. With each careful step down the staircase, her boots stuck to the filth layering the stone. Stale, dusty air dried her tongue and throat. The booming beat of her heart throbbed in her ears, her chest nearly bursting from apprehension. She squinted against the darkness as the subtle sweep of feet across concrete echoed through the silence. She raised her machete, pointing her flashlight at the source of the commotion. Shadows scurried from the bright glare, and two figures raised their arms to shield their eyes, wincing from the sudden glare of light.

One stood in front, partially obstructing the other from view. He had a blue checkered long-sleeve shirt and dingy jeans. Thick mud clumped around his shoes. His lip trembled, and his eyes were swollen and bloodshot. Fear chalked his dark complexion. A round, green eye peered over his shoulder. It was a girl. She had freckles and short, unkempt hair, tousled with grime and red.

They must be around my age...

"Why are you doing this?" It was barely a squeak, like a mouse caught in the shadow of a predator. "Please, please don't kill us."

"Let her go," the boy demanded. He hardened his brow, frowned, and then stuck his chin out. Courage swelled in his heart, but fear caused his voice to break. "Kill me if you must, but let her go."

"Please." Tears flushed dirt from her reddened cheeks. "Don't kill us."

"I have to," Celeste managed to mutter with a croaky voice. Her hands trembled, but her fingers tightened around her blade's handle. "If not you, then it'll be me."

"We don't have to go down that road," the boy began, but the girl's shrill and despondent cry cut him short.

"She killed Kayla! She killed her with no remorse!" Her troubled gaze fell from the blinding light. She practically spat, then muttered bitterly, "She'll kill us too. Murderers don't feel pain."

Murderer? "I only killed because you're people threatened me first!"

"We were on edge because of recent attacks!" The boy savagely defended. He balled his shaking hands into fists. "They would have never hurt you."

"I don't believe you!" *I can't.*

"Then don't," the boy whispered, struggling to remain calm. Tears overwhelmed, and his face twisted with grief. He knew he stared death in its face. "But it's true."

Part of her heart yearned to spill his blood. *Prey does not plead for mercy from wolves.* But as she raised the machete, uncertainty loomed.

Could he be right?

Caught in the whirlwind of bullets, pain, and death, survival had been her only thought. She wanted nothing more than to find her way through this forsaken town, away from the malevolence which once plagued its streets and homes. Now, she wanted only the comfort of the trees, the warmth of her own bedding, and the melodic sounds of a fire spitting and crackling while she dozed by its radiance. Exhausted, wounded, and numb from the constant blood, she longed to rest her weary head on her wolf's fur as they lounged in the dewy grass, basking in the morning light. She wanted nothing more than the chill besetting her heart.

He's right.

The icy thought pierced her broiling mind. It was an anchor around her ankles, pulling her beneath the crimson waves of death's bloody ocean. She drowned in its malignance, lusting for a nightmare she couldn't wake from.

Every confrontation, Caden attacked first.

She'd ignored the sickened twist in her gut, choosing ignorance behind a thinly laced veil of safety. He was erroneous, but she had latched to his fallacious tale of losing family and his camp. She continued believing his nonsense, even after glimpsing the darkness he harbored behind stormy eyes.

Caden killed the man after he'd stopped attacking me. A bitter taste fouled her tongue like rancid bile. *He shot the one who lowered his rifle.*

I killed the others.

Kayla. Jer. Bill.

Guilt panged like an illness. "You have to get out of here."

"What?" The boy shook his head in obvious disbelief. "I don't understand..."

I'm going to vomit. "There's no time. If he's alive, he'll find you."

Please be dead. Through the disgust, she thought briefly, *would I still be alive without him?*

Does it matter?

"Why are you doing this?"

She tried not to let her voice waver when she spoke quietly, "For once, I have to do something right."

What would you think of me, father?

"Don't believe her!" Screamed the freckled girl, still cowering behind the dark-skinned boy and clutching his red shirt tightly. "She's still going to kill us!"

They cringed at her approach, quickly shuffling against the wall and away from the bite of her blade. She jerked the flashlight toward the soiled curtain. It was brown, stained from years of accumulated filth. The window was surprisingly intact but also sullied with a layer of dirt. It was just within arm's reach, so she pushed against the panel. It wouldn't budge, and neither would the bolt securing the window panel to the frame. It had long rusted shut.

"Damn it," she mumbled, cursing her soured luck. Striking the dirty glass with her machete handle, it cracked at first, then shattered into curved shards that fell around the frame and floor by her boots.

"Okay," she finally whispered, "you two go through the window and get out of here."

The boy's eyes shifted from their salvation then back to her, still wary. "What about you?"

"I'm going to distract Caden." *Hopefully he's already dealt with.*

"We can't trust her," the other girl stated flatly.

"We don't have a choice," the boy whispered back. He grabbed her hand, running his fingers across hers as he said, "We stay here, and we die. At least this way we have a chance."

"You think she'll let us go?"

"If she wanted us dead, I have a feeling we'd already be bleeding. She wants to help. I know it. We can trust her." He turned back, nodding sharply, but she glanced awry and tried to speak past the lump forming in her throat.

"Just make sure you get out of here alive."

"Thank you," the girl whispered, wiping the tears from her doleful green eyes.

"I hope you make it out alive, too," the boy began, before his forehead burst in a spray of red. They cringed, spattered by the warm mist as the boy's body collapsed and *smacked* against the cold, stone floor. The girl wouldn't stop screaming.

It took a moment for Celeste to gather her riotous thoughts, provoked into panic by ensuing fear.

No!

There he stood, at the edge of the staircase, his dark coat soaked with blood. He smiled luridly with crimson stained teeth, staring eagerly at the boy's corpse with cloudy eyes.

"I like my meat young," Caden whispered, licking his lips and raising his pistol again. "And tender."

"No," the girl whispered, hunched over the boy's limp body. "Wake up. Please!"

Caden's low, rumbling chuckle smothered her sobs like a predacious growl from the shadow's depths. A vulturine grin spread across his blood smeared face.

"Celeste, ya disappoint me."

"Put the gun down, Caden," replied Celeste with a tremulous tone. "We can end this without more bloodshed."

"It's almost over," he promised coldly. "I knew I'd find ya here, especially with that mutt scratchin' at the damn door."

The distraught freckled girl kept bellowing, "Wake up, you have to wake up!"

Celeste whispered through gritted teeth, "You're a coward."

"And yer a lil naïve bitch." His guttural words were like a cold, steady blade pressed against her throat. "Ya wanted blood, princess. No point denying it now."

"Oh my God..." The tearful sobs continued. "Come back to me..."

"I never wanted this!" Celeste steeled her heart, unable to tear her gaze from his haunting eyes. "I never wanted innocent people to die!" She winced from the raspy, raucous laughter trialing her desperate assertions.

"Nobody's innocent in this world, darlin'!" He licked his lips again, smearing more red throughout the grime. Chills danced along her skin and down her spine, raising bumps on her pale flesh. "Bein' a sweet, pretty lil thing yerself... Well, ya should know that already."

"You don't have to do this!" *This is hopeless. I have to do something!*

"I always finish what I've started, girlie."

"No... Baby, wake up, please!"

His dark eyes flickered from Celeste to the girl on the stone floor cradling a bloody corpse in her lap. The corner of his mouth twitched in annoyance, but his honeyed words cooed through the chilling black, "I'll give ya one last chance to help me, Celeste. We make one *hell* of a team."

She answered with a tremulous voice, "You make me sick."

"Please..." The girl muttered weakly.

"Oh, for the love of God," Caden muttered. His sardonically twisted grin fell to a malicious frown. "Will ya *shut up?*" He nudged his pistol to the girl sprawled over the boy's limp body.

Celeste blurred through the dimly lit room, her bloody blade carving through the shadows. It chopped through empty air. Caden sidestepped her swing with a scowl plastered on his filthy face, but her shoulder rammed into his gut. Toppling over, his pistol discharged with a bright, blinding flash. It *popped* against her ears and rattled her mind, and the bullet gouged the stone floor by the wall.

She yelled for the girl to run, or at least tried to. Whether the words formed and spilled from her tongue or slurred into a garbled scream, she did not know. Anything past the wailing screech left in her ears from the blaring gunshot became muffled whispers she couldn't discern.

RUN! Her throat burned as she yelled, her mind ablaze with the thought.

The machete's edge plunged for Caden's flesh. His head snapped sideways, and the blade *clanged* off the stone stairs. Before she managed to lift the machete again, Caden drilled his fist against the side of her head. The force of the blow nearly knocked her to the floor, but she struggled to keep him pinned. She lost her grip on the machete and resorted to pummeling him with fists. He laughed at her onslaught, then struck her again.

Black blotted her vision after her face *slapped* against the floor. Disoriented, her fumbling fingers pushed the fallen machete further from her grasp. Caden twisted his hands in her sweater, grappled her, and then heaved her off the ground. Thrust against the wall, the back of her head bounced loudly off cement.

A foggy curtain obscured her thoughts. Her mind roiled with pain, and everything melted together in a stream of dulling colors. Another blow loosened teeth in the side of her mouth, forcing blood to spew from her lips. She struggled, but he slammed her against the concrete again.

"Ya thought I had a kind heart, eh?" He hissed, pushing his knee between her thighs. "Thought I'd help ya for nothin'? Who the *hell* ya think I am, girlie?"

Only blood flowed from her gaping mouth.

"Truth is, I lost who I was when my own kids were slaughtered." Warm, rancid breath warmed her ear as he whispered softly into her hair. "I became a bloody *monster*. For years, I was alone with those thoughts." He leaned away from her, smiling brightly through the black.

Still dizzy, the room continued to tilt and blur together, but over his shoulder, she could faintly see the movement of shadows.

"So, a bloody monster is what I am!"

It was the girl, pulling herself up the wall toward the window.

Yes!

"And really, in a world full of them, that's how ya survive, princess. Ya become a monster, like me." He almost laughed, and she quickly shifted her eyes back to him. "C'mon, Celeste. I know ya want more *meat*."

They both heard it at the same moment. A small gasp, followed by a *crunch* of shattered glass. Caden twisted his neck and cursed loudly, settling his voracious gaze on the girl.

Celeste reached for him and clawed at his face with her dirty nails. She jammed her fingers into his eye, bursting it. It sprayed her hand with sickening warmth. He howled, but grabbed her wrists and pushed her back against the wall. He turned with his pistol drawn, but the girl had already vanished through the open window.

"Bitch!" He screamed hoarsely. He glared back at Celeste with a bright, bloody eye, and the last thing she recalled was being struck in the head with his pistol.

Blood. It gathered in her mouth, spilling through her parted lips to the concrete. *Why am I still alive?* Thoughts were lost in a haze of disorienting black. Old and new wounds alike were leaking crimson with each unsteady pump of her heart. Pain jolted through her torn body with every shiver from the cold embrace of the concrete floor. Opening her eyes slowly, the room blurred into view. He was craning his neck out through the broken glass, swearing loudly and stomping his foot in anger like a spoiled child wailing against a mother's will. Blood splattered with each kick of his boot.

I must have been dazed for only a few moments...

The machete was far from her reach, obscured by shadows somewhere near the bottom of the stairs. Her revolver remained empty, uselessly tucked away in its holster. *My knife.* She reached and fumbled to grab her belt with clumsy fingers.

There it is.

Before Caden could turn his head, she ghosted through the unforgiving black. She leaned close to the floor, brushing her fingers along the bloody cement. The blade glinted as she sank through the bright beam from her fallen flashlight. Caden laughed when her shadow eclipsed the room. Her muscles strained, but propelled her forward. The knife sliced through his dark coat, barely nicking his flesh through the fabric. He rapped his knuckles against her cheek, drilling her back to the cement. The contents of her sweater spilled across the floor along with her knife.

Damn!

"Ungrateful bitch! I don't like my food escaping!" He snarled angrily. Then, "What's this?"

He bent his knees and crouched close to her, keeping his pistol level with her head. Plucking one of her fallen items from the cement floor, he grinned and opened the cover.

"Dictionary?" Amusement trickled through his tone. "What an *interesting* read. Does daddy make ya go through this crap?"

Hatred burned through her chilly veins. "Give it *back*."

He sneered, "That kind of sentiment makes ya weak, Celeste. A killer like yerself should know better."

Paper crumpled inside his fist. Ripping the pages from the spine, he scattered them around her. His laughter boomed over her furious cries as he tore more pages loose.

She pushed herself up, swinging a small and bloody fist at his face. His own fist struck her first. She was back against the cold cement with his fingers twined in her hair, forcing her face into the sticky blood pooling by the corpse. He breathed into her ear, pushing against her with his groin.

"Ya had a fire in yer eyes; a ravenous hunger only blood could fulfil, a lust only death would satisfy. Whatever hate that had withered yer heart helped it blossom into a reaper's scythe, a harbinger of death." His warm, malodorous breath nauseated her weak stomach. "I like a killer bitch."

She struggled beneath his vicelike grip, but he only whispered, "I like when they fight as well."

Dirt and sweat smothered her tongue with a foul taste, then her mouth pooled with blood. Her teeth ripped up bits of his grimy flesh, and he wailed with pain. He proceeded to bash her head with his fist until she released her bloody hold.

She couldn't breathe. Writhing under his crushing weight, another dizzying blow forced her head to bounce off the cement.

Smack.

She tried screaming.

Smack.

Again, she succumbed to the numbing black.

The cold cement against her skin roused her from a battered slumber, but it was the pain that kept her awake. It was like a knife with a fiery blade twisting inside her guts, carving down through her smooth, pale flesh. Her thighs were inflamed, surely charred from whatever dreadful fire spread within her. Frigid fingers clenched her throat tightly enough to strangle any scream or tearful plea.

Caden was between her legs, grunting loudly and rocking his hips against her bared flesh. Her sweater had been torn, the ripped fabric now splayed around her with several of her belongings. Droplets of salty sweat splashed her face and soured her tongue when she gasped for breath beneath his strangulating weight. He heaved heavily, spattering putrid, bloody drivel on her neck and abrading the skin on her back with every violent, impenitent thrust.

"Bitch," he wheezed breathlessly into her ear, carelessly groping and pinching her skin with a sweaty, calloused hand.

No!

She fought madly, and when raking her nails across his filthy skin did little but garner a rough, cavernous bellow, she bucked her legs and pushed against his chest. She thrashed against his forceful mount, but he pushed harder. She screamed as the pain flared, rekindling the fiery burn between her legs.

From the unseen reaches of the darkness came a ghostly, disembodied growl. The rabid snarl resounded through the empty room, and Caden cursed, pulling away from her a moment too late. Through the black came a flash of fangs then spilling blood. A ragged scream roared through her ears. Caden tumbled over her, covering her with sticky blood and clumps of flesh with strands of hair still poking through the torn meat. He was struggling with the wild attacker on his back while she writhed madly, finally forcing herself free. She rolled through the bloody muck and scrambled to her feet – only to nearly collapse from a sharp, stabbing pain in her guts. She staggered, bracing against the wall.

What the hell?

Like the tears welling and falling from her eyes, blood slowly trickled down her thighs in crimson streaks.

It was painful to pull her jeans back up, but she did so quickly. Caden was still screaming, his face covered in blood. A flap of his torn scalp covered his ear, and a shadow tugged at the dangling flesh with white fangs.

Aurous!

Her machete had fallen somewhere by the stairs, and it only took her a harrowing moment to fumble for it blindly. Her legs refused to move quickly, and the pain was enough to make her retch along the wall.

C'mon!

Light trickled through the doorway. She could see the glowing moon behind parting clouds, and the faint twinkling of stars. The crisp, chilly air soothed her battered bones and bloody abrasions.

She was finally out.

She fell to the muddy ground, unable to bite back her bitter bellows. Like a lonely, howling wolf, she cried out under the pale moon. Her hands were awash in blood, and she knew the same stains sullied what little remained of her soul.

Exhaustion managed to subdue her. Unable to stand or move her battered and broken body, she toppled into the mud and feigned rest. She wished vainly to flee, to escape far from this hellish nightmare. She wanted the pain to end, for the fulsome memories to burn from her ravaged mind.

Most of all...

"I want to survive!"

"Then hurry up!"

It was the freckled girl. Her clothes were torn and muddy, her red hair crudely tied back under her hood. Her hands were still slick with blood, but she uncurled her clenched fingers, which Celeste warily accepted. After pulling her from the mud, the girl glowered. Under the moonlight, her green eyes were resplendent through gathering tears spilling gently down her freckled face.

"I'll never forgive you for what you've done," she whispered accusingly.

I'll never forgive myself. "I know."

Never.

The freckled girl wiped her eyes. "You should be dead. Not them."

Celeste only nodded, blinking back tears. She looked aside, afraid of the pain emanating from the girl's gaze.

"But you saved my life." The girl mustered a halfhearted smile. "So... Thanks."

"You should have left." It was all Celeste managed to mutter. *Why didn't you?* But she didn't have to ask. *I thought I had nowhere to go. After I'd lost everyone.*

"I wanted to," she whispered, casting a nervous glace over Celeste's bare shoulder. "But I heard what was happening."

"Oh," breathed Celeste. Aware of how exposed she was, her face burned against the cold night air. She covered her chest, blushing brightly and shifting uncomfortably.

Seeing her shiver, the girl slipped the old, musty coat off her tiny shoulders. "I'd give you my sweater, but it's my favorite." She stepped closer, reaching out with one hand and brushing against Celeste's arm.

She recoiled like the violent kick of a discharging gun. Her heart lurched, her blood like ice creeping slowly through her veins. She was there again; his cold fingers twisting around her neck, his sweaty, pallid flesh slapping against her bruised thighs. He was a beast, clawing his way inside of her. She fell to the mud, screaming.

The girl stared down at her with wide, wondering eyes. "You're bleeding."

Whispered so delicately, Celeste barely heard her words. When she gazed down at herself, she saw the dark blotch spreading across her jeans. The sickening ache throbbed between her legs, and she vomited again.

"You need this." The girl tossed the coat on her lap. It was no longer warm, but it stopped the cold from piercing her bare flesh. She pulled the coat close, standing despite the protests of a battered body.

It was distant, but they both heard it.

Gunshots.

Aurous!

She turned, but the girl yelled and reached out for her once more. Celeste stopped, avoiding the girl's touch but staring back at the dark, verminous house.

"I have to go back!"

The girl shook her head, speaking in a shaky whisper, "If that man is still alive, he'll kill us both!"

"My friend..." She choked.

"The dog?" The girl tried to smile. "I let him in. He was scratching at the front door, howling madly."

"You did?"

"There was nothing else I could do." She lowered her gaze, shifting her round, green eyes away from Celeste's dark glare. "I have no weapons... I was never a fighter."

"Thanks," Celeste said, trying not to sound bitter. "You saved my life. But I have to go back for him."

"We don't have time!"

She listened a moment longer, straining her ears for any sound. No more gunshots, no howling or threatening growls echoing from the shadows.

Aurous... Dying wouldn't bring him back. *A wolf survives to hunt again.* She blinked away her frozen tears, and turned back to the freckled girl with a stony glare. *Help the pack.*

I owe her that much. "Let's go."

The fog had receded into night's chilling blanket of darkness. Moonlight struggled to penetrate the veil. Streets were frosting from the gelid sleet, the concrete like sheets of ice under their boots while they ran through the pitch black.

The girl chattered breathlessly, rambling between gasps and laboring to steady her voice. She told Celeste her name was Melina, and for as long as she recalled, she'd lived in Antler Creek. Six months ago, the town had bustling streets and a thriving community, with roads patrolled and maintained by the military controlling the neighboring city. In recent months, she explained as they rounded an icy corner, the highways were unpatrolled. Without the military's power, efforts at quarantining the infected or slaying the shadowed creatures failed, and they were soon overrun.

"Antler Creek was decimated," she continued, huffing frantically for air. Her freckled face burned as red as her bound hair, and gleamed from perspiration. She led Celeste down a vacant road, away from the concrete streets she'd taken before. They were only a block or so away from the house, but Celeste still felt the emanating chill, smelled the fetor of Caden's breath while he heaved his filthy body overtop of her...

She shuddered.

"... almost a month."

Celeste blinked stupidly. "What?"

"I said," Melina explained between deep, rasping breaths. "The creatures hunted us first, killing travelers along the highways and outside of town. The virus infected others. They came back and spread it through town... It happened so fast..."

"Why didn't everybody leave?"

Father always said it was better to find a new home than die trying to save the one you have in vain. Belongings can be replaced. People can't. But her heart ached at the thought of her mother's torn scarf. *But he wouldn't avoid those wolves...*

She shrugged slightly, hunching her shoulders and frowning. "I wanted to. My parents... They were killed last year. I was with Leo's family. The boy..."

"I'm sorry." Celeste's voice cracked.

"They wanted to stay. Defend their town, their homes. Once we lost a lot of people... Everyone started to panic. Some left, others were turning up dead. *Murdered.*" The last word she muttered with clear distaste, like the letters themselves were putrid and left a disgusting taste in their wake as they tumbled off her tongue.

Caden. His toxicity plagued Celeste's thoughts until her mind reeled.

"That *man* was finally found responsible, but never caught. Then the killings stopped. But the sickness didn't." She stopped suddenly, pointing ahead. "We can hide there for now. I know there's dry clothes at least."

There was a small building not far from the dirt road, nestled behind a brown house in the trees. The house itself was decently maintained, with only a few broken windows that had been patched, and a barricaded door. It was small, almost no larger than the shack behind it. Impossibly dark, yet Melina seemed to know where she was stepping, so Celeste quickly followed her lead.

"This was our old house," she whispered, eerily answering Celeste's silent questioning. "Leo's mom was always prepared for the worst. She even boarded up the house so no one would loot it. I told her to write 'Infected' on it, like the others, but she didn't want them to burn it down while we were gone." She sniffed, surely struggling to wipe away her tears. "She was adamant we'd be back shortly."

Once they were in the shack, Melina eased the door shut, concealing them in tomblike darkness. The floor *creaked* underneath their shifting weight, and Celeste couldn't stop shaking from the chill.

"I don't have any light," Melina said, fumbling through the black.

Celeste replied with chattering teeth, "Better we don't have any."

"Right." More shuffling, until Melina said, "I found something. It might not fit, but it's dry." She reached out blindly, trying to hand off the bundled clothes.

Celeste smothered a scream as something brushed against her arm.

Melina stepped forward when Celeste jumped against the wall. "It's okay," she whispered. "Just clothes." She held them out a moment longer until Celeste reached out to grab them. But Melina pulled her close.

Celeste struggled at first. *No!* Every thought screamed, urging her to flee and shroud herself within the night. Her fearful heart hammered against her ribcage until she was certain it would burst through her chest. Yet, she didn't resist. She melted into Melina's arms, embracing her gentle warmth.

Aurous... I need you.

"I'm sorry," she whispered again, crying into Melina's shirt. It was damp and musty, but welcoming. "Why are you helping me?"

"Leo always tried to see the good in people," she replied softly. "And he saw something in you, I know it. I do too."

"I'll get you out of here." Celeste wiped the runny snot off her lip, smearing a green streak along her sleeve. "I promise."

Melina nodded. "I know a way out, through the back roads. We used to go on hikes up into the mountains."

"No," Celeste interjected quickly. "I need to get to the city."

"The highway? Why?" Before Celeste answered, Melina said quickly, "But it's too dangerous."

"I have to get to the city." She grabbed the bundled clothing and began peeling the cold, damp material off her numb skin. "You said the military stopped patrolling the highways. That means something must have happened in the city, right? I have family there. I need to know." The new clothing wasn't warm, and the fabric was coarse enough to scratch as she slipped it on.

"It's not far from here."

"Where were you going to go before?"

"North," Melina replied. "Kayla had sent scouts to make sure the roads were clear, but none had returned. That was yesterday."

That must have been him... The first man to attack her on the outskirts of town would have likely been one of those scouts. Caden had killed him, assuring her the man would have killed her otherwise. *That man had tried to say something the moment he stopped attacking me...* She wondered if the sundered corpse she'd discovered in one of the run-down buildings had been a scout also.

"We can make it to the highway," replied Celeste, adamant. "But the longer we stay here, the more we risk. If my... if that *bastard* is alive, he'll find us. We have to go now."

The mud hasn't concealed our trail much, she grumbled silently. *And I'm out of ammo.*

"Okay," Melina agreed, though uncertainty crept in her tone. "We can keep to this road until the turnoff. The highway isn't far from there."

Celeste cautiously ventured outside first. The machete shook in her trembling hand, her eyes darting nervously through the pale glow. Rapid breaths fogged the air around her, dissipating quickly like wisps of smoke in the airy night. She could feel the warmth flowing from Melina as the freckled girl kept close and mimicked her movements. They passed the dark, empty house Melina had once called home. Celeste tried imagining the sun's bright shine cascading down the mountainside and into the trees, spilling through the windows of the house to warm the occupants inside. She longed for the love of her home, one she barely recalled through the pain in her heart and the bloody blemishes on her soul.

"There," said Melina, pointing to the horizon ahead. Snow capped the jagged mountains reaching into the dark sky, glistening from the moon's pale light. It was hard to see, but she squinted through the hazy night and spotted the sinuous path carving through the snowy trees. From where she stood, it seemed insurmountable.

"Don't worry," Melina said, sensing Celeste's worry. "There's a few roads leading up to it. We have to go around the cliff, though."

"I figured," Celeste replied, not bothering to mask her disappointment. "I don't know how much strength I have left."

Melina glanced back at her former residence. "We could see if Leo's parents left anything behind."

"That would be," Celeste began, until her heart chilled and silenced her agreement. Melina heard the strange disturbance as well. She jumped then clutched Celeste's coat. Celeste pushed her back, trying to catch her breath and steady the bladed weapon in her tremulous hand.

Where did it come from? Fear fueled the panicked *thumping* of her heart. *Damn!* She could see nothing but trees and mud. Then she heard it again.

It began at a distance. At first, she thought the peculiar sound resembled the raging waters of a river. *What the hell?* Then she saw it.

Like Caden's frigid fingers were slipping around her neck once more, her throat tightened with fear as she yelled for Melina to flee. She spotted the shadow charging through the mud toward them, and she reeled, bracing against whatever malevolent creature it was.

It jumped at her.

Every instinct of instilled survival burned deeply, urging her to swing the blade in defense. But she fell to the clutches of consternation. The blade slipped from her fingers as the shadow's fangs gleamed and its claws slashed at her chest. She fell back into the mud.

By the time she realized what sort of creature it really was, her face had been coated with thick, foamy slime.

Aurous!

The wolf kept nudging his cold nose into her neck. She wrapped her bruised arms around his damp fur, pulling him close. "I'm so happy you're alive."

"It's just your dog," Melina whispered, clutching at her chest but still trembling.

"This is Aurous," Celeste replied. She tried her best to brush the sloppy mud from her clothes. He looked up at Melina with a lolling tongue.

At her puzzled look, Celeste offered meekly, "He's got a bit of wolf blood in him."

"He's quite big," Melina admitted, patting the wolf's head gently while Celeste leaned over him. "What is it?" Melina asked, noticing her companion's frown.

"Blood," Celeste whispered. "It looks like a graze."

"Those gunshots we heard earlier..." Melina bit her lip. "But that man... He has to be dead."

She tried not to sound frightened as she muttered, "He has to be."

They hurried down the muddy road with trepidation heavy in their hearts. Shadows chased them, enclosing around them as the ghostly moon descended behind the mountainside. Her boots were wet, and so were the bottoms of her jeans. The revolver bobbed in its holster, brushing against her hip while she ran. To her dismay and regret, her belt felt oddly light and strange. She'd lost most of her belongings in the struggle, and it cut deeper and pained worse than anything that bastard inflicted upon her. *My father's knife and rifle, my bow... Son of a bitch.*

Thud.

She heard it through their boots slopping about in the muck. It took a moment longer to find the source of the thump. By the time she'd plucked the shaft from the mud, she heard the familiar *twang* of a bow-string.

"Move!" She yelled, grabbing Melina's coat.

Thud.

Another arrow plunged into the mud by their feet.

"Celeste!" The bellow rattled her bones, sending shivers crawling down her spine.

No!

"I ain't done with ya!"

"It's him!" Melina shrieked, burying her face in her coat. "Oh God, he's going to kill us!"

"Go!" Celeste pushed against her, but the freckled girl went limp. Her hands were clasped together, and she mumbled words Celeste didn't want to hear. *I'm not dying!* "Run, Melina!"

Thud.

The third arrow came dangerously close to her head.

"I can't," she breathed, but Celeste shoved her again.

She turned, fiercely glaring through the darkness and gripping her bloodied machete tightly. *I'm not a coward!* Her guts burned, but she gritted her teeth and yelled back, "Let us go or I'll kill you myself, Caden!"

"Listen here, bitch!" He called back with a hoarse voice. He wheezed as spoke through the shroud of shadows. "Ya know I only want what's mine, darlin'!"

"I'm not giving her to you!" Turning back to Melina, she whispered, "You have to go! I'll buy you some time and then meet you at the highway. Take Aurous with you. Please!" Melina opened her mouth in protest, but Celeste already averted her eyes. "You hear that, you bastard? You don't get her!"

"Ya don't get it, do ya?" His rasping laughter sickened her even more.

"Celeste..." Melina whispered quietly, barely audible over the wolf's threatening growls.

"I don't want her," he said. She heard his footsteps along the muddied road echoing with his laughter. "Not right now, anyway."

Her heart lurched. Through the curtain of black, he stepped through with his pistol raised and his lips inching up into a smile. Part of his scalp still dangled down his face in bloody strips of flesh.

"I only want ya, Celeste."

Aurous kept growling at her side, and Melina whispered again, "Celeste..."

"You have to run, Melina," Celeste insisted, lowering her weapon. She flinched at the hollow *click* of Caden cocking his pistol.

Father...

"I can't," came the fearful reply. Her voice broke as she burst into tears. Aurous snarled and howled, snapping his frothy teeth.

She stared, horrified at what silenced them all.

It was hunched over, crawling with twisted, elongated limbs that ended in deadly, curving claws. Bony quills protruded from its spine. Muscles rippled and bunched, flexing under each swift and long stride. Its mouth opened to jagged teeth, and it glared ravenously with deep, crimson eyes. It was a shadow, swimming through an ocean of black toward them. She barely glimpsed the monster carving through the night, but she knew what it was. It had been the source of her nightmares as a child, the reason she used to fear the darkness after the sun had fallen. The reason for her family's heartache and loss.

The source of my suffering.

It's a Hunter.

"My, oh my," Caden whispered, chuckling deeply and licking his lips. Anticipation gleamed through his muddy eyes. "This is getting interesting."

TWELVE
BÊTE NOIRE

Recreant thoughts stormed her mind, but her father's blood boiling through her veins warmed the chill of effusing fear. She reached behind her, gripping Melina's hand tightly. *We have to run!* She sprang for the trees, dragging the listless girl along with her.

Melina was dead weight, an anchor dropping into the ocean mid-sail. Her head bobbed limply, her eyes nearly swollen shut and red. She slipped, tripping over her own boots and pulling Celeste back down into the mud with her.

"Melina!"

Aurous snarled, and Celeste could hear the creature's claws ripping through the road as it charged them. She gripped her machete, baring her teeth like her wolf and crouching over her fallen friend. *I'm not dying without a fight!*

She flinched. Two gunshots roared through the night, and the bullets punctured the monster's umbral scales. With a growl like blood gurgling in the back of its throat, it turned and gnashed its fangs at the man and his pistol.

"They're mine!" Caden screamed over the raucous bellow of his gun.

Celeste hauled Melina back to her feet, but the languid redhead wouldn't tear her hollowed gaze away from the abhorrence. A tiny sob escaped her pursed lips, and soon tears streamed down her freckled cheeks.

"Kayla said they were all killed." She spoke between shallow breaths, but the tears wouldn't stop. Like a shuffling zombie, she stumbled through the woods after Celeste. "She said..."

"I don't think that one was from around here," Celeste replied, feeling the blood drain from her face. Aurous growled as she continued, "It's been following me for a long time."

I'm sure of it now. She thought back to the lone cabin in the woods. *That man... He transformed and slaughtered his family. He... It... has probably been following me ever since.* What was it her father had always told her? *"They wait for the perfect moment to strike, when you're injured or separated from everyone else – they won't stop until you're dead. They'll hunt you endlessly. And they won't let anyone else have their kill."*

Am I the one it wants?

"What do we do?" Melina asked in a small, shaky voice.

Survive.

"We get to the highway." Another gunshot echoed through the trees. "And fast," she added quietly, cursing the bastard's tenacity to live.

I can't face another monster tonight.

Like scattering prey, they scurried through the trees, breathless and nearing the brink of utter exhaustion. Her chest burned as if her lungs seared over a vicious flame. Her limbs ached. She squinted, peering past the dense thicket.

"Which way?" Celeste asked, smothering the panic in her tone. She dared a glance over her shoulder. Nothing was following them. *Yet.*

"Not far, I think," Melina whispered. Breathing heavily and clutching at her side, she winced and hunched over. Red hair dangled loosely over her bleary eyes. "Gas stations. Turn off. Then Highway." She thrust her finger past Celeste, pointing into the black. All Celeste perceived were endless shrouds of shadows and trees. Perfect cover for them to lose Caden.

But perfect cover for a monster to hunt as well.

"Let's keep going then," She said, shaking the grim thought from her head. Smiling, she reached for Melina's hand, but the frightened redhead looked up with wide, hopeful eyes. Then her face blanched.

The monster's wail carried past their trembling bodies, haunting the velvet night. The wolf growled, his glossy, black fur bristling as the piercing shriek engulfed Celeste in fear she'd thought conquered.

Don't give up now!

But her muscles were petrified, she couldn't move. Bloody eyes gleamed back at her through the shadows. The Hunter found them.

"Run!"

They were no longer under the glare of the moonlight. Darkness swallowed their surroundings. Trampling through the thicket, craggy bark ripped her sweater and scraped her skin. Melina stumbled through the muddy soil, squealing like a rat crushed by a hawk's talons. Celeste refused to release her grip on the girl's hand. She screamed, but Celeste dragged her to her feet.

The Hunter advanced through the forest like a stampede of wild beasts. The ground trembled from its monstrous paws *stomping* into the dirt. Bony claws scythed through the thicket; they were showered with chunks of bark and splintered wood, the Hunter's curved claws lunging for their tender flesh.

The wolf's thin lips parted in a snarl. He became a blur, a black blot darting through the night. He jumped, raking his fangs across the Hunter's thick hide, but they barely pierced the monster's scaly armor. Celeste fumbled for her machete.

The wolf ripped into the Hunter's skin and clawed through to its flesh. The monster wrenched its neck, its fangs slashing madly for the small beast. The wolf darted away, stumbled, but lunged again. Another gash across its thick scales, and the wolf jumped back, waiting for the monster to strike. A riotous roar rumbled through the woods and the Hunter charged. The wolf limped between the trees, leading the hulking monster far into the night.

"Aurous!" Celeste belted out desperately, calling after her wolf. *He's too weak to escape!*

Melina gripped her friend's hand, twining her fingers tightly with hers.

"We have to go!"

"I won't leave him!"

"Come on!"

Treading a sinuous path through the muddy forest floor, Celeste could barely lift her legs. Her muscles were like cement beneath her bruised skin.

I can't keep this up.

"Melina..." She began breathlessly.

A chill gripped her spine. "CELESTE!"

No...!

Melina's fingers slipped from her grasp, and Celeste tumbled through the watery muck, pain jolting through every wound.

"Oh, darlin'!" Caden's haunting call echoed around her like a lingering chill. "Where are ya?"

"Melina!" Celeste whispered over the fearful *thumping* of her heart. "Melina!"

Where did she go?

"I'm gonna find ya, princess," he snarled, grinding his carious teeth. "So we can finish what we started."

Not if I have anything to say about it, asshole. She bit her lip until blood squirted through the split flesh and warmed her tongue. She trembled from the frigid muck soaking through her clothes, but waited in the murky mud. *Keep talking.* His voice carried over the *slop* of his boots through the soft, watery earth.

There he is. She raised her machete...

Long, slender fingers slipped through the ebony curtain. A crushing grip strangled the scream belting from her ragged throat. Battered from her grasp, the machete *plopped* uselessly into the muck.

"Ya realize what sorta trouble ya caused, girlie?"

Blood dribbled down her thin lips from her gaping mouth. She croaked weakly, writhing desperately when he forced her head below the muck. As his grip loosened, cold, thick sludge seeped down her throat and filled her burning lungs. He pulled her to the surface briefly, then plunged her beneath again.

"I don't want to kill ya!" He yelled, curling his fingers through her hair and yanking her from the mud. She gasped wildly, weakly throwing her fists as he snarled, "I want to help ya! Set ya free!"

Melina, Aurous... Did you make it out?

"I wanted to show ya what really dwelled within yer wicked heart!"

Revolted, she spat the clumpy dirt from her mouth and muttered with disdain, "I'm not the wicked one."

Like minced meat, the right side of his face had been torn and shredded, oozing thick globs of stringy crimson down a rising smile. "All I had to do was set ya down that fiery path, Celeste, ya did the rest yerself. Killed without question. Murdered in cold blood. Ya nearly severed that bitch's head. Innocent people, might I add."

"That was you!" She screamed, clawing at his hands around her throat. "You tricked me!"

"I told ya some sob story any wanderer could have made up!" She nearly vomited, sickened by the rotted stench of his mouth as he dragged his rough lips across hers. "I told ya what ya wanted to hear, so ya could soothe yer aching heart. It felt good, didn't it? The warm blood on yer hands, the symphony of screams in yer ears... The feeling of *meat* in yer belly."

"You're a goddamn monster!"

"Yer the monster," he whispered harshly, spattering sickly warm saliva on her cheek. "*My* monster."

"Screw you!"

"It was so easy," he said with a laugh, relishing the feel of her battering fists. "Hunting everyone in town once I came here. They were already panicking from Stalker attacks. I picked them off, one by one. A man's gotta eat, ya know. They tried bravery, holding out until the military came again. But the patrols wouldn't come, and they won't ever again. They're gone, baby girl. I was never gonna help ya get there, because there's nothing *left*.

"I killed the townsfolk until that blonde whore ya shanked discovered everything. I slipped away, releasing the last of the infected. They tried to leave, but I sent *you* in to slaughter the rest of the bloody cowards."

No...

But she knew it was true.

"My puppet, Celeste," he said, pulling her close. "My..."

Warm blood flecked her face. Caden lurched forward with a heavy grunt. She fell with him, crushed by his limp body and sinking through the marshy dirt. Mud gurgled in the back of her throat when she screamed. She thrashed against the grip around her arm, but inhaled sharply as the brisk, cold air nipped her skin. She sucked in another breath, then retched a murky stream.

"Celeste, come on!"

She gasped wildly, calming her burning lungs with frigid air. Wiping the mud from her face, she nearly screamed. Caden glared back at her through the mud. His dark eye had been clawed to sludgy flesh in his socket. He was motionless, with a fresh river of red rushing down his minced face.

Melina dropped the bloodstained rock from her trembling hand. "Is he dead?"

"I think so," Celeste whispered with a torn voice. She stood still a moment longer, watching for bubbles or ripples in the murky mud-water by his mouth and nose. "He's not breathing."

She gathered her nerve and reached down, catching a shade of red through the muddy surface. She yanked the bow and quiver from his shoulder, then reached for the pistol on his belt. *I'll make sure of it...*

Like a lunging snake, his arm *snapped* forward through the mud and clutched at her coat. She jumped back, her fingers fumbling with the slick weapon. She slipped from his grasp and fell into Melina. Both girls tumbled into the slop.

"Get up!" Celeste screamed, pushing against her fallen friend. Melina reached for her hand but Celeste cocked the pistol instead. Ferocity fueled her ailing soul. Anger jarred her blood-soaked mind.

I want to kill him myself!

She stared into the barrel of her own hunting rifle.

Caden was sprawled in the mud, propping himself up with his elbows. The rifle glared at her, taunting her and dangling death before her eyes.

He pulled the trigger.

The blare of gunfire blinded her. Another earsplitting roar resounded through the night. The tree next to her ruptured and split after the bullet drilled into the bark. Her trembling finger hovered over the trigger until she was thrown back into mud. Melina forced Celeste to her feet, and they both ran into the darkness.

Bullets whistled past; they ripped into bark and chewed through trees or sank into the mud by their feet. Like the screams haunting her nightmares, she heard a ragged, ghostly wail carry through the unsettled trees. *Hunter!* The chill in the night air pierced her skin like icy knives through her flesh. *We have to hurry!*

"The road!" Melina croaked. "There!" They burst through the trees and their boots *slapped* against the concrete. Once again, they basked in the eerie moonlight, wheezing and gasping for air. "It's not far! We can still lose them!"

Shadows swirled around them, threatening to swallow them in nothingness. Fear fueled her sore muscles, and she ran until she discerned the outlines out of the few old buildings littering the roadside. They passed giant signs resting high above them on rusting metal poles. The words or pictures, if any remained, were illegible in the dark. They trudged past the empty buildings, hearts clamoring for an end to their nightmare, but crestfallen and certain death would be waiting with welcoming arms.

And it was.

Teeth ripped her coat as she threw herself to the ground. Both elbows bashed against the concrete, then she rolled, narrowly evading the bony, serrated claws ripping through the solid ground. The Hunter bared its gnarled fangs and roared.

Her gun countered with its own snarl, bucking three bullets into the monster's distorted snout. The bullets ripped through its scaly flesh, but it snapped its elongated muzzle and roared its frustration, spewing wads of meaty saliva through the air.

A flash of tawny eyes and white fangs. A blur of silky black. The wolf darted past the Hunter again, thrashing near its bony quills, then weakly melting back into the night. The monster reared its malformed head, and Celeste quickly squeezed the trigger. Lead ripped into its neck, but the wolf attacked as it turned to face her. Aurous dragged his fangs across its scaly armor before disappearing into the darkened depths of the night.

"GET BACK HERE!"

It was a hellish melody. Caden's bellow opposed the Hunter's ghoulish wail. The rifle discharged like thunder rumbling from a storm cloud in the distance. Bullets ricocheted past after striking the pavement. Melina screamed.

She yelled for Aurous and grabbed her friend's arm. The wolf limped from the shadows and Celeste opened fire at the Hunter and Caden. Melina pulled her through the doorway of an old building, and they quickly ventured deeper.

There was an intact door further inside. Beyond that, a narrow hall that soon expanded up into a wide, open room. Empty crates were stacked against the wall, and torn rations of packaged food were littered across the floor. Nailed boards stretched across the windows, except two in the far corner. Moonlight glared through the stained glass, beaming brightly against the white, tiled floor.

"What do we do?" Melina asked, wincing and clutching her shoulder. Celeste didn't answer. She was searching frenetically, but found little else other than a few stones and crumpled pieces of garbage.

"This will have to do," she muttered woefully. She grabbed one of the stones, looking back up at Melina. "I have a plan – Melina! Are you alright?"

"It hurts," she replied quietly. "But I'm okay." Streaming tears betrayed her brave words. She had her hand clasped over her shoulder with blood seeping through her fingers.

"You've been shot!"

"I know." She cursed through chattering teeth. "Ow. It hurts."

"Okay, hold on, Melina. I'm getting us out of this."

Celeste tugged at her collar, exposed her bandaged shoulder, and carefully parted her mother's torn scarf. She shut her eyes tightly and clenched her teeth, thrusting the jagged stone into the wound. A muffled scream escaped her, and pain flooded her mind while blood burst from the split scab like water spilling from a cup. She dropped the stone and cupped her hand, catching most of the gushing crimson. She smeared it along the doorframe and floor.

"What are you doing?"

She closed the door. "Putting an end to this madness."

"How?"

"Come here!" She hissed, reaching for Melina's hand. "Aurous! Go!"

It was a bellow any beast would cringe from. Like a dull blade through flesh, the ragged roar pierced their hearts, flooding their veins with fear.

"Celeste!" Caden wrenched the doors open, slamming both against the wall. He eased through the doorway with her old rifle in his hands. His filthy fingers coiled around her father's fading bloodstain. His one eye peered down the barrel, glaring at the wolf nearly ensconced in shadows. "Yer only makin' it worse!"

The wolf's growl echoed, rumbling through the empty room. Caden gritted his teeth, nudging his rifle toward the moonlight spilling through the far grimy windows. He smiled, narrowing his brow and licking his crimson-stained teeth. The wolf's ears flattened and his lips curled in a menacing snarl. "Ya can't protect her now, ya damn mutt!"

Celeste raised the pistol. She inhaled sharply, trying to soothe her frayed nerves. The weapon trembled in her hand, and Caden twisted his bloodied head to find her diffident gaze. His dark eye widened. Her finger hovered over the trigger as he turned.

I can't do it!

Time never stopped. She'd often heard her father describe the feeling, how it was in the moments he thought he would die. It was like time would crawl, he'd say, like every moment stretched impossibly long and unfolded slowly. It wasn't like that for her. Caden moved quickly, dragging the rifle through the air with a raspy, triumphant laugh.

Daddy... I can't do this alone.

"Bitch!" Caden hissed through a venomous smile.

Warmth reached across her numbing hand. Blood slickened her skin. Melina's fingers curled over hers.

They both pulled the trigger.

One bullet pierced his gut. The second bullet chewed into his hip. Then final shot hit above his knee, leaving a bloody patch of torn skin.

He screamed first, reeling from frustration and sudden pain. Then he tried to lunge. Droplets of blood pumped from the wounds and fell to the floor like sanguine rain. He hit the ground, scrambling to lift the rifle.

She ripped it from his grasp, stomping her boot down on his bleeding thigh. He bellowed again and clawed for her coat. Wresting from his desperate clutches, she pulled the doors closed and jammed the rifle through the curved metal handles. She twisted and lodged the weapon, then ripped the bolt free.

"What... what the hell are ya doin'?" He coughed, drooling red down his chin. "Goddamn..."

She leaned against the doors, breathless and weak. Exhaustion heaved her eyes shut, and she slumped against cold metal, but her shoulder throbbed fiercely. Blood soaked through her coat and trailed down the metal doors.

Caden gurgled on blood when he spoke. "Answer me... Ya monster!"

She remained silent, letting the subtle sounds of death creep into the room. Claws dragged across the floor, carving through the tile as the monster stalked the corridor.

There you are.

The frame cracked and the metal by the door handles bulged. The Hunter wailed and screeched, hurling its massive body against the metal barricade.

Aurous howled, and Melina yelped with every loud thrash against the doors. Celeste masked her fear with steeled eyes.

"It's over now," she said, pulling her bow back over her shoulder. She led Melina to the agitated wolf, and together they hoisted him through the opened window. Melina needed help climbing through as well, hindered from the pain in her chest.

"Ya can't leave me here!" Caden cried. The metal doors shook from the Hunter crashing into them. "Ya can't! I... I was trying to help you!" More blood squirted through his clenched teeth. "I wanted... to save you."

"Caden," she whispered softly, her words like poisonous barbs. "I hope you enjoy hell."

"Bitch!" He yelled hoarsely, clasping the wound in his gut. Crawling along the floor after her, his leg smeared a trail of red across the white tiles. "I'll kill ya!" She ducked through the window and closed it behind her.

She hoped his spilling blood and craven screams would resonate warmly through her soul and cleanse some of the blood staining her hands. Instead, the chill remained deeply rooted in her heart. Her eyes blurred from tears she was weary of spilling, but she disappeared into the unforgiving night.

They were almost to the highway.

PART III.
HIGHWAY (EARLY WINTER)

THIRTEEN
TOOTH & NAIL

UNDER A resplendent morning sun, flakes of falling snow shimmered like stars on a clear, dark night. The white glitter coated the rocky ravine at the edge of the road, and clumped along the tops of trees daring to take root inside the bluff. Green pine needled through the snow, and branches were astir with cheery birds chirping through the evanescing chill.

The warmth did little to pry the glacial grip from her bones. Her clothes were in tatters, sodden from rainfall and mud. The saturated fabric clung to her like a soggy, uncomfortable layer of numbed flesh. Muck pooled in her boots.

Their muscles ached, burned, and grew stiff from the old; yet they continued staggering breathlessly up the steep highway. The steep road snaked across of ragged mountainside. Brush and growing thickets covered the edges of the sinuous concrete, like the enclaving forest slowly reached out to reclaim its lost greenery.

Melina leaned on Celeste, stumbling along the slushy road. Red curls fell over her pale face when she hunched over and wheezed, her mouth agape like a fish out of water. Celeste dragged her through the slush, ignoring the redhead's enervated thrashes.

"I can't... keep running," she whispered, pulling against Celeste's unyielding grip. A worried whine rumbled in Aurous' throat. She gazed at the trotting wolf and met his stare with a halfhearted smile. His tawny eyes swam in radiance like the brazen sun.

"We have to keep going," Celeste mumbled through trembling lips. "Just a little further."

For the entirety of the day, they kept their sluggish pace, but Melina's breathing worsened. Her shortness of breath progressed into wheezing gasps. Even the freckles on her face paled with the rest of her wan complexion. Celeste helped steady her balance when she lurched across the road, eyes fluttering and head lolling. The girl teetered on the brink of exhaustion, and Celeste wasn't sure she possessed enough strength to keep both of them moving.

Behind them, mountain peaks bulged through a thick fog blanketing the valley at the bottom of the serpentine highway. Aurous would slowly trot back into the mist, only to reappear further ahead after limping through the trees. His usual game, though he lacked the vigor to bound through the woods as he pleased. As their stride slowed to a weary shuffle, the wolf burst through the fog, leaving swirling white wisps in his wake. His foreleg buckled, but he swayed and growled playfully. A patch of red dangled in his frothy jaws. Crouching low, he wagged his curved tail. Then he growled again, displeased with her impassivity. Her nose wrinkled and her eyes widened at the bilious odor.

Blood.

Yet her stomach groaned and twisted painfully from the sickly sweet scent. Her mouth eagerly pooled with saliva. Aurous cocked his head, staring at her with shining eyes. He dropped the bloody meat, and gave her a familiar growl she knew meant, *you know the drill, you get whatever – but save me the guts.* He licked his thin, pink lips.

Sunlight ebbed as the fiery sun descended behind the mountains. Besieged by shadows, she hauled Melina away from the road, their boots now slopping about in the muck of the hillside. She found a patch of dense shrubbery under the watchful guard of pine and oak, keeping the highway within view. Melina shivered and curled up against the base of the tree, and Celeste leaned against her with two stones in her hands.

Let's see if I can do something. She struck the stones together.

An hour passed. Sparks would occasionally flash, though no flame would catch on the bunched brush. She hurled the stones into the darkness, her frustrated cries startling Melina awake. As the girl trembled, Celeste silently cursed her stupidity and huddled closer, vying for the dull heat emanating between them both.

Aurous pawed the dead rabbit and growled, a warning of his growing impatience. She sighed, but decided satisfying their bellies held more importance than dozing off against the constant throbbing pain.

Without her knife, the job was messy. She had to wiggle her fingers into the rabbit's puncture wound and tear its warm flesh like opening a zipper on a fur coat. She gagged, but scooped the steaming guts into her hand and *plopped* them on the ground for Aurous. He lapped up the murky juices secreting from the entrails, then devoured them greedily. Without a fire to cook the meat, she remained wary about eating it. Her father had warned her many times about sickness from undercooked meat. Though it wasn't a guarantee, the risk loomed over her hunger-riddled thoughts.

Last thing I need is more uncontrollable vomiting and a weaker stomach. She shuddered unexpectedly.

After a moment's deliberation, she conceded to her stomach's grumbling arguments and ripped a piece of pink flesh to eat. She chewed the tough, stringy meat and choked it down, then spat out the slimy blood coating her tongue. She frowned at the lingering, piquant taste, but her stomach groaned in appreciation.

It wasn't so bad... She convinced herself.

Celeste spent most of the evening rousing Melina from a catatonic state. The girl looked up with fluttering eyes and spoke with garbled words Celeste was unable to decipher. When she pressed the back of her frigid hand against Melina's forehead, worry wormed into her mind and rooted along with other dismal thoughts. *She's burning up...* Yet, the fragile girl remained pale, her red hair slick with dripping sweat.

It took hours of coaxing, but Melina finally choked down few mouthfuls of raw, bloody meat. She chewed slowly then dozed, only to be roused again and forced another mouthful. Celeste kept plucking pink ribbons of flesh until Melina feebly shook her head and leaned back against the tree. Her eyes heaved shut and she sighed, then went limp and slumped against the dirt. Panic brewed inside Celeste, her unblinking eyes staring through the aphotic thicket until she was certain Melina's chest rose and then fell occasionally.

She's still breathing.

Her heart *thumped* deeply with relief. Aurous crawled between them, offering what little comfort he could. He blanketed Melina with his jet black fur and nuzzled up against her.

Celeste disregarded her remaining dignity and quickly scarfed down the remaining bits of meat. Blood spattered her cheeks and dribbled down her chin. She was like a wolf, nudging her snout deeper into a bloody carcass, gorging on the flesh peeling from its bones. She saved an ample amount of gristle then tossed the rabbit back to Aurous, who happily snatched it out of the air.

The night smothered them with unrelenting darkness. Snowy tree-tops and overgrown shrubs obscured the haunting glow exuding from the moon. Eerily silent, only the shallow wheeze of Melina's breathing filled the cold air around them. She strained her eyes peering through the shadowy night, shivering with the pistol cocked in her lap. Exhausted and sore, she yearned to rest her bruised muscles and dull the ache in her bones. Yet, even as she thought no more tears could fall, she buried her face into her wolf's fur and silently wept until daybreak. It still wouldn't glut the pain welling in her soul.

It seemed colder by morning.

Celeste found herself stumbling through the trees, away from their makeshift camp. She pulled her coat closed, hoping to trap the fleeting warmth. She stopped behind another thicket and winced, biting her tongue quickly to stifle a pained yelp. Her thighs were still swollen and bruised, with bloody lacerations carved into her pale skin. Shielding the wounds from sight, she crouched and relieved herself.

Bastard, she cursed bitterly.

Melina still couldn't break her fever. Soaked with sweat, her face burned deep red, and her eyes rolled to the back of her head when Celeste attempted waking her. Eventually, she hoisted the girl to her feet, but Melina barely sustained her balance for long. She toppled over into the dirt, and Celeste struggled to help her up again. The wolf was clearly displeased with their plodding, but too fatigued and wounded to venture further ahead.

They emerged from the wooded mountainside to a highway smothered in white under dreary, leaden skies. The cold crept through her clothes. Her fingers were stiff and refused to uncurl. The skin on her face numbed. Melina fared worse; her lips were blue, and perspiration from fever soaked through her clothes. She languished and reeled, nearly dragging Celeste down with her.

She can't travel in her condition. Melina swayed again, but Celeste ducked under her arm for support. *But we can't get trapped in a blizzard without shelter.* They had to keep moving.

Hope faded quickly. Heavy snow began to fall and stick to her clothes. It gathered in her boots, soaked her wool socks, and puddled by her toes. *Damn it.* The chilly breeze amplified to a brumal gale as they rounded the mountain. The growing tempest fanned snow in their faces, swirling it around them until they were lost in a haze of white.

Spoke too soon, she cursed nervously, biting her lip. *We're going to freeze.*

At first, she became wary of the shadows dotting in the distant blustering snowfall. She hesitated, stopped, and waited for movement. *Nothing.* Uncertainty poisoned her optimism. She wondered what the snowy curtain concealed, and her mind was rife with vain wishes. *A large animal for us to hunt? Shelter?* She frowned. *People?* Her heart quickened with irrational fear. *... Caden?* She shook her head quickly and dismissed her paranoia.

After a few more steps, Melina collapsed into a mound of snow, so Celeste dragged her through the flurry. She yelled, abandoning caution as she approached the shadows. Her cries carried with the piercing howl of the wind, but they garnered no reply.

Shelter!

Or at least the best she could hope for. The first shadow blurred into view. The vehicle wasn't rusted and old like the few she'd seen littering Antler Creek. It was a truck, with metal bars encasing the windows and tires almost as tall as she was. The glass was smashed, scattered along the inside of the seat. Snow had started sprinkling through the bars, coating the interior with icy white.

Might as well sit in the damn snow.

The second was a light colored van with frosting windows, and a door partially wedged open. She peeked inside after propping Melina against the back bumper. Cocked and poised, the pistol trembled in her hands.

One bullet left. If anything happens, I have to make it count. Aurous whined, curling up on Melina's lap to shelter the girl from snowy gusts.

The van was empty. It wasn't an ideal shelter, but it would do until the storm eased. *If it ever does...* She quelled those incessant, grim thoughts and tried not to remember the long, brutal mountain winters with her father. *At least we're out of the wind.* She dragged Melina inside, waiting until Aurous shook the clumpy ice and snow from his black fur, then closed the door behind her.

The wolf crawled between them. It was cramped, but the seat extended across the entire width of the van. Stuffing bulged through the split seams, and the remaining material was rough and stiff with grime and cold. It wasn't nearly as empty as it seemed at first glance. She scoured every dark crevice and managed to find an old T-shirt and frozen, oily rags stuffed inside the dash. She also searched for a key, hoping to start the vehicle and somehow heat the interior. *If it works.* When she found nothing, she squirmed through the part between the front seats and burrowed into the wolf's damp fur. The wind howled its fury outside, and her teeth chattered along with the wintry chill. She rubbed the rags between her hands until her palms were stinging.

"I know it's not much," Celeste mumbled, covering Melina's chest and neck with the warmed rags. "But it'll help keep the chill away." She made sure the T-shirt was as thoroughly warmed and comfortable before pulling Melina's muddy boots off then wrapping it around her legs and feet. Shifting in his seat, Aurous yawned. Celeste peeled off her own wet boots and soggy socks.

"Just a bit of rest, alright boy?" Mimicking the wolf, she yawned as well. "Then we'll get some food."

She didn't doze for long.

Her stomach groaned. Whenever she would move them, her fingers would ache, causing her to wince and cry out. She reached for her bow, careful not to stir Melina. *I'll let her rest. We can travel after the storm passes.* The van had grown slightly warmer. Fog crept across the edges of the windows. It wasn't enough to chase the festering chill from her bones or dry her boots, but the tepid air burned her skin, and Melina had finally stopped shivering.

Now if only her fever would diminish. Snow billowed with the howling wind, whiting out the windows and burying them inside. *It's getting dark.*

She finally caved from the wolf's throaty whines. Aurous pawed at her lap impatiently, groaning and growling while nipping at her sleeves.

"I don't want to leave her," she started to protest, running her fingers through his coarse fur. The painful twist in her gut from the thought of food burned a bit of purpose through her jaded muscles. "But we won't survive without food, right boy?" Aurous panted and lolled his pink, frothy tongue.

"I'll be back soon, I promise," she whispered softly. She squeezed Melina's warm fingers, then slid the door open to the cold and blustery evening.

Her boots were still uncomfortably wet, and she sank with each step. Snow swirled from the wind, pelting her with ice. The wolf bounded across the frozen sea of white like a deer hopping through the forest. *He must be feeling stronger after eating and resting.* She tromped through his makeshift path and followed him up the wooded mountainside. The branches bowed from the heavy snow along the treetops. Aurous plunged his nose into the white fluff, leading her deeper into the woods.

She must have circled the same thicket a dozen times. Aurous had faded into the shadows growing from the ensuing night. His growls carried down through the trees, and she knew he was goading her to quicken the hunt. Something else caught her eye; familiar gnarled branches covered with brown leaves, like the shrubs she used to find in her father's garden.

Berries!

Her elation quickly abated as reality set in. Whatever had grown there would certainly be foul and rotten by now. Grudgingly, she trudged through the snow to see for herself.

To her surprise, she found a handful of shriveled berries dangling from the twined branches. She ate one. It was tart, and definitely rotted. The mush stuck between her teeth and coated her tongue with a bitter taste, but she pocketed the rest and searched for more along the snowy forest floor. She brushed the recent snowfall away from the base of the nearest tree, peering closer at the tiny claw marks in the frozen ground. Grinning, she used her nails to scrape away the dirt concealing the treasure she knew lurked beneath. Plucking the light brown, oval shells from the frigid earth, she began thrusting them in her pocket along with the withered berries.

Feels like a lifetime since I've had walnuts. She checked a few more trees but uncovered no more signs of buried nuts.

"Some squirrel is going to be mad," she murmured. "Aurous!" She called, already knowing he was gone, enjoying the thrill of an exciting hunt. He would return, no doubt, with a rabbit's haunch between his bloody teeth.

I should be with him, helping him hunt. She sighed and began descending the snowy slope back to the highway. *I'm so goddamn useless...* Plagued by iniquity, she lowered her gaze and stomped on. *It's my fault Melina is hurt. I can't be selfish and abandon her.* Though, Celeste became increasingly uncertain how much longer they would be able to survive. The storm may pass in a few hours, but the temperature would continue to plunge. *The city is still inconceivably far.* Lost in her own morose musings, she barely heard it.

Voices.

"... So goddamn cold, ain't it?"

"Colder than a witch's tit."

Someone huffed. "Witch's tit would be more welcomin' than this, I bet."

She ducked. Slinking through the trees along the edge of the snowy highway, she spotted them; two figures lumbering through the thick powder. She'd emerged from the forest further up from Melina than she'd hoped.

"Hey, check it out," one of them whispered.

"What?"

"Vehicles. Straight ahead. You see it?"

"Yeah."

"Might be somethin' we can use."

One of them coughed then muttered, "Alright." They shuffled through the snow a bit more. "Let's not dawdle, okay? *She* may have set us free from the prison, but she made it clear if we weren't fighting for her, we were against her."

"They won't patrol this far down," the other countered.

"Queen Bitch said her next move was to secure any other nearby cities."

"They won't be traveling in this weather."

"Let's take advantage of that then."

She stumbled through the snow, remaining within earshot.

"I'll check the first car," one of them ordered, pointing toward the van. "You check that one. Maybe we can find some damn clothes or something."

"What, that stolen coat not good enough for you?"

"I got bloodstains on it from slashing that bastard's throat."

Someone laughed. "It's a nice coat."

"I wanted it," the other asserted, "but I didn't want his blood all over the damn thing."

She reached for her bow then quickly stopped, wary of her reaction; the blustering winds were too strong to lob an arrow through and strike her targets accurately, and her pistol only had one bullet left. *If they have any firearms, I'm dead as soon as I miss.* She clenched her teeth to stifle their chattering. *If I don't do anything they'll find Melina!* She scurried back up the slippery mountain slope, they're muttered musings of murder haunting her panicked thoughts.

Scampering through the trees, she tried outpacing the scavengers. The van wasn't far, but neither was the wanderer. He waded through the thick blanket of snow toward the vehicle while she quickly darted through the trees, where the snow only reached up to her calves. She followed the trail back to the highway and crouched, cautiously keeping her hand on the pistol. She slowed her pace near the van and peeked over the gathering snow. The man was calling over his shoulder, yelling and laughing at his companion. She bolted through the smothering white and eased the door to the van open. She pulled herself inside and crawled up to Melina.

Sweat still plastered the girl's freckled face and clung to her damp clothes. She had curled into a ball, pulling her knees close to her chest in an attempt for warmth. Celeste shook her catatonic friend, trying to wake her.

"Melina!" She hissed, keeping quiet. "We have to leave!"

Crunch. Crunch. Crunch. The front door opened, and Celeste pressed herself against Melina and held her breath, fearing to make any sound. Sounds of the wanderer rummaging through the compartments flooded the interior. She reached for her gun.

Too loud, she thought. Her throat tightened. *Damn it!* She stared at the faded red paint of her bow that had fallen to the van floor.

"Ah," the man breathed, hunched over the front seat. His ungloved fingers squirmed through the ashtray that slid out of the dashboard, procuring a burnt, white stub from its depths. He propped himself up on one elbow, fished a small, grey item from his pocket, then lit the stub. Inhaling deeply, he then breathed out a thick cloud of stale smoke.

She carefully twined the bowstring around her palms. When the wanderer began easing himself out of the seat, she lunged.

She slipped her arms over his head, pulling the string around his neck. He grunted, first from surprise, then from the makeshift garrote silencing any words after it dug deep into his throat. Skin bulged and blood streaked when she hauled on the bowstring, her legs pushing against the front seat for leverage. The man's head bent back and he clawed at his throat, attempting to pry the wire loose. His mouth gaped, and she tightened the noose-like hold with dwindling strength. He surged forward in a desperate struggle, yanking her from Melina's lap. Her hips crashing against the seat stopped her from being thrown into the windshield. The bowstring nearly slipped from her grip, so she wrenched the garrote, twisted, then heaved on it again. The man bucked his legs while she strangled the terrified scream trying to escape his parted lips. Convulsing once more, he slumped. His chin tucked against his chest, then he fell forward on the steering wheel.

The horn blared through the howling blizzard.

She grabbed his coat, frantically pulling him away from the steering wheel. He fell over the console, his head dangling above the lit stub burning into the van's floor.

Not good!

"I'm comin', bro!" The other man wheezed, then opened the driver door.

She blindly fumbled for the pistol. *Where the hell is it?* Her fingers traced across the smooth leather surface of her quiver.

The man called out again and shook his friend's shoulder. "I smell that. Don't hog all the smoke, man. You said you'd share the next time you... What the hell?"

Like fangs piercing into the flesh of prey, she plunged the arrow tip into the man's neck. It bit into his skin, burrowing down into his shoulder. He reeled, bellowing furiously. He fell back through the open door and tried to pull the arrow free. The barb snagged deep in his flesh, so blood pumped, squirted, and gushed with each forceful tug.

He crawled through the snow and quickly reached into his coat, but she was already upon her prey. She struck his arm aside before he raised his weapon, then clawed at his face. He screamed, blood pooling around his eyes. He reached for the pistol again. She wrestled it from his bloody fingers and leaned away from his thrashing fist. She raised the pistol above her head, gritting her teeth fiercely while the man writhed beneath her.

"Please don't!" he shouted, voice unsteady and broken from fear.

It was too late. The pistol bashed his face. His nose split open, flattening with *splat* of blood. He continued pleading, but she brought the weapon down again like a hammer strike. The next blow cracked and shattered the man's scarlet teeth. He gurgled and spat out bloody fragments, then she struck him again. Then again, and again... until his face turned into a sludgy pile of red meat.

"I'm sorry," she whispered. Steam puffed from the blood staining the snow around her. The pistol fell from her hands, her fingers slick and dripping red.

"I'm so sorry."

FOURTEEN
BUTCHER

ASHEN CLOUDS and falling flurries blotted out the setting sun. The glacial tempest raged through the mountains, smothering the highway with white and sealing them inside a desolate, wintry tomb. Branches bowed from collected ice, snow fell through the brittle pine. Even sheltered within the trees there was no escaping the wind's icy claws.

She moved closer to the writhing fire in hopes of chasing the chill from her bones. Her eyes strained against the heat, but she kept her gaze firmly set upon the grey item in her hand. She rolled the metal across her palm, then flicked the lid open; a small flame burned from the opening momentarily before the lid *snapped* shut.

Her fingers were suffused with red.

For two days since her encounter with the scavengers, they'd wandered the highway at a pitiful pace. Melina's condition no longer declined, but neither did the sickness dissipate. Fever burned like the fire they leaned over for warmth, and their disorientation rendered navigation exceedingly difficult through the impossibly thick snowfall. The storm refused to quell its chilling wrath, forcing them to seek shelter in the thicket until it passed.

They were layered in the bulky clothes she'd looted from the scavenger corpses and huddled near a fire barely lit against the snowstorm. Melina sprawled across the ground, bundled with most of the garb, her eyes clenched shut and freckled face dripping sweat. The wolf snored between them, resting his head on Celeste's lap with his back against Melina. He whined and shifted, aggravating his wounds. She peeled her gaze from the flame's luster. His tawny stare mirrored her own worry; the hunger would kill them long before the cold managed to. She shivered then yawned, weary of the bitter frost creeping through her clothes.

The lighter rolled between her numb fingers, her attention once more lost to the fire. Entranced by the flickering edges of flame, her eyes dragged shut. The *crackling* branches burning in the pit startled her awake a moment later. She gasped from the panic swelling in her chest. The gun quickly slid from her belt, her finger arched over the trigger; her eyes darted to each side, the gun following her gaze.

Nothing, damn it!

She eased the gun down, breathing slowly. Aurous, grunting his disapproval, shifted back into her lap.

I have to stay awake. She'd barely slept since leaving that bloodied town behind.

Pain jolted through her muscles whenever she moved, but her belly ached worse. The blizzard made hunting scarce, with no creatures foolish enough to venture through the arduous mountain storm. The wolf hadn't bothered wandering far from their makeshift shelter, preferring to conserve what little energy he had and remain warm by the fire. She cleaned and dressed his wounds as best she could. And despite her various injuries and aches, she gathered as many fallen branches and ripped the brittle ones from dying trees around them. Some she threw in the fire pit and others she propped around the thicket, reinforcing the barrier between them and the callous wind. She struggled to keep the fire alive, and had already sacrificed part of her shelter to fuel its fleeting warmth. She shivered from the wind drifting through the thicket, and tried not to doze off again.

"Celeste."

She barely heard it; the wind smothered the whisper with its howling fury. It was almost a growl, a threatened wolf warning another pack of its territory. She strained to see through the blinding dark surrounding them.

"Celeste."

A bloody eye glared back at her through the shadows.

No... Fear strangled her thoughts. *It can't be him!*

"CELESTE!"

"Celeste?"

Her eyes shot open. Her finger brushed against the trigger, the gun glaring across the diminishing fire. Melina peeked through the make-shift blankets bunched around her and whispered softly, "Celeste, are you okay?"

She shook her head, but replied, "I'm okay." The corner of her mouth twitched into a smile. "It's good to see you're coherent again."

"I feel like crap." Melina shivered. "And I'm cold."

"Want my coat?"

"No," she replied quickly. "It's fine. I just can't sleep. I'm so hungry."

"Hunting has been slow," Celeste admitted sheepishly. *Not like I've been able to accomplish much.* The wolf yawned in her lap. *Without Aurous, we would have starved days ago.* "If the storm eases up by morning, maybe we can get lucky."

Melina nodded, eyes fluttering. Celeste thought she'd fallen asleep until the fatigued girl mumbled, "Tell me something, Celeste."

"What?"

"Where you came from."

Celeste bit her lip. Fresh blood dripped from the cut. "I can't remember much about before the outbreak. Bits and pieces, mostly."

"I don't remember much either," Melina said meekly, nuzzling up to Aurous. The wolf groaned his delight. Celeste tossed the last of her gathered tinder into the voracious flame.

"I lost my mother and brother quite early. Sometime after the quarantines failed and the mutations occurred." She nudged the soft snow with her boot, pushing a clump of white closer to the heat. She watched it melt into slushy muck. "They were infected, but my mom didn't want my brother to go through that horror."

"I'm sorry," whispered Melina, sorrow drowning her words. "I lost my family to it as well."

"Their passing broke my father, but he tried to stay strong for me. His idea of survival meant isolation deep within the mountains, living off a land that could barely sustain us any longer. Dry summers and devastating winters." She couldn't stop the spreading smile. "I hated it, nearly every damn day. But I would give anything to wake up to our daily chores and mundane routines again."

"We always miss what we've taken for granted." Melina blinked the tears from her eyes. They trailed down her face slowly, soaking into the collar of her shirt. "I despised Leo's family for making us stay during the recent outbreak in my town. They wouldn't leave, hoping to wait it out and praying the military would rescue us like they always had. In the end, it cost them their lives."

Celeste looked away. Guilt panged through her brittle heart. She tried mumbling her apologies, fearing to betray her stony demeanor. Melina only shook her head.

"I spent weeks in silence, refusing to speak to them," she continued. "They weren't fighters by any means. I didn't even get to say goodbye. I spent too much time hating them. I miss them so much right now. I can't even remember the last time I told them how much I loved them all."

"I miss my father," Celeste admitted, echoing her companion's agony.

She flinched and her muscles tensed. Her frigid fingers curled around the weapon instinctively as warmth spread across her hand. She almost pulled away from Melina's touch, then grasped the girl's hand tightly.

"Tell me about him."

She shuddered and steadied her lamenting heart. Though the tears welled in her eyes until the firelight blurred into a dim, orange glow, she spoke teeming with pride. "He was a survivor. He did whatever he had to in order to protect me and his family. He was gruff, surly, and always had a frown on his face. But he was wise and full of kindness; more than he dared admit. Knowledge was true power to him, though he wasn't afraid to work with his hands." She laughed. "I used to hate waking up in the mornings, I couldn't stand the tedious chores he'd force me to finish. He made me dismantle and clean my gun so often I could accomplish the task in my sleep. He taught me how to shoot almost any type of weapon, what he knew about fighting, hunting, gardening – he used to make me read a book about *words*." She chuckled softly, wiping her eyes. "Can you imagine that? A book comprised of words... *about* words!"

Despite the faint smile etched on her face, regret festered deep within her mind. *My dictionary. Knife. Scarf. Gloves. Almost all of it is lost.* Though she still had a few of her mother's rings tucked safely in her jeans.

"He sounds nothing like Leo's father," Melina admitted after enduring a bitter silence. "He was a passive man, putting his faith before the well-being of his family. He believed God had a plan for us all."

Celeste snorted, but she grinned and stoked the fire with the last brittle branch she'd gathered. "My father wasn't very religious, but he always seemed to talk of my grandmother's unwavering faith."

"Do you remember her?" Melina asked. She brushed the red hair from her eyes, then buried her hands into the wolf's fur. "Your grandmother?"

"Very little." Celeste tossed the branch into the eager blaze. "I recall her laughter. How warm and resonating it was. Most of what I remember came from stories my father would tell me."

"She believed in God?"

Celeste nodded. "She believed in something. My father once told me she used to believe that crows held the spirits of our departed loved ones, giving them a chance to watch over us again."

"That's strange," Melina said, then quickly added, "I'm sorry, I've just never heard of anything like that before."

"It's okay." Eyes misting, Celeste smiled. "I never believed in it much."

Melina voice cracked as she replied through the lump forming in her throat. "I didn't believe in God. Leo did, and so did his family, but I could never understand it. Blind faith and foolish hope..."

"Unreciprocated love," Celeste added bitterly.

"It seemed so foreign. Unrealistic. When they would pray... I sat with them, closed my eyes and folded my hands, but it was just pretend. I had nothing to say to someone I didn't believe in." Melina sniffed, wiping her runny nose on her sleeve. "I believe now. At least... I want to. I want to know Leo and his family are watching over me and loving me from afar. I want to know that someday I can be with them again."

"It's a nice thought," Celeste managed to say.

"Maybe you should hold on to that too, Celeste," Melina said, meeting her gaze with radiant, green eyes. "Maybe your father never fully left you."

Is that true, father?

She'd been so certain of his presence on more than one occasion, it seemed foolish in itself not to believe. The pieces of her heart longed to feel whole once more. To know her mother, father, and brother were together... and waiting for her to leave the pain and worry of a troubled world behind to finally become whole again.

Are you all watching over me, making sure I stay alive just a little longer?

I want to believe... but why do I feel so alone?

"Because I am," she whispered quietly to herself, morosely responding to her own heartache.

Aurous growled his worry, gazing at her with eyes like glowing embers from the firelight. She tussled his fur, and looked back to Melina. She had shut her eyes, her head drooped to her shoulder. She breathed softly, and her lips quivered from the chill, though her freckled face still flushed red and dripped sweat. The fever still raged.

"At least I have you two," Celeste mumbled, smiling weakly as she stood to gather more tinder for the dying fire. "We'll survive together."

Morning came painfully slow. Again, she found little rest. Memories unraveled like nightmares through her jarred mind, until she feared to even blink lest she drift into a slumber and succumb to whatever horror awaited her inside. Instead, she kept the fire sustained and burning brightly through the wintry night, trying to chase the shadows from encompassing them. They were shivering, vying for warmth while the wind snapped its chilly jaws and numbed their skin.

Melina's fever didn't ease by sunrise. Celeste unzipped her companion's dark coat and pulled back the frozen stiff sleeve. An inklike green scab ballooned over inflamed flesh, bulging out from her shoulder.

The bullet wound! Celeste forced her to shift on her side, and Melina gritted her teeth in apparent pain. *No exit wound...* She grimaced. *The bullet is still in there.*

"This is going to hurt, Melina," Celeste warned with a soft, apologetic voice. The girl's eyes fluttered in response. "I'm sorry, but this is the only way."

She's once seen her father with an infection from the same type of wound. *That was on our way to the mountains,* she remembered, wincing as the flames lapped eagerly at her fingertips. Her skin burned.

So long ago.

Her father had encountered bandits and refused to surrender the limited supplies he'd managed to scavenge. She remembered being swept into his arms as gunshots blared through the dark night, jostling in his grasp. Blood. There had been a lot of it. Days after their narrow escape, the bullet wound he'd sustained became infected, making him feverish. He'd showed her how to clean and properly dress an infected wound. The bullet fragments, he said, would be fine if they didn't lodge within the muscle. She cleaned as best she could, then drained the wound. Her father always maintained she had saved his life.

It feels like a dream I can no longer recall once I've woken, she thought, frustrated. *I barely remember my past.*

"Brace yourself," she whispered, tracing her fingers along the edges of her wound. She pushed against the swollen scab.

A stream of dark yellow burst through her fingers, and splattered the inside of Melina's coat. Viscid sludge drained through the split scab like an overflowing dam. She wrinkled her nose at the putridity and gagged. A scream pierced the howling wind as Celeste skimmed a fresh clump of snow over the bubbling wound.

"I'm sorry," she whispered woefully. "I know this might make it worse, but doing nothing is killing you." Another scream rivaled the stormy wail as Celeste pinched and drained the wound again. *There.* She packed more frozen fluff around the wound to dab it clean.

I've already risked adding to the infection, she thought. She scrubbed her hands vigorously with snow. *Any longer and I might as well kill her right now.* Soiled slush dripped back to the ground. *I can't lose her too.* She reached into the smoldering fire pit.

"Melina, we're just about finished, okay?" Celeste braced Melina's shoulder, then pressed a glowing ember onto her oozing wound.

When the girl bellowed in pain, the wolf echoed his own with howl.

Dissipating clouds revealed effulgent skies reaching far beyond the mountain peaks. Sunlight beamed through the trees, caressing her with warmth. Snow drifted down from the branches above, glimmering as it swirled along with the chilling breeze. They strayed from the highway, keeping to the wooded hills instead; the sinuous road remained in sight, but she preferred traversing where the snowfall had been hindered by the giant trees and branches full of hearty pine. The continuous inclines and impenetrable thickets were exhausting – but her socks and boots remained dry.

Might be tedious, she thought sorely, *but it's better than freezing to death.* Not that they didn't dangling over the edge of dissolution.

A terrible ache pulsed through her fingers whenever she moved them. The flesh on her hands became swollen and purple, refusing to warm even by a fire. Her toes numbed. Her skin tingled from the chill like the icy breeze pierced her clothes and pinched her flesh.

"I'm so hungry," Melina quavered, losing footing in the snow. She slipped, thrusting her hands deep into the frigid fluff so she wouldn't tumble back down the slope. "Damn it…"

"I know," Celeste murmured. Her stomach grumbled in reply as well. She clasped Melina's trembling hands in hers, trying to capture a sliver of warmth. "We'll find food."

Their earlier discovery only strengthened the ache in their bellies. Melina had stumbled across a withered patch of gnarled branches tucked between two thin trees with bark as white as the snow around their boots. Before she could devour the few rotted but frozen berries she'd plucked from the ground around the plant, Celeste batted the shriveled red fruit from her hand and pulled her companion away from the trees.

Baneberry. Celeste explained the dangers of its toxicity, but even her stomach urged her to tempt fate by groaning eagerly at the thought of eating them.

"There's more snow the further we go into the mountains," Melina said, becoming increasingly winded the further they trudged. "Less chance of finding food."

"I lived in the mountains most of my life," Celeste replied. She squinted through the bright glare of the sun, spotting a shadow darting through the trees ahead. "We'll find more game deeper in the woods."

"I hope so."

Celeste tried to smile. "I promise."

I hope it's one I can keep.

"I need to rest," Melina whispered wearily. "Please."

"Of course."

At *least it's nice today.* The sunshine was a welcome change but the cold still chilled them to their bones, and their stomachs burned for sustenance. She'd clumped snow inside an indented rock and placed it near the fire earlier that morning, warming enough water to barely wet her tongue. A tedious task she'd been thankful to accomplish.

Father, I still remember what you taught me. Surviving without water was impossible, but I can go without food for weeks. She shivered. *Maybe days, considering these wretched conditions.*

"I'm going into the woods with Aurous," Celeste said, tightening the string around her bow. Her fingers grazed the blood still stained into the stiff wire. Her throat tightened painfully. "It won't take us long to find something to eat."

Hopefully.

"What should I do?"

Celeste hesitated. Melina pressed her back against a tree and slid down the trunk until she crouched over the frozen dirt. Welling tears made her green eyes shimmer. "I don't want to be alone," she whispered timorously.

Celeste reached into her pocket. "You're in no condition to exert yourself," she said, clasping her hands with Melina's. "We won't be long." Melina gripped the grey lighter Celeste left in her palm. When the redhead nodded, Celeste said, "start a fire, and get everything ready for a meal."

"Okay."

"One last thing." Celeste pulled one of the pistols from her belt. "Just in case."

Sprinting quickly through the snow, each labored breath fogged the air around her. She'd lost sight of the wolf inside the dense thicket, but immediately spotted his tracks stamped into the snow. There were other prints to her left, and a patch of muddy snow where animals trampled the ground foraging for food.

He's healed nicely. She'd noticed he favored his foreleg, and limped when he would bound through the snow in a giddy daze. *He's faring far better than I am.*

His tracks veer off to the right. Her frigid muscles *creaked* with the bowstring as he pulled it back. *The other tracks lead further into the woods. They're fresh. They can't be far.* The wolf was setting a trap. *All I have to do is wait.* The arrow trembled between her fingers. *Then we can finally...*

It chilled her like the wind's frosty breath, like shivers slithering down her spine and heart. It almost mocked her with its incessant laughter. She spotted it, obscured by the shadows of the pine, glaring down at her with a beady little eye. It cawed again, reveling in her gaze. A moment later, another crow called to her. It was perched in a branch adjacent to the first. A third crow joined their raucous symphony, settling its accusing stare on her like the others.

What the hell? She closed her eyes, shaking the uncertainty from her mind. *Focus on what's important.* Her own piercing screams were buried under their clamorous cries.

A blur of brown burst through the piney thicket. She raised her bow, but the frightened creature nearly collided with her. She fell back into the snow and the animal darted through the trees behind her. Aurous dashed after it, stumbling, his teeth bared and ears flat against his head. Another moment and they both disappeared into the brush.

"Damn it!"

She pushed herself up and raced after them, ignoring the startled caws of fleeing black birds. Snow impeded each quickened step down the slick slope. Darkness polluted the clear skies as the sun slipped behind the mountains. Shadows chased her through the trees, expanding and attempting to swallow her in a pool of night.

She ran blindly within the growing darkness, nearly hurling herself off the edge of the winding trench. Snow smothering the landscape obscured the danger beneath its blinding white blanket, but now *heard* it. Like the static of a radio without a signal, the river hissed as water flowed beneath the snow and ice inside the trench.

A river. She exhaled a shaky breath. *I shouldn't be so careless.*

Maneuvering down the slippery slope, she spotted tracks along the snow leading across the river and curving back into the trees. *Aurous doesn't know when to stop,* she grumbled inwardly, smiling despite the wolf's foolhardiness. *He's exerting himself too much.*

The last rays of sunlight glared off the ice after she brushed the snow away. *What was it dad had said?* Pain struck each thought like knives piercing her brittle mind. *Thin and blue, fall right through – White like clouds, always allowed.* She grinned, stepping onto the ice.

She made it halfway across before catching her boot on a frozen wedge and dropping like a stone onto the thinly veiled surface. Her elbows painfully *smacked* off the frozen river, and the air was forced from her lungs. She grunted, then swore loudly. Ice split beneath her weight and water seeped through, soaking her coat and pants. She clambered up the slushy shoreline and gasped for air that wouldn't fill her lungs. She was too cold, shivering wildly and crossing her arms over her chest.

Damn it. She tried to stand. *I have to find Aurous!*

Disorientation swirled the bleak, wintry landscape into a stream of dimming darkness. *Melina...* Overburdened with fatigue, her eyelids sagged shut. *I have to...* She reeled, glimpsing a shadowed figure approaching her through the blurry white.

Dad?

It was the last thought she recalled.

"Are you going to wake up, little one?"

She opened her eyes to garish light, discarding the slumber she'd succumbed to so abruptly. She groaned, expecting pain to flood every crevice of her being. Instead, she sat up and squinted, blotting the flame out with her hands. The shadowed figure sat across from her.

"You look tired." The stranger's coarse voice chafed her ears, but she basked in its familiar warmth. "And like you've been through hell."

She smiled, replying, "I have, father." Hope flourishing, she thought, *I'm safe.* "But I'm alright now."

"No," he replied, his sharp frown drooping through a blood-splattered beard. Even the firelight failed to penetrate the darkness swimming in his eyes. "You're not."

Fear chilled her heart. "What?"

"It's your fault."

"What is?"

"Everything." Hatred seethed from his whispered words. "The pain that you feel. The hurt you've caused that little girl."

"I didn't..."

"The blood is on your goddamn hands!" He learned toward the fire, black eyes glaring over dulling light. "They deserved to live as much as you, so why are you still alive? Your mother... Your brother... Why did they have to die instead of you?"

"I would have gladly taken their place!" Her tremulous voice nearly broke. "I would have!"

"What about mine?"

"You have no idea how much I miss you, father."

He grunted. He shook something in his hands, but a shadow cast from the burning flame obscured the object. "Then why did you insist on leaving?"

"I never wanted you to die!" Endless tears streamed from her bleary eyes. "I never wanted this hell!"

"I told you what was out here, what had happened to this world."

"I need you, father!"

"It's too late." Firelight glared off the glass in his hands. He uncorked the bottle and raised it over the fire. "To a world long gone to hell," he whispered. Crimson stained his neck and clothes, still seeping from his torn flesh. "And to the blood you'll forever bathe in."

"Stop it!" She screamed, covering her ears and burying her face in her lap. "I'm sorry! Forgive me, please, I'm so sorry!"

"Celeste!" Something kept jarring her mind, provoking another wave of nauseating pain to thrash against her battered body. She opened her eyes to more firelight.

"Celeste, thank the Lord." Relief flooded someone's tone, their whispers muffled by the crackling fire. "I thought you would never wake up."

Celeste was about to respond when she shifted her weight to sit up. A terrible scream tore through her ragged throat. She howled like a wolf under the haunting glare of the moon. Her fingers and toes ached like she'd plunged them into a blistering flame until flesh bubbled and burned. They were wrapped in whatever material Melina had ripped from her clothing. She was on her side with her hands placed near the fire. Her feet were nestled under Aurous while he lounged near the warmth. The wolf looked as weary as she felt, with gilded eyes that lost their luster and shine, and fur still stained with frozen blood and grime.

"You and Aurous were gone for a long time," Melina stated. She rubbed her hands together for a quick spurt of warmth before stoking the flame. "It took us even longer to get where you had fallen."

Red strands of icy hair fell over Melina's eyes. She brushed the stiff bangs from her sight, then tossed another stick into the greedy fire. Her face seemed weathered and worn, like she'd aged decades since their escape from Antler Creek. She frowned, deep lines curving around her mouth.

"When I saw you just lying there in the snow... I thought you were dead." Melina smiled instead. "You said you were getting us food," she prodded playfully.

Celeste wanted to reply and assure her friend that everything would be fine. *Empty words,* mused a rancorous thought. *False hope.* Beset by flourishing darkness, she knew it would be another fool's errand to try and procure more food. Her stomach cramped. *Not like I can hold my damn bow right now.*

"We'll try again tomorrow," was the only thing Celeste muttered in response. For now, she craved rest to soothe the incessant *thumping* in her head, as well as the burning ache in her fingers.

For once, she slept soundly. Her mind weaved no dreams to plague her broken heart, nor conjured wicked nightmares that plagued her even after she'd woken.

Not that the pain in her wounds subsided. A quick inspection of her hands confirmed what already lurked in the back of her mind.

Frostbite.

Dark blots swelled from her fingertips and nails. Like it had been chafed raw, her blackening skin began peeling, revealing pink and tender flesh beneath. The pain rendered her hands inert.

Melina occupied her morning by preparing as much water as she could. It wasn't a lot - a few mouthfuls every couple of minutes - but it was easier on their stomachs than snow.

Warms my belly as well. We need a damn water bottle... I wish I had my pack. They drank their fill and slaked their thirst before traveling further.

Celeste kept her hands bound tightly and tucked in her coat. The warmth pierced her tender skin, but she gritted her teeth against the pain and followed Melina back to the highway.

The cold and dismal day seemed endless. Her mind writhed from her throbbing fingers and the pain in her feet, like shards of glass minced her flesh with each step.

Aurous returned from a day's hunt, only a gaunt rabbit dangling from his jaws. He dropped the bloodied brown animal by their feet, happy to share but growling his irritation at the lack of warmth for him to sprawl by lazily. He sat, impatiently, while Melina, still woozy and sickly, bustled to start the fire.

After an hour of shivering miserably in the cold, they managed to sustain a flame long enough to catch upon the greenery propped above the tinder. As they tore the carcass open and peeled the stringy meat from its bones, Aurous lapped up blood and piled organs steaming in the snow by his paws. Hunger urged her to scarf down as much meat as her belly would allow, tempting her with satiation and relief. It took patience, but she roasted chunks of rabbit and savored the redolence of its sizzling meat. They ate, then slept soundly while the wolf watched over them.

The next day was a disorientating blur. She could no longer move her fingers without crying out in agony, and her clothing and boots remained dry only by the fire. The snowfall seemed heavier and the wind unforgiving. Exhaustion dogged their every step.

"I'm so tired," Melina whispered. She stopped trudging through snow to catch her breath, hoping the cold air would salve her burning lungs. Only her eyes peeked through the clothing bundled around her, yet she still trembled from the cold. "I can't..." Her eyes fluttered before she reeled and toppled into Celeste.

"Melina," Celeste murmured. She wiped the frozen fluff from her eyes and bit her tongue to stifle the scream as her hands throbbed painfully. "You have to get up." The girl stirred, trying to open her eyes.

Aurous began growling. Chills rippled through her thoughts as she followed his gaze, glimpsing a shadowed figure down the highway. The wolf parted his lips and flashed his white fangs, but hope resonated through her heart.

Dad!

No... The foolish thought withered from her mind.

A hoarse bellow erupted from the shadowed stranger, like a ghost wailing through the night for the living to take notice of its perennial suffering.

It can't be...

Caden.

Scarlet skin gleamed like a lit flare when he stepped through the shadows and into the fiery shine of the setting sun. Torn and clawed through, the flesh on his face dangled past his chin. Black blemished the edges of his wounds, and blood dried to his neck and clothes. He gritted his stained teeth, extending her old rifle at her. His ragged voice carried over the growing bluster as he *snapped* the bolt back.

"I knew ya wouldn't make it far without me!"

Frothy saliva rained down from the wolf's snapping jaws. His black fur bristled and his shoulders bunched. He sprang through the snow after the madman.

"Aurous! Come back!"

Mockery poisoned his laughter. "Ya think I want to deal with yer goddamn mutt?"

Her own cries resounded with the blast of the rifle in his hands. A flash of light and then red streaked across the frozen highway behind Aurous. The wolf collapsed into the snow with a shrill yelp. Ignoring the pain jolting through her fingers, she tore the bandages loose and reached in Melina's coat for the pistol.

She pulled the trigger and bucked a bullet from its barrel. Red misted the air as it struck his abdomen, but he kept his pace while aiming down the rifle's sights. Another deafening blast engulfed the desolate mountainside.

A bullet *thumped* into the snow beside her, spraying her with frozen mist and blurring her sight. She tried firing the pistol again – *click*.

She screamed, with as much pain as fury. "Damn it!" She cocked it again but lost every thought to a numbing and disorientating black.

Her jaw hurt. So did her entire head.

She grunted in pain, blood spurting past her cracked lips. Fingers twisted her hair and yanked her from the snowy road.

"There ya are, princess!" Caden exclaimed, expelling rancid air with each word. "I knew ya couldn't resist me much longer!"

She screamed and struggled against his bestial clutches, but she might as well have been a rabbit dangling from a wolf's jaws.

This has to be a nightmare! Please, wake up!

"Look at me!" He pulled her head back and hissed in her ear, spattering warm and putrid saliva on her neck. "I wasn't gonna let some little girl and her bloody *whelp* take me down after what I've endured."

Blood speckled his tainted skin when she spat at him. He ignored her. "Six years. Six *goddamn* years I spent in that hellhole! Imprisoned! I won't stop until every last bastard has paid the price my family has!"

"You're a goddamn liar," she muttered. "Everything you spew out of that asshole you call a mouth is complete *bullshit*."

He chuckled, and his tongue slithered into her ear. "We were wanderers, myself and my wife, along with my young son, Conner. For years after the disaster, we survived like that, staying out of people's ways and never taking what wasn't rightfully ours. I never crossed a single person!"

"Hard to believe considering your charm."

"Still a snarky one, huh?" He pulled harder on her hair, forcing himself on top of her.

"I was a good person, Celeste, even when the world had ended. Do ya wanna know what changed, girl? I came back one day to find them dead. Slaughtered. Not just killed, but *mutilated.* They were torn to pieces. I followed the tracks that led away from their camp and found a military unit with my family's stolen belongings." His eyes darkened as he stared into hers. "I just wanted them back, Celeste. So I tried to kill them all."

"I didn't succeed, even though it was all I wanted. To gain vengeance and finally unite with my family in death. I was captured instead of executed, and thrown in the military prison for *six goddamn years!*" His sudden outburst of laughter grated her ears. "I *still* remember the day the military outpost in the city fell. A few months ago at the most. *Oh, what a sight it was;* all the blood and guts, the dying screams, and the destructive flames – it was the sort of chaotic beauty I'd been dreaming of. It was the vengeance I'd been waiting for."

"The military had been slaughtered throughout the city after the attack, but that couldn't deter me. I could still strike fear in the hearts of those the military had sworn to protect from monsters now roaming this earth. *We* are those monsters, Celeste. Both of us." He licked his grimy lips, smiling broadly. They both heard the horror wailing through the night. "So let's go to hell together."

Through the pullulating darkness came a thunderous roar, the howl of a beast feverishly desirous for blood.

Hunter!

Panicking, she painfully battered her fists against the mangled flesh of his face until he delivered a sharp blow of his own. His knuckles rapped off her chin and dazed her. He hauled her to her feet, fingers still twined in her hair and nearly ripping it from her scalp.

"Look what we have wrought!" He yelled, cocking his head back in a frenzy of depraved laughter. "All the blood on our hands culminates in death! Look, Celeste! I said LOOK!" A scream escaped her as he jerked her neck. "Ya shoulda finished me when ya had the chance, Celeste!"

"No," she whispered in horror. She watched helplessly as the wolf stood, crimson streaming through his black fur, to confront the shadowed creature. Weakened, Aurous tried lunging but the Hunter struck first and raked his glistening white claws through the wolf's flesh. Blood sprayed across the creature's scabrous scales. Its pace never wavered; hell's fire glared at her through its eyes, and its scythe-like claws left a trail of red through the disturbed snow as it charged.

"Aurous!"

"Better be worrying about yerself," Caden hissed. "We're next on the menu. Before I bite the bullet watching the Stalker rip ya to shreds, I'll have a bit of fun with the redhead. Don't matter if the cold already killed her. Makes it less of a struggle if you ask me. There's something lovely about the cold embrace of a corpse beneath you..."

"Go to hell!" Celeste screamed, writhing under his clutches.

"I'll see you there, love!" She collapsed by his boots, dizzied from another sharp blow. The Hunter wailed, and Celeste closed her eyes tightly, awaiting the fatal strike.

She thought it was thunder from a clamorous storm, the angry bellows of a tempest growing over the mountains – but it was an explosion of gunfire. Each deafening blast rattled her bones. Black blood spritzed from every rupture wound the bullets inflicted, but the creature roared and turned its ravenous gaze on its attacker.

It almost resembled a tank. Giant wheels chewed through the compacted snow and shattered the ice around it. Solid steel encased the vehicle's body. Even the tinted windows were covered with thick bars and rusted wire mesh. A large barrel swiveled on top of the green vehicle, then another round of bullets erupted through a flash of blinding light.

Projectiles ripped through its armored skin. Flesh ruptured and blood burst; more bullets sawed through its skull until its malformed head exploded into a mist of putrescent black and jagged fragments of bone. The Hunter collapsed, mangled and lifeless. Smoky wisps trailed into the air from the creature's wounds.

"What the..." Caden began to mutter. He reached for Celeste and pulled her close, thrusting the rifle barrel into her spine. "Who the hell is this?"

The vehicle rolled to a stop not far from the Hunter's corpse. Its engine rumbled the frozen ground beneath them, until quickly sputtering to a stop. Except for the whistling breeze, the highway plunged back into uncertain silence. Moments passed before one of the doors opened.

A strong voice boomed and echoed through the barren highway. "Drop any weapons you have or we will open fire!"

"Ah," Caden breathed into her ear. "Let's see how many rounds we can squeeze off before they kill us."

"Wait," came another voice. Quiet, but commanding, laced with enough fire to sear deep within Celeste's mind. "Lower your weapons."

"Yes, ma'am."

Crunch. Crunch. Boots stomped down into the snow, and then the door slammed shut. A slender figure stood by the vehicle, with a long, dark coat whipping behind her waist like a flag rippling from the wind. Flowing curls of black hair fell past the fur-lined edges of her hood and bunched in ringlets around her shoulders. Smooth skin, tinged with an olive complexion, and a piquant grin carving up her face; she radiated elegance. Tenebrous eyes, like an extension of the night itself, caught Celeste in an alluring gaze. She approached slowly, slipping sleek gloves over her fingers, walking like there wasn't a clump of snow blemishing the highway pavement. She ran her eyes over Celeste before her shadowy gaze settled upon Caden.

"The bitch," he whispered, recognition widening his one good eye.

The woman's cerise lips parted with a small laugh. "The vagrant."

"Fancy meeting ya here."

"These are my roads," she warned, purring with a silky voice. She licked her lips. "I told you what would happen if I found you wandering them."

"Ya can't banish me from every place I step foot in," he growled in reply. "Ya free me from that prison then try confining me to another!"

Arching her eyebrow, she said, "I gave you a choice, murderer. Fight for me or leave these lands." She narrowed her nebulous eyes. "Otherwise you die."

"Don't call me a *murderer* like we're not cut from the same cloth."

"You're comprised of nothing but filth," she said, shifting her dark gaze to Celeste. "Did he have a tear in his eye when he spoke of how his family was murdered? Or how he needed to bring those responsible to justice? Maybe he tried convincing you his daughters were raped by the military and then killed."

"Shut up," he hissed.

Her mouth twitched with amusement. "Maybe he fed you the tale of being the sole survivor of a bandit attack, watching his fellow soldiers fall to an onslaught as he was captured."

"I said *shut up.*"

A fearful yelp squeaked from Celeste's lips as he jammed the barrel into her spine.

"You know what I heard from his former guards? A patrolling unit stumbled across a camp, locating only one survivor. The rest had been savagely killed and partially eaten. The man responsible was the lone survivor, who attacked the unit and managed to kill several of them before being subdued. They should have executed him on the spot but... one of the men he killed happened to be a general's son, a fresh faced boy on his first military excursion. Poor bastard," she muttered, gesturing to Caden. "Killing your own family and wishing for death, only to have your pitiful existence prolonged."

"Ya don't know shit!" He yelled and pulled Celeste's head back, exposing her throat. Cold metal kissed the back of her neck. "One more bloody step, I'll blow her spine out and then take ya down before that fancy gun can fire on us both!"

"What makes you think I care about the girl?"

"Then just leave us be, *bitch*, and let me finish what I started long ago," he muttered.

She didn't answer. Her eyes wandered over Celeste, stopping at her jeans. "Is that from him?" She asked, steeling her tone. Celeste looked down at the blood stained into her jeans.

Yes, she wanted to say, but her tongue refused to unravel like a tightly wound ball of yarn. Though her spilling tears already admitted plenty.

"Take him down," the woman ordered tersely.

Caden screamed a string of curses before a single gunshot forced him silent. The bullet slammed into his chest, pierced his flesh, and shattered bones in his ribcage. It lodged deep in his lung, and his next words were incomprehensible gurgles as blood gathered in his throat. As his fingers slackened, Celeste tumbled into the snow away from him. He fell back clutching his wound. Thick globs of blood pumped past his hand.

"I told you, rogue," the woman said as she stepped over Caden. He was writhing through the snow, reaching for his fallen rifle. She nudged it away with her boot, then slipped her hand into his tattered coat. "I would show you no mercy." She pulled a weapon from his belt.

"You," the woman called, turning her head to Celeste. "It's your kill, girl." She extended her arm. In her clutches, gripped firmly with slender, gloved fingers, was her father's machete.

That bastard found it... Sickened, she couldn't move or even open her mouth to speak. *I just want to forget about it all.*

The woman pursed her blood-colored lips. She slathered her words in venom, muttering, "Girl, always finish what you've started."

Fixating her predacious eyes on Caden, the machete gleamed above her head. His one eye widened in horror, and his mouth opened in a raspy scream. Blood gurgled in his throat. He extended an arm in vain defense, but the machete cleaved through his flesh and wedged into bone. The woman jerked the blade from his partially severed arm, a spritz of blood blemishing the snow by her boots.

"Ya bitch, I'll kill ya!"

He continued screaming until the blade sundered his arm, and plunged through his chest. Bones split and blood gushed past the handle. He sputtered weakly, still trying to curse them both while she hacked through his neck and head until there was nothing but mangled flesh beset by hellish red snow.

"So, girl," the woman finally said, catching her breath and wiping the beads of sweat forming along her brow. "Finish what you started. Remember that."

She turned, still clutching the bloodied blade tightly. "But you're either with *us*." She pointed to Caden's mutilated corpse with the machete. Crimson dripped into the snow. "Or with *him*."

PART IV.
CITY (LATE WINTER)

THE ASCENDING sun glared over the mountain peak, piercing through the black veil of night. Shadows scurried from its incandescence. Celeste shivered under the tepid glow, only aware of the ache lingering beneath each thought. She was *still* cold.

"Advance on my signal. And nobody opens fire unless I say so."

Like a whisper in a boisterous crowd, the firm order was overwhelmed by the wind whistling noisily through the branches above. Her mind seemed lost in the distance, shrouded in fog like the mountain mornings she lamented for.

Why can't I purge my bones of this chill?

"That means you too, rookie," someone sneered, tone riddled with mockery. "Or are you having issues with following orders?"

Eyes blurring, she blinked, then followed the figures preceding her through the thicket. She attempted utter silence, but snow clumped around her boots and *crunched* beneath every cautious step. She paused momentarily, straining to hear any sound through the dense greenery. She heard nothing but footsteps from her comrades, and the whispers of contempt from the boy trudging along behind her.

"Don't know why we're wasting time with a brat like you," he stated flatly, raising his voice as she continued walking through the trees. "Can barely lift a rifle, let alone use one. What did you shoot back there?" He clicked his tongue, whistled as though he were impressed with her shortcomings, then chuckled breathlessly. "Yeah, I watched you at the range. Could barely wound a target five feet in front of your face."

His blunt words left welts along her pride, but she bit her tongue and shook the snow from her coat. She cursed once she realized she'd lost sight of the others. *Of course.* She knew not to let him rile her, no matter how much she hated that he was right. *I couldn't shoot the broad side of a barn anymore.* She smiled slightly, recalling the familiar saying her father used to tease her with. *So long ago,* she thought, lamenting. *When I was too young to hold a gun properly.*

"Wonder why they even gave you a gun," he continued in a barbarous tone. Wisps of stale smoke curled into the air from the end of his lit cigarette. He rolled the tip along his tongue, grinning as she glared over her shoulder. "More of a liability than anything. Probably shoot one of us before scouting is finished." His pale, sky-colored eyes darkened. "Or maybe you accidently shoot yourself."

She stopped and turned, voice brimming with anger. "Are you threatening me, Abbot?"

He scoffed, sniffled, and wiped his narrow nose. A stream of snot smeared along his sleeve. "Merely stating the obvious possible outcomes of this excursion. We all know *why* you're here, mountain girl."

There was no avoiding his poisonous trap. "Because you're an even lousier shot than I am?"

"You're her new *pet.*"

It was Celeste's turn to grin devilishly. "Is that jealousy, Abbot? It's not very becoming."

"She'll grow weary of a useless little doll, given enough time to pursue other interests."

"Abbot, I'm not impressed."

"What?"

She cocked her head, arching her finger over the pistol's trigger. She watched his eyes trail down to her weapon. He exhaled a cloud of smoke and tossed the burning stub by her boots. "Your childish behavior," she muttered quietly. "It's not flattering."

"I'm not very impressed either," he retorted, mumbling as he lit another cigarette. "You keep taking your eyes off the target."

Her eyes darted back to the rustling brush, her pistol cocked and poised a moment later. Two gunshots blared against the morning silence, followed by Abbot's sneering laughter after she'd almost jumped out of her own skin.

"Help me!"

A man stumbled through the frozen thicket, traceries of blood welling where thorny branches pricked his bare flesh. Uncurling his stiff fingers and reaching for Celeste, his chapped lips parted in another plea. A patch of torn and ribboning flesh dangled where his other arm should have been, warm blood still steaming as droplets spattered along the snow. Grime sullied his otherwise pale skin, and a row of carious teeth lined his blackened gums. His eyes widened, icy blue like the frozen waves of a pristine mountain river – but all she saw was a swirling sea of black threatening to engulf every thought in a darkness she'd never escape from again. Hell stared back at her through those eyes.

His eyes.

Caden. She wanted to scream.

Another blast resounded through the trees. Blood misted the air, streaming down the man's neck like a river of death. He gaped and clutched at his throat before collapsing into the snow. Gurgling, he tried to speak, but sputtered blood until Abbot pulled the trigger again. The gun spat out another bullet, thrusting it deep into the man's skull in a splatter of red. The man, now lifeless, stared through Celeste with his blue tinged eyes...

"Or you'll get yourself killed," Abbot chided with a smile. "Either way you're useless." He leaned over the bloodied corpse, wrinkling his nose. "Smells like a shithouse. What was this bastard doing way up here?" He shrugged and slipped his gloved fingers into the man's pocket. Procuring a silver chain, he whistled his delight and chortled. "Not bad for a quick kill." He eyed Celeste playfully. "One of us has to eat well tonight."

Damn it. Again, she'd been left with little to trade.

"Come on, Abbot. You looted the last one." She'd long grown tired of rice and potato rations, having scarfed down the plain food every evening since her arrival at the city.

She discovered rather quickly that trade ruled the city's society, whether for better food, clothing, bedding, or weapons – everything was up for trade. During her first scouting mission, she'd found a package of cigarettes in a run-down shelter outside of the city. Abbot had quickly claimed the package, handing her a bottle of filtered water instead. She'd shrugged and accepted the water since she didn't smoke – only to find out later back at camp that he'd traded the cigarettes for sweetened snacks and warmer clothing.

Arsehole.

"Pull your own weight, rookie."

She rolled her eyes. "Go to hell, Abbot."

"After you," he shot back. "*Princess.*"

Anger boiled through her tone. "Do you have some sort of problem with me?"

"Yeah," he riposted, voice laden with disgust. "You should have been left to die on that highway. There's no place for weaklings on this planet anymore, especially not in this unit. So why don't you screw off and scurry back to whatever inbred mountain shithole you crawled out of."

"Or what?" Her fingers tightened around her revolver, brow furrowed at the pompous bastard. "You're going to kill me?"

"Maybe I will."

Danger crept into her words. "I'd like to see you try."

"What do you know about the world, little girl? You shouldn't speak unless you want a bullet where your mouth is." He snickered, narrowing his eyes. "Do you know how many people I've killed? Three. Well, four now, considering this unlucky bastard. You wouldn't have the guts to pull the trigger. You *don't.* Sheltered within the mountains your entire life... Give me a break. Lose the attitude before I break if off you."

Her lip curled in a threatening snarl, heart drumming angrily against her chest. She wanted to wring his neck, to feel the warm, sticky blood around her fingers after burying her blade in his flesh...

"About time you wised up," Abbot muttered. "Before you got hurt."

He flicked his finger over his rifle's trigger, and her gun trembled in her hand.

"Enough!"

They both averted their eyes, shifting nervously as the voice boomed through the tension. Silence reigned afterwards, but even without her stern order, the very presence of her shadowed eyes would have commanded their full attention. Through the snow-fringed verdure, the woman emerged, her honey colored skin glazed from falling snow. She pursed her ruby lips, regarding them both thoughtfully and letting her dark perpetual gaze find their eyes.

"Well," she finally said. Black curls bounced around her shoulders when she turned to the corpse then back to Abbot, who bit his lip anxiously. "It seems like you both finished the job."

"I-it was me, Vega," Abbot quickly stammered. "I took the kill."

Her glacial tone bit like the wintry mountain wind. "I thought I told everyone to give the girl a chance to prove herself."

"She wasn't taking the shot, ma'am."

"Perhaps she was bettering her aim," Vega replied. Her eyes narrowed dangerously, scanning the wound in the dead man's neck. "Instead of wasting ammunition."

Abbot opened his mouth in response but quickly snapped it shut; his face burned a deep red. A hearty laugh erupted behind them, reveling in the rebuke.

"Jesus, Vega," the man said after his laughter died. "The poor lad's going to piss himself."

The woman smirked. "I know. Abbot, I've taught you better than this."

"Yes ma'am," he said quietly. "Don't make them suffer. Always aim for the head first."

"Good boy," Vega purred, running her fingers through his unkempt blonde hair. "Now, return to me what isn't rightfully yours."

He began protesting, intending to counter her demand with pleas – she knew that. She saw it written on his pallid, perspiring face. Fear. Fear of her disappointment.

He gulped nervously, reaching into his pocket with a tremulous hand and relenting possession of the glimmering, argent chain.

"Help your father carry our gear back to the vehicles," she ordered sternly, quickly pocketing the chain. "Sort out what you want between yourselves."

"Thank you, Vega."

"Michael," she said. The other man scratched his scruffy chin, offering Abbot a hearty slap on the shoulder as he sulked past. "Meet up with Unit B once you've secured everything. Radio in, then head back to the city."

He nodded sharply, but his eyes shimmered ambivalence. He asked, "What about them, Vega?"

"I'll take the girl and show her what true power is." She softened her eyes when she looked at Celeste. Smiling, she replied, "And I have a promise to keep."

The morning chill began to pierce her mittens, stinging the tender flesh on her fingers. Her boots filled with chilly slush as Vega guided her through the wooded landscape. Red blemished the snow and small trees around the makeshift campsite, and soon the smell of death pervaded the crisp, winter air.

A tent lay partially buried in the snow, trampled and stomped into the icy sea of white. A hastily dug fire pit smoldered and spewed clouds of black smoke into the treetops. Bloody corpses were splayed around the campsite like discarded, tattered dolls.

"Where are the others?" Celeste questioned, eyes darting through the trees. *They vanished.*

"They're hunting, little one," Vega replied firmly.

"This isn't like any hunting I've ever done," Celeste whispered to herself, though the crisp breeze carried her complaints.

"Because," she replied harshly, her tone gritty and cold. "I'm the one being hunted."

"I don't understand."

"You will." Snow *crunched* under her boots. "First lesson, girl. Loyalty. Always have it. First for me, then for those who watch your six."

"Ma'am?"

"Pay attention!" Vega hissed, lowering her eyes.

More boots tromped through the snow; four guards had circled through the trees, surrounding them, their weapons raised and glowering at them.

"Vega," one of the men called out, snarling through a frosted scraggy beard. "You should have foreseen this."

"I did." She anchored herself in the clumpy snow, letting the wind whip and snap her coattail behind her waist. The parting black fabric revealed twin pistols holstered to her belt, but her hand fell instead to the ebony blade curving down her thigh. Hooked teeth fringed the edges, resembling a crude saw more than machete. The blade was thick near the end like a cleaver, thinning near the leathery handle. "You speak loudly."

"I made my dislike of you no secret." His stiff, greying hair dangled over his face like jagged icicles. "You made a terrible mistake ordering them to their deaths."

Her voice never wavered, the ferocity raged through each word she spoke. "I did what I had to."

"You ordered their slaughtering!"

"They were soldiers. They knew the risks."

He scoffed and ignored the spillage of tears from his own eyes. "There's always a risk of death, Vega. But what you did was order them to suicide. Without telling them!"

Her fingers thrummed impatiently against the gleaming handle of her blade. "Your point?"

"That ya don't give a *shite* about anyone but yerself," another guard gibed, his heavy accent slurring his words. "That ya'd rather send us off to die than fight and spill blood on yer own."

"Strong words from former captives." Her demeanor remained stony, but her eyes seethed anger. "Do not forget who gave you freedom."

"You got lucky!"

"We're tired of this shit!"

"We don't want yer bloody war, Vega," the accented guard stated flatly. "We don't want yer leadership."

"You don't have a choice," she promised. "Either you're with me or you die."

"Yer not in the position to talk shite."

She licked her cherry lips. "I can't wait to taste your blood."

"You're only going to taste yours."

"Just kill the bitch already."

"I will," said the first guard. He pulled the lever, cocking his rifle. "I want you to know, Vega, this is for my brother and everyone else you sent to death for your foolish revenge. We just wanted to be free but now we're prisoners under another tyrant. You wasted lives so you could secure weapons we didn't even need, land we didn't even claim. Buildings we burned instead of living in! Forcing us to stay in a gutted city running on dwindling power. You're not a leader, you're just another walking corpse." He stared voraciously at Celeste. "I'll make sure your girl is... taken care of."

Vega's fingers tightened around the handle. She eyed the nearest guard, muttering with a smile, "You're first."

Thick snow didn't impede her; she sprang like a pouncing wildcat, unsheathed her ebony blade in a quick, fluid swing, and lodged the weapon's serrated teeth into the accented guard's hand. A scream tore through his throat when his fingers fell into the snow in bloody clumps of flesh. His rifle erupted, firing harmlessly into the white with a loud *crack* echoing through the wooded hills.

She silenced his pain by slipping her fingers around his throat. Blood streaked where her nails pierced his skin. The blade plunged into his gut, thrusting and twisting. His eyes bulged with disbelief. He fell back into the snow, disemboweled, his guts steaming in a sludgy pile by his feet.

"Jesus Christ," the first guard muttered. "Shoot the bitch!"

Celeste reached for her weapon when they all opened fire on Vega.

But she moved like a ghost, as if bullets passed through harmlessly, and veered off somewhere into the undisturbed snow or up into the cerulean sky. Their faces blanched, but their guns bucked and roared continuously. She burst through the cannonade like an angered demon. Black hair flowed behind her like an ensuing shadow. Her blade lunged for the next man's neck; a curtain of blood fountained over his rifle as the barrel burst into Vega's gut. Crimson splattered the man's face. He tumbled into the snow, clutching at his throat in a vain attempt stop the vital fluid from pumping out of the wound like water down a pouring down a ridge.

"To hell with this!" Another guard yelled, his brown hair slickened to his face with sweat. He dropped his rifle, letting it dangle by his side from the strap around his shoulder. A knife then flashed through his hands. His desperate eyes wandered to Celeste. "I'll kill them both!"

Celeste stiffened. She tried to reach for her weapon but she couldn't move, couldn't scream; her lungs refused air. Like a bear fattened off berries, rich vegetation, and salmon, the burly man lumbered through the trees after her, but displayed neither the skill nor prowess that Vega had. He dragged himself through snow like wading through swamp water.

"Girl!" Celeste heard Vega yell through the deafening silence. "Shoot him! Now!"

She couldn't, so Vega did.

The woman reeled, clouding the air around her with fresh powder. Gunshots blared. Blood spurted through the first wound inflicted on the man's leg. He stumbled, but kept charging. Two more bullets bit into his leg and waist, then his chest, rendering his mighty bellow into a gurgled cry. Red misted behind him like a bloodied comet's tail before the last bullet pierced his neck. He finally collapsed by Celeste's boots, limp and lifeless.

"W-what," The last guard stammered, dropping his weapon. It sank into the powdery white. "What the h-hell are you?"

"I told you, Emmerson," Vega replied. She wiped the blood from her face, smearing red along her cheek. "My land, my rule. My *war*."

"Please," he begged, his back slamming against the frozen trunk of a tree. Tears frosted his eyelashes. "I won't question it again. I won't, I swear."

"Problem is, I don't believe you. You're a liar, Emmerson." She nodded to the corpses and blood staining the blinding white landscape. "You promised these people their so called freedom, when all you delivered was their deaths. You scoff at my decisions for ensuring those who inflicted so much pain on our people suffer at *our* hands, yet you line your men up for slaughter like cattle. Any others who also followed your word will receive a similar fate."

"No, please, it was my fault," he continued sniveling. "I take the blame."

"How noble of you," Vega admitted, flicking her blade and splattering the snow with droplets of blood. "But leadership doesn't suit a coward." She stopped in front of him, letting her dark eyes pierce into his like shadowed daggers.

"I'll do anything..." Emmerson whispered with tears brimming and leaving frozen streams down his cheek. "Please... Anything. I don't want to die here."

"How many more?"

"W-what?"

"Careful, Emmerson," she warned. "You get one chance. How many more?"

"Twelve," he confessed quickly. "They're waiting by the fueling stations. We were supposed to meet them after disposing of you."

"What next?"

He grunted, "We'd cut the power, eliminate those under your influence and then liberate the city."

"You placed a lot of faith in a simple plan."

"We just wanted our freedom, Vega. Surely you understand..."

"No," she interjected. Sunlight glinted off the blade as she raised it above her head. "We were already free." He crossed his arms over his face, screaming hoarsely and pleading as the blade descended like a hawk with piercing talons. Emmerson recoiled from the spray of his own blood. Warm slime coated his face and he sagged into the snow, now clutching at his sundered arm. His elbow ended in jagged bone and dangling strands of bloody flesh.

"You... bitch," he wheezed. His head lolled and his eyelids fluttered; slushy blood clumped under his severed arm. "I can't..."

"Enough." Her venomous words riddled his mind with fear. She nudged her bloodied blade under his chin. He stared up the gleaming ebony face of death. "This is what will happen: you will go to your people and tell them what has transpired here, and you will convince them to leave unless they wish to share the same fate as your comrades. This is my land, and if you want no part of this war, you either leave or die by my blade. Now you run, boy." The kiss of her blade left bloody rivulets across his skin as it caressed his neck. "Run and tell them the Devil shall stay on her throne."

His eyes widened, but he closed his gaping mouth and stumbled to his feet. He plodded away weakly, leaving a trail of blotted red in the snow.

"He thought it would be easy," she remarked, musing to herself as Emmerson stumbled and bled into the forest. "He's going to think hell is on his heels for as long as he lives... however short that may be."

"I... I don't understand."

"Blanks. I made sure that was the only ammo they had."

Vega turned, glowering. Celeste sundered her mind trying to digest the deathly scene. "And I told you to shoot him." Celeste shivered, her gaze lost in slushy red. "Take it in, girl," Vega warned, her tone gelid like the mountain winter. "Because the next time you disobey me and fail to prove your loyalty, *this* is what will happen to you."

When Celeste didn't answer, Vega purred sweetly, "Now come along. I made you a promise, remember?"

Sixteen
Bonds

"You'll have to excuse Abbot," Vega offered, finally breaking the brewing silence. She spoke softly and casually, as though Celeste's altercation with the arrogant boy was the sole horror still stained upon her mind.

The engine roared like a hungered beast and the vehicle chomped through the thick snow, misting the windows white and jarring the seat beneath them.

"He's a good kid. Brave, skilled... Though, he lacks manners and common decency." She yanked the steering wheel, jerking the vehicle to a tilt as they slid around a corner. Though Celeste was jostled into disorientation, she could see the city lights in the distance, shimmering like stars through an inky, evening sky.

"He's an asshole," Celeste said without masking her petulance. "That one armed man didn't seem to be a danger to anyone."

Vega admitted flatly, "By all rights, he probably wasn't."

"Then we're no better than murderers."

That garnered her a glare from Vega, her dark eyes flickering like the shadow of a flame. "We are *not* murderers."

Celeste remained undeterred, incapable of satiating the suspicion pooling in her thoughts. "We could have saved him."

"Absolutely not." A curt response, to which Celeste began to protest. "You witnessed it. The man was bare assed and freezing in the snow.

Not only that, but he was dying from blood loss as well as exposure. His camp fared no better. There were other bodies, frozen solid. Whomever the man had been, his mind had long receded to a primal survival state. But, for whatever foolish reason, he didn't eat the departed."

"Love," Celeste blurted out, unable to contain the spilling words. "He loved his family too much to sully their corpses."

Vega grimaced, as though Celeste's words were a taste of fouling meat in her mouth. "And it made him *weak*. The humane decision was to ease his suffering with a bullet."

"Then why was I different?"

"There are more than just monsters living in this world now, Celeste," Vega explained after a moment's hesitation. "There are those who seek to keep these lands shrouded in darkness. Well, it's my duty to bring light to this world again. We're at war, girl. A seemingly endless battle. Monsters, and the bastards that created them."

"Created?" Celeste asked, her interest piqued.

"Some would see this virus weaponized still. An unstoppable army and the power one could wield with it, to reshape the world to one's liking... A formidable temptress to say the least."

"I don't see how that involves saving my life."

"Like I said, we're at war. I need all the soldiers I can get."

Celeste shrugged. "I already told you, I've never killed before." The lie tasted bitter on her tongue.

"We both know that isn't true. You have blood staining your soul, little one." Vega's nebulous eyes momentarily glimmered like the dazzling city lights. "Death shadows your every step. I know a killer when I see one." Celeste tore herself from Vega's abyssal gaze. "I also know remorse. It's time to forgive yourself, Caylee."

What? "Who's Caylee?"

A moment passed before Vega's lips twitched into a smile. "Apologies. My former second-in-command, I'm used to traveling with her on scouting missions."

"Former?" Celeste dared to venture, but was instead met with stark silence.

The vehicle squealed, sliding to a stop near the barred entrance to the city. Wired mesh layered the front of the gate, laced with barbed wire along the top. Behind the metal stood what appeared to be a solid wall – however, it was a series of wooden frames and stone slabs erected along the perimeter of the city limits. The razor-wire discouraged any sort of climbing, and as far as Celeste saw, there were no entrances or exits other than the two designated gates at either end of the city.

Regularly patrolled as well, she mused quietly, watching Vega nod at the two armed guards by the wired gate. *At least we're somewhat safe.*

For now.

"You should feel safe here," Vega muttered, watching Celeste's gaze trail along the fence while they drove through the gate. Celeste tried not to betray her unease through a steeled demeanor as a chill danced down her spine.

Get out of my head.

"You're not a prisoner here. There's no need to plot your escape."

"You've fortified this city well," remarked Celeste. "Seems like it could withstand a war."

The woman chuckled quietly, smiling sweetly, "It already has."

The first few streets were barren, with only a few hollowed or burned out structures and soldiers on duty, clad in black with thick vests and weapons extending further than their arms. Most buildings had been plundered for anything useful, until only skeletal metal frames and rotting floors remained. Towers were found behind the fence and between various gutted structures, looming like giant trees over the city and its outskirts. The closer they drove to the heart of the city, the livelier it became. Large buildings and even houses were no longer decayed and scorned; most seemed newly repaired or freshly painted the previous season, with shoveled driveways and intact vehicles. Windows were lit and dazzling, promising warmth and comfort to those who ventured inside. Fire burned in barrels along each corner, flooding the streets with an eerie glow. People bustled along the frozen sidewalks, and vendors were tending to their counters. An array of goods piled behind hagglers, and even through the engine's steady rumble, their voices boomed as they shouted, laughed, and mingled together. There were drunken guards with bottles raised above their heads, who stumbled, cursed, and sloshed liquor up their sleeves.

No younger people, though... no children.

Vega steered through the crowded street, and slowly crept toward a building that resembled a mountain reaching into the skyline more than a manmade structure. Metal bars twined over the copious curtained windows, but the drawn shades still emitted faint light. The brick layering the exterior of the building was dark as tanned leather. They drove past the support pillars and through the darkened opening of the building's basement.

Whytecliff Hospital. Finally.

Dimming lights did little to brighten the drab cement dwelling. Vehicles were parked and abandoned with their doors ajar, bloody footprints trailing to the sealed doors across the lot.

"This way." Her silky voice bounced off the cement walls. "This is a vulnerable place," she continued, raising her voice to smother her echoed footsteps. There was no discernable way to open the doors; no handles, latches, or even hinges. "A hospital and talented doctors can be the difference between keeping soldiers and losing them." There was only a small device latched to the ceiling. A lens glared back at them, humming, spinning into focus. Vega jutted her chin and stared into the camera. At the slight nod of her head, the sealed doors slid open.

"Follow me."

The doors closed behind them. Vega leaned against the railing, letting Celeste slake her curiosity from the selection of buttons along the panel. It was dizzyingly bright. Lights glared against the white tiled floor. Vega smirked, then pressed her thumb against one of the middle buttons.

"I almost forgot," Vega said, digging into her coat pocket. With the silver necklace now coiled around her fingers, she handed it to Celeste. "Something to trade with, my dear."

Celeste shook her head. "Thanks, but no. I didn't take the shot or loot the body. It would only give Abbot more of an excuse to dislike me."

Vega smiled, but shook her head. "Prideful girl, but foolish nonetheless. Still... admirable."

"You know, I always knew what an elevator was," Celeste said, weary of the silence growing between them. The floor jostled abruptly, and her chest seemingly swarmed with butterflies. "I always knew what it meant. The word, I mean. But I could never recall what one looked like. I'm sure I've been in one before... well, when the world was normal." She had to smile. It was almost foreign. "It feels weird."

"I prefer the stairs," Vega replied dully. "But this is the only way in and out of the hospital."

"There are a *lot* of lights on."

That earned her a grin. "We have a *big* generator," she replied, sarcasm dripping from her tone. "We fixed the dam years ago. Supplies more than half the city with power. It took a long while to reconnect most of it, and many street posts are either completely broken, or gone altogether. We salvaged what we could. It ended up being quite a bit."

"It's amazing," she replied, genuinely awed. Too many years she'd spent with simplistic supplies, and though she longed for those days in the mountains, the city filled her with a sense of wonder she couldn't easily dismiss. Regardless of whatever shadows lurked in its depths. "It truly is."

When the elevator jerked to a halt and the doors eased open, Vega led her into the corridor. Maps of the building's interior were strewn across the walls, along with bulletin boards and various coded warnings she'd never seen before. Benches and chairs leaned against the wall but the blood staining the floor like splattered red paint rendered any comfort into unease. Lights *hummed* and *buzzed,* some blinked out into darkness, only to flicker brightly a moment later.

Posted to the side of the elevator, a guard sat with his elbows propped against the table, his hands lazily placed atop a mounted rifle. The weapon sat perched on a swivel with ammunition cartridges piled near it; other guns and knives were scattered across the table as well.

"Ma'am," the soldier grunted before turning to Celeste. The barrel of his gun followed his hardened gaze. "Weapons on the table, miss."

With a quick nod from Vega, Celeste unstrapped her machete and pulled the revolver from its holster. He raised his eyebrow curiously, but after her insistence that she was no longer armed, he waved them along.

"Security reasons." Vega gestured down the corridor. "Just a little further."

They passed gurneys with rumpled white sheets, streaked and blotted with dark blemishes, and other dimly lit corridors stretching further into the hospital. Few doors were ajar, but she could only glimpse curtains or empty beds, along with multiple machines she'd never seen before. Some *hummed* noisily as she passed, others *dinged* with every passing moment.

"Room 217." Vega curled her blood-colored lips into a smile. "She's expecting you."

The room was as dreary as the rest of the hospital; dimmed lights and drab paint, machines crowding every corner, and black wires snaking along the walls. Yet, like sunlight peeking from behind clouds and shining through an aphotic haze, Melina's smile brightened the entire room with its radiance.

"Celeste!"

With a grin plastered on her face, Celeste rushed to the bedside, embracing her old friend.

"You've recovered nicely!" She peeled herself away from comforting warmth. "You look amazing!"

Green eyes dazzling, another smile inched across Melina's freckled face. "So do you!" Beside her bed, a shadowed blur growled and nipped at Celeste's hand. "Someone else has missed you more than I have."

"Aurous!" Celeste buried herself in the wolf's black fur while he slobbered his excitement on her neck and sweater. "I'm glad you're both okay." He whined as she squeezed, and tears stung her eyes when she prodded his bandaged wounds. *He's still so hurt.*

"I'm thankful you are," Melina whispered, a trickle of fear in her tone. "They wouldn't tell me anything about you, or if you were coming to see me. Until..." Her green eyes shifted to the doorway, where Vega positioned herself with her hands placed on her hips, and her lips pursed. "Well, until *she* told me this morning."

"Vega," Celeste responded. "She's the leader of this place."

"What is this place, exactly?"

"A fortified city. The one the military used to regain control of these lands."

"So, they're military?"

Interjecting quickly, Vega replied, "Yes, we are." An empty smile, then, "Welcome to Whytecliff City."

Melina's own smile had long faded. Rekindled anger burned in her eyes as she asked bluntly, "Where were you when our city fell to the infected?"

"Melina..." Celeste began.

"Where were you when the survivors barricaded themselves inside their own walls because they were hunted by monster and man alike?" Venom seethed from her words. Aurous whimpered, nudging her hand with his snout until she snatched it away, balling them into fists. "Tell me!"

A terrible silence crept between them until Celeste said, "We were starving and freezing, and I couldn't get another fire started." She swallowed past the lump forming in her throat. *Lies.* "We were about to die from exposure... Vega came along and took us in. If it hadn't been for her, we would have died. She saved our lives."

"Not soon enough," came Melina's bitter response.

"Melina!"

"Let the girl speak," Vega said, steeling her tone. "I owe that much, at the very least."

Melina sounded resentful, fury masking her brittle words. But her lip trembled and her voice wavered when she demanded again, "I want you to tell me."

Vega's eyes glimmered. "As you wish, little one," she conceded. "There is a prison within these city walls, housing criminals awaiting execution – murderers, bandits, raiders – anybody deemed a threat to civilian life. There was a coordinated breakout and they hit us hard. They overtook the prison within hours, securing weapons and gear before beginning a full frontal assault within the city. It took all the manpower we had to retake these buildings and not let it all burn to the ground. The soldiers we could once spare to patrol the highways and neighboring towns were no longer expendable." She shot a dangerous look at Celeste. "This is why we kill without mercy, now." Turning back to Melina, she said, "We made a difficult decision, but maintaining control of this city was top priority. For that you have my most sincere apologies, but not my regret."

"That's where Caden escaped from," Celeste whispered, shuddering and averting her eyes. Aurous lolled his tongue at her.

"Yes," Vega agreed. "The man you described was one of the criminals meant for execution."

"Then it's a good thing he's dead," Melina said. Her voice softened but hatred still flared throughout her words. "Nobody could survive an encounter with that monster."

Vega ignored the nervous glance from Celeste. "A monster killed by a monster." Her blood-colored lips twitched. "How fitting of an end." That seemed to coax a small smirk from the redhead.

"I'd like a moment with her, please," Celeste said softly, casting her eyes to the glossy linoleum floor.

"Of course," Vega responded. "I'll wait outside."

When the echo of her footsteps faded, Celeste dared to meet Melina's bright green eyes.

"Are they feeding you well?" She finally asked, unsure of what else to say.

Melina shrugged. "Potato soup. A few vegetables. Nothing special, but nothing to complain about. Though, I wish I could have a little more."

No use making her worry. Since they'd arrived at Whytecliff, Vega informed Celeste of how their society worked. Trade would yield what she wanted, and so would hunting and farming. Stealing was strictly forbidden, and though you would be fed rations every evening, there would be no more than a pittance unless properly earned. *Abbot made sure he had enough to trade for meals, ammunition and whatever else that weasel could want,* she thought bitterly. *I've been making sure a portion of my rations are given to Melina and Aurous. Maybe I should have taken that necklace...*

"I'll see what I can get for you," she finally answered. Offering her friend another smile, Melina's eyes twinkled and returned the warmth.

"Thank you."

Aurous meekly pawed at her leg. "I'll get something for you as well," Celeste said, tousling the wolf's fur.

"I think he's been going a little crazy," Melina said, chuckling lightly. "Unable to move much, being cooped up in here with me all day."

"He probably won't to leave your side until you're better."

"I appreciate it. Truly, I do." A small sigh escaped her chapped lips. "But they won't even allow me to take Aurous outside of this building and let him pee. Some nurse comes in and takes him outside every few hours. She says I shouldn't be exerting myself while I'm healing but... I don't know..." She lowered her voice into a whisper. "Are we okay here?"

"I think so." *I hope so.* Masking the fear dwelling in her heart, she replied firmly, "I'll make sure we are. If not, I'll get us out of this city. Safely."

"I know. It's just the barred window isn't the same, I'd like to feel the fresh air and wind. No matter how chilly it is outside."

Celeste couldn't stop smiling. Her chest blossomed warmth. "I'll see if I can arrange something."

"Thanks again."

"Of course," Celeste responded, a bit too quickly. She placed her hand on Melina's, but averted her gaze when her face burned red. "I have to go, but I'll be back to see you both later. I'll be sure to bring some food."

It was difficult saying goodbye, and she had to fight past the tears welling in her eyes as she embraced them both and closed the door behind her. Her heart panged for Aurous, and guilt settled in her belly like an arrow shaft buried deep in her flesh. *I should be taking care of him, of Melina. They're hurt because of me.*

Vega leaned against the wall, waiting with her shadowed eyes to the floor.

"You lied." It was all she said, lifting her head slightly to peer through black curls.

"I told her what was necessary."

"She certainly seemed strong enough to handle the truth."

Celeste lowered her voice, but hardened her words. "She would only worry about what he might have done to me, or that if he stalked us along the highway for days to finish us off, he might not truly be dead but only lurking in the shadows. Waiting to taste our blood. No, it would only cause her more harm than it would good. She *doesn't* need that."

"Are you sure you're trying to protect her?" A smirk spread across Vega's tanned complexion. "Or perhaps convince yourself it never occurred?"

Through gritted teeth, Celeste muttered, "Whatever the reason, he's dead. It's over."

"You're right, it is. Though, through no action of your own. Now, I assume you'll be able to find your way back to your quarters?"

Pride stinging, she replied, "I think I know where it is."

"Good. Go home and change out of those dreadful clothes. New ones will be provided for you in your room soon. I expect you to join us for dinner tonight. Tomorrow's a big day."

"Yes, ma'am."

Vega smiled darkly. "Good girl. Now if you'll excuse me."

Celeste watched the woman ghost down the corridor. Her hips swayed, her long legs nearly intertwining with each elegant step. Vega turned her head once more before rounding the corner, and smiled again.

So much for my relaxing evening alone. She sighed, already weary of the day, and turned to walk back to the elevator.

A malodorous scent flooded her nostrils. She nearly gagged as she covered her mouth, wincing and wrinkling her nose in disgust. *Smells like rotting flesh.* She almost retched. *Worse than rotting flesh.* Further down from Melina's room, she glimpsed a shadow at far end of an adjacent corridor. She glanced back to the elevator, but the guard had his head turned, distracted. She slipped down the other hallway, muffling her footsteps and pressing her body flat against the wall. She passed other rooms, each with closed doors and curtained windows. The smell became stronger and more pungent the deeper she ventured. Her boot squealed as it slid through some sort of muck pooled across the floor.

Blood?

"Just what the hell do you think you're doing down here?"

She gasped, clasping her hand on her mouth to stifle the brewing scream. Her heart lurched inside her chest. "Damn it, Abbot! You scared the crap out of me!"

"Good," he sneered. "You don't need to be here." His oily skin glistened under the pale light. He rolled a cigarette between his fingers, the stale stench of smoke exuding from his mouth while he spoke. "Stop poking your nose where it doesn't belong. Screw off."

She narrowed her eyes. Her heart quickened, thundering in her ears as her blood boiled in anger. She turned away, mostly to stop herself from pelting him with as many fists as she could throw. His mocking laughter trailed her retreat back down the corridor, taunting her as he unlatched the door and slammed it behind him. She glanced back once he was gone, and only then did she see it; red smeared across the walls and bloody handprints stained to the floor. Even her boots were soaked in its filth.

What the hell is going on here?

Seventeen

Ghosts

The city seemed alive; a nauseous swirl of smoke, sweat, animal entrails, meat and liquor. Boisterous crowds gathered, raising glasses full of drink. Others cheered and brayed, strolling past on the slick sidewalks. Wisps of snow trailed the armored vehicles advancing further into the city, their barred and tinted windows shadowing the operators inside.

I've never seen so many people before. Celeste eyed the streets with a sense of wonderment. She'd spent the first few weeks recuperating from her wounds, proceeding directly to training and scouting afterward. Only now did she have a chance to satiate the brewing curiosity, to devour the city sights with wide, dazzled eyes. She was in awe; faces blurred past, and a cacophonous roar of voices flooded her ears.

Father, what would you have thought of all this?

A resentful whisper hissed through the clamor, chilling her heart. "I would have thought my daughter to have more sense than to get me killed."

Chilly air frosted her lungs when she gasped quickly. "No," she whispered. Her eyes darted through the crowd, but her father remained hidden. *He's not really here.* "I wanted to see the world, but not if it meant leaving you behind."

"But this is what you wished for, is it not?" Demanded the disembodied voice. "This is what you wanted!"

"No!" She yelled her response, balling her fists. "I didn't want this! I didn't ask for this!"

When she opened her eyes, she found puzzled glances and peculiar whispers, all directed toward her. She stood, fists trembling and eyes shimmering, staring through a sea of faces she couldn't recognize.

I'm losing it.

"I know what ya want, miss," a low, husky voice rumbled through the murmuring of the crowd. She turned, hand falling to her holstered revolver. A grubby, thick man stood behind a large wooden table. A tattered blue tarp whipped and snapped against the winter wind above him, and fallen snow frosted the glass on the table's surface and peppered the man's dingy facial hair. He scratched at his cheek with a finger poking through the split in his glove, picking his reddening skin with filthy nails. His mouth parted in a greedy grin as his piggish little eyes trailed down her legs.

"What?" She asked stupidly. Her face burned with embarrassment. "Excuse me?"

"Got what ya need right here," he muttered with a slur. He wiggled his fat sausage fingers over the glass on his table. "Fer trade, of course. A beautiful little creature such as yerself needs a fine blade to match."

She nudged the machete handle on her belt, replying slyly, "I already have a fine blade."

"Fine? That wretched ol' thing?" He even snorted like a pig when he chuckled. "That slab of rust couldn't slice through melted cheese."

"It slices *fine.*"

Grinning, his cheek bulged. "Sentimental heirloom, I presume?" At her stony stare, he clasped his hand and continued babbling, "I understand completely, miss. Nothing like a good ol' trusted blade by yer side. Seen its fair share of entrails, has it? Carved into a few too many unlucky basterds?" His ballooning neck rippled as he nodded his head. "Yes, yes, a good blade becomes family, I'm well aware of the bond one can forge with steel."

"It was my father's," she blurted out quickly, though her skin prickled with fear as though her words may summon his rapacious spirit.

"Ah, yes, a family treasure," he wheezed. "Yer a good girl fer keeping it! But yer pa wouldn't want ya stuck with a dull blade when ya need to cut something."

"I don't have much to trade," Celeste insisted.

"Empty yer pockets and lemme see what ya have."

He scoffed at her revolver, remarking its age and worn handle, but praising the lengths she'd gone to care for it. A bracelet twined with strands of rope he dismissed with a wave of his hand. Bullets, he had plenty. The distinguishing rings her mother once adorned were worthless in his beady eyes. In spite of the chill, sweat gathered along his brow until droplets spattered down his round cheeks. Close to shooing her away in attempts to attract customers who perhaps had something of value to trade, he glimpsed it.

"What's that lil gem?" He asked, smudging the glass with his fat fingers. He snatched the ring before she grabbed it off the table. He held it close to his eye, inspecting the gleaming emerald meticulously. "Interesting!"

"That's not for trade," Celeste said adamantly.

He whistled his disbelief. "Are ya certain, lil one? This here is one rare rock."

"Rock?"

"Diamond," he replied with a shrug. "Clarity's nice, though I'd need my specs to make sure of its cut..."

"As I said." Celeste narrowed her eyes. "It's not for trade."

He gaped at her for a moment, a fat fish out of water, then reluctantly plopped the ring back into her outstretched hand. Firelight glared off the green diamond as she slipped its gold band around her finger. The pudgy man grunted his disapproval.

"I'd give ya any weapon in my shop," he offered, his voracious gaze on her fingers and sweat setting an oily path down his face. "Anything yer able to carry."

"I can't," she said, turning away and vanishing back into the crowd. "Sorry!"

She shivered, discontented with the winter's frigid lashes. She pulled her coat closer as the wind picked up, spinning the ring around her finger with her thumb.

Mother.

A sweet fragrance drifted through the chilly wind, coiling around her senses and blossoming through her mind.

Flowers?

She looked up, encompassed by the shroud of black sulking between two buildings. She'd wandered far from the sidewalk, trudged through undisturbed snow, and now stood with strands of her carmine hair whipping against her face, staring into the abyssal night. Bright eyes glared back at her, the same glimmer she'd seen countless times in her dreams.

"Mother," she whispered breathlessly.

"Selfish girl," came the sinister response, hissing like an agitated snake. "Always thinking of yourself."

"That's not true," she said, shaking her head with disbelief. Part of her burned to call out, to scream that her mother would *never* say anything to hurt her – but somewhere, deep inside the back of her mind, she knew the voice spoke truth. *If I hadn't been so persistent about leaving, he might still be alive.* The thought pierced her lamenting heart. She quickly stepped back, nearly slipping through the snow. Strands of darkness slithered and swirled around her. She couldn't help but scream.

She sucked in an icy mouthful of air. Her heart thundered and pumped fear through her veins. She yelped with fright a second time after nudging a passerby with her shoulder. Stuttering her apologies, she found a nauseating blur of faces staring back at her. There must have been hundreds of them.

"That's her isn't it, the one they found frozen on the highway?"

"I heard they found her with a pack of wolves, acting just like a beast herself."

"No, she was fighting a pack of wolves when she was rescued."

"That's stupid. She was just a wanderer."

"Abbot said she was snarling like a wounded wolf when they took her in, half-dead and frozen."

"Why keep her alive then?"

"I heard she's Vega's new pet."

"Another?"

"Yeah, you know that woman's lost her..."

"Shut up! Don't bad mouth the queen, she'll have yer head."

It was too much; too many voices, too many thoughts flooding her battered mind. She pressed her palms against both ears, clenched her eyes to halt the bursting tears, and didn't stop running until the murmuring crowd and populous streets were far behind.

By the time she reached her new dwelling, her lungs burned in spite of each chilling breath, and the muscles in her legs throbbed fiercely. Reaching the front gate, she was stopped far from the barricaded doors of the building.

It was large, quite possibly a former apartment complex that had been gutted and armored. Debris littered the property surrounding it; remnants of demolished walls and supplies to continue bracing the fenced gate. There were more guards on duty than she cared to count. Some partially obscured by the darkness, ghosting along the edges of firelight with their eyes darting through the darkness, others standing idly by the gate, their weapons drawn as she approached with her hands in plain sight. Faint light glowed from the windows of the building, but hers remained shrouded in darkness.

Home, sweet... home.

"Evening, Celeste. Bit chilly tonight," one of the guards remarked pleasently, lowering his rifle at her approach. "You're home a little late this evening."

"Hello, Jeremy," she replied, offering a weak smile. Though weary, she was still pleased with his genial greeting. "No more so than I'm used to."

She pulled the revolver from its holster and emptied the bullets from the chamber. They rattled in her palm, then she handed them to Jeremy. His took the handful of metal casings, a smile curving up his smooth, tanned skin. She continued, "Visiting the hospital. The walk home took a little longer than I thought it would."

"Right," Jeremy said with a nod. "How is your friend?"

"Friends," she corrected, wiggling a finger at him. "And they're doing fine. No, I still won't introduce you to her."

"She sounds like a peach," he said, grinning stupidly. "If she's anything like you, I enjoy her already. Any more ammo I should know about?"

"You know that's the only gun I have, Jeremy."

"Don't mean that's the only bullets you have."

She rolled her eyes and patted her jeans, replying sarcastically, "You can come search me if you like."

"Tempting," he mused, winking at her. "But I'm prone to believe a pretty face. Go on, enjoy your evening, beautiful."

"Don't work too hard, Jeremy." She grinned, holstering her revolver and ducking through the gate.

The walls of the building, interior and exterior, were fortified and braced with enough steel to withstand any firepower short of a large-scale detonation. The windows were the only weakened attribute to the complex, but even they were barred on either side, layered with enough razor-wire to diminish visibility. The inside corridors remained cold and unwelcoming, with dimming lights and barred doors. There were two rooms at the end of the hall on the bottom floor, the kitchen and the pantry. Only those close to Vega resided within the complex, and seemed to enjoy a higher luxury than others crowding the streets and warming themselves in smaller dwellings. *As if I needed another reason to be disliked.* Vega had insisted she sleep near her rooms, and even gave her the chamber adjacent to hers. Besides Abbot's blatant display of jealousy, temperament from the others fared from mild, puzzled glances, to scornful mutters after Vega took her in.

They call me weak. Her thoughts were like bitter bile fouling her mind. *Maybe I am.* Ascending the stairwell slowly, her disgruntled laugh resounded with her footsteps.

Maybe I should have died on that highway. I certainly deserved worse.

Melina. Hope glimmered from that thought. *Aurous. They needed me.* She smiled. *They still do.*

Just like I need them.

In contrast to the dismal tomblike appearance of the complex, the rooms were lustrous and bursting with beauty. Azure imbued the walls that were nearly covered with framed paintings of landscapes she'd never seen before; sandy ledges with an endless stretch of sea, forests with bright colored plants, and trees with animals she'd only heard of in stories, and other wondrous swirls of colors she craved to reach out and feel. Where her cabin felt sparse and quaint, her new abode was exquisitely furnished, adjourned with chairs and cushions almost too plump and perfect to sit on. Elegant patterns had been stitched into every fabric surface. Tassel trim lined the edges of her bedding sheets, and the blankets were smooth as silk. Lamps with leather shades emitted a calming glow, but a chill had settled in the room from hours of disuse.

I could crawl under the blankets, she thought, already tempted by her bed's promised warmth. *Sleep until someone wakes me to eat.* She grumbled quietly, slipping out of her boots and crossing the coarse carpet. She sighed, nearing the edge of her bed. *Or I can refrain from my endless nightmares.*

Solvent, reused oil, a toothbrush with twisted bristles, a silky cloth, and a few bore rods; her cleaning supplies were dwindling, the last remnants of one of her only trades now scattered across the table. *I miss that canteen. I hope Michael is enjoying it at least.* She sighed wearily, cursing her welling pride for refusing the necklace. *It should have been mine. Abbot's just a bastard.* Although anger ceased spilling through her mind like a flooding river of hate, the whisper in the back of her mind strengthened. *I couldn't do it... I couldn't kill him.* She slammed her fist down, rattling the table. *I wanted to help him. I'm sick of all this blood.*

Pieces of her revolver were strewn across the table. Her hands trembled until she slammed them against the surface again. She knew better than to attempt even the most mundane of chores in her agitated state. There she differed from her father; where he would throw himself into thoughtless tasks and stew in his anger, her mind was unable to cope with an immeasurable deluge of rage. Something inside begged her to quench her thirst, to satiate the need for blood...

No!

She shot up, toppling the chair. It tumbled to the carpet, the back end crashing against the wall, scuffing the dark paint. She pulled her sweater off, tossing it on the table in a crumpled heap with her gloves. She dropped, her palms flat and face inches from the floor.

I'm better than that.

Pushing, she straightened her arms, then abruptly dropped back to the floor.

I don't need to hold on to this hate.

Her muscles tingled, burning with more exertion. Her fingers clawed into the carpet, a mess of scarred skin and dark, mangled flesh. They were stiff and sore, but she learned to work through the pain. She kept going, gasping for breath and losing count of her movements. Sweat slickened her face.

I'm not a killer. I'm not a killer. I'm not a killer!

"Yes you are," drawled an accusing voice. She clenched her eyes shut, gritted her teeth, and kept to her routine.

Ignore it. Not real. Not real.

"If you had never left the mountains," the voice continued. "I could *still* be alive."

She cried out, her muscles stiff as stone. She sat, catching her breath and staring into the face of her demons. Narrowed eyes glared back at her, the boy's dark skin melting into the shadows shrouding behind him.

Leo...

"You took her away from me," he snarled. A rivulet of red trickled from the bullet wound in his forehead. "You destroyed everything she's ever loved!"

"I didn't mean to!"

"That's always your excuse, isn't it?" He barked back, blood staining his teeth red. "You helped that monster, Caden. You're no better than *him*."

"I'm not like him!"

"You have the same soul," whispered Kayla, thrumming her skeletal fingers on the hilt of the knife. The blade was still buried deep inside her neck. "Putrid and black, twisted in the bowels of hell."

"She's right," the woman with the cross necklace accused, clutching her daughter's bloody teddy bear in her arms. "You could have helped people. Instead, you chose to let us all suffer!"

"No," Celeste pleaded, desperate to shut the voices out. "I didn't want to hurt anyone!"

"*A soul as black as coal*," Her mother sang, voice riddled with disgust. "*Try as she might, she'll never be whole.*"

"No..."

"You should have died on the highway," her father growled. "Died alongside that monster."

"One in the same," Leo whispered.

Celeste yelled madly, "I'm not like him!"

Her heart froze from the chill crawling through her. "Oh," came another voice, raspy and voracious. "But ya *are* like me."

Caden's torn face blurred into focus through the shadows behind Leo, his tongue slathering his lips in bloody saliva. "*Princess.*" Bony fingers reached for her, eager to worm across her warm flesh.

"No!" She screamed, reaching for her sheathed machete. Confronting the ghosts, she raised her blade, only to find a familiar face. Her heart raced, and her mind lost control of the torrent of panicked thoughts.

Blood, she felt a part of her mind whisper. *Spill blood.* Her fingers tightened around the weapon's handle.

"Whoa, baby doll, calm down," Michael reasoned, easing both armfuls of bunched fabric onto the bedside. He slowly raised his hands, saying gently, "You're okay, Celeste. It's just us."

"I told you she was crazy!" Abbot yelled, his own blade unsheathed as well. He was glaring at her, lips curled in disgust. "We should'a put a bullet in her already."

Celeste lowered her blade. "I'm... Michael, I'm sorry."

The older man shook his head, offering a warm smile. He gestured to the clothes on the bed. "Don't worry yourself. No harm, no foul, right? Vega wants you dressed appropriately for dinner tonight. It is a feast before our soldiers march to reclaim fallen cities tomorrow."

Celeste barely heard him. "Right," she whispered in response, dropping the machete to the carpet.

"Aw, hell," Abbot cursed, sheathing his blade. "Vega can *keep* her little pet project then."

Michael assailed the boy with a hard look. "Enough, Abbot." He turned back to Celeste, asking quietly, "Do you recall where the dining hall is?"

"Yes," she replied. Michael nodded and nudged Abbot, who glared, then slunk through the doors. Michael eased the doors shut behind them.

Her hands wouldn't stop shaking. She intertwined her fingers, bracing against her chilling heart.

What the hell is wrong with me?

She frowned. The clothing on her bed was made of material she'd never felt before. It was smooth, not as fine as silk, soft as bunched cotton. The top was pearly white, with buttons twinkling under the lights, and designs carving down the dress in black stitching. The bottom was tufted, swirls of dark like a starless night with gold lace on the fringes.

A dress.

"I've never worn a dress before," she blurted out to herself.

Last time I even saw one was on mother... Or was it? Her memories blurred together until she forced them beneath her thoughts. *If only you could see how ridiculous this thing looks on me...* She turned in the mirror, twirling the dress around her pallid legs.

Ugh... Dark spots blotted her skin. *Of course my legs are bruised.*

"What does one even wear with a dress?" She mused, wiggling her toes into the shaggy carpet. "Boots? Shoes?" Her snow boots were at least two sizes larger than her feet, and appeared awkward protruding from the bottom of her dress like clown attire. The tip of her sneakers poked through the lace as well, looking ragged, torn, and filthy compared to the elegance of her dress.

"Matter of fact," she mumbled, bunching a handful of hair in her fist. It was like brittle straw jabbing her palm. "What should I do with this rat's nest?"

After careful deliberation, she pulled her dark hair into a tail and smoothed her frayed bangs. She hauled on her snow boots, unwilling to catch more of a chill than she already had. She stared at her reflection for a moment. Her father's eyes peered back at her, a dark, chalky brown.

She smiled.

As she closed the doors to her room, she glanced further down the corridor, unease ballooning through her thoughts. *Pet project...* Abbot's infuriated words bounced around her skull. *What did he mean by that?* The doors located at the end of the corridor seemed to be screaming to her, calling and begging to her flaming curiosity. *Survival, right?* The dark part of her whispered. She found herself moments from slipping her scarred fingers around the handles.

What am I doing?

Locked. "That's that," she muttered, defeated.

No.

She hesitated, but crouched and reached into her boot instead.

I'm sure it's still here... Ah!

She wormed her finger through a slit in the lining of her boot, fishing out two small metal pins twined together with thread. *Hairclips,* she thought with a cocky grin plastered on her face. *Glad I kept them.* She unthreaded them, pulling one open and bending the edge slightly. She twisted the other end into a makeshift handle, enough for her index finger and thumb to grip. She left the other hairclip closed, but still bent one end.

It's been awhile.

She peered into the lock; dirty, old and probably rusted, but nearly identical to the model her father forced her to learn with. *Thanks, dad.* She slid the open hairclip between her teeth, then carefully placed the second into the lock. Applying slight pressure, she nudged the angled end of the other metal pick inside the lock as well.

Patience. Her father's words echoed through her mind. The first pin inside the lock was loose, so she pushed the metal pick further, pushing the second pin gently.

Stuck!

Smiling, she eased the pin up with her lock-pick until it *clicked* into place. Dampening her celebratory excitement, it took several moments longer than she'd hoped to locate the second stuck pin. Her hands were trembling, jolted from nerves. As her fingers numbed, the last pin *clicked* and the lock turned quickly.

She stepped into Vega's chambers.

It reeked of liquor, and a fragrance she couldn't name, but recognized from her father's clothing years ago. Coats, boots, and leggings were disheveled and tossed carelessly around the room. Most were uniforms or material with dark blots patterned into the fabric. Unkempt sheets crumpled along the bed, musty and stained, seemingly undisturbed.

I've only seen her here occasionally, she remembered. *And never at night.*

Faint light peeked through the wired mesh around the window. More uniforms lined the closet; checkered and stripped shirts with long sleeves and countless buttons. Suits, ties, and sleek, black pants.

These aren't women's clothing.

Searching through the drawers and bedside, she found a pile of women's clothing stuffed under the sheets. Though, what she glimpsed on the countertop chilled the blood in her veins.

Beside the half-emptied bottle of liquor, a stack of old papers nestled neatly inside a brown folder. Slipping past the cover was a single document. Eyes widened, she pulled the paper loose and read:

WHYTECLIFF HOSPITAL
Experiment 439-12
Subject: Female
Age: 15
Strain: MSV–M46
Tests: Unable to fully mutate host or control;
Resulting in lack of control, damaged specimen.
Recommend immediate elimination.

Like the depths of haunted darkness, a ghost stared back at her through the photograph clipped to the paper. Her heart pumped icy shards, her mind drowning in a torrent of fear. One of the figures in the photograph resembled Vega, though she appeared younger. The surface was faded, but she discerned smooth, dark skin and a smile not yet beset with wrinkles. Her eyes even seemed brighter, not a deluge of darkness.

But it was the girl beside Vega that seized her gaze. Scarlett hair fell over her face in tousled curls, her eyes a deep shade of brown. Her lips pursed, almost pouting with her arms crossed over her chest. A black dress flowed around the girl like a stormy cloud.

The same dress as mine...

It's like I'm staring at my own reflection. She flipped the photo between her fingers. Scrawled with pen on the back, '*My loving daughter, Caylee*' along with the year '08.

With a tremulous voice, she whispered dolefully, "I have to get us the hell out of here."

"I'm glad ya changed yer mind, miss. But I'd prefer ya choose quick-ly."

She barely heard. The noisy drum of her heart beat in her ears dispelled his muttered words, but the metal glinting from the firelight captivated her attention. She pressed her fingers against the table, peering inquisitively until the fat man irritably told her to *stop* smudging the glass. She then jabbed her finger at one of the blades.

"Let me see that one," she finally said. The man rubbed his hands together, chasing the chill from his skin. He stood still another moment, focusing his piggish eyes on her.

"Don't try anything funny."

"Wouldn't dream of it," she replied.

He slid the glass case open with his pudgy fingers and selected one of the knives. She took it from his meaty grasp. The sheath was smooth, made of fine leather, and laced tightly along the edges with stringed wire. *Homemade,* she thought, tracing a gloved finger across the wooden handle. Dappled brown and gold plated. *Luxurious, but not much for grip.* She eyed the vendor, shaking her head slowly.

The man's neck wobbled like a rippling pond as he cleared his throat and informed her, "That's a fine blade. Pretty enough for a princess."

"I'm neither a *princess,*" she responded tartly, shoving the sheathed blade back into his clutches. "Nor in the need of something *pretty.*"

Princess, she seethed inwardly. *I'm really getting sick of that.*

"Aye, miss, but all blades have a sense of beauty," he grumbled back. "This one makes a lethal companion." He handed her another, wrapped in soiled rags instead of a sheath. "Elegance, balance, and makes one helluva belt piece."

"It's nice," she admitted reluctantly. It bore a wooden handle as well, tinged lavender with various grooves carved throughout. Peering closer, she discerned the pattern of leaves and gnarled bark twisting into a trunk with roots reaching to a pearly hilt. The argent blade was curved slightly at the tip and sharpened enough to slice through the tip of her glove. "But I want something quick and brutal. Efficient."

"Then maybe this one is more yer style," he replied with a sly tone. The sheath in his hands used to be a fine, dark leather, but years wore it down into craggy flap of tattered hide. The knife itself fared no better; cheap paint chipped from the rusting hilt, and grime sullied the handle from years of apparent misuse. Serrated along the back with jagged teeth, the blade ended with a wicked upward curve. She slipped her fingers into the grooves around the handle, then grinned.

"I'll take it."

The man shook his head, scoffing while he conceded. "As you wish." Uncurling his fingers, he thrust his sweaty palm in her face. She refused his demand with a small shake of her head.

"I want a gun as well," she demanded, hardening her tone and giving her best attempt at a frosty glare.

"Yer joking, I said one weapon," he began babbling furiously.

She relented, smiling from his outburst. "Just a small pistol."

Red faced, he arched his brow. "How small?"

"The smallest you have," she replied, "and some ammo."

His neck bulged as he tucked in his chin, staring blankly at the rack of guns behind his table. After a moment, he selected one. "As much ammo as the gun carries."

"Fine." She bit her cheek, relishing the warmth it spilled on her tongue. With a heavy heart, she stared at the green gem in her palm, drowning in melancholy. *I love you, mother.* Her mind reeled when it fell into his greedy clutches.

She hurried down the busied sidewalk, palming her pistol and clutching the blade to her chest with the other hand. Muddied snow sloshed around the gold trim of her dress, dappling the black fabric and soaking the jeans beneath.

"Frilly piece of crap," she muttered sullenly, ignoring the quizzical glances. "I'd prefer sweatpants instead."

As the mountainous hospital loomed over the buildings around her, she slowed her pace. The crowds withered to lonely drunks and shuffling wanderers. She steadied her breathing, crouching low and tucking the sheathed blade into her boot. It was snug, and the leather bulged from the hilt. But it was obscure enough. She bestirred herself at the first raucous bellow resounding through the street, a familiar laugh which grated her ears.

Michael!

Snow slickened the sidewalk. She darted through the wall of darkness and into the unwelcoming alleyway, her boots slipping through the slush. She bit her lip, smothering the pained yelp as the blade wedged into her foot.

"... We have nothing to worry about," she heard Michael growl through his raspy chuckles. "We've been watching them. They're days from here, not in a position to make a move against us. We'll have the upper hand by marching on them at dawn."

"Right," someone barked back, clearly distraught. "But Vega is so concerned..."

"Do not speak ill of our leader," Michael snapped, his tone menacing. "She will get what she wants. After what we've all been through... it's only fair."

"We've all suffered, Mike."

"Aye," he chuckled again. "And soon we make the rest of them pay. They won't escape their own creations."

"I still don't like that plan," the other man grumbled.

"Ah, but it's the *future*! They call it a sickness... we know it's a weapon."

"It destroyed our world."

"No," Michael replied sardonically. "It gave us a new one."

They wandered out of earshot, and a sickening silence befell the street around her. She peered through from the shadows, making certain no other surprises lurked through the dimming streets.

Come on, Celeste!

Panic roared through her mind. *Weapons...*

She folded back the gold trim lining the bottom of the dress and lifted the flap. Her jeans were partially soaked, but she'd long forgotten the aching chill settling in her bones. She nestled the small, silver snub nose inside the waist of her jeans. *It's now or never.*

There weren't many guards earlier. She exhaled nervously, balling her shaky hands into fists. *This will be easy. In and out. Without anyone noticing.*

Easy.

Her heart sank like a stone to her belly when she reached Whytecliff Hospital.

Crap.

Surrounding the armored vehicles and armed to the teeth with machine guns, blades, and enough ammunition to fight a small war, there were dozens of guards. Seemingly garbed in the night itself, the soldiers stood idly in the misty darkness, yet kept their hands near their weapons, silent except for the various superior officers barking orders. Her widened eyes scanned the vehicles, which were outfitted with metal bars on the interior like rolling prisons, with thick chains dangling down the grimy walls. The metal extruded from the ceiling and coiled along the floor, ending in bulky shackles and serrated hooks nearly twice the size of her own head.

What the...

As if sensing her presence, heads turned and eyes wandered through the dark street before settling on her shadowed figure near the gate entrance. Her lungs swelled with air but she couldn't exhale, and she scowled to keep the fear from chalking her face. Striding through the gate, she kept her hands away from her waist, the guards nudging their weapons at her. Nerves jarred, sweat began misting her brow.

No one stopped her. The guards at the gate waved her through, and one even winked after running his eyes down her dress. *Creep,* she thought, mustering a half smile but wanting to claw out of her own skin. The soldiers gathered around the armored vehicles, either servicing the engines or restocking the ammunition, paid little attention as she strolled past with the trim of her dress dragging through the muddy slush. Yet, it seemed as though every eyeball within the vicinity burned into her back, studying her movements to the hospital entrance.

The bottom level of the building had been gutted and remodeled into a lot. There were other vehicles, most former ambulances or vans specially refitted for gurneys and corpses. Flattened duffle bags with sealed zippers piled beside the elevator door. A deathly redolence swamped her nostrils, and her stomach writhed from its putrescence. She masked her nose with a gloved hand and winced. *Disgusting.* Blood seeped from the black material into a dark, slushy puddle around it. *Body bags.* Her eyes darted to the ceiling at the familiar *hum* of the camera focusing its lens. She mimicked Vega; she stuck her chin out and glared above her, letting a disappointing scowl twist her lips. After a few seemingly endless moments, the elevator doors slid open.

She finally breathed again.

Once inside, her finger hovered over the button Vega pressed on their first venture through the hospital. Trying to steady herself, her mind screamed for her to flee, to hide and never look back at the hell she'd gone through. It was almost too much.

Wolves don't run from prey, she reminded herself, clenching her jaw shut. *And we don't leave our pack behind.*

The button lit up under her touch.

"Is that your plan?" She closed her eyes as his voice drifted through her mind. "Guns blazing? More death?"

"No," she whispered back. "No more death."

A chortle of disagreement. "You know there's no other way."

"Than what do you suggest I do, father?" Her words were drowning in a steady stream of sarcasm. "Skulk away in the shadows and pray I survive?" She rolled her eyes, weary of the ache beginning to thrum against her mind. "That's not what you would have done."

"Now you're getting somewhere," he agreed. "So, it's time to think. What would I do?"

She smiled, whispering, "Thanks father," as the floor jerked to a stop and the doors slowly opened.

There were a *lot* more guards than she had anticipated. She stared down the hall, her eyes skimming across the various weapons each soldier carried. *Steady,* she thought, trying to calm her erratic heart.

"Um – Miss?" The guard behind the table began, noisily clearing his throat. It was the same man as before, his stern eyes probing hers. He had his hands wrapped around his weapon, with his finger tucked against the trigger. "Visiting hours are over."

She spoke quickly, stuttering as her tongue dried like a grape shriveling in the sun. "I-I'm aware, but I came to say a quick goodbye before the feast. I won't see her for a long time."

"I understand," he stoically replied. A loud *creak* pierced through the crowd's murmuring as the machine gun shifted on its swivel, staring her in the face like a cornered beast daring provocation. "But this floor is off limits for the night."

No, she roiled inside, *this isn't happening!* But her mouth curved into a frown. "You made me come all the way up here just to turn me away?"

"The cameras are silent, and by the looks of it, you don't have a radio." A sly remark, dripping impatience.

I have to get in there.

"Really?" She sighed irritably. "You're going to waste *her* time?"

"Protocol," he replied adamantly.

"Alright," she said with a shrug. "Why don't you just use that radio and see for yourself then."

Take the bait, arsehole.

He stared at her a moment longer before reaching for the radio. *Damn it,* she cursed silently. She strained to hear any response through the *hissing* static.

"Alpha Team, do you copy?" Again, he asked firmly, "What is your status? Over."

"She's obviously busy," Celeste stated, much to the guard's growing annoyance. He finally sighed wearily, jerking his thumb down the hallway.

"Room 217. First, weapons on the table," he muttered. After she'd emptied her belt of her machete, revolver, and its ammo, he arched a brow and asked with a dreary tone, "Is that all?"

"Same as last time," she replied.

"Be quick," he warned. She nodded her thanks, making her way through the throng of armed soldiers.

Even through the uproar in the corridor, Melina managed to rest. Kinked hair bunched around her face, cascading down her neck like crimson waves as she stirred slightly. She breathed in deeply, shifting under her blankets before settling back into the warmth with a long sigh. Aurous lolled his tongue as Celeste eased the door closed behind her, muffling the discord of voices. His sunny eyes brightened when she ran her fingers through his bristled fur. She was careful to avoid his injuries.

"You still don't like strangers," she commented quietly, glancing over her shoulder at the door. "I don't either. That's why we're getting out of here."

"Celeste?" Melina mumbled groggily, rubbing her eyes against the dim light. "Back so soon?"

"Hey," she greeted, forcing a casual tone. Melina smiled warmly. It was like sunshine bathing the room with a warm, aureate glow. *Like blooming flowers.* "We - I mean..." She stumbled over her tongue. "What I was trying to say..."

Damn it!

Worry glazed Melina's green eyes. "Are you okay?"

"I don't know." It was all she could muster.

Aurous whimpered, thrusting his snout into Celeste's hand until her fingers itched behind his ears. Melina bit her lip, casting her dulling eyes to the floor. "I have been feeling a bit odd about this place."

"Me too," Celeste agreed. "Which is why I think we need to leave."

Celeste averted her gaze when Melina asked with a small voice, "Are we going to be allowed to just leave?"

"Probably not." Her words summoned a chill to encompass them.

"What if we're leaping to conclusions based on paranoia," Melina reasoned. "Maybe after all we've been through... it's just hard for us to accept a bit of normalcy."

Maybe... "Except this place is anything but normal." *The forbidden rooms. Strange documents. This goddamn dress.* "It's more than just a bad feeling." *Pet project...*

"I'm grateful for their help. Really, I am," Melina assured her. "I wish I could repay them somehow. I mean, they saved my life. *Our* lives."

"I know."

She looked up with fiery eyes. "But I'll follow you if you really think we're not safe." She reached out, curling her fingers around Celeste's hand. "I trust you."

Her words sparked a flame of determination in her heart. "Alright," Celeste replied. Loosening the collar of the dress, she said, "I'll find out what's going on." She pulled her arms through and slid the top down her waist. The tufted black bottom crumpled to the floor like an empty sack around her knees. "If there's danger, we'll leave. Quietly. Then - What is it?" With sparkling green eyes, Melina met her gaze with another heartwarming smile.

"That dress looked nice on you," she said. "Much better than those old jeans."

After stripping a layer of her clothing that smothered her with humid warmth, the cold air whisked over her perspiring skin and cooled her, but her face flushed red.

"I like my jeans." *And the dress makes me stick out like a sore thumb.*

"They're nice too." Melina quickly glanced at the weapon Celeste pulled from her belt. "What is that for?"

"It's for you," Celeste replied grimly, thrusting the small pistol in Melina's lap. She clasped the girl's hands around the weapon and held them both tightly. A burden she would help carry. "*Only* for emergency."

Melina nodded, stiffened her trembling lip, and slipped the pistol beneath her sheets. "Alright," she replied, her voice sturdy like mud. "Where are you going?" Her eyes shimmered behind welling tears, betraying her fear and taut nerves.

"I'm going to find out what this place really is." Aurous growled when she stood, but Celeste ruffled his black fur and whispered, "She needs you here, boy. I'll be back. Stay with her." He nipped at her cheek, slathering her skin with drool.

"Please be careful."

Celeste muttered quietly as she eased the door open, "You too."

As she thought, discarding her frivolous garb allowed her to slip unnoticed into the array. She even pulled her hair back and tucked it under her hood to shadow her face. One quick glance down the hall revealed the doorman to be distracted with another guard, so she ghosted through to the adjacent corridor, following the sickly stench poisoning the stale hospital air.

No guards. She peeked over her shoulder. *No one posted by the hall.*

"Maybe there's nothing wrong," her father whispered in her mind. "Maybe you're safe."

She made her way toward the bloodied door at the end of the hall. "You were never the assuming type." She reached for the handle, twisted it, but the door wouldn't budge. "Or the type to use keys."

Except this lock was too sophisticated for her.

Damn it.

Annoyed, she nudged the bottom of the door with her boot, and it shifted open. Startled, she found a second, albeit makeshift, lock; a jagged block of wood forcibly wedged under the door. As she thought, the deadbolt would have been too difficult to pick or even force open.

It works fine... She closed the door slowly. *So why wasn't it locked properly?*

Sight was nearly extinguished. A bitter chill swamped the darkened stairwell, almost blanketing the unmistakable malodorous scent. *Blood.* It rotted her nose. She gagged, her stomach lurching violently. She smothered her face with her sleeve and descended the stairs quickly. Her boots slapping against the cement reverberated through stairwell like an outburst of applause, but curiosity swelled in her chest; she couldn't fight it, she had to know.

Wolves are not prey, she asserted strongly. But all the doors inside the stairwell were sealed shut.

Except one.

At the bottom of the stairwell, she came across a hatch on the wall reinforced with thick steel, and several locks she'd never seen before. Fading numbers lined along the face of the hatch.

Keypad entry? Perplexed, she examined it a moment longer before noticing the cold air bursting through the slit in the wall. The hatch was unlocked, slightly ajar.

Trap. Every thought teemed with danger. It was almost too easy. In a quick, fluid movement, she yanked the sheathed knife from her boot, then slipped through the opened hatch.

The overwhelming stench in the corridor and hallway had been nearly unbearable; the noisome cloud she stepped into made her retch. Its putridity caked her mouth with a foul, feculent taste, and vomit gurgled in her throat. She blinked past the tears attempting to sooth her stinging eyes.

Disgusting.

The small opening grew into another corridor. Beset by multiple rooms, chalky light beamed through the windows, casting an eerie shine down the drab passageway. She paused at each window she passed; most were like the rooms found on higher floors, full of machinery, tubes, wires, and gurneys. Others were lined with tables against the walls, with various tools and instruments scattered across them. Serrated knives, scalpels, hooks. There were forceps, pliers, hammers, shears – along with large power drills and circular saws. Bloody rags piled loosely in the sinks. Crimson stained the interior walls and floor like hellish paint splattered by death. She wandered through the corridor until she spotted it.

Strapped to one of the gurneys, there was a figure secured to the bars and concealed under layers of bandages. Its face was masked. Like an old, infected wound, bare patches of its flesh darkened, spreading through and staining the pale pigment. Needles were wired from machines and pierced through to veins, flushing discolored liquid from various vials into its bloodstream.

She thumbed through the papers piled near the edge of the desk. Blood dappled the first few pages. Names, dates, experimental effects. The same as the files found in Vega's room. *MSV-14W, MSV-2a, R6...*

I'm going to be sick.

It keeps going on and on... No.

What she read next chilled her heart.

Experiment 539-04

Subject: Melina / Female

Age: 17

Strain: MSV-HOST4b (Direct Blood Transfusion)

Results: Commence experiment immediately.

"This can't be happening."

The machines.

She tracked the wires and bloodied tubes along the wall to another entryway; a wooden door leading into small, windowless room. She gagged on the warm fetor.

Another figure remained partially concealed by the shadows. Chains and shackles hanging from the walls like dangling argent serpents latched around the figure's neck and waist. Metal rods protruded through the flesh on its legs. It hissed when the dim light streaked through the abyssal dark.

Charcoal black skin. Mangled bone twisting through mutilated flesh. Dead eyes.

Infected.

It lunged at her – or at least, it tried. The chains stiffened around its neck. Its teeth snapped harmlessly at the stale air between them. Bloody saliva frothed, bubbling down its bony chin. Each shoulder ended in ribbons of tattered flesh. Maggots squirmed through the sludgy flesh by her boots. Carious teeth were still chattering madly when she closed the door and left the creature in utter darkness.

I have to get us out of here!

She hurried past the various machines surrounding the gurney. Dials whirled, screens flickered than brightened; the lab was coming to life. Lights lit up above her.

Crap!

Like an unwanted burden, the knife weighed heavily in her palm. She balanced it, flicked her wrist, and tucked the old blade against her forearm. Peering past the door, only shadows lurked inside the corridor. She held her breath, straining to hear anything through the constant *hum* of the machinery behind her.

Her eyes darted to the other entryway, the last door at the end of the corridor. She'd heard it; an echo, almost a whisper. Distant. *No...* It was a scream. A pleading cry muffled by the cement walls.

It was similar to the room before; dreary walls streaked with blood, chains and shackles extending from the walls. Prison bars and cages.

People.

Some were strapped to gurneys, like the other, latched behind steel mesh. The skin on their faces peeled from the bone like rubber Halloween masks, their limbs severed and organs piled in bloody lumps on the floor. Mutilated corpses littered the room, some fleshy and pink, tanned and dark; others putrid black and rotted. The stench *still* made her heave.

Someone wheezed, muttering incomprehensible words.

The knife trembled in her grasp, but her mind clamored for blood. *Survive.*

It was another cage.

It spanned the width of the room, barred and layered with razor-wire. The barbs reached through the interior as well, snaking up the walls and already stained red from oceans of blood.

Someone shuffled through the shadows, breathing shallowly and avoiding the glare of light. Eventually, he shifted into view, squinting through the bars. A sallow complexion across a concave face, grime and blood staining his naked flesh – he resembled a corpse inside a coffin.

"You don't seem like one of them," he muttered weakly, his voice hoarse. "You don't belong here."

Fighting past the fear gushing through her thoughts, she asked, "What is this place?"

"Hell." There was an outburst behind him, a riot of screams and garbled words, pleas and frenzied threats. The metal bars rattled and the razor-wire shook. Blood sprayed from the prisoners gripping the piercing barbs.

"This is insane." Her voice quavered. She reeled, trying to regain her dwindling composure. "Melina..."

The prisoners wouldn't stop screaming. Their cacophonous voices bounced off the cement walls, assailing her mind until she made no sense of any rational thought. She squeezed her eyes shut, rubbed her temples and swore loudly.

"Let us free."

The man stared at her through the bloody steel mesh. Desperation flourished and darkened the blue hue.

"We can fight our way out," he offered through the riotous noise after a few moments of her silence.

Cold metal of her blade nipped through the sleeve of her sweater. "What makes you think I need help getting out?"

"Fear of what you've discovered here," he replied quietly, grinning with chapped lips. "I can see it in your eyes."

"I see darkness in yours."

"I never claimed innocence."

She retorted, "So far, you're not convincing me..."

"We're going to die, alright?" He finally shouted back, frustration gleaming through his calm demeanor. Unsteady silence rushed through the throng of prisoners. "We're experiments! They're butchering us, performing tests on us! Experimenting!"

Already figured as much. "Why?"

He hesitated. Then his eyes shifted as he replied, "Evolved soldiers. Unstoppable monsters. An army that can never fall."

"I've seen many monsters fall," she sneered. "I'm sure I'll see many more."

But he shook his head. "No, you don't get it, do you? They're tampering with the virus, developing new strains with unforeseeable consequences. They're creating weapons."

And they're already difficult to kill on their own... She shivered. *Defeating an army would be inconceivable.*

She narrowed her eyes. "How do you know all these details, what they're trying to do?"

"Because we're the soldiers," he answered, broken tone teeming with pride. "And this is *our* city."

"It's ours!" Another ragged voice cried out.

"Bloody raiders!"

"Savages!"

"Goddamn monsters!"

She scoffed. "I don't believe you."

"Girl," he said, strangling his desperation with anger. "I know all this because we're the ones that held the raiders captive and performed God-awful shit in these dungeons. But we did it with a purpose! We were trying to battle the infected, to find a way to either weaken them or completely eliminate the illness. We... we lost control. They attacked us, overwhelmed the building. Soon, whoever they didn't rape or slaughter was thrown in here, to suffer the same fate as they had."

He was right. This is hell.

"If you don't get out of here," he continued, "you'll be next. They don't give a shit who you are, or how innocent you claim to be. They'll butcher you like all the others. They're savages."

Every troubling thought she'd had since waking up in Whytecliff City flashed through her mind. *How do I get out of this?* It was impossible to calm her doleful heart. *What can I do?*

You survive.

"Alright," she decided quickly. Courage flowed. "We're *all* getting out of this hellhole."

"But this hellhole is where you belong."

Ice crept through her veins.

No... She turned, peering over her shoulder at the shadow obscuring the entryway. Thrusting a pistol toward her, Abbot stepped through the dimming light, his ghostly pale face twisted with a smirk.

His words were drowning in magniloquence. "I'll make sure you never see the light of day again." He cocked the pistol and sneered. "*Bitch.*"

"I KNEW you would never fit in with us," Abbot jeered with scathing words. "You're an inbred mountain whelp. Too weak for this world."

She spoke, feigning bravery. "You don't know the kind of things I've done."

"You haven't done shit!" He snarled through a malicious smile, delighted at her fearful flinch. "You survived on luck alone. Begging for scraps like a wayward pup, clutching onto Vega's coattails to ensure your pathetic life lasted just a moment longer. It's *sickening*."

"What about you?" She shot back, indulging his grandiosity. "Sniveling and pouting like a child, concealing your cowardice with a weapon." Her barbs barely pierced his pride.

Abbot, you bastard. She buried the blade in her sleeve, her widening eyes never leaving his. "You left the doors unlocked."

He forced a chuckle, grating her nerves. "I knew you couldn't resist poking your nose where it doesn't belong." He licked his lips, and wiped the sweat greasing his skin. "I never trusted you. An outsider should *always* be killed, especially weak, useless bitches like yourself." He shrugged, his grin widening into a smile. "Maybe pass you around until you taste and smell too foul..."

That boiled her blood. "Or maybe I open this gate and let these prisoners have *you*."

"You make a move," he responded sinisterly, tightening the grip around his pistol. The barrel trembled slightly. "I'll make sure to paint them with your brains."

Through gritted teeth, she asked, "Why don't you get it over with, Abbot?"

I'm sorry, Melina. Aurous...

"No," he whispered. "Vega needs to know of your treachery."

Images of a curved, ebony blade carving through tender flesh and blood spritzing into the snow flashed through her mind. Thoughts reeled from the screams of terror and disbelief echoing in her skull. *"Because the next time you disobey me and fail to prove your loyalty, this is what will happen to you."* Vega's whispered promise shattered the tumult in her mind; it was a poisonous threat had seeped into Celeste's heart, which now fueled the fear jolting through every nerve.

I'm not going to die here!

Abbot was practically snickering as he spoke into his radio. "Yeah, I found that mountain girl in the lower levels, snooping around the restricted areas. Someone's going to have to alert Vega. Over."

"Copy that," someone replied through the hissing static, clearly annoyed. *"We'll secure the other girl. What is your current location?"*

"Oh," Abbot began, his lip curling into a malicious snarl. "I'll bring her in..."

The fire coursing in her mind burned through reasonable thought she still maintained; the wolf inside her howled its fury, bent on survival at any cost or measure. She snapped forward, twirling the knife handle in her palm before thrusting the blade's edge toward Abbot.

His vulgar words were lost to her fury. He shouted, pistol trembling, and slowly stepped back to the doorway.

She didn't care. She wanted blood.

As she thought, the fear of killing without Vega's permission caused him to discard the gun a moment before the blade drove into his belly. Except the knife snagged in his coat. It tore, but no blood spilled through the frayed fabric. She cocked her head, his fist grazing across her cheek. The blade carved through the air for his neck.

He grunted, managing to bash her forearm with his. With her nerves jarred, the knife slipped from her numbed fingers. It spun wildly across the cement floor. She reached for it, the handle brushing lightly against her fingertips.

A boot collided with her ribs, forcing the air from her lungs. Pain spread like wildfire. She opened her mouth to scream, but he kicked her into silence.

"No matter what kind of feral beast you think you are," he muttered breathlessly, his words drowning in the sea of prisoner screams. "You're still a little girl. A goddamn pampered *princess*."

She snarled, lunging like the beast he didn't imagine her as. Every forceful kick intended to rupture the organs in her belly, but she gaped breathlessly and reached between his legs. His muscles stiffened. She didn't give him a chance to hit her again; she clenched her fist and twisted.

He screamed, but this time involuntarily. As he stumbled away from her crushing grip, she bloodied his mouth with two solid blows before he managed to regain his composure.

Frustration welling, he charged. Fingers desperately snatched at her sweater, and he tucked his head down and rammed her chest with his shoulder. She slipped along the cement, sidestepping the initial collision. His unwavering grip intertwined them, and they tumbled toward the floor.

Abbot crashed into the prison bars, rattling the cage and razor-wire. The floor embraced Celeste, breaking her fall. Her face *smacked* loudly off the cement. Dazed, she spotted the knife within arm's length. Desperation roared through her mind, and she reached for the discarded weapon. But his fingers found their way around her throat.

"I'm going to kill you!" he shouted, his face flushed red. "I'm going to... What the hell?"

Bloody, filthy fingers wormed through the metal mesh, twining around his hair and clothes, forcing him against the gate. His arms flailed, and he thrashed uselessly against his fleshy restraints.

"Now, girl!" someone yelled through the bars. One prisoner stared back at her, his arms streaked with red as he reached through the razor-wire to subdue Abbot against the bars.

Abbot parted his mouth to scream, but only managed a wordless gurgle when the knife sank into his belly and carved up against his ribcage. A river of scarlet burst past the blade.

Help me, he mouthed with bloodied lips. He stared past her, skin pallid like undisturbed snowfall. Darkness shadowed the cerulean blue of his eyes.

Caden, the fear in her whispered.

"Nobody's going to help you," she snarled, sliding the blade between his ribs. Warm blood spilled over her hands, her penchant for death fulfilled.

"Abbot!"

The blade tore free from the boy's gut. She turned, bloodlust surging, and confronted another weapon's glare. Michael shoved the twin barreled shotgun at her, his face contorted and ravished with grief. Enmity radiated from his eyes.

He pumped the forend to his shotgun. She tossed her blade.

The blast smothered the raucous jeers, and the buckshot tore through the ceiling. Her knife had sailed lopsided through the air, battering Michael's face without drawing blood. He'd flinched, however, nudging his shotgun upward.

She dashed through the dusty debris raining down from the ceiling. Just as her hands slipped around his weapon, he batted her to the floor like a useless doll. Her vision flashed white as her head bounced off the cold cement.

"You goddamn murderer!" Hands enclosed around her throat and squeezed. Her head felt like it would burst from the pressure.

"Enough!"

Michael loosened his grip, hunched his shoulders, but snarled, "She killed my boy."

Gelid words fell from her tongue, chilling Celeste like no mountain winter could. "Then I shall deal with her personally."

"No!" Defiance boomed with his voice. "Following you is what got him killed!" He towered over Celeste, disgust plastered on his face while she sucked in ragged breaths and rubbed her throat. "This *girl* has clouded your judgment, Vega!"

"My sight remains clear. Does yours?"

"He was your boy, too! Maybe not flesh and blood, but damn it Vega, he was your boy!" Tears drizzled to the bloody floor. "Then you discard him like an unwanted toy when you come across this whelp! You can't fix the past! She will never be your..."

"Choose your next words carefully." Shadows swirled through her glare. "What happened to your boy was unfortunate, Mike. I am sorry." Eyes drifting to the floor, her icy gaze melted momentarily.

Michael clenched his fists, spitting while he hissed furiously, "That's it? A simple apology? I want her head!"

"I will *not* give you blood."

He retorted madly, "She's not your daughter!"

The ground heaved under them all. The floor roiled violently, lurching beneath their feet. Vega stumbled. Michael fell into the wall when he lost his footing, like the floor itself had been pulled out from underneath him. Celeste scrambled through the bloody muck.

"*This is Bravo, I repeat, this is Bravo!*" A panicked voice blurted through the hissing static of the radio. "*We're under attack!*"

Through the settling dust, Vega's voice thundered, "What is your status?"

"*There were multiple detonations across the city, and we have enemy combatants in the-,*" someone reported, before distorted static blared through instead.

"Bravo, do you copy?" The pistol slipped free from the holster on her belt. "Damn."

Coughing and expelling dusty debris from his lungs, Michael confronted Vega, misty-eyed but snarling viciously. "I warned you that this distraction would cost us everything! We had a plan, Vega! We were supposed to be outside the city limits by now!"

"Then it's time we leave," Vega suggested coldly. "It's time for you to stop being *weak*. The girl comes with us."

Michael snarled back, "You never loved me! You never cared for my boy! We gave up everything to fight for you! We stayed in this hellhole that almost killed us, denied our own people freedom so you could expend their lives for your cause, and butchered those who disobeyed! I loved you, Vega, but you let this girl ruin everything we've fought for! You're too lost in your own grief..."

They both flinched from the blast blaring against their eardrums.

Celeste stood by the gate with Michael's fallen shotgun in her hands. Smoke funneled from the end of the sawed off barrel. No blood spilled to the floor. Instead, she had directed the blast at the bolted latch, hoping to shatter the lock and open the gate. The shells mangled the metal but the latch remained sealed; she pumped the forend and pulled the trigger again.

Nothing happened.

"Now you see," Michael hissed. His hands blurred to his belt, then a pistol gleamed under the flickering lights. "This is one whelp that needs to be put..."

He grunted, collapsing to the cement floor. A sickly spray of red warmed her face. Celeste smeared the blood along her sleeve, staring up in disbelief as Vega lowered her pistol. Wisps of smoke swirled through the putrid air. Her blasé, shadowed eyes wandered over Michael's bloodied corpse. Speckles of red dappled his beard. His ghostly gaze stared across the floor at Celeste, lips still parted with an unspoken insult.

"Love was the distraction," she whispered morosely. Her perennial gaze found Celeste. "I'm so sorry you had to see that, Caylee. He didn't understand."

"Neither do I," Celeste mused, darkening her tone.

She raised the shotgun and Vega shouted; but her words were lost to the clanging clamor. Fiery sparks flashed when she bashed the stock of the shotgun against the gnarled metal latch. Two more strikes until the lock shattered into jagged shards and the heavy gate shifted.

The prisoners flooded through the opening; it was a malefic river of grimy flesh, blood, and putrid waste. Waves of rot poured into the room, a blur of anger and rancor. Vega screamed her daughter's name, then raised her pistol and fired into the crowd.

One prisoner faltered as he ran. He collapsed, blood fanning the face of another behind him. The next stepped over the fallen prisoner, a maddened cry ripping through his throat. Two bullets sank into his chest, the third into his skull. More bodies dropped.

Click. Click. Click.

Emptied, she holstered her pistol. Her ebony blade slashed through the crowd. Blood burst across the floor, then she vanished, evanesced by shadows.

One man was fishing his severed fingers from the puddled red by his bare feet. Another clutched his entrails as they slipped through the gash in his sunken stomach. Two more nursed wicked lacerations across their chests.

"Do not stop!" Celeste roared, thrusting her death slickened blade into the air. "We fight our way out or we're trapped just like before! We kill them all!"

They stirred, but remained uncertain; a few followed Vega to the corridor, but their screams emanated from the darkness, howling their pain through the hall like disembodied spirits.

"Girl," a familiar face whispered. Blood streaked down his arms from torn flesh. Some had even spattered across his filthy face. The prisoner who had helped her kill Abbot. "They may be soldiers but they are weak."

"We can't wait," she hissed back, her own words muffled by the *thumping* of her erratic heart. Pursing her lips, she almost sneered, "I'm not dying down here! I'm not letting them win! You can stay if you want, but once she closes that door, you may never get out again!"

Fire roared through her tone. The wolf in her snarled, "I choose to be predator, not prey!"

"You heard the girl!" One prisoner responded. The others rallied, their cries thundering through the room. "We can die down here like prisoners, or we can fight as free men!"

Celeste was lost, drowning under waves of malevolence. Blood was all she could see. There were guards stationed at the far end of the corridor, some beginning to seal the reinforced door and others with their weapons directed down the passageway at the ensuing chaos.

Gunfire erupted. Blood sprayed through the crowd and bodies dropped around her, but the cries of fury never quelled. Guards vanished under the vengeful tide of whirling prisoners, crushed beneath waves of rot. Screams were silenced by sharp *claps* of flesh pummeling flesh; the guards were stomped and pulped into the cement floor, reduced to sickening puddles of blood, broken bones, and mangled meat. The other guards abandoned their efforts to seal the exit as their comrades fell to hell's thrashing. They ran up the stairwell, squealing like pigs from the slaughterhouse.

A few prisoners grabbed whatever weapons they could find on the guards, others stripped their battered corpses of any clothing to drape over their own bloody flesh before continuing their charge. The deluge of malice roiled up the stairwell.

One of the last remaining guards stood in front of the exit, his pale face pleading tearfully with the camera above the door. He bashed his fist against the metal and screamed until his voice cracked. He didn't even fight when death swarmed. Instead, he placed the barrel of his gun inside his mouth and pulled the trigger.

They were trapped.

No!

"They've barred it from the outside!" Her anger subsided into fear. "We can't escape."

"The hell we can't," the first prisoner muttered, turning to the throng of filth behind him. "Let's break this bloody door down!"

She recalled the metal latches and the sophisticated lock and couldn't imagine what other measures they undertook to further secure the facility in her absence. *Especially after Abbot told them I was down in the sublevels.* There would be more guards as well. It didn't matter; the hinges held and the lock remained sturdy. The door itself wouldn't budge from the battering bodies, but instead crumbled through the wall and collapsed in a cloud of dusty smoke.

Someone had been crushed beneath the rubble. Another guard, partially pinned but lifeless, lay beneath the concrete rocks. The others dashed for the corridor, abandoning bravery in favor of safety.

Celeste anchored herself in the rapid flow of the human sea. She screamed, certain the flesh in her throat tore and ripped with each hoarse bellow. But they wouldn't halt their mindless rampage. The wordless howl smothered her voice.

No!

It was like the vicious roar of thunder as lightning split the sky. Through the throng of grime, she caught glimpses of bright flashes, misting blood, and falling prisoners. She watched, horrified, as three men rounded the corridor corner. Their bodies were then ripped apart by the cannonade. Limbs scattered and blood spouted from continuous wounds; their bodies burst like fleshy balloons against the machine gun's wicked wrath.

The mechanical whirl of the machine gun died, and a dreaded silence poisoned the surviving prisoners. Her mind outpaced her speeding heart.

"We need to figure out a way around that gun," she began.

Two muffled gunshots and a rabid growl; she was certain the faint sounds brushed against her dulled senses.

Melina! Aurous!

She ejected from the crowd like a bullet bursting from the barrel of a gun. Pain, fear, even the thought of death – everything that would have scorched her mind and stilled the bravery welling in her heart seemed of little importance now. Blood splattered up her boots as she bolted through to the main corridor.

The machine gun bellowed its fury, howling its thirst for her blood. Bullets chased her, chewing through the wall behind her and shredding a trail of destruction in their wake. She lurched forward, colliding with the ground. The wall showered its gutted debris over her as the bullets sawed through it above. She gasped for air. Her lungs clogged, and her mouth caked with chalky dust. The settling rubble flushed tears through her eyes, then clumped as mud around her lashes whenever she blinked.

The machine gun whirled to a stop once more. She scrambled to her feet and continued her desperate dash. Her boots slipped through the debris as though running across a smooth ice. She heard a distant shout, muffled by the loud ring in her ears, and the *clap* of the machine gun firing. Then the walls exploded around her.

Something burned into her shoulder. She wasn't even sure if she screamed. The pain was there, her lips parted, and her lungs fueled a desperate cry for survival; but all she heard was the eruption of bullets bursting the walls apart.

She propelled herself through the window; glass shattered and lead ripped through the frame. Jagged shards carved bloody trails through her skin as she tumbled across the floor. She glimpsed a shadow through the disorienting blur, but the floor seemingly jostled beneath her feet.

Someone screamed.

Melina!

Except it wasn't her. It was a guard, a boy not much older than her, crouched against the wall with his hands buried in the wolf's fur. Aurous snarled and snapped his jaws wildly, raining saliva over the boy's face. He held the wolf back, but only just; Aurous raked his claws through the guard's legs, tattering the fabric of his jeans and ribboning the tender flesh beneath. The boy was gritting his teeth, straining to brace against the wolf's strength. Blood and sweat sullied his smooth skin. The wolf nearly closed his jaws around the boy's throat.

"Aurous!"

The wolf growled, but relented. The boy dropped his arms to the floor. He cried out, relief flooding his tremulous voice.

"Oh, God," he whispered through his tears. "Thank you. Thank you. I'll do anything... Please, I'll help you get out. I know how..."

Her knife carved through his throat with one thrust. Blood jetted from a gash in his neck that even his hands couldn't clasp closed. He gurgled for a moment and stared up at her with wide eyes, bewildered as life flooded from his severed veins. Fear tainted his chestnut colored eyes. He slumped forward, spilling his last tears as the knife entered his heart.

She heard a small gasp behind her. She reeled, streaking red across the wall. Melina curled up beside the bed. Trembling, she held the snub nosed pistol in her hand, still leveling the barrel with the dead boy's corpse. Tears streamed down her freckled face, her red hair slickened from sweat.

"I couldn't... get a clear shot," she mumbled, staring blankly at the blood pooling across the floor. "But I-I killed the other."

So she had.

Celeste found the other body, crumpled by the doorway with a single bullet wound in his face. There wasn't much blood. Clean kill. Though, it had been her first, and Celeste knew the bitterness that weighed on one's soul. But something else demanded her attention.

She plucked a weapon from the guard's belt.

"Cover your ears!" Celeste yelled over the thundering machine gun fire. She leaned out of the window, shielding her face. Debris clouded the corridor from the machine gun's rage. "Enjoy, you son of a bitch."

She pulled the pin and tossed the grenade.

For a moment, nothing happened. Then the detonation tore through everything. Walls fractured and split, the floor lurched and rumbled, and smoke billowed through the halls to smother their lungs.

It took her another minute to collect herself. She was sprawled across the floor, her mind a swirl of a blurring thoughts she couldn't grasp. Through the ringing in her ears, she heard the distant sounds of someone screaming. She stumbled to the doorway, which was now just a crumbling frame poking out of the wall.

Corpses littered the hall, beset by severed limbs, bloody chunks of flesh, and settling debris. The blast demolished and caved in part of the wall surrounding the gunmen. The surviving prisoners had rallied together and slaughtered the remaining guards, butchering the gunmen with their own weapons.

"You did well," one of the prisoners remarked, stepping over a mangled corpse to greet her. "The hospital is ours again."

"The city has yet to fall," Celeste muttered in reply. Her bleary eyes stared through the wired mesh layering the window. Fire. Smoke. Screams. The city was still under siege.

"Aye," he replied, yellow teeth flashing through his grin. "But you freed us. We owe you a debt, one that may never be repaid. But the honor is ours if you join us in our fight."

"For now," Celeste conceded. "But we're leaving after I kill Vega."

"They said there was an attack on the city," Melina informed them. She had her arms around the wolf and her head buried in his fur. She trembled, but spoke strongly. "It's our chance to escape. To leave this madness behind."

"After I kill Vega." The words tumbled from her tongue again before she could stop them. Hatred poisoned her tone.

The prisoner grinned, wrinkling his grimy face. "Type to hold a grudge, are you?"

"Her tyranny needs to end."

Always finish what you've started.

"Then I'm coming." Melina pushed herself up, but Celeste quickly refused. "No. I'll get you away from the city but I'm going back for Vega."

She glared at Celeste, pursing her lips. "I'm not letting you leave me again!" Welling tears made her green eyes shimmer like raindrops falling through sunshine. "I don't want to be out there alone."

Her heart lurched. "Then maybe you should stay here."

"What?"

"This place is secure. There's only one way in and out." She nodded to the prisoner. "He said it. This building is ours for now."

"What if the attackers outside get in?" Melina asked, worry creeping through her words. "Or what if Vega or her followers get back in?"

"Not gonna happen," the prisoner chimed in, flashing his yellow teeth with another smile. "That's the real military out there. You have nothing to fear from them. These imposters don't stand a chance." He clasped his hands, rubbing them together with excitement. "The cavalry has arrived!"

"You'll be safe here for now," Celeste reassured, squeezing her friend's hand tightly. "I told you I was getting you out of this city."

"How do you know?"

"Because," she replied. "I promised."

Reluctantly, Melina whispered, "Okay."

"Plus," Celeste added, glaring at the former prisoner. "If I don't return, he'll make sure you get out of city. From there, you'll be fine."

Shrill laughter burst from his foul mouth. "I respect you, girl. I really do. A helluva lot. But what makes you think I wouldn't harm this poor soul?"

"I'm not worried," Celeste said. "Despite her objections, she can take care of herself."

"Is that so?" He prodded, amused.

"Yes."

Aurous stirred beside her. His fur bristled, his lips twitching into a snarl.

"And if she can't, *he* will."

The wolf bared his bloodstained fangs and growled.

The prisoner kept smiling, whispering coldly, "Time for you to finish the hunt, then."

Twenty
Reaper

Celeste pulled herself up from the frozen muck, spitting the grit from her tongue. It was a foul taste she didn't wish to think about, let alone experience. *Blood and dirt,* she thought darkly, *I'm never eating meat or potatoes again.* She swayed, not bothering to brush any of the filth or slush from her garments, and quickly checked her weapons.

Knife. Gun. It was all there. As the ringing in her ears subsided, she heard voices and people approaching. She dashed through the rubble and away from the chaos.

The blast had taken her by surprise, hurling her into disarray. She was thrown through the icy snow and falling debris. She'd only just left the relative safety of the hospital gates, wading through the slushy blood and stringy flesh of slaughtered guards once thronging the parking lot. Even their armored vehicles were debilitated; gnarled metal twisted around the front like an unfurling metallic flower, and smoke billowed from the torn engine inside. Each vehicle had been forcibly ripped through. Her eyes barely digested the massacre when the explosion struck.

She cloaked herself in shadows, held her breath, and watched the soldiers advance through the smoke. Their weapons extended every direction. They were outfitted in the same black gear that Vega's soldiers were, except the attacking force had a strange crest under the left shoulder. *At least there's somewhat of a distinction.* Though it mattered little; she'd likely be killed the moment she was spotted, regardless of who happened to lay eyes on her. *I'll just have to remain unseen.*

Easier said than accomplished.

Gunfire became a constant hum against her eardrums, and explosions reverberated through the city, momentarily dampening the accursed melody of screams. She ran blindly through the city's backstreets and alleyways, avoiding swarms of militia and roads wide enough for armored vehicles.

I just want Vega. Nobody else.

But there were soldiers *everywhere.* She watched from afar as the drunkards once cheering loudly into the clear night sky were plunged into riotous confusion. Their buildings erupted and crumbled around them. They unloaded clips and shells into the onslaught of soldiers. Bodies kept *smacking* against pavement.

There were too many opposing soldiers, and fight valiantly they might, the drunkards were a disorganized, scattered mess. One by one, they were gunned down in a storm of a bullets and thunder, and their angered, sometimes tearful cries resonated through the blasts.

I can't get caught.

Her eye caught the glint a moment before the blade slashed through the air. She dived, bashing and skidding her elbows across the cement. Pain jolted through her wrist when she whirled and reached for her gun. Her fingers numbed and she cried out, unable to ignore the pain flushing up her arm.

"I knew you'd follow me," Vega whispered softly, thrusting the blade in front of Celeste's face. "But if my girl wants the crown, she'll have to *earn it!*"

Celeste hooked her boot behind Vega's leg. The woman stumbled, quickly regaining her balance. The ebony blade chopped through the snow as Celeste rolled, unsheathed her machete, and sprang to her feet.

"Enough talk," she growled, wrenching her scarred fingers around the handle.

Then she lunged.

She heaved the machete, swinging the old blade like a baseball bat. Vega leaned back, arching her spine. The machete blade carve through the dappled brick beside her. Wine lips parted in a curvaceous smile. Her eyes, black as a starless night, beamed furor. The machete slashed harmlessly through the air once more, bouncing off the opposing alley wall. Vega took a sole step back, then parried the third wild strike. A storm of sparks erupted as her jet blade slid down the edge of the machete, then ripped it from Celeste's grasp. It *clanged* against the pavement out of reach.

"My girl will have to do better than that!" Vega declared, carving her blade toward Celeste's neck. She managed to duck, avoiding the blade's deadly kiss. Throwing herself into Vega, they both crashed into the dappled brick.

Vega grunted, bracing against the girl's clench. She raised her blade, bringing the handle down on the back of Celeste's head. A meaty *crack* echoed through the alley.

Celeste's grip faltered and her balance wavered; Vega battered her to the pavement, but nearly caught a blade to her own belly the next instant.

The front of her coat ripped like it burst from the seams, but the machete only tore through the fabric and snagged on her coattail. Vega pushed away from the wall, pivoted, and pulled Celeste along with her. She stumbled, refusing to loosen her rigid hold.

Crack. Vega drilled the handle of her blade into her unprotected face. Celeste and her machete tumbled to the ground.

"That was clever," the woman remarked, sighing lightly, almost dreamily as if lost in the warmth of a fond memory. "Forcing close combat to retrieve your weapon."

"It's a shame," Celeste sputtered, letting blood drain down her chin. "I didn't spill your guts to the pavement."

"How many more tricks do you have up your sleeves?"

"Plenty."

Vega grinned wickedly and narrowed her shadowy eyes. "Don't forget who taught you most of what you know, Caylee!" She bolted forward, but before she could swing, Celeste's revolver was clear of its holster.

The silver barrel trailed her movements, but Vega was too quick; she lurched to the ground and rolled, sprang from the pavement, then pushed off the dappled brick to hurl herself through one of the stained windows along the side of the building. It was like a shrill scream resounded through the alley as the glass shattered and burst.

With both weapons secured to her belt, she heaved herself through the window after Vega. Shards of glass razed her scarred fingers when she gripped the window pane, and *crunched* beneath her boots when she dropped into the lightless building.

It took a harrowing moment for her eyes to adjust. Blurred outlines of various furnishings cluttering each room, curtained or dingy windows fringed with a dull glow like cooling embers and shadows ebbing from the pale light trickling through – it was all she could see, a murky haze of nothing.

"So," Vega's phantom voice echoed throughout the shadows. "My girl wants to play rough!"

The mechanical *click* of the pistol filled her ears, then a searing light flashed. Celeste already propelled herself through an adjacent entryway. The bullet ricocheted into the wall, and they were flushed into darkness again.

The floorboards creaked beneath a hurried step and shattered the heavy silence. Rolling to her feet, she let the revolver buck. She caught a glimpse of Vega darting through the flash of light, gleaming ebony blade raised and ready to slash a bloody trail across her neck. The wall splintered and burst when the bullet veered past Vega and pierced through the brittle wood instead. As darkness inundated, she panicked and pulled the trigger again.

Light glared, another bullet tore through the makeshift paneling – but Vega had vanished. Disappeared. *Keep it together!* Fear gravened into her heart now coursed wildly through her veins. *She's not a ghost,* she reminded herself, balancing the hefty machete blade in her hand. *She's not invincible.*

She heard nothing through the familiar *thump* of her heavy heart, and her own rapid, unsteady breathing. The floor jostled beneath her. The malefic melody of erupting gunfire, detonations, and undulating screams throughout the city became but a distant thought she couldn't dwell on.

Where the hell are you, Vega?

Every shadow seemed to stir, every inky corner a possible shroud. The darkness appeared to melt and reach for her; Vega burst from the murky curtain, thrusting her shadowed blade like a spear into her shoulder. Pain flared after a stream of warmth soaked through her torn sweater. She pushed away from the blade's sharp bite, her knees buckling. Vega advanced, spinning her blade and spraying Celeste with her own blood.

Pain subsided to rage. Celeste charged, but there was no way to avoid the blade's razor kiss. She felt cold metal split the flesh on her arm as she rammed into Vega. They tumbled through the darkness, rolled across the blood slickened floor, and collided with the wall. Pain forced the air from Celeste's lungs into a soundless scream. Vega leaned over her, blade raised.

Writhing madly, Celeste averted the first two strikes; Vega's blade hacked into the wall like a butcher cleaving meat. She bucked underneath the woman's hold.

An odd fragrance sweetened the stale air.

"You're not strong enough!" Vega yelled, bringing her blade down like a guillotine strike. "You never were!"

NO!

Something inside her roared; the survivor in her blood, the wolf in her soul. She snarled, gritted her teeth as if baring wicked fangs, and then thrashed against the woman's iron grip. Blood pooled where her nails dug into tanned skin and raked across a fleshy throat. Vega lost her footing, her blade chopping wildly into the floor. They fell again, tumbling along the wall and crashing into the cluttered furniture.

Vega flowed to her feet with ease, but Celeste stumbled as if the floor jarred uncontrollably beneath her. It took a moment for her to realize it actually *was*. A steady tremor rattled the walls and agitated the throb in her head. Another explosion tore through the city.

"You won't survive on luck alone," Vega snickered wickedly, dissolving into the shadows. "Show me where you real strength lies. Prove to this world what you're capable of!"

Through the smoke, blood and grime, the sweetened aroma faintly brushed against her sense. It was like a patch of wildflowers blossoming in her nose.

Light pierced through deluging shadows as the doors swung open. Smoke funneled through the passageway and blanketed the room with thick, black smog. It smothered her lungs and burned her throat.

She's trying to smoke me out. Part of the building seemed aflame, and she couldn't discern any other entryways or windows through her disorientation. *Looks like there's one exit.*

She crouched under the clouding smoke, muffling her face with her sweater and fumbling through her coat for ammo. *She's waiting on the other side of the door.* She loaded the cylinder and snapped it back into place. *I just need...*

The redolence of wildflowers overwhelmed her nose again. There they were, propped inside a glimmering glass vase, with curled resplendent petals that were a swirl of violet and white.

Keep watching over me, mom.

When Celeste, revolver poised and machete unsheathed, slipped through the smoky curtain and stepped back into the chaotic city streets, her heart dropped. She quickly counted a dozen or so soldiers, each armed with a blockade of weapons, closing in on the entryway. They tensed at the sight of her, barrels glaring as each rifle leveled with her chest.

"Now you see!" Vega declared, shouting from the midst of advancing soldiers. "What one can accomplish with true strength!" She smiled wickedly, caressing her wine lips with her tongue. "Kill her."

"Ma'am," one of the soldiers said, lowering his weapon. "She's just a kid, and not with the enemy. We're under attack..."

Vega's cold words pierced through soldier's booming voice. "Betrayal is an enemy trait." She raised her pistol, thrusting the barrel toward the soldier's head.

The soldier's head snapped back. Blood misted the crowd as he collapsed. Vega stared at his corpse, momentarily bewildered, before tracing the bullet's trajectory to Celeste's smoking revolver. There was a cry from one of the other soldiers, and they all readied their weapons. Vega smiled, and eagerly stared up the barrel of the revolver.

Before the volley erupted, the street shuddered beneath them, as if the city itself feared the ensuing massacre taking place within its walls. The pavement fractured and split, cracking like glass from the giant lumbering into view.

It was easily as wide as the street, larger than any of the other vehicles she'd seen inside the city. The wheels were small, but bunched together under a rolling track that chewed through the pavement as the vehicle advanced. It wasn't crudely armored with steel plates and razor-wire, but ironclad in a thick metal hide already scarred with bullet marks and gashes which barely scratched its murky green paint. There were no windows, only a small turret with long, twin barrels jutting from the sides.

"Crap," Celeste cursed in a whisper, watching the turret angle both barrels at them all.

Then it opened fire.

The weapon roared with unimaginable power, its thunder surged against their eardrums. Fire jetted from each barrel as blasts tore through the mob of soldiers. The ground erupted under their feet. Celeste was hurled to the rippling pavement, her ears ringing and mind drowning in turmoil. She moved, avoiding the warm, scarlet mist and settling rubble obstructing the street. There were bodies strewn around her, and flesh minced from shrapnel or charred from the spreading flames. Muddy blood leaked through the shattered pavement. Dismembered limbs were scattered. Screams, if any, were lost to the hurricane howl of the weapon cannonade.

She pushed past the few remaining survivors. Some rallied and opened fire on the vehicle in a vain, desperate attempt to fight, others scrambled away from their imminent demise as another blast engulfed them all.

She was thrown off her feet and into the piling rubble. She couldn't breathe. Coughing and expelling the sooty mucus from her throat, she watched helplessly as the last soldier stumbled through the smoke, his weapon dangling loosely at his side. Blood smeared his gear and face, despondent eyes wide and lost to the horror unfolding around him. His boots sloshed listlessly through the tattered flesh and puddled entrails of his comrades. She shivered as his gaze fell over her, his fear entrenching upon her mind and spreading through her thoughts like a deadly plague. Another blast thundered through the wreckage and ripped the soldier apart. Everyone was dead.

Except Vega.

The woman emerged from the abyssal shadows, her olive skin glistening with blood. She darted through the demolished streets and smoggy smoke, her torn coat bunched into a ball and clutched to her chest like a sleeping babe. The turret swiveled, dogging her steps but lingering a moment behind. The turret fired, shifting the vehicle, and ruptured the street with another blast.

It was too late; she leapt up the armored plates, ducked out of the turret's sight, and crawled along the edge of the giant.

Vega crouched near the turret barrels, bracing against the steel dome and hatch. Several panels along the top of the tank-like vehicle were pried open from the inside. Rifles and other high-caliber weapons jabbed through the latches, and the enemy opened fire on their own vehicle.

Sparks streaked from bullets pelting the armored hide like hail against a tin roof. Celeste ducked, partially shielding her face as whizzing lead missiles ricocheted into the wreckage around her. Vega hunched her shoulders, unfolding the coat in her arms. Her hand then blurred to her mouth. Tenebrous eyes bore into Celeste's, and bloodied lips parted with another deadly smile. A metal pin dangled from her clenched teeth. She dropped the grenade into the makeshift satchel.

Vega launched through the gunfire, shrouding herself in her tattered shirt while a storm of bullets followed. Blood spat across the pavement rubble as she landed, stumbled, then bolted away from the vehicle.

A sickening realization settled upon its occupants; the gunfire ceased, and a metal hatch swung open, flooding the street with screams and panicked cries. Nobody made it out.

A ball of flames burst and engulfed the vehicle in a fiery haze. Torrents of smoke surged from the ruptured metal, suffocating her with the smell of burning flesh. Her body numbed. Pain pierced her ears like a shrill shriek.

Everything was a nauseating blur. She stood, barely, skin scorching from the billowing flames, and eyes stinging from the smoke. Boots slopped through guts. She wiped her face, smearing black along her sleeves.

Black.

Chills coursed through her, as if plunging deep beneath frozen waters.

Dark blood. Horrified, she wanted to scream. *This can't be happening.*

But it was. Black puddles bubbled and frothed like murky boiling water. Corpses stirred. A loathsome clamor arose from the bloody muck; gurgling wails, splitting flesh, and rupturing bones.

Infected.

Dark masses of putridity clawed through the fleshy remains of their former selves. Shadows thrashed along the surface of the macabre ocean, rising like black smog streaming into the night air. Jagged crimson bones glistened through cloudy patches of torn flesh, serrating their bodies like the edge of a toothed blade. Their dead, sunken eyes searched for blood.

A voracious gaze settled on her, then another turned to snap its jaws at her. They found their prey. Her muscles were rigid, her blade more like an anchor weighing her arm to her side. They lunged, scything their bloody bone claws. But terror consumed her as she awaited the reaper's strike.

Move!

The familiar nudge against her mind flushed purpose through her thoughts, boiling her blood and thawing the fear from her heart. Instincts predominated.

Attack before cornered!

With one long stride, she cleaved through the first one's neck. It growled as the machete sawed through its tattering flesh, retching dark blots up the face of her blade. It thrashed its bony fists blindly while its head lolled over its shoulder. More flesh tore from its partially severed neck. She pivoted and sank her blade into another. Bones snapped. The creature fell and gnashed its razor teeth. It struggled feebly, squirming its near limbless body beneath her blade. The turret had previously torn the former soldier apart, mangling what remained.

There were too many. Snarling, waling, spewing frothy black saliva. Swinging their bony fists like drunken brawlers in a seedy bar.

Know when to run!

They screeched, swarming her like a nest of agitated hornets. She slashed wildly. Blood streaked. Boots stomped through the massacre as she dashed through the damned horde.

She lost track of how many strikes slipped through her guard. Bruises, gashes, lacerations – drowning in a frenzy, she numbed against the pain and fear, shoving against the shadowed mass converging on her warm flesh.

She reeled, firing the revolver. Two shots punched through the remaining clumps of flesh on one creature's head, but lodged against a grimy skull. She lowered the barrel, squeezing the trigger again. Its kneecap burst through the tattered ribbons of its pants. A boggy stream of blood poured to the ground, and its leg *crunched* in half, mid-run. It didn't stop. It clawed up her jeans in a fitful rage. She stomped its limps into the pavement wreckage before sprinting for the nearest intact building.

Turbid smoke concealed the street like a smoggy curtain. She squinted through the roiling irritant, spotting two more vehicles lurching across the rubble.

Let them deal with this mess.

The ground rumbled, and gunfire blared and dulled her hearing. The first door she approached was locked, and the next one as well. The infected shrilled, scrambling through the gunfire and lunging for their prey. She rammed her shoulder against the door. Part of the frame splintered, and she burst through the entryway.

She slammed the door and braced against it. The lock had ripped through the framing, so it wouldn't latch shut and stay secured. She heard them, screeching through the gunfire clamor and clawing at the dingy wooden door.

The stale air burned her ragged lungs. Sweat pasted hair to her face like soggy paper. The creatures thrashed against her strength, hammering the door like a battering ram. Bony fingers wiggled through the ruptured frame. Her strength dwindled.

A fight it is then.

She grimaced, then pushed away from the door.

They funneled through the entryway, a confused inrush of rage, lunacy, and insatiable hunger. Her blade minced flesh. She hacked through the surging frenzy, lopping off limbs and grinding against bone. She howled with them, lusting after their blood as they did hers; fury bereaved her of any coherent thought beyond kill.

There were *still* too many, and her body already strained past its limits. They would fall, collapsing into puddles of their own muddy blood, only to writhe along the ground after her. Others swung their stumpy limbs and snapped their teeth as if already rending away her scarred flesh.

Reeling, she ducked into the adjoining room and they swarmed through the door after her. The terrible roar of gunfire hadn't ceased; bullets burst through walls and windows, shattering glass and splintering wood. Firelight beamed through the ruptured walls like streaks of blood. Another room, lightless and abounding with shadows, welcomed her fearful flight.

I'm trapped!

A blur of white lashed out through the shadowed shroud. Movement came a moment too late; she jerked her head back, but still caught the blow across her face. Skin split and blood warmed her cheek. The machete snagged on something behind her, tangling when she slashed at her relentless attacker. She fell, swarmed by flurries of fists and battering bones. A scream pierced through the ringing in her ears.

Her attacker collapsed in a spatter of blood. A shadow slithered through the darkness. Dizzying light blinded her. A loud blast rocked her eardrums, and a bitter metallic smell burned her nostrils. Another blast thundered against her chest, another corpse fell.

Celeste barely scrambled to her feet before she propelled through the frenzied infected. She embraced the floor again, skidded across the hardwood like a stone skimming over water, and then crashed violently into the furnishings.

An earsplitting wail escaped the torn lips of an infected soldier. It towered over her, mouth widened. Droplets of sludgy saliva rained from its gleaming fangs. She lifted her blade and swung, battering uselessly against armored bone. Before she fell to its rapacious clutches, a dark, blood soaked blade carved through its face and partially severed its jaw. It lurched from the blow and slammed to the floor, still struggling under the blade.

"Get up and fight," a somber voice hissed through the shadows. "Or die yet again!" A blinding light flashed from the barrel of a gun. The infected soldier stopped squirming, his incoherent sputters trailing into a quiet gurgle.

Celeste slipped through the bloody muck, her machete slashing through empty air. Her eyes adjusted to the eerie glow, searching through the dim haze. The infected wailed for her blood. Hell's stampede launched through the entryway after her.

Her pulse pounded, dulling their horrific cries. Before an infected soldier swung its bony limb, she cleaved through its outstretched arm and nearly severed the entire appendage. It dangled uselessly, but the soldier's bloody half-stump reached for her with phantom claws. She leaned back, letting the infected creature fall past her. Then she hurled herself into it.

Shoved unexpectedly, it stumbled and flailed its arms like a rotted bird trying to take flight. It screeched madly, then regained its balance as the blade blurred through its neck. It collapsed, and its head hit the floor with a *thud* then rolled past her boots.

More materialized from the shadows. She slashed through their frenzied fists and ravenous jaws, immersing herself in the fury that followed. Warped, bony knuckles grazed her face. She thrashed her blade against pummeling fists, and shoved a rabid soldier toward the woman in the doorway.

Balance wavering, Vega recoiled from the unanticipated blow. Her blade battered its fist, barely biting into its mangled flesh. She stumbled from the clumsy strike then hacked through its leg, and as it fell to the floor, its neck. It didn't stop there. The corpse clambered up her legs like a fleshy ladder, heaved itself up, and clawed into her bloodstained clothes. Like the hood of some cadaverous sweater, its head dangled loosely down its back, hanging by its partially severed neck.

Her throat is exposed, Celeste's predacious thoughts echoed. *Go for the kill!*

The moment Vega turned her back, Celeste gave chase. She sprang, teeth gritted and a growl rumbling in her throat. Her blade leapt for the woman's neck.

But a hollowed gaze found hers as Vega spun on her heels. The thrashing corpse twirled with her like a ghoulish dancer, before flinging from her loosened grip and colliding with Celeste.

Teeth snapped at her neck, and the corpse battered her chest. She shoved it aside, crouched, and leapt at Vega. Like fangs on a lunging snake, the blade sank into the woman's leg with an upward thrust.

Vega snarled like a threatened beast and leapt away from the steely bite. Celeste couldn't match her speed; it took moments to steady herself, raise her blade, and dart her eyes around the shadows only to realize Vega had once again receded out of sight.

But she was far from alone.

Screaming their fury, the remaining infected struck from the darkness. She ducked under their malformed fists and bolted across the lightless room. They sloshed through the bloody muck after her.

With the last of her strength, she lifted her machete and whirled; the blade tore through the dead soldier's neck. Its legs buckled and its body went limp. It slid into the wall as the other stomped through its corpse. Breathless, the blade was impossibly heavy in her hands. The infected corpse slashed at her with jagged, skeletal fingers.

Vega severed the soldier's arm with one fluid swing. Celeste grimaced against the throb in her muscles, letting hatred fuel her movements. She slashed at Vega, but the woman slipped a punch through her guard. Knuckles crushed her lips, bursting blood from the split skin. She tumbled back through the entryway.

Screaming maniacally, the infected soldier shoved through Vega and charged for Celeste. Dizzied, she ducked under another swing, and its bone cudgel thrashed into the drawers above her head. Jagged, splintered wood, chunks of plastic, and mangled silverware; she shielded her face from the showering debris and braced for the creature's strike.

Vega threw herself into the infected soldier. They crashed through the splintered countertop, and Vega pummeled the creature into the ruptured wood as though a maddened, raving corpse herself.

Celeste drove her machete into Vega's back. Or at least tried to. The woman lurched sideways, and Celeste buried the blade deep into the wreckage.

Sable eyes bore into hers, rooting fear deep into her heart.

Vega twirled her scarlet tinged blade while Celeste pulled hers free; the machete's dull edge *smacked* against Vega's skull before the woman could thrust her blade into Celeste's belly. Serrated teeth ripped through her arm instead. A fresh flow of warmth spread through her sweater.

Vega grunted loudly, stumbling into the counter. Celeste winced, but gripped her machete tight by her side. A desperate, defiant cry erupted from her as she charged.

Vega braced. She leaned back, forcing a cupboard door open. The machete blade speared the makeshift shield, rupturing the wood. Vega drove her heel into Celeste's chest, propelling her away from the infected soldier's sudden strike. Machete in hand, Celeste stumbled into the rubble while Vega hacked the corpse into a dark pile of stringy flesh.

"The weak do not kill the strong!" Vega stormed savagely. Her usual stoic façade faded to a dismal frown, and her nebulous eyes momentarily burned bright with anger as she muttered to Celeste, "You can't keep hesitating. Sooner or later, you'll have to make your move."

Face flushed and breathless, Celeste threw herself forward in a flashy lunge. Sparks flashed as Vega's blade viciously greeted her aimless swipe. The blow jolted the machete and rattled her bones. Vega's blade corkscrewed around hers – once, twice, then finally on the third, the hilt slipped through her fingers and left a dent in the tiled floor when it landed out of reach. A triumphant smile arced across Vega's blood spattered face – which quickly fell into an astonished gape.

"This *was* my move," Celeste hissed gravely, thrusting her old knife deeper into Vega's tender belly. "And it's just the beginning."

"I-I commend your newfound strength and resolve," replied Vega, muttering through the blood pooling in her mouth. "But you're right, my girl. This is *far* from over."

Vega pulled herself free of the blade's grip in her gut. Blood spouted from the wound. The woman leaned against the kitchen ruins, muddy scarlet streaming through her fingers from clasping the wound shut with one hand. With the other, she dangled a spherical device by a small metal ring.

"Here's my next move." She flicked her wrist, pulling loose the ring and pin. The grenade dropped to the ground, the weighty *thud* muffled by stomping boots as they both scrambled through the darkness.

Celeste propelled through the nearest entryway. Descending like a falcon's dive, she snatched her fallen machete like unwary prey. A terrible roar followed. Her eardrums rattled then seemingly burst; an ardent blast erupted and scorched through the room. She was thrown to the floor then buried under smoking debris. Everything crashed down around her.

The first coherent thought trickling back through her addled mind had been death. Momentarily certain it had finally claimed her, she almost succumbed to the numbing black her mind feebly struggled against.

No, she thought grimly. *I wouldn't be in this much pain.*

Everything hurt. Bones, muscles, bruised and spongy flesh. Lacerations, gashes. She couldn't tell if bones were broken or muscles were torn. Movement was near impossible; she writhed and wormed, but the rubble tightly enclosed around her, a suffocating coffin.

"... Couldn't survive that, the whole damn building nearly collapsed in on itself."

Voices, dulled and stifled by the debris, trickled through her ringing ears. "I'm sure I saw someone in the windows, Pete." A familiar, mellifluous tone.

"Even if there was," replied the man named Pete, "they probably got crushed under all that wreckage."

"We have to check..."

"In case you haven't noticed, Jeremy, the entire city is under siege. The North Sector has fallen and the South undoubtedly will as well. We have to rendezvous with our squad and get the hell out of here while we still can."

"Jesus, Pete," said Jeremy. "You can be one selfish asshole."

"Why the hell do you think I'm still alive? Let's go, douchebag, before you get us killed gawking at a pile of rubble."

"Yeah, we're supposed... Hey, what the hell is that?"

"Goddamn, man. What now?"

"There!"

Celeste had been clawing her way through the rubble the moment she recognized Jeremy's voice. Attempts at yelling only filled her mouth, throat, and lungs with dirt and debris. Panicking, she squirmed until the cold air pierced her skin, and air rushed through to her aching lungs. She gasped wildly as a rigid grip plucked her from the rubble like a battered flower.

"Shit," Pete said. "You were right."

Jeremy ignored him. "Celeste?" He helped her balance, steadying her while she reeled and expelled the grime from her mouth.

"Jeremy," she finally croaked out, her voice raspy and broken. "Thank you."

"Holy Christ, Celeste," exclaimed Jeremy. "What the hell happened?"

She grinned weakly, sarcasm lacing her words as she responded quietly, "Bit obvious, isn't it?"

He chortled, "Yeah, just a little." Then seriously, he added, "Look, the city isn't going to last, rebels are overwhelming our forces. We have to get out of here quickly."

"Rebels," she repeated with a distasteful mutter. "Right."

"Come on, you can come with us..."

"Aw, hell no!" Pete interjected suddenly, hands blurring to his weapon. Before she responded, he thrust the barrel of his rifle toward her. "Celeste. I recognizes this bitch's name!"

"Pete, what the hell?" Confused, Jeremy faced his comrade, but Celeste merely glowered.

"This is the little whelp they were talking about on the radio!" He yelled back, his young face twisting into a vengeful frown. "The one that broke into the lower levels!"

"Pete," Jeremy said calmly. "That hardly matters at the moment. We need to get out of here!"

"May not matter to you, rookie," he replied, tone venomous and cold. "But I'm a goddamn soldier, through and through. I follow orders. Vega told everyone to shoot on sight." He peered down his sights, clenching his rifle tight. "Keep warm in hell," he snickered cruelly to Celeste.

Her fingers twitched, hand hovering over her holstered revolver. *I won't be able to draw in time.* Her heart plummeted to her belly. *But I'm not giving up without...*

She cringed when a loud *crack* startled her. A thin rivulet of blood trickled through the small hole in Pete's forehead. He gaped for a moment, eyes dulled and partially closed, before his legs buckled and he fell to the pavement.

"God, he was an unbearable asshole," whispered Pete, almost too quietly for Celeste to hear. His oceanic eyes shimmered regret. Then he turned, brimming purpose and saying, "Now, we can get out of here."

She wanted to ask him why, to know his reasoning behind dispatching a comrade to aid someone they were ordered to eliminate. She wanted to thank him, let him know a familiar face warmed the chilling fear engulfing her mind. Or berate him for his blatant foolishness, for endangering his life to protect hers, someone he barely knew. It all swirled through her mind, a blur of thoughts she couldn't focus on. Words were smothered by confusion before they tumbled from her tongue.

Then warm blood spattered her face. She flinched, screaming as Jeremy grunted and stumbled into her. Two more quick bursts echoed through the street. More blood warmed her face. Slender fingers slithered through his hair, gripped tightly, then yanked his head back; slashed with a dark blade, blood cascaded from his neck like a descending claret curtain. He stumbled, then collapsed near Pete, gurgling on his own blood.

"No..." Celeste whispered, tears blurring her sight.

"Yes," responded Vega, her gelid tone forcing shivers down Celeste's spine. "Love is a distraction. Love is a weakness." She gestured to Jeremy with her blade. The dying boy writhed, but his movements slowed. "Now finish it. No more distractions."

Love isn't weakness. It can't be.

Or is it?

Father always maintained it had been what kept him strong for so many years, the love he felt for his family. Even after mom and brother were gone, his beliefs persisted, saying their love kept him alive. But it had also darkened him, fractured his heart, and soured his mind. I watched him wallow in his despair, howl his fury, and glare at me with cold eyes. My very presence was a constant aching reminder of what he'd lost. He'd cared for me, but even the loss overwhelmed that. He'd spent his remaining years clinging to loving memories and the ghost of hope long faded.

But love gave me hope, purpose. A reason to struggle when death waited for me to fall. Love kept me by father's side, even when he'd lost himself to despair and despised company for weeks without end.

It surged within her now. Her heart drowned in a spate of it. *Aurous.*

Melina. Strength blossomed. *They made me stronger. I fight for them.*

"You're right," Celeste finally whispered, tears streaming down her face. Her hand fell to her revolver. "No more distractions."

I'm sorry, Jeremy.

He stopped struggling. The last of his blood drained past his hands, and he went limp, still lost in her sorrowful gaze. His skin darkened rapidly, as if invisible fists pummeled and bruised his flesh. The corpse convulsed before her revolver erupted and recoiled in her hand. The bullet drilled through Jeremy's skull and his spasms ceased. He was finally, truly dead.

"Now," she said, indifferent. "It's just you and me."

Vega smiled, licking her bloodied lips. Her eyes beamed avidity as the ground rumbled beneath their feet like it threatened to rupture and split. A laugh like shattering glass carried through the uproar.

The streets teemed with them; vehicles lurched across the streets, ripping uncontrollably through the wreckage like derailed trains. Armored, windowless, and easy twice the size of the turret-vehicle – yet no discernable weapons or firepower on any of them. Instead, large metal hatches covered each side, similar to the reinforced steel door securing the basement of Whytecliff Hospital. Steam jetted and puffed into the air like dwindling fog. The hatches slid open.

There were countless of them, serried and shrouded in shadows, bony quills, and serrated claws. Bloodied eyes burned through the night like flickering, hellish flames.

Terror gripping her spine, she whispered fearfully, "Hunters."

An army of them!

"Well," replied Vega, bemused. "Looks like we're not alone after all."

TWENTY-ONE
HELL INCARNATE

SHADOWS STIRRED like gathering storm clouds while guttural roars thundered. Waves of darkness rose and crashed to the pavement, surging and inundating from metallic tombs.

Fear swept through Celeste like a rush of icy water. Horrified, she witnessed the outpouring of malevolence, the streets benighted by battalions of living nightmares, embodiments of hell itself. Their appetence resonated as terrible howls. Their jaws snapped perniciously, and their haunting, crimson eyes searched the city for prey.

The malefic horde howled like tornadic winds. Bloodcurdling cries and screams rose with the horrible tumult, shrilling from the dwindled ranks of soldiers entrapped by hell's shadow.

The Hunters charged.

It was a riotous bloodbath. Claws mangled and minced. Vehicles recently disembarked were upturned, torn through, and shredded like old paper. The screams of its occupants, if any, went unheard through the uproar.

Smaller vehicles burst through the chaos, resembling the few she'd seen patrolling the city before. Their turrets *boomed* and flashed in a brilliance of fiery light. Armed soldiers, thrown into the same bloodlust frenzy as the monsters around them, leapt from the moving vehicles in an attempt to barricade the Hunters from the rest of the city. Turrets provided cover fire while the soldiers formed along the fringes of the congested streets.

"You see," declared Vega, waving her blade excitedly. "This is strength; to fight when all seems lost and hopeless, to sacrifice everything you love in hope of change." She raised her blade, shouting madly through the pandemonium, "We fight for the ones we've lost, our blood that was spilled, and the hell we'll always live with! Kill them all!"

They couldn't hear her; their hearts were not stirred by valiant words, nor were their spirits raised by the bravery and hope steeling her tone. Her voice was but an echo through the caliginous symphony. But their eyes had found hers, battening from the brimming anger in her soulless gaze. Her furor spread to infect her fellow soldiers like a prideful disease. Her shouts may have been lost to the clamor, but as she propelled into the monstrous mass, their cries rallied to strengthen hers and drown out the cacophonous howls of bloodthirsty beasts.

Celeste stared after Vega, revolver trailing. The woman disappeared under the shadowed spate. She surfaced a moment later, slashing her ebony blade against bony quills and scimitar claws. Soldiers dove into the tempest after her, screaming through their gunfire and thundering turrets.

Hunters collided with the blockade of tender meat. A plethora of lead punched into armored scales, and razor bones ripped through flesh in return. Tank-like vehicles plowed through the predacious throng. Turrets manned by blood spattered soldiers screamed with unbridled fury over the peal of discharging weapons. Blade clanged against claw. Bodies fell – bisected, beheaded, severed into unrecognizable clumps of meat – or scattered through the air as shadowy mist when claws and fangs cleaved through the crowd.

Celeste stood while the maelstrom unfolded, disconcerted from the horror and death consuming the city. The revolver trembled in her hand as she stared, mouth agape. Her heart *thumped* fear as the conflict boiled over her.

The Hunters were coming.

A primal urge growled inside her, snarling and howling through her mind until fear ebbed like light from a dying flame. *This is my world.*

My kill!

Abandoning thought, she dived into chaos.

Claws descended for her flesh, thwarting her mindless charge. She lifted her blade to deflect the strike. The force of the blow flared pain through her wearied muscles. Her shoulder burned, nearly dislocated. Her heart hammered adrenaline into her veins.

Twirling, her revolver bucked two bullets into the monster, but the lead barely pierced its thick armor. In the fiery light, fragments of metal glinted through the scales. It opened its snout, bared twisted fangs and frothy, black saliva, and then bellowed its hunger.

But she heard nothing between the constant high-pitched ring of her damaged ears and the beat of her accelerated heart. Even the blare of her own revolver erupting in her hand was but a muffled echo down a long and distant corridor.

Another bullet tore through the Hunter's agape jaws. Black blood spurted, and it staggered but then roared with anger again. Claws raked through the cement as it readied a pounce.

The ground rumbled before beginning to burst. Turret-fire ripped into the cement and carved a sinuous path of destruction toward the Hunter. The vehicle circled them, turret swiveling and firing madly. The Hunter roared when the weapon overwhelmed it. Scales split, bones cracked and shattered – but the Hunter still charged for the vehicle. Wheels smoked and burned into the rubble as the vehicle sped out of the monster's reach. The turret blasted the Hunter's flesh and bones apart. Finally, the monster dropped as most of its entrails slopped out of its mangled body like supplies spilling through a rip in a rucksack.

The turret's victory was cruelly short-lived; three more Hunters surged against the vehicle, upturning it and tearing through the armored metal. Then their voracious appetites growled for her blood.

Shadows blurred. She fired another shot, then holstered her revolver. All three Hunters roared, ripping through the wreckage. She stood defiantly, but even the wolf inside her whispered, *there's a time to fight, and a time for flight.*

RUN!

She reeled, and a Hunter lunged. It slashed through the cement a moment too late, but followed her maddened dash for the heart of the hellish throng. The rest gave chase to the feeding frenzy.

Soldiers corralling the creatures were torn apart. Ranks were ripped through and vehicles destroyed; acrid smoke from burning flesh and spilled innards suffocated the streets. Tears soothed the stinging in her eyes, but death burned into her nostrils. She gagged.

Two soldiers on her right both fired rifles, darting around the shadowed monster behind her. The Hunter roared, turned, and slashed its curved claws. One soldier slipped around the monster, opening fire on the base of its malformed skull. Bellowing rage, it swung a hulking arm and flailed. His comrade sprinted around the behemoth while the other became the distraction. The second soldier lifted his rifle and peered down the sights. Then he screamed. The monster's neck twisted back so its bloodied eyes could glare into his.

His comrade cursed loudly and squeezed the trigger to his rifle. Indifferent to the bullets pelting its scaly armor, the Hunter arced its neck and sank its gnarled fangs into the soldier. It wrenched the body and severed it, then turned to the other with flesh ribboning down its snout.

She ran, shutting out the man's petrified scream as the Hunter descended upon him as well. His blood spilling and seeping into the wreckage did little to garner her interest. Her predatory gaze combed through the shadowed horde and blurred faces while she dashed into battle, her blade lunging and hacking anything in her path.

Bullets *zinged* and *whizzed* past her head. How many followed the balm of her untainted blood? How many soldiers aimed their weapons into the horde, only to nearly fill her with lead in lieu of a Hunter, or came back as an infected, mangled corpse to screech and wail for death?

She didn't care. Her eyes finally settled upon her prey.

Vega immersed herself in the frenzy, blade swinging and pistol firing. Claws scythed and fangs gnashed, but she struck then blurred out of sight before the monsters could react. Soldiers rallied wherever they spotted her. They provided cover fire, or hurled themselves at Hunters and became fleshy shields while she dashed through the horde. Celeste lost sight of the phantom woman, drowning in a tidal wave of human meat, blood, and scaly armor.

More turrets erupted in a fiery cannonade, propelling into the battle or besetting the abyssal pool of swarming Hunters. Soldiers thrived and converged on the shadowy mass. Yet no matter how many Hunters or infected fell to their impressive onslaught, there seemed to be no end to horror. Vehicles were overrun and torn apart. Turrets fired into the crowd of monsters until Hunters and infected wrenched open hatches and slaughtered the occupants. Tanks, blasting their twin barrel-cannons, were demolishing buildings and toppling them over like sandcastles crumbling from ocean waves.

She'd lost sight of Vega. In fact, she'd lost sight of damn near everything. Bodies dropped around her, whether malformed and mutated, or bloodied and severed. Swirls of shadows and bone, gunfire, and blades – a dizzying and chaotic blur of death. Screams and savage roars pierced her muffled ears. Gunfire. Her lungs ached from the smoke and putrid burning flesh. Pain scorched her chest with each deep *thump* of her heart.

There!

Vega emerged, her olive skin and clothes smeared with black blood. Her ebony blade struck claw. She bolted between Hunters, lacerating her shoulders and arms along their bony quills. The behemoths followed her, stampeding through the wreckage and dead.

Celeste hurled herself into riotous slaughter. Impassive eyes riveted Vega's as the woman cleaved a bloody path through the jungle of meat.

Infected fists studded with bony barbs were intent on pummeling her while she ran. Some were even reaching from the bloody muck and rubble, bodies severed and torn but still thirsting for blood. Celeste pursued Vega deeper into the massacre.

The further she ventured, the more monsters thrived. Claws like wickedly hooked blades nearly sundered every limb with one strike, skeletal fists battered against her bruised body, and piercing teeth snapped for her flesh. Gunfire incessantly beat against her eardrums. She couldn't navigate through it all. There were too many, monsters and soldiers alike.

An infected corpse lunged for her before being ripped apart by a turret's bullet barrage. She dove behind an advancing group of soldiers. More infected clogged the street around them. Desultory gunfire followed.

Too many! They were enclosing around her. *I'll either be stomped into a puddle of blood or killed by reckless aim.*

Scrambling to her feet, the sounds of their tormented screams battered her eardrums. She dashed behind the guards, skimming the razor edge of her blade across the tender flesh of their legs. The first two fell as their knees buckled. The third stumbled, turning to face his hauteur attacker, only to quickly realize his fatal blunder as the infected fell over him with a flurry of gangly limbs.

Vega! She glimpsed the woman briefly, her vengeful gaze burning into alluring, shadow eyes. *She's daring me to follow.* She gritted her teeth. *But she's too far. I'll never make it.*

The ground rumbled and an engine roared loudly.

Not on foot.

It was a smaller vehicle with six large wheels caked in blood and guts. Its body was slender, but reinforced with armor like the others. Two turrets were mounted on the top. It rammed through anything in its path; the infected were dragged under the monstrous rubber, crushed, and splattered into a muddy mist.

Jumping on to the back of vehicle wasn't difficult, it was maintaining a solid grip on the blood slickened armor which proved laborious. She clenched her fists tight, careful not to slop infected entrails and blood on her wounds. Disastrous. The vehicle jostled and her boots slipped through the muck. The air was slammed from her lungs when she lurched forward, crashing into solid steel. Momentarily disoriented, she peered quizzically through metal bars and spotted the sullen face of a seasoned soldier. He shouted something she couldn't discern through the clamor. It took a few seconds for her mind to snap back into her skull.

Her hands fumbled for any sort of latch; the soldier was behind a mesh of metal and steel bars, wrapped around him and the weapon as makeshift armor. For confidence more than protection. Bullets could easily pierce the thin strips of steel, and the various openings made a direct attack a frightening possibility. Which is why she thrust the barrel of her revolver through such an opening and splattered the man's brains all over his own weapon. She finally pried one of the steel plates loose and slipped inside the confines of the turret.

Holy crap. She pulled the body off the weapon, letting the former soldier slump against the curved steel. *This is a big gun.* It easily matched her height. Serried barrels clasped together by large metal rings protruded from the makeshift armor. Rows of bullets dangled from the weapon, bunching and piling on the floor, glimmering gold. It was heavy, even propped on a swivel. Tiny hands slipped around the handle of the mammoth weapon, and she sneered down the massive sights.

To hell with this place! She squeezed the trigger.

At first the barrels rotated slowly, then they *whirled* into a blur; bullets burst through flashes of fiery light, chomping through flesh and shattering bone. The vehicle rolled deeper into the horde. Grunting, she struggled to swivel the hefty weapon. Like a spinning blade, the bullet stream sawed through flailing corpses. Rendered into puddles of flesh, the infected succumbed to the turret's onslaught, but the Hunters stormed through the cannonade.

Her scream mimicked their bloodthirsty howls, ragged with savagery. She glared down the sights and the weapon surged in her grasp, its recoil *pounding* against her chest. Bullets punched through scaly armor and ruptured craggy bone, but glowing, ember eyes bore into hers.

Another vehicle swerved to her left, both machine guns *whirling* and erupting in quick, deafening blasts. The monster collapsed, and victorious bellows boomed from the vehicle's occupants. Using her weight, she leaned and forced the weapon's fury on them.

A torrent of bullets tore through the wheels and carved up into the metal armor. Rubber exploded into a cloud of shredded ribbons. The vehicle lost control, swerved into the mass of monsters, then abruptly lurched across the wreckage. Weapons, steel plates and soft, fleshy bodies – it all became clumps of gnarled metal and blood as the vehicle rolled violently, crushing the soldiers and their makeshift turrets.

The Hunters pullulated. Shadows thrashed against the vehicle, clawing through the armor and clogging her escape. The barrels to her weapon slowed and dulled the blare in her ears. She watched helplessly as the soldier on the other end of the vehicle frantically pried the steel plates loose to the hatch. But the Hunters converged on them. Claws and bone ripped through the pitiful armor and soldier's flesh before the panicking man freed himself.

Bony points pierced the steel armor around her.

Too many!

The giant machine gun had been rendered useless. The vehicle heaved and rocked. She grasped the metal mesh, straining for balance. Pulling herself through the pried hatch, she tumbled back to pavement as the wreckage came crashing down around her.

Shadows surged after her, but her legs couldn't carry her quickly enough. It was a violent flood, impossible to outrun. She heard the collision behind her, the quickened gunfire and screams, the sickly noise of sundering flesh, and the shrill screech of bloodlust.

I need to get out of here!

Two soldiers obstructed her path, weapons firing into the charging horde. She crouched low, machete swiftly clearing her belt. One soldier had his head turned, his attention focused elsewhere. His comrade noticed her a moment too late; her blade impaled his chest, wedging between his ribs, and plunging into his flesh. He fell with a gurgled scream, now motionless under the weight of her blade. His weapon slipped from his grasp into hers.

THUMP!

Before the first soldier investigated the reason for his comrade's scream, the shotgun in her hands tore through his spine and flesh with a forceful blast. *Crunch.* She pulled the blade from the first man's ruptured chest cavity, then bolted for one of the buildings.

Jostled, she unwillingly, and roughly, embraced the ground while a vehicle careened past. It collided with the entrance to the building, bursting through the walls and fracturing the support. Part of the structure collapsed in on itself, burying the vehicle and its occupants under suffocating rubble. Debris choked her lungs. Her eyes searched for another escape, but her frantic gaze settled on burning crimson. The Hunter snapped its jaws as she lifted the shotgun.

THUMP!

The bright blast ripped most of the scaly flesh around the Hunter's malformed snout. Strings of meat and gristle slopped down its face. Still snarling, it snapped at her again. She pumped the forend and fired.

THUMP!

Bone glistened, and a skeletal snout parted with an earsplitting howl. She squeezed the trigger again – nothing happened.

Crap.

The emptied shotgun dropped to the ground while she reached for her blade. The Hunter arced its neck back, readying its lunge. More black sludge slopped around its ruptured scaly flesh. Another howl, then abrupt silence. The creature went limp, *smacking* its colossal skull off the concrete by her boots.

"Keeping your head in battle," Vega approved, wrenching her blade from the nape of the Hunter's fleshy neck. "Smart. Fighting when you could flee... Admirable, but as always, foolish."

"I've had enough of your lessons," Celeste snarled in response. She steadied her breathing, despite the adamant burn in her lungs. She wasn't willing to display the fear teeming though her mind. It was a potential dagger to her heart. "It's time we end this madness."

Her laugh shrilled through the chaotic clamor. "I told you, it's *far* from over! The best part has yet to come, my dear!"

"It's over, Vega!" Celeste screamed. Anger boiled over, spilling through her veins. "The city has fallen!" Fingers enclosed around the revolver. "And so have you!"

"There it is! The fire in your eyes settling to darkness, the cold breaching through the warmth encompassing your soul!" She smiled wickedly, shadowy blood dribbling down her chin. It streamed from her nose, now crooked and split along the middle from a recent break. "This city falls when I say it does!"

She launched herself into the frenzy, and like that, she was gone.

Not this time! Celeste dashed over the mangled corpses, scanning the battle raging around her. She spotted the woman ghosting through the crowd, slithering quickly through the shadowed blurs and struggling soldiers.

She's trying to escape!

Infected beings lashed out at her. Hunters roared, and the ground trembled under their stampeding charge. Gunfire deafened as it erupted by her head. Vehicles discharged their weapons, paying no heed to fellow soldiers in a desperate gamble for escape. She ran through it all, her own screams bellowing soundlessly through hell's terrible roar.

Vega bolted for her own crowd of soldiers along the edges of the street. They were providing constant cover fire, tearing through any fleshy being approaching their ranks, infected or otherwise. Bullets were *zinging* past her ears or *slapping* into meaty bodies around her.

The bitch grinned back at her. Thrusting her arms into one of her soldier's chest, she shoved the unsuspecting man into Celeste's path.

The soldier grunted, surprised, then shouted his frustration when he stumbled off balance. He looked up, almost apologetic at his bluster, until he caught Celeste rapidly approaching out of the corner of his eye. Before he could lift his weapon or even open his mouth in protest, her blade cleaved through his neck. She kept pace and pushed through the soldiers who now turned their weapons on her in vengeance.

She didn't care. They would soon answer to the hell that followed her. Screams haunted the spurts of gunfire as the Hunters giving chase to her descended upon the rank of soldiers instead. Shoving through her fellow soldiers, Vega continued to carelessly expend any life in a scramble to save her own.

There was a steady influx of soldiers, both on foot and jammed shoulder-to-shoulder inside armored tanks. Some paused, momentarily bewitched at the sight of their leader dashing from battle, before turning and marching with vigor into death's awaiting arms. Others murmured between themselves, possibly questioning the reason for to continue marching toward their imminent demise if their own leader wasn't willing to do so. Someone shouted her name, even reached out as she ran past. A blur of black and a streak of blood; the man lost his arm, screaming loudly enough to stop other soldiers in their tracks. Vega was gone, leaving only bloody footprints through the snow.

Still, Celeste pushed on through the confusion. Two shots rang through the crowded street. Blood steamed as it fell to the snow. A man collapsed beside her, blood bubbling in his throat.

Another shot bellowed.

Zing!

Soldiers were thrown into an uproar. Some marched on, while others desperately searched for the source of the commotion. It didn't matter. Hunters breached the barricade of soldiers behind her. Panic struck. The bravery once riddled throughout their hearts withered and died, poisoned by terror, betrayed by cowardice. It was a mad scramble, a discord of former comrades. They were flooded with diffident thoughts and bowel loosening fear. Hunters surged through them, bloodying their claws and fangs.

It felt as though she were swimming against a tempestuous current, battling waves of haphazardly marching soldiers. Gunfire became sporadic, turrets were destroyed along with most of the vehicles. People were even running into buildings to escape the madness, only to be hunted by the infected and slaughtered out of sight. Still, some soldiers hurried to the battle and willingly leapt into the open jaws of death.

Through the winding streets and sinuous alleys, she relentlessly pursued Vega. The soldiers rushing into battle dwindled to a mere trickle, with some even screaming their indomitable fear and retreating. The horrifying clangor of war resonated through the emptying streets. Shrilling infected, Hunters roaring their bloodlust, and the dying screams of the living. It was a feeding frenzy.

She stepped into the lightless alley, and was quickly greeted by a single bullet. A loud *crack* echoed, followed by the projectile ricocheting into the pavement. Lead burst from her revolver in response. There was a grunt, and the sound of someone collapsing to the pavement. Then a bright flash engulfed the alley.

A scream involuntarily escaped her. Blood. It was streaming from her hip and soaking her jeans. She fell against a building wall, clasping one hand over the wound. It stung, enough that she gritted her teeth to stifle another brewing scream.

Damn it... That one hurt.

It was exceedingly difficult to ignore the pain. Her left leg wanted to buckle under each step. *C'mon, Celeste. Keep moving.* The bloodthirsty screech of infected resonated through the city. *It's time to end this.*

She staggered through the darkness, revolver poised, and finger trembling over the trigger. A faint glow pierced the darkness ahead.

Vega... Where did you go?

She slowed to a cautious amble. *Voices.* Someone barked orders, strict and rough in tone, words harsh and voice grating. Flattening herself against the stone wall, she peeked around the corner, revolver still cocked and eager.

There were three vehicles, each the length of a bus and the width of a tank. Armored, but with no weapons, they only contained large steel hatches along the side.

Carriers, she surmised quietly. *More Hunters.* They obstructed the front entrance, beset by dozens of soldiers garbed in black with red patches. Smog billowed from exhausts and hatch doors. *Why would they use monsters to clear out the city?*

Better question, she grumbled inwardly, fumbling through her pockets for ammunition. *You must have known how powerful the military really was.* Nestling the last bullet in, she snapped the cylinder shut. *Just what is your endgame, Vega?*

What are you planning?

The alley ended near the main entrance to the confined city. Behind her, nothing but darkness and distant screams – the fighting simmered into slaughter. Debris from a demolished building barricaded the street to her left. Straight ahead, an impossibly tall fence scalable only if one had little fear of the wire's razor embrace. Any attempt and the wire would ensnare clothes and skin, piercing barbs promising to shred through the flesh of any foolish struggler.

She could have only gone one way.

The crowd of soldiers, at least a dozen or so, congregated by all three carriers. There were gaps of darkness between vehicles which the moonlight couldn't perforate. As her bleary gaze fell over entrance, she spotted a figure slumped against the fence, the fuzzy outline of someone crouched in the swirling shadows. Ready to strike.

There you are.

It took a few gulps of frigid are to mend her frayed nerves. Her eyes never strayed from the soldiers. They chattered amongst themselves, seemingly oblivious to the deathly pandemonium further into the city. Or they remained indifferent to slaughter, desensitized to the putrid stench of blood, meat, and innards now spoiling the crisp winter air.

Apprehension fluttered inside her chest like butterflies. Leaping from the depths of darkness, she scurried across the wreckage of the road. Then the butterflies seemed more like a swarm of hornets. Each carefully placed step begged silence, but rubble shifted and collapsed from her weight.

The road seemed unusually large. It stretched impossibly long, like no matter how quickly she ran, she'd never close the gap between her and the other side. Voices fueled her fear further; someone laughed deeply, and others shouted over the raucous laughter. Terror swept through her, chills nipping her skin like frostbite.

She didn't stop her desperate scramble until colliding with the fence. She pressed up against it, breathless, letting the sharp embrace of steel chill her skin through her bloody sweater. Then she ghosted toward the entrance.

Flattened against the fence, she leveled the revolver with the shadow ahead. The soldiers were no longer in view, but their uproarious voices reverberated through the street. She heard them all shouting over each other, a garble of slurred words like drunkards stumbling home after a night of drink.

"You see them bastard rebels runnin' to their deaths?"

"They should have retreated when they had the chance. Running to a slaughterhouse. Nothing brave about that shit."

"... Why the rebels even stayed, beyond me!"

Another boisterous laugh. "Bloody fools didn't even reinforce any of the defenses."

"They had access to all that firepower, and barely put up a fight." Someone scoffed, mockingly disappointed. "They deserve to die."

"Right," another one chimed in. "We won't even need to bring in the next platoon."

"You hear they found Stonem?"

"General Stonem?" Someone asked incredulously. "He was overseeing the project when the rebels escaped and decimated his troops. There's no way he survived."

"I served under him," came a gruff response. "He'd die before surrendering to rebels."

"I heard him, clear as day," a burly voice growled. "He and his imprisoned troops escaped the confines of the hospital right before our counterstrike against the city."

"No shit." More murmuring, amazement seizing their tones.

"General Stonem. Always a devious bastard."

"Apparently had help. Someone on the inside freed them."

"I'll be damned..."

Project?

Voices became whispers as her pulse pounded in her ears. Revolver raised, she cautiously approached the slumped shadow. It didn't stir from the snow groaning beneath her boots, or from her harsh, hissing whispers. It remained motionless, even under the nudge of a cold barrel. The figure's head lolled to the side, slipping further into the snow.

The first thought to permeate her mind, *she's already dead.* Instead of drowning under relief, frustration raged to anger. She practically snarled, disgusted by the carrion in front of her.

What did you die of, Vega? She peered closer, her eyes adjusting to the dim light. *The bullet wound or stab wound...*

Fragments of broken bone poked through the mangled meat. Dark blood stained the snow under the body. Wisps of blonde hair speckled with dark blood dangled over his hacked-through face. There was another wound in his neck, a gash deep enough to nearly sever the head. Blood still dripped into the snow.

Fresh.

"... Check on Peterson, he's been taking a piss for a bit too long. Don't want any infected creeping up on us," A rough voice called out.

Crap!

"Yeah, yeah," someone muttered. Behind her, snow *crunched* loudly. "Freezing my ass off out here... Hey, Peterson! Where did you... What the hell is this?"

Bursting from her revolver with a bright glare, a bullet was her response. A yelp carried through the gun's echo. The man staggered, clutching his shoulder as blood seemingly spilt from the red insignia on his uniform. He fumbled for the weapon on his belt with his other hand, shouting for his comrades.

Damn it!

She'd missed, but wasn't about to waste another bullet. She had little to spare. She twirled and dashed through the slushy blood. Two gunshots chased her into the night. Both ricocheted off steel and *zinged* by as she ducked through the entrance.

"It's the Bandit Queen!"

"We've got casualties! Rebels are escaping! Find and kill them!" Someone yelled as she disappeared into the night.

Vengeful cries pursued her up the wooded hillside. There were two paths leading through the forests outside of Whytecliff City – at least two she was aware of – but only one contained bloodied corpses. Vega was leaving a trail of breadcrumbs for her to follow – with flesh. The corpses stirred as she approached, their haunting hisses rasping through the forest.

The machete sank through the skull of the first corpse before it fully transformed. She wrenched her blade free then turned to the others, but their relentless charge had already begun.

The infected wailed and screeched as they ran; soldiers behind her shouted for her blood, infuriated with her attempted escape.

Have fun getting through these bastards!

She arced her arm, then swung her blade at the next infected. It stumbled through the snow, clawing the air as it slipped past. Unable to swing again, she gouged the corpse's leg. Her blade clipped bone. Without slowing, she bolted through the trees, and their hungered wails were silenced by the eruption of gunfire. The cannonade lasted moments, but blinded her with its incandescence. Swallowed by complete darkness, she hurried up the winding path. Then another row of bodies slipped into focus.

More?

She stopped, machete trembling in her hand. They rose from the bloody slush like shadowy ghosts, wailing their desolate melody of blood thirst. She exhaled a shaky breath, unable to calm her nerves. Revolver cocked and machete held tight, she rushed through the infected crowd.

She never aimed to kill, merely hinder. Her machete carved through their legs. Her revolver discharged whenever a snarling corpse lunged. They screamed their rage, dead eyes fixated on her. Then gunfire erupted again.

She left the clamor behind until her own ragged breaths and rapid pulse deadened its chaotic echo. The moon barely penetrated through the treetops, its ashy light beaming through disturbed patches in the snowy canvas above, like faint beacons leading her through the lightless woods.

It started as a murmur, like the babbling brooks she remembered from the mountains, which quickly amplified into a rippling gurgle as she ran through the trees and off the beaten path.

Why would you come here?

It was like the constant revving of a giant engine; a plume of chalky mist rose from the water surging down to the river below. She approached the edge cautiously, carefully placing her boots atop the icy surface. A giant wall spanned the width of the water. Water pooled behind it like a lake, easily doubling the river's size. But only a trickle of water flowed through, cascading down the wall's surface into the roaring current below.

The dam.

"But why here?" She repeated, her voice croaking through chapped lips.

And where the hell are all the guards?

No more corpses littered the walkway or the path leading up to it. *But there's blood.* The slushy muck slopped up her boots. She gripped the steel rail, the gelid bite barely registering through her scarred skin. She closed her eyes and steadied her breathing.

C'mon, Celeste, she convinced herself, *you've seen enough crap to haunt your nightmares for the rest of your days. Not scared of a little height, are you?*

Despite nearly slipping twice when crossing the icy walkway, she clenched her eyes shut and allowed the railing to guide her across. The river's rush was deafening; even through the ringing still prevalent in her ears, she heard the turbulent flow of the river resonating below her. When the railing arced downward, her eyes snapped open to the edge of the walkway. There were no stairs descending from where she stood. She had to ease over the railings and gently cross the rickety scaffolding against the side of the dam. After climbing down, she readied both weapons and gazed into the misty woods.

Did she escape to the mountains? Her eyes settled on the building looming in the shadow of the trees.

The maintenance building. She cocked her revolver and hurried to its doors. *What are you trying to do?*

Bloodlust and fury fueled each step in her myopic approach. So consumed by barbarous thoughts, she didn't see it; razor fangs snagged her sweater, tore the fabric, and grazed her skin in one furious chomp. The blade jarred painfully in her hand as it batted uselessly against a bloodied skull.

Wrenched from her grasp, the machete landed in a pile of snow. The attacker screeched and continued its assault.

She fell back, boots sliding across ice. Two shots burst from her revolver, punching holes into the infected soldier's chest. As it pounced, another round tore through its face. Then another. The corpse fell over her, lifeless, but spilling putrid black ooze over her clothes.

"Disgusting," she muttered, nearly retching with each reluctant breath. The fetid air fouled her tongue.

It was a woman. Well, used to be. A slender frame like Celeste's, she was apparently the same height as well. Her throat had been slit. She groaned and winced. Her body throbbed with pain she couldn't just brush aside as a mere nuisance. Still, she staggered to the doors, careful to keep her eye on the corpse slumped against the wall. The head was entirely bashed in. More bodies piled by the building, garbed in black armor and red insignias. None mutated, but all dead.

The doors *creaked* as she eased them open with a nudge of her revolver. The silver barrel glared through the darkness first.

Empty. So far.

It wasn't long before a faint shine burned her bleary eyes. She followed the wan glow, then paused at the end of the corridor. Blood dappled the floor. Uncertainty quelled the tempest in her heart. Her lungs ached for air.

"So," came the viperous whisper. "You survived."

Pull the trigger!

Keeping her revolver poised, she slowly eased through the doorway. Hatred urged her to pump a few bullets into the woman's skull. Vega was standing, back to Celeste, blade hanging by her side. Blood still dripped down the ebony steel. Her black hair flowed down her shoulders, spattered with crimson and streaked with ash. Her clothes were sopping from innards and blood.

"Alpha team," she remarked, mumbling quietly. "I admired their bravery. They reveled in being cavalry, the heroes turning the tide of battle. They waited patiently while their comrades fought in the city, eager for my command to march onward. I assume you met their corpses on your journey here? Brave souls."

"You killed them," Celeste muttered, her voice tremulous. The only words her tongue would spill. "*You* killed them."

"They fought for our freedom," Vega replied, inimical. She glanced over her shoulder, a smirk spreading across her bloodied skin. Shadows inundated from her callous gaze. "They died for their vengeance. As I live to fulfill mine." She turned slowly, letting the blade slip through her bloody fingers and *clang* against the floor. Extending her other arm, she said, "We were meant to survive, my girl. Fated to this moment since our paths intertwined along that desolate little highway. I knew I would find you again, daughter." Uncurling her fingers, she revealed the small device; small, irregularly shaped, but similar to the radios used to communicate through the city. Though, it held no speaker or dials. Just an antennae protruding from the top and a switch along the side.

Celeste glanced over the device, responding coldly, "I'm not your daughter."

Vega smiled lovingly, clutching the device tightly again. Her eyes however, burned like a sinner's soul within flames. "Aren't you?" She asked wickedly. "Without the warmth of my embrace, would you have survived that treacherous highway? Without my hospitality, would you have lived comfortably amongst my people? Food, clothes, training; it was all offered to you while others had to work, like you were an extension of myself. And who would care for your wounds, no matter how small or insignificant? Tell me, who else would let you soak their nightgown with tears as the vengeful nightmares of your iniquity plagued every sleeping moment?" Blood trailed down her chin from the corner of her mouth. Like parting clouds revealing the faint glow of a starry sky, something shimmered in Vega's eyes, something Celeste had never seen penetrate her apathetic façade. Love. "Who else but a mother?"

Through gritted teeth, Celeste hissed, "You claim you cared, but you left us all to die like vermin!"

"No!" Her response boomed through the empty building, echoing down the dark corridor behind her. "I left you there for purpose! You finally found your strength, amidst so much despair! You were weak, battered, and broken! Now you can withstand hell's army! Don't you feel it? It's power!"

"It's nothing," she replied harshly, "but a knife to my throat."

Darkness purged any glimmer of emotion from her eyes. "Yet here you are, abandoning everything you hold so close to your heart."

"I'm going back for them!" The muscles in her arm ached. The revolver trembled. "After I rid this world of a tyrant."

"Me, a tyrant?" A shrill laugh engulfed the unsteady silence. "I'm the lesser of two evils, girl. This is just the beginning. There's no going back from here, you've made your decision."

"You're a monster," accused Celeste. "But in no position to stop me."

Vega licked the blood from her lips and replied sweetly, "I told you already." With her thumb, she flicked the switch along the side of the device. The cover opened like a latch, displaying a bright red trigger underneath. "The city falls on my command only."

Detonator? "So, you plan to flood their escape?"

"Escape?" Another shriek of laughter. "No, girl. Then the city would be salvageable."

Her thumb twitched as it hovered over the device trigger. "This will decimate the remnants of their army along with the entire city and its surroundings. It'll start beneath the dam, shatter the wall, and flood the river again. Once the first explosion is triggered, the rest will follow. Anything within the walls will be buried under rubble and then water. An icy tomb."

"You're bluffing." *That's her style.*

"Michael was the expert." She almost smiled, as though for a moment she recalled him fondly. Celeste remained haunted by his blank stare, his mouth forever parted with unspoken words. "He rigged the old sewer system, under the guise of finally having water running through those old rusted faucets."

"Someone would have noticed," she insisted. "No way would anyone else allow this."

"Some knew," declared Vega, impassivity clouding her tone. She glanced at her blade on the floor. "I slit their throats after they helped Michael set the explosives."

She offered another sweet, but weak smile. "Yes. I told their comrades they had been sent to gather Intel on the military camp and unfortunately killed in the line of duty. What I saw as declaration of bravery, their surviving kin saw as slaughter. They were... easily dispatched, as you witnessed."

"It *was* slaughter."

"It was necessary, as you will understand one day when you're leading your own people in battle."

She's mad.

"How could you do this? Your comrades, the people that believed in you, that are fighting for you right now... You'll sacrifice them all just to kill a few military soldiers?"

"Like you said, this is only the beginning. This is the spark that will flare into the fires of rebellion, one that will rid this world of true tyrannical rule. A twisted regime that we've lived under, suffered because, and watched loved one's *die* from. One of monsters, both in the shadows and lurking within the hearts of men."

"My life, my friends... We would have died for your twisted vengeance!"

"No, daughter," Vega replied, her voice soothing, but cold. Dead. "I made you harness your fears as strength, forced you to overcome the hatred pooling in your heart. I helped you gather the courage to fix this world, I made you fight your weakness."

"I wasn't weak!" Her face flushed, exuding sweat and soaking her hair to her face. "I wasn't..."

"You were *weak*," interjected Vega, malicious tone chilling Celeste. "Cowering when you should have been fighting. You were prey." She grinned wickedly, glowering as she whispered, "*Not* predator."

"No..."

"Yes. The mother had to shoulder the daughter's burden. *Again.*"

"I could have killed him!" She yelled in response, spilling tears she thought would never flow again. "Caden deserved to die by my hands!"

"You didn't do it."

"I wanted to!"

"But you didn't!" An unexpected outburst. Dark eyes glared from under a furrowed brow, but glistened despondency. "You had a gun! You had a gun and you couldn't pull the trigger! You were too scared... and you died! You shouldn't have died... He killed you, but you could have pulled the trigger and lived!"

She extended her arm to the side, letting her thumb brush against the device trigger. Her desperate smile broadened, and she shouted triumphantly, "But I found you! Destiny set us on similar paths for this very moment! My daughter! Nothing can keep a mother from..."

The abrupt blast silenced Vega, spraying her face with muddy blood. She gaped for a moment, staring into the revolver's barrel as it erupted again. The second bullet punched through her chest. She grunted loudly, staggered as her legs buckled, then collapsed. The device slipped from her grasp. She fumbled for it blindly, her lungs refusing air.

"There," Celeste stated coldly. She nudged the device further out of reach. "I pulled the trigger."

"C-Caylee..." Tears streamed from her dulling eyes.

"Celeste." The final bullet lodged inside the woman's skull.

Staring at the lifeless corpse, no satisfaction flooded her heart. Relief never blossomed in her chest, never warmed the gelid grip hatred had on her soul. It was ... empty.

Dark blood gushed from Vega's wounds.

Despite her piqued curiosity, she quickly gathered the device and wrapped it inside her blood soaked sweater. She tucked the bundle under her arm, leaving Vega on the floor, dead in a puddle of her own blood.

I have to get out of here fast. She raced through the dark corridor, boots resonating off the walls. *Sneak back into the city. Get Melina and Aurous out...*

But what do I do with this device?

Once outside in the starry winter night, the wind's frigid touch nursed her aching wounds. Collapsing into the snow seemed welcoming, a comfort to dull her pain to a slight tingle and numb her to the hurt. Instead, she staggered to the trees and away from the frozen path and walkway. She dropped to her knees, letting the snow melt and soak through her jeans. Then she started digging.

It took her longer than she'd hoped. Her fingers had long numbed, but the burning ache spread through her palms and wrist. She clawed through the frozen dirt until the tips of her scarred fingers stained crimson. She buried her sweater and the device, noted the mark she made near one of the trees with her blade, then silently hoped her weary mind wouldn't obscure these details upon recollection. She remained there, crouched under the trees and propped in the snow, the items previously packed in her sweater now splayed in her lap. A small kitten ring, an old rope bracelet with brown, frayed strings, and the map from her father.

This is all I have left... She pushed through the pain in her muscles and braced against the chilly wind. *But I also have my new family. I need to get back to them now. Unseen.*

Muscles throbbed as she started for the walkway. Hope spilled from her heart.

I'll find a way down the embankment and cross the narrow river below. Ice should still be thick in some spots. Then I-

The sound of shouting voices startled her.

She quickly fumbled for her revolver but the *roar* of gunfire and the sharp jabs that followed engulfed her mind and body with enough pain to drive her down to the snowy ground. She gasped, then cried out as her body seemingly burned within. Blood soaked the snow beneath her.

"Hold your damn fire!" Someone shouted roughly. "I want to see if it's the Bandit Queen."

Snow crunched loudly as someone approached. Another cry escaped when they nudged and rolled her on her side. Warmth spread down her clothes.

"It's not her. Doesn't even look like one of 'em. Christ, she's so young." The man leaned down, reaching for her spilled belongings. "Unintentional, girl. Apologies." He rummaged through her rings and bracelet. "Any means of identification? Name? I'll inform your kin, this way they can properly mourn..." His voice trailed off into a bewildered curse. She focused her blurry vision.

Her map, blood-spattered and torn, lay carefully unfolded in his gloved hands. Scouring the stained paper, his eyes widened first with disbelief, and then recognition. "Where did you get this?"

"It's mine," she managed to mutter, spitting blood from her mouth. "My... father...." Her vision blotted, but the pain numbed as more blood pumped from her wounds.

Dying isn't so bad... she thought, somewhat bitterly. *I love you, Melina, Aurous. I'm sorry.*

Mom, dad... Brother. I'll see you soon.

"Holy hell!" he barked, enraged. "You and you! Put a bullet in the bastard who couldn't keep his finger off the goddamn trigger!"

Someone pleaded quietly, tearfully, before two gunshots tore through his words.

"Get me Mengele, now!"

"He's right here, sir," someone replied immediately.

"What is it?" asked a gruff voice. Recognition spurred fear long rooted inside her mind.

"Her." He paused. "Accidental G-S-V. Can you save her?"

She wanted to scream as rough fingers prodded the wounds in her gut, but she couldn't take her eyes away from his.

"Maybe, given the proper... *Medication.*"

No...

"Then do it."

A grunt, then, "She needs treatment now."

"Then let's move her." The man giving orders leaned closer, breaking her fearful gaze. *Odd.* For a moment, she saw her father. "Ma'am, my name is Lt. Jordan Cavarly, but I believe you already know who I am. We're going to get you fixed up, so stay with me. This man right here is going to help you."

"You're going to be just fine," the other man assured, puckering his lips as he inhaled smoke from his cigarette. His face seemed heavily scarred, like a blade had carved his flesh into meaty puzzle pieces. Like stitches that hadn't quite healed yet. Blanched skin, cold, blue eyes and light hair – the face from her nightmares she'd long forgotten. Someone she thought dead. The monster responsible for her family's constant suffrage.

The Blonde Man.

His scarred lips spread into a malign smile. "I promise."

End of Book One

She awoke to blinding light.

The mechanical *hiss* was a whisper at first, pervading her mind, probing deep inside her skull for any thought beyond the velvet curtain of unconsciousness. She stirred, eyes unfocused, her body unresponsive and strangely numb.

Lights flashed, dimmed, and blinked through the aphotic fog obscuring her vision. *Gunfire*, she instinctively thought, heart drumming against her chest. The tips of her scarred fingers tingled. Blood rushed through her veins, and feeling slowly returned. She bolted upright.

Like a snake crushing prey, wires had slithered and coiled around her wrists, neck, and ribcage, securing her to the bedframe with a rigid, iron grip. She tried screaming, but instead choked from various tubes clogging her airway.

Familiar pain ached like blisters across her skin. Barbs and needles snagged her flesh, but she ripped wires from her chest and neck, ignoring the alarming *screech* of nearby machines. Coughing, she pulled the hose from her throat. Finally free, she leapt over the bedside.

Where am I? Her feet slapped against cold, tile floor. Stark white walls, crinkled curtains drawn across the only window, and a door with no discernable handle. Panic rooted deep in her thoughts and blossomed into terror.

The door *clicked*, shifting.

She sprang for the opening. Her fingers enclosed around the unsuspecting stranger's coat, smearing black marks across the bleached material. Flummoxed, the stranger gasped, eyes wide and staring into hers. Then a scream pierced her ears.

"Code Seven!"

Her fist silenced the shrill words bursting from the stranger's lips. A whimper followed the sharp blow, but footsteps echoed beyond the door. She glanced over the stranger's coat, then her fingers slipped into the front pocket. Gripping the pen with her bandaged hands, she pressed the pointed tip into a soft, fleshy neck.

"Don't move," she warned, digging the pen deeper.

"Please," the stranger, a woman, whispered. She was trembling fearfully. "We're here to help."

"Shut up."

"Dear girl," a voice carried past the door, calm and reassuring, smooth like water down a parched throat. "She's right. You are in a safe place, there's no need for alarm."

Her fear refused to simmer. "Don't believe you."

"Look." The door, already slightly ajar, opened more. "There's nobody here who wishes to harm you." The opening revealed a corridor, a brightly lit passageway with sunlight beaming through windows and doors. Troubled whispers filled the room, brewing from the crowd gathering around the door.

She tugged the collar of the woman's coat, propping the frightened hostage like a shield between herself and the pack of unwelcome guests. Another whimper escaped the stranger's quivering lips. But there were no rifles aimed at her, no soldiers garbed in shadows with their weapons poking through the doorway. Only a row of women, clad in the same white outfit as the one in her clutches. Bewildered faces gawked back at her, their hair neat, trimmed, and proper, and cheeks flush with red powder.

They look like dolls, she thought meekly. *Not fighters.*

Still, she tightened her grip around the hostage.

"Ladies," the man in the midst of the crowd whispered quietly, shooing them aside like nosy children. He kept his unblinking, coppery eyes steady with hers, but a hint of fear drained the color from his face. Though, his voice carried through the room, unwavering. "There are no weapons, no restraints, and certainly nobody strong enough to try and hold you down."

He edged through the doorway, his arms raised by his shoulders. Grey stubble, unruly from neglect, covered his chin. He was slender, almost gaunt, with indented cheeks like he steadily puckered his lips. Round, grubby glasses slipped down the bridge of his oily nose.

"Will you allow poor Annie to stand?" He offered a small smirk, then nodded over his shoulder and added, "Now that the hens have finished clucking?"

Her eyes scanned over his attire. Nearly identical to the others, though he appeared more professional, dressed in formal wear under his lab coat. Florescent light even gleamed off his unblemished, leathery shoes.

Gruffly, she asked, "Doctor?"

A curt nod. "Yes." He took another step. "How about you let her go, and you and I have a little chat?"

She shook her head, shifting toward the door. "No."

He chuckled, warily. "It's okay, I'll keep my hands up."

"No," she repeated, looking down at the woman in her clutches. "Save her."

The man cocked his head slightly, confused and gazing over the woman named Annie. Then his mouth gaped.

"No!"

The pen plunged into Annie's neck. The doctor leapt forward, cradling the woman in white as she slumped to the floor, face drained of color and mouth parted in a soundless scream.

Dropping her bleeding hostage, she dashed for the doorway. Frantic yells were lost under the sound of her labored gasps. Her guts burned. Her muscles froze.

Sunlight glared through the windows, blinding her as she stumbled down the drab white corridor. Someone reached for her, their hands grasping vials and needles. Despite her weakened state, her knuckles found a target. A solid blow connected with their face, staining her bandages red. Her desperate scramble to freedom continued.

Perfume hung heavy in the corridor, stinging her eyes and nostrils. *Nothing like the flowers mother used to wear,* she thought grimly, scrunching her nose in disgust. *Pampered princesses.*

"There she is!"

The moment she rounded the hallway corner, she stared into the barrel of a rifle. Her feet slid across the cold tile, then stumbled to a halt.

Soldiers, faces obscured behind goggles and masks, surged forward.

Crap!

She turned, fleeing back the way she came. Heavy boots stomped after her, mimicking her erratic, speeding heart. But the corridor of women became overwhelmed with soldiers as well. They flowed like a rapid river of shadows, waves of armored men threatening to pull her beneath a violent, ebony surface.

No harm, right?

She stood, surrounded, heaving from her impractical escape. Sweat rained around her face.

"Stand down."

The gravitas forced each weapon to lower. She stared through the throng of soldiers, glimpsing the stern eyes of her uncle. His freshly shaved face revealed the set of scars lining his chin like her father once bore, and for a moment, that's who she saw.

"Celeste," he called out, his face brightening with a genuine smile. "I'm sorry we weren't here when you woke up."

Someone else squealed her name with excitement, red hair bouncing through the sea of black, a streak of fire spreading through the crowd. She smiled back at the approaching warmth, then recoiled from the cold draft in her soul. Like a clear sky suddenly blemished with storm clouds, murky, blue eyes glared at her. Patches of scarred skin trickled blood. The monster of her past, her nightmares.

The Blonde Man!

"No!"

Her eyes snapped open.

Sunlight twinkled through the ripped tent-flap, rousing her from a troubled daze. She blinked, her vision blotted, then groaned and shifted under her blankets. Everything ached, and she craved rest without the tainted touch of fear. Pain plagued every waking moment, then stalked her while she slept.

I need peace.

Beside her, a warm body stirred.

"Are you okay, Celeste?" A soft, honeyed voice soothed her frayed nerves. "Was it the same nightmare?"

Memory. "Yes," she replied quietly in a broken voice. "Hospital." She dragged her tongue across her chapped lips. She was parched.

A delicate chortle of laughter followed her response. "I'd feel a bit guilty too for what you did to that poor nurse."

"She didn't die," Celeste countered, a bit defensively. "I just needed to get out."

"You nicked an artery."

The corners of her mouth twitched into a frown. "Nothing serious. She's already back on duty."

"You know, you probably should have apologized," Melina whispered. "Maybe send some flowers or something."

It was a gentle, but daily rebuke. *Maybe I am overflowing with guilt,* she thought bitterly, recalling the statement from Melina she'd callously dismissed as foolish. *Maybe I should...*

Faces flashed through her mind; bloodstained skin, hollow eyes, mouths twisted with endless screams of agony.

She shook her head. *Get it together.*

"I wasn't meaning to press."

Her heart simmered, then swelled with warmth. "No," she lied feebly. "Just cold."

"I can fix that," her companion purred lightly, crawling across the cold gap between them.

She nestled into the comforting embrace, burying herself deep in the patchy, wool blanket. The rickety cot beneath them trembled like a frightened child and dug into the dirt when she shifted her weight. Melina's breath tickled the back of her neck, soothing like a balmy breeze. Her spine tingled with shivers.

I want to sleep like this all day.

Except she couldn't.

Like a wet, soggy cloth soaking her face, a frothy tongue slathered her with drool.

"Ugh," she sputtered, wiping her lips. "Good morning, Aurous."

The wolf propped his head on the edge of the cot, his nose poking her cheek. He growled playfully, then nipped at her blanket. Black fur clumped around his neck, tufted from his shedding coat. His tawny eyes shone into hers.

"I get it," she said, sighing. "Bathroom."

Melina pulled away, and cold crept between them once more. The redhead teased her with a mellifluous giggle. "Like you, he's not one for waiting patiently."

Worming out of the blankets, she groaned and pushed them aside.

Pain rocked her abdomen. She stood, one hand clasped on her stomach, bracing against the bitter chill that had settled in the tent during the night.

"You should rest," Melina began, another gentle chastise.

"I'm okay," interjected Celeste. She kicked her boots, hoping to startle any critters residing in their depths. "Really."

"You're still recovering from being shot!"

"A few grazes." Her slight grin extended into a broad smile. "Nothing serious." Though, the pain shocking her nerves and muscles begged to differ.

But her freckled companion whispered gravely, "But you almost died."

"I'm still here."

"Only because they had excellent doctors."

They. Disgust welled in her heart. *Military.*

Shadows beneath the cot stirred. Bloody, ravenous eyes glowed through the veil, waiting, observing... *Stalking.*

Her cheeks warmed from the foolish thought. *There's no monsters under my bed.* Kinked strands of carmine hair bounced when she shook her head. *Enough.*

"They left scars," replied Celeste, stubbornly.

"That wasn't from..."

She growled, "Not those. On my stomach."

"It doesn't look as bad as my shoulder," countered Melina. She wrinkled her brow, pursed her lips, and averted her eyes from Celeste like her presence was no longer cared for. Her finest scowl.

The beauty in Melina's sullen gaze coaxed a smile back from Celeste. "I'm taking Aurous outside. I need the fresh air."

Melina slouched her shoulders, conceding. "Fine," she said. "At least let me check your bandages."

"Later," Celeste promised. She wiggled her chilly toes into rough, woolen socks, then slipped into her stiff boots. The cracked leather had been wiped clean, now only scuffed from the dusty winds of a torrid summer. However, there were a few distinct red splotches on the tips of her laces.

"Hold on," Melina quickly called out. Celeste poked her head through the tent flap, and the redhead said, "I'm coming with you."

"Really," Celeste replied. "I'll be okay."

Her green eyes shimmered like lake water on a clear day. "You're not exactly a *people* person."

Like billowing smoke, ashen clouds drifted through the sky along swirling wind currents. Jagged mountains loomed over the ruins of the nearby city like rocky, predacious jaws enclosing around carrion.

Tufts of torn up grass clumped to the dirt around her boots. The previously glossy meadow had been trampled into a sinking pit of mud, with rainfall, wash water, and waste coagulating around the various tents and temporary structures erected along the roadside and field. It reeked like a sewer.

Aurous spurred through the puddled mud, tongue lolling and giving chase to the chunk of meat she'd lobbed over the tent. He darted through the crowds bustling across makeshift walkways and gathering around the simple structures, then disappeared under the beige canopy of tents.

She breathed deeply. Despite the odorous camp, she was thankful to leave the fusty confines of her tent and stretch her sore muscles. Daily, her body ached. Her restlessness and refusal of pain medication only prolonged her recovery, maybe even hindered it. But she couldn't afford to dull her mind with drug, not like her father had. *To hell with their doctors,* she thought. *Dad was up and moving days after an injury even without medication.*

Countless bullet wounds, lacerations, broken bones... infections. She grimaced, then bit her lip. *Maybe I do need rest...*

A sudden shiver surged through her.

"It's getting cold, again," whispered Melina. She pulled the collar of her coat tightly around her neck. Red curls bunched around her freckled cheeks. "Doesn't get warm until the sun rises over the mountain peak."

Celeste nodded. "The chill makes my wounds ache." *And my bones.*

"Do you want to see how the city is faring?"

Her words swam in distaste. "I'm not staying here long."

"You said that a few months ago."

Mud splattered their tent as a row of soldiers marched through the soggy soil. Celeste remained silently thankful their boisterous chants concealed the sound of her teeth grinding in irritation. She lowered her eyes, both to obscure her face from their wary gazes and to avoid staring at the barrels of their weapons. Her heart wouldn't stop racing.

"I know," was all she meekly offered, her voice trembling. She gathered another chunk of meat as Aurous barreled around the tent, his lips stained pink from the previous bloody treat. Over the tent the meat sailed, with Aurous trailing through the mud after it.

"Well?"

"I still want to leave."

Melina suspired, then, "I'll go with you, wherever. You know that. But I think you should give your uncle a chance."

Celeste glared from under a rigid brow. "You didn't see what they unleashed in the city." She bit her lip, immediately regretting her careless words.

Melina clenched her teeth, settling her accusing, green eyes on Celeste. "Because you *left* me in a building with former prisoners. *In the middle of a warzone!*"

Guilt burrowed into her heart. For weeks she'd agonized over abandoning her wolf and Melina for impetuous revenge, sickened by the lust of battle worming back into her mind. She would drown under the bloody waves of her memories, wake feverish from nightmares, yet crave the fear that would vanish after Melina's comforting embrace. Melina knew of her unease, at least partially; the redhead was aware the fight had changed her – that Vega had *changed* her – but she'd been trapped in the confines of the hospital, oblivious to the destruction Celeste forced herself to tread through. Horror had risen from the spilled blood of men tainted from Vega's touch. *Loosen that thread from the web of deceit and death she wove, and it leads right back to the military.*

My uncle.

Melina sensed something else was amiss, but Celeste refused to divulge her troubled secrets. She still hadn't informed anybody of the charges Vega had placed under the city. *In Melina's eyes, I'm callous and cold, with little feelings for anything beyond blood.* Her eyes misted. *Maybe it's true.*

"I'm sorry." She couldn't make it sound sincere enough.

Soft, delicate fingers brushed against the jagged grooves scarred into her hands. Melina squeezed and commented lightly, "You've been avoiding everyone for months. Just give it a chance, that's all I'm asking. Get to know the camp." She shrugged. "It's not that bad, really. And everyone is nicer than the few I met at the hospital."

Her scars tingled. "Alright." She grinned, wiggling a finger at her companion. "One chance."

"I'm glad you agreed," Melina said, raising her voice over the clamor and smiling sheepishly. "Because I told them you would be ready today."

Celeste turned toward the commotion. Monstrous wheels ripped into the earth, spinning and jetting streaks of mud through the campsite like clumpy rain. The engine bellowed like a shadowed beast, thrusting the armored truck across the thick slop slowly devouring their tents. The vehicle carved to a halt near them.

Green mottled the black paint in countless swirls and patches, resembling tangled verdure in the woodlands. The windows weren't barred, but translucent, which she found rather peculiar until glimpsing the gouges in the thick glass from bullets. *Barely a dent.* The vehicle was large, with an engine loud enough to rumble the ground gently under their feet as it idled. Not weaponized like a tank, but outfitted to transport troops or cargo. *Or beasts,* she added silently.

The vehicle door swung open like a heavy gate. It was almost as though her father jumped down into the mud, splattering his jeans with the filth as he trudged through it to greet her. Scars blemished his smooth, shaven face, and his bright eyes were a stark difference to her father's dark, chestnut colored ones. But his tousled black hair, lanky limbs with ropy muscles, the curve in his jaw, and pallid skin resembled the man she recalled as a child. For a heart wrenching moment, she wanted to call out to her father and fall into his embrace.

Instead, she bit her lip nervously and nodded. Her uncle, however, smiled so broadly as he approached that she thought his cheeks would certainly ache afterward. He opened his arms and greeted her warmly.

"Celeste! It's good to see you up and about!"

"Be careful," warned Melina, narrowing her catty eyes at his attempted embrace.

"Ah," her uncle breathed, clasping her shoulders instead. Celeste managed to grin in reply. "You look better than you did trying to flee from the infirmary."

Her throat was dry, so her voice cracked when she spoke quietly, "I was confused. I'm sorry about that girl. Annie?"

Her uncle waved his hand, dismissing her forced apology. "She's a tad frightened, but otherwise completely fine. She was quite displeased, mind you. But after reminding you that you were more than capable of taking her head right then and there, she wisely closed her mouth."

"So," Celeste interjected, eager to change the subject. "What am I ready for?"

"Oh?" Her uncle turned his gaze to Melina. He smirked. "The darling little nurse-to-be didn't inform you yet?"

"Mr. Cavarly," said Melina, giggling. "Learning how to change bandages and clean wounds is a far cry from becoming a nurse."

"Please, call me Jordan."

"Yes, Mr. Ca-, Jordan. She needed as much sleep as she could get."

Irritated, Celeste asked, "Will somebody please explain what is going on?"

Jordan clapped his hands together and rubbed vigorously. Another smirk carved up his face. "I knew you'd become restless as you healed, especially if you're anything like my brother."

I've been restless about leaving.

"So," he continued, "I've decided to give you a job, if you want it. A responsibility."

"A job?" She raised an eyebrow, already recalling the mundane chores of her old mountain life. "What kind of job?"

"Something to suit your... special needs, of course." He gestured to the vehicle behind him. "Hop on up, and I'll show you what I mean."

"Wait!" Melina called out, coaxing Aurous away from the truck with another string of meat. "We have to change your bandages!"

For the first time in ages, Celeste gave her a true smile. "I'll be fine. Something to look forward to when I get back." Then she climbed into the truck after her uncle.

They left the campsite and bypassed the ruins of the city. The vehicle motored through the thicket overgrowing across the edges of the road, snapping branches and brittle leaves under the rigid tread of its wheels. Her head throbbed as the cacophonous engine roared through her ears.

It was as though the windows were frosted. She could squint and discern the blurred outlines of other campsites they rolled past, and the mountains in the distance, but features, signs, and even the road beyond a few feet was impossible to view. Instead, her uncle kept his gaze upon the console just above the padded steering wheel. A small monitor with a split screen displayed the street ahead of them and behind. Cameras must have been mounted on the exterior of the vehicle.

But the shadow in her reflection corralled her attention to the glass. She tugged at her shirt collar, exposing her neck and shoulder. Black blemishes dappled her pale skin like careless strokes of a paintbrush. Swirling, shadowy scars consumed her neck and carved up her cheek and eye, then disappeared into her hairline. The right side of her face appeared smooth, but closer inspection revealed black pockmarks in her skin, and her minced hands were stained with the same caliginous taint.

"Don't worry about it," her uncle shouted over the engine roar, sensing her disgust. "Barely noticeable." The vehicle jerked roughly as he slammed his palm against the gear stick to shift. The engine sputtered, then thundered loudly. "Feel lucky, little niece of mine. Not many people survive a near-death infection like that."

I'm sure most of them turned, she thought with a shudder, averting her gaze from her reflection. *But I still look like a freak.*

"I still can't believe Mengele and his team were apart to stitch you back together," he said over the engine clamor, shaking his head with disbelief. "There you were, full of bullets and bleeding to death. Then we find out you'd been infected, probably for hours. It was a miracle they managed to halt the transformation. At first, I'd thought you a lost cause, just a girl caught in the cross fire. Or perhaps a fleeing bandit. Though, you looked far too young and delicate. They only seemed to keep the rough sons of bitches."

"I remember," she replied quietly. Her uncle didn't hear her, and she just stared at her scarred hands instead of responding again. *I remember begging for an end to the pain. To let death claim me. But it didn't.*

"Christ," he swore. "That goddamn map... Your father was an asshole, you know that? Big, bleeding heart, but a mean prick. He promised he would never speak of me after the travesty the military caused during the initial outbreak. He was a damned good man. I'm glad he lost some of his stubbornness with old age."

Celeste snorted, genuinely pleased. "He didn't lose it. Sorry uncle, but he didn't speak of you until the night he passed." Her eyes lowered even further to stare at the muddy floor. "After months of begging him to leave."

"Right," her uncle replied with a laugh. "Of course, his little princess would be the only exception to his bullheaded stance."

"He told me the military executed those displaying symptoms of infection, whether they were transforming or not."

"We did." His jaw tightened.

"Why?"

He hesitated, peering at her from the corner of his eye. "People were panicking. They thought it was a hoax, that we were enforcing martial law on citizens merely to control them. They fought back. But that was when the full effects of the sickness were becoming known. Certain people transformed into... terrible beings. Others only partially. It was pandemonium, and a terrible decision."

"Do you regret giving the orders?"

"I didn't give the orders," he replied, defensively. Then, "But I regret taking part in the slaughter."

"What about using those *monsters* on the bandits?"

He almost snarled, "Look, Celeste. We only infected volunteers with a controlled form of the sickness, those too weak or injured to fight otherwise. The bandit queen took it too far; she infected all of her soldiers, knowing once they were killed most would likely transform. It was a dirty way to fight, but sometimes you bring fire against fire. It was a desperate act to seize the city with minimum casualties, especially when the *bitch* was conducting experiments and tampering with the sickness. Your father would never have agreed, but it had to be done."

"Dad stayed mad at you all these years, you know."

He smirked, though his eyes betrayed the hurt rooted deep inside. "I bet your mother was all too happy about that."

She shrugged. "I don't remember her hating anybody."

"Oh, she hated me. A demon, I am. Her words, really. Spiteful little minx."

"She was a beautiful woman," growled Celeste, drumming her fingers on her lap. "I miss her."

Face flushed red, he muttered, "Right, of course. She had a fiery spirit, that's for sure."

Maybe you're the arsehole. "So," she said, feigning boredom. "What is this job you want me for?"

"The job is more or less a new responsibility and honor."

"Honor?"

"And thanks."

"I don't understand."

"It's a reward for killing the bandit queen and releasing the prisoners in the hospital basement. Stonem accepted on your behalf." Her uncle winked at her. "He said you'd be more than eager to begin."

She narrowed her eyes, unable to quell her bubbling curiosity. "Eager to begin what?"

"Leading your own squad."

After leaving the road and parking near the woodlands, they disembarked the giant vehicle, with her uncle shouldering most of the bags taken from the backseat. Celeste grabbed one, and struggled to steady it in her tremulous grip. Then she waddled after her uncle, careful not to further agitate her tender wounds.

I should be in bed still.

Pine needles jabbed through her shirt and scrapped her skin as they ventured under the thick branches and stepped into clearing. She stopped, her boots shifting in soil, then eased the bag to the ground.

"There you are," her uncle state proudly. "Your very own squad."

Strangers turned to face her.

"This is her?" One of them asked incredulously. "Queen Slayer?" The girl huffed, tracing her slender fingers across the barrel of her rifle. Sandy hair flickered over her cold eyes and dangled down her slender face as she shook her head. Her sun-kissed complexion seemed to glow through the gloomy clearing.

Apparently amused, the largest one of them remarked, "Small." His throat rippled as he spoke, jiggling like the fat under his tight fitting clothes. His arms bulged out of the sleeves of his shirt. His head was shaved, apart from the middle which stood in rows of spikes. He squinted to gain a better look. "Real tiny."

"Alright, enough," her uncle barked, bemused. He jerked his thumb toward the light haired girl. "This is Snyder, rifle expert. And that giant of a man calls himself Twist."

"Hi," he greeted, his voice dull like a simpleton. "Queen Slayer."

Muttering to her uncle, Celeste asked, "Why do they keep calling me that."

"The woman you killed, Vega," he replied quietly. "She's been the cause of plenty suffering for us, and many of their parents, friends, or relatives lost their lives at her hands. You're a legend for killing the phantom woman."

One of the other strangers stepped forward, pushing her rifle behind her hip. Black hair kinked around her shoulders, tousled as she walked. Wide, ginger eyes stared at her with wonder. White teeth flashed behind her growing smile. She extended a greeting, and after a moment's hesitation, Celeste took the girl's tanned hand in her own and shook.

"I've been looking forward to meeting you. You're like, wicked cool," she practically exclaimed. At a sharp glance from Jordan, she quickly added, "Ma'am."

"Kiss ass," the girl known as Snyder hissed.

The tanned girl ignored her. "I'm Nadie. Machine guns, survivalist. You name it."

The large, tubby man chimed in, "I'm Twist."

"Right," Celeste said. Her gaze fell over the remaining of the strangers. "Anyone else have the urge to share their name?"

"Clark," a small, wiry boy called out, shooting his hand into the air like he waved to her in the distance. "Not sure what my role is yet, but I'd love to stick close to you, beautiful."

Face burning red, Celeste opened her mouth to respond before Snyder sneered, "Really? Look at those ugly black marks on her face."

Clark shrugged and pulled his hood down. Shaved head, smooth face, lean, muscled frame – he was young, but confident, and looked every part a soldier. *True military brat.*

"She's still cute," he countered smugly.

Blood soured her mouth as she bit down on her lip again. She looked back to her uncle, but his gaze remained indifferent. *He wants me to prove I can handle it,* she reasoned. *Like a leader. I have to be hard on them. Firm. Prove that I'm capable of leading and ensuring their survival as a unit.* A tingle danced along her spine. She could almost hear Vega purr her agreement in the back of her skull.

"If you think infection is sexy, than yeah," Snyder commented with a shrug of her small shoulder. "She's *hot.*"

"They wouldn't let her out if she was contagious," Clark stated loudly, then hesitated. "Would they?"

"Shadow marked," sneered Snyder. "It took a monster to bring down a monster."

"Are you always this cheery?"

"Only one good days."

Clark laughed, but Snyder idly tapped a finger on the hilt of her knife.

"Enough!"

Her voice boomed through their clatter, resounding like the heavy *thump* of a discharging rifle. Startled into silence, they let their eyes slowly wander to her. The wind breathed between them like the haunted whispers of a ghost.

"I don't want to hear another word unless I ask you to speak."

Celeste's mind reeled. Frustration boiled over to rage, and her heart surged madly. The primal part of her mind roared for the blonde bitch's blood, for her knife to carve the bumptious smirk into a petrified frown. To bloody her dainty features. Yet outwardly, her demeanor remained stony, their eyes averting from her apathetic stare. Power flushed through her veins, dizzying her like too much drink.

"Alright," she said, looking toward the last two men she didn't recognize. She pointed a scarred finger to one, a hulking man with more muscle than body and hair longer than hers. A polished, gold plated shotgun leaned against his massive shoulder. He grinned through a prickly black beard. "You. Details."

"Name's Harn," he drawled in a thick accent. "Shotguns. Explosives. I admire your work, little warrior. I look forward to spilling blood with you." His neck bent in a slight nod.

She returned the gesture, then turned to the man beside him. Slicked hair, tinged brown like a chestnut, curled around his mousy eyes. Dark stubble speckled his creamy skin. The corner of his mouth twitched, almost offering her a smile.

"Colbat," he said. The lull of his smooth voice seemed to calm her frayed nerves. "Sniper. I'm a brilliant shot, but I'd be more than happy to prove it to you right now."

"Right," replied Celeste. She cleared her throat, then, "But not necessary at the moment."

"Major," Snyder began, lolling her head at Jordan.

"Lieutenant-General, now," he corrected, abruptly silencing her. "And I'm no longer your commanding officer. In this field, you belong to her."

"Great," the blonde muttered bitterly. "So I am stuck taking orders from a *shadow spawn*."

Celeste clenched her fists, then spoke through gritted teeth, "And I told you not to speak unless I said so." Anger burned through her like flames consuming tinder. Snyder set her jaw and pursed her lips, ever defiant.

"Drop!" Celeste barked suddenly. Snyder flinched, and the fresh faced boy named Clark chuckled lightly. To him, she muttered, "You too, hotshot."

They both stared back at her, unblinking.

"And do what exactly?" Snyder questioned.

"One hundred push-ups," Celeste replied coldly. "Training starts now."

"M-ma'am," Clark stammered, grinning stupidly. "We do countless exercises during our morning routines. Wouldn't our time be better spent on shooting or blade dueling? I heard you were an expert with a machete."

"Two hundred," came the bitter response. Celeste narrowed her eyes until the boy gulped and dropped the soil. Snyder grumbled, then followed his example. She gazed over the others, then demanded they drop to the ground as well. They were wise enough not to mutter any snide remarks.

"How many for us?" Twist asked with a dull but innocent tone. He heaved into the dirt, then rolled to his belly. "Lots?"

"Just go until I say stop."

She heard Snyder click her tongue. "A leader ordering us into the dirt when it looks like she couldn't perform a single push-up to save her life."

Arms uncrossed, Celeste's hand brushed over her holstered revolver. Her muscles tensed. Snyder's gaze lifted from the dirt to calmly fixate on the silver gun. *I can't kill her.* Her heart pumped deeper at the thought of it. *But I can break her goddamn skull...*

But she eased her hand away from the revolver, and shifted her boots in the soil. Then she dropped to her hands and pressed against the ground. Pain burst free from her wounds and burned through her entire body, but she pushed against the dirt, then lowered again. Her arms pumped. The others were quickly outpaced.

"Holy hell," Nadie whispered, quickening her own pumps. "Shut you up, blondie."

"You're just used to the filth," she countered coldly. "Your people scrub it for a living."

"Yo, I'm Native, not a goddamn Mexican." Nadie grumbled quietly, "*Môniyâw.*"

"What the hell did you just call me?"

"If I reach one hundred before you," huffed Celeste, her face dripping with sweat. "You're doing two hundred more."

Snyder bit her tongue, and Celeste wouldn't tear her gaze away from the irreverent girl. Her muscles strained, but she pushed on. Then she noticed black blemishes in the grassy soil below her.

Blood.

Her wounds had torn open, and tainted blood soaked through her bandages clothes. Dark rivulets trailed down her arms and hips, dripping into the soil. Still, she didn't stop.

When she finally did, her belly ached and her clothes were stained black. The others slowed their progress staring up at her with a mix of apprehension and uncertainty. Snyder cringed in disgust.

"Commander," Nadie began.

Celeste cut her off sharply, "Finish, and then we'll move on and test how well your aim truly is."

She turned away from them, her face draining of color. The sounds of their grunts and breathless chatter faded, and the landscape twisted into a whirlpool of colors. She staggered back to the truck with the help of her uncle.

"Brilliant," he said, though she barely noticed. "You established yourself as a serious commander from the start. They're a promising bunch, but they need discipline. I'm glad we picked the right leader."

He leaned her against the truck. If there had been any food in her belly, she would have retched over the giant wheels.

"It's in your blood, you know. To lead. You're going to be great." He met her gaze, and his light eyes brightened with pride.

Grinding her teeth against the incessant pain, she muttered darkly, "I'm going to need those meds."

About the Author

Tyler is an aspiring writer from western Canada, striving for a degree in English. With a penchant for strange horror and science fiction, he began crafting his own dystopian series in his spare time, but now devotes all precious hours of a day to writing an assortment of genres. He is currently completing the second installment to *The Wild Hunt* trilogy, *Wolf Blood*.

www.ingramcontent.com/pod-product-compliance
Lightning Source LLC
Chambersburg PA
CBHW070432170726
48291CB00002B/460